NEMESIS

THE WRATH OF CHAOS

SHANIA SCICHILONE

BOOKS BY SHANIA SCICHILONE

The **Fates Divine** Series

A Fate of Smoke and Ash

A Fate of Gods and Fire

The Wrath of Chaos Series

Nemesis

READERS DISCRETION

A NOTE FOR READERS,

NEMESIS is an Adult novel and should only be read by mature readers. This book contains sensitive content, and it is advised to review the list of content warnings provided. You can find the list on the author's website at www.shaniascichilone.com under the tab "BOOKS: CW - The Wrath of Chaos". Readers discretion is advised.

GUIDE

Character Names

- Astraea Sirenstar — Ah-s-t-r-ay-ah S-eye-r-in-s-t-ah-r (she/her)
- Ravena Ruinoak — R-ah-v-EE-n-ah R-ooh-in-oh-k (she/her)
- Aurelia Nox — Or-ay-l-EE-ah N-aw-x (she/her)
- Asher Aidos — Ah-shh-ur Ay-d-oh-s (he/him)
- Aspen Aidos — Ah-s-p-eh-n Ay-d-oh-s (they/them)
- Malek Azadiron — M-ah-l-eh-k Ah-z-ah-d-ur-on (he/him)
- Calix Lightcrest — C-ah-l-ih-x L-eye-t-k-r-eh-s-t (he/him)
- Juniper — J-ooh-N-ih-P-ur (they/them)
- Valentina — V-ah-l-eh-n-t-EE-n-ah (she/her)
- Theo — Th-EE-oh (he/him)
- Emir — Eh-m-EE-r (he/him)
- General Solbourne — G-eh-n-ur-ah-l S-oh-l-b-or-n (he/him)

- Darius Blackfare — D-ah-r-EE-us B-l-ah-k-f-ay-r (he/him)
- Eagan Whitlock — EE-g-in W-ih-t-l-aw-k (he/him)
- Zade Yarrow — Z-ay-d Y-ah-r-oh (he/him)
- Rana Yarrow — R-ah-n-ah Y-ah-r-oh (she/her)
- Sun — S-uh-n (ze/zir)
- Freya — F-r-ay-ah (she/they)
- Indigo — In-d-ih-g-oh (she/her)
- Devi — D-ay-v-EE (she/her)
- Zoya — Z-oh-y-ah (she/her)
- Parineeti — P-ah-r-EE-n-EE-t-EE (she/her)
- Imani — Ih-m-ah-n-EE (she/her)
- Jade — J-ay-d (she/her)
- Aziz — Ah-z-EE-z (he/him)
- Zoren — Z-oh-r-eh-n (he/him)
- River — R-ih-v-ur (he/him)
- Tariq — T-ah-r-ih-k (he/him)
- Nasir Lazaroth — N-AH-s-EE-r L-ah-z-ah-r-ah-th (he/him)
- Leander Lazaroth — L-EE-ah-n-d-ur L-ah-z-ah-r-ah-th (he/him)
- Atlas Loupart — Ah-t-l-ih-s L-ooh-p-ah-r-t (he/him)
- Fenrir Vale — F-eh-n-r-EE-r V-ay-l (he/him)
- Vizhen Shadesteele — V-ih-j-ih-n Sh-ay-d-s-t-EE-l (she/her)
- Ronan Shadesteele — R-oh-n-ah-n Sh-ay-d-s-t-EE-l (he/him)
- Keziah Shade Steele — K-eh-z-EE-ah Sh-ay-d-s-t-EE-l (she/her)
- Oshin Sylva — Oh-sh-ih-n S-ih-l-v-ah (he/him)
- Storm Ceypre — S-t-or-m S-ay-p-r-ah (she/her)
- Remi Ruinoak — R-eh-m-EE R-ooh-in-oh-k (he/him)

Celestial Names:

- Meka'al — M-eh-k-ah-ah-l (he/him)
- Valre — V-ah-l-r-ah (he/him)
- Sybìron — S-ih-b-ih-r-on (he/him)
- Verulane — V-eh-r-ooh-l-ay-n (she/her)
- Cyraea — C-ur-ay-ah (she/her)
- Ophaeus — Oh-f-ah-y-us (he/him)
- Zephrðn — Z-eh-f-r-on (he/him)
- Casteìð — K-ah-s-t-ay-oh (he/him)
- Vitur'en — V-ih-t-ur-in (he/him)
- Theçerra — Th-eh-s-air-ah (she/her)
- Rykkel — R-ih-k-eh-l (he/him)
- Ahemì — Ah-h-eh-m-EE (he/him)
- C'tarð — K-t-ah-r-oh (she/her)
- Urðra — Ooh-r-or-ah (she/her)
- Aegliðs — Ay-l-EE-oh-s (he/him)
- Phaðs — F-ay-aw-s (they/them)

Dragon Names:

- Nemesis — N-eh-m-eh-s-ih-s (he/him)
- Orion — Or-eye-on (he/him)
- Nyx — N-ih-x (she/her)
- Idris — Ih-d-r-ih-s (he/him)
- Erubus — Air-ooh-b-us (he/him)

Places, Things, & Species:

Eterì: Elemental power

  Oasòs: Heaven/Haven

  Healing: Using your eterì to coax someone else's eterì to work to heal said person.

Outer Edge: An impenetrable wall the dragons built to keep themselves safe—also known as **Frèire.**

Asherian War (1st War): When the dragons were cast from Oasòs to Earth.

Bonded: A person who bonds cosmically with a dragon, the pair sharing the same eterì and a mind-link.

Mind-link: A unique power shared between bonded, which allows them to read one another's minds.

Soulmate: A unique counterpart, which is thought to be predestined by the universe. Two people meant for each other.

Soul-bound: When soulmates claim one another, their souls become bound for eternity.

Territories: The regions of different species.

Celestials: The gods of the universe who rule eterì.

Legacies: Demi-celestials.

Dragons: Large beasts with leathery wings, scales, and claws.

Fae: Super-humans with heightened senses and physical capabilities.

Lycanthropes: Super-humans who can transform into large wolves.

Orcs: Super-humans who are larger in height and mass, with tusks and superior strength.

Vampires: Immortal super-humans who have heightened senses and survive on blood.

Nymphs: Super-humans of nature. (Subspecies include: **Empusae** (Empusa)—*Shapeshifting Nymphs*, **Aurae** (aura)—*Wind nymphs*, **Dryads**—*Tree nymphs*, **Naiads**—*Fresh water nymphs*, **Nereids**—*Sea nymphs*, and **Oreads**—*Mountain nymphs*.)

Orc Lands — *Iceland* — (Leaders: Vizhen & Ronan Shadesteele)

Lycanthrope Enclave — *Scotland* — (Leader: Atlas Loupart)

Nymph Wilds — *Ireland* — (Leader: Mabon Ma'at)

Vampire Empire — *Netherlands* — (Leaders: Nasir & Leander Lazaroth)

Fae Court — *England* — (Leader: Asher Aidos)

Legacy Compound — *France* — (Leader: General Solbourne)

Lycanthrope Enclave — *Spain* — (Leader: Fenrir Vale)

Celestial Language (With Translation):

Freìre — Freedom

Eterì — Power

Oasòs — Heaven

Ka'aìh — Of

Mìiyre — Mine/My

Cðh'ide — Heed

Sù'vðq — Summoning

Bokontaì — A divine decree with no exact translation, meaning that a pair has made an oath to their fated mate and become soul-bound.

SIXTEEN CELESTIALS RULE OVER THE ETERÌAN SECTORS

THOSE BORN OF CELESTIALS HOLD ETERÌ IN THEIR VEINS –
AN ELEMENTAL POWER DETERMINED BY ONE'S ASTROLOGICAL BIRTH SIGN

AIR:
MEKA'AL – CELESTIAL OF DREAMS (AQUARIUS)
VALRE – CELESTIAL OF SKIES (LIBRA)
SYBÌRON – CELESTIAL OF TIME (GEMINI)

EARTH:
VERULANE – CELESTIAL OF LOVE (TAURUS)
METRÌVA – CELESTIAL OF HARVEST (CAPRICORN)
CYRAENA – CELESTIAL OF HUNT (VIRGO)

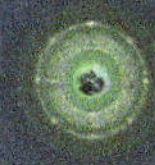

FIRE:
OPHAELIS – CELESTIAL OF FORGE (ARIES)
ZEPHRÒN – CELESTIAL OF WAR (SAGITTARIUS)
CASTEÌÒ – CELESTIAL OF PLEASURE (LEO)

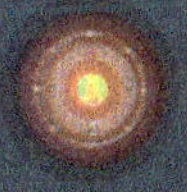

WATER:
VITUR'EN – CELESTIAL OF SEAS (PISCES)
THEÇERRA – CELESTIAL OF PEACE (CANCER)
RYKKEL – CELESTIAL OF ETERNITY (SCORPIO)

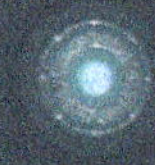

SPIRIT:
AHEMÌ – CELESTIAL OF DEATH
C'TARÒ – CELESTIAL OF WISDOM
URÒRA – CELESTIAL OF FATE
AEGLIÒS – CELESTIAL OF VOLITION

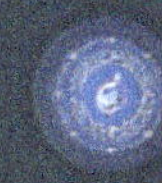

SPIRIT ETERÌ IS RARE, AND THEREFORE DOESN'T REQUIRE ONE TO BE BORN IN A SPECIFIC BIRTH SECTOR.
THOSE WITH SPIRIT ETERÌ ARE RULED BY ALL FOUR CELESTIALS.

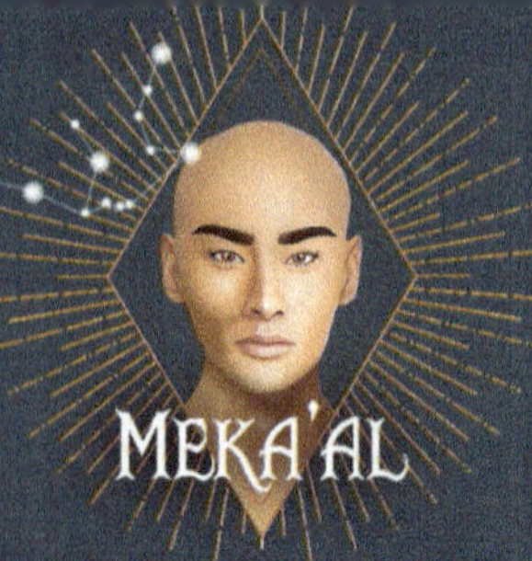
MEKA'AL

VALRE

SYBÌRON

VERULANE

METRÌVA

CYRAEA

OPHAEUS

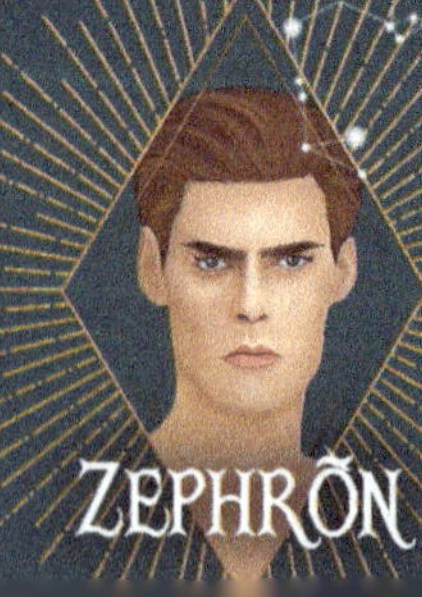
ZEPHRÕN

CASTEÌÕ

UITUR'EN

THEÇERRA

RYKKEL

AHEMÌ

C'TARÕ

URÕRA

AEGLÌÕS

FREÌRE

PROLOGUE

There haven't always been dragons scouring Earth.
'Tis the dawn of a new era, born of creation and oblivion.
The dragons, fueled by an insatiable thirst for vengeance, have risen.
The legacies, beholden to celestials, are obliged to expunge the world of
the beasts' lethal fury.
With Fate in peril, our time in this realms-crossing war is on the brink
of extinction.
When the stars align, one must concede, lest they plummet into chaos.

CHAPTER I
ASTRAEA

Rumbling echoes all around me as I take cover behind a felled dragon. Amidst the tremors of the earth and the death-gasps of both friends and foe, my thoughts are barely coherent. With the cliffs so exposed, there's nowhere else to hide. I am bait, shivering in plain sight. Gathering my courage, I do the unthinkable—when the chance comes, I slice the horrid crimson-red beast's abdomen wide, yank its entrails until they fall to my feet, and, ignoring the throbbing in my bones, crawl into the belly of the beast.

I can feel my heart pounding fast in my throat, and I'm afraid to breathe as I huddle in the carcass. With the heat of seeping guts and the putrid stench, it takes everything in me not to scream, or vomit. I clamp my hand over my mouth, trying to ignore the rising bile. It's the only way to stop my panting, ensuring no others can hear me.

The beasts are everywhere. Though the cliffs are drenched in the blood of my enemy, far more of my allies lie below, in the rocky soil and the English Channel. The area is too open to set up camp in a place with no ward or protection. We should have known we were tempting fate. What had Solbourne been thinking?

As was the custom every second Thursday, we'd been travelling for supplies and trade. We were a skilled group of soldiers, and General Solbourne took charge during the trip by stern-wheeler. He and I worked closely together for years, learning from each other and preparing for a second inevitable war. The Asherian War had taken everything, and all the people of Earth had to begin anew.

Solbourne was content to set up camp and sleep on the cliffs before crossing over to the Fae Court for trade, but I was against it. We'd argued for the last half hour. Being asleep and out in the open with very few soldiers and insufficient weaponry didn't sit right with me. I had tried convincing everyone to stay in the boat for easy escape, but he insisted they wanted to stretch their legs and sleep in their tents. After all, we had arrived an hour early, and the fae wouldn't be expecting us until noon. Nevertheless, I obeyed the general's orders and helped him set up an encampment atop the chalk-white cliffs. Surrounded by the Normandy coastline, we were highly vulnerable.

Had I known that my *eterì*—the power that was more a part of me than my own heart—would fail upon this cliff, I would have steered clear.

Inside the dragon's cavity, I stiffen at a heavy *thump*. My eyes widen as I spot a dragon, black as pitch, mere feet away and sniffing the carcass. My ears begin ringing, my spirit eterì stirring. Why was it coming back now? I grow dizzy, my power pulsing in and out, hesitant. My body unintentionally hitches forward, and I pray to Oasòs for a swift death—though it doesn't find me.

As the ringing dies, the fog clears from my head and I hear shouts of horror that soon narrow to individual voices. I recognize the agonized cries of my fellow soldiers, and a shooting pain ravages my heart.

"Astraea!" I hear from afar.

Malek. He is still alive.

The black dragon abruptly takes off, lifting into the air. I'd dodged that fury, but only at the cost of diverting its interest toward my friend. It's going to find Malek.

No. I cannot allow it. I am done with cowardice. Though I didn't know how terribly this mission would transpire, I came willingly, and with bravery in my hands. Just because my eterì has vanished does not mean I will yield in battle. These monsters, with iron talons and fire-breath, will not get the chance to kill yet another of my allies—certainly not Malek, my friend.

With the burden of life and death ever present on my shoulders, I carve my way out of the carcass and stand on shaking feet. I slide my hands up over my face, brushing the bloodied hair from my eyes. I flick the gore off my fingers before summoning my silver blade. I let it sit in my hands, taking a deep breath as it balances. The cool metal is an excellent relief from dragon flesh and fire.

It's time to finish this.

My mind is suddenly stolen, my eyes going white with eterì —a divinatory guidance bestowed.

Embrace not death. Seek instead solace in knowledge. Let wisdom be your guiding light as you navigate the challenges ahead. Have faith in your instincts, for they will lead you to greatness.

TERROR FILLS ME, and I feel ice cold as my vision is restored. I watch with dread as the black dragon carries my friend toward the Outer Edge. My eterì returns to me with fervour the moment Malek and the beast leave my sight. I swallow heavily, and my eyes find livid dragons waiting to pounce, their prey dead at their feet. They gather around me, eager to fight. With my head held high, my eyes tapering with stealthy vision, I let the wind carry me forward.

The dragons, now demolished, never saw what was coming.

CHAPTER 2
ASTRAEA

My legs tremble as I near the giant gated doors of the Compound. Sweat soaks through my clothes as I reach the old stone steps. The solitary trip back on the sternwheeler had been a blur, the rough five hours feeling at once like twenty and none at all.

My sister Ravena spots me first. "Astraea! What are you doing here alone?" Her curly brown hair bobs up and down as she runs toward me. Countless shocked gazes swing toward me. I quiver inside, but refuse to show weakness in front of my peers. I stand tall, a pillar of strength in the face of hardship.

"Raea, why do you look like you've seen a ghost?" asks my youngest sister Aurelia.

Darius Blackfare, a tall orc legacy responsible for the Intelligence Division at the Compound, descends the stairs, followed by four armed guards. "What's the meaning of this, Lieutenant-General?"

I clear my throat, raising my chin. "I couldn't save them," I answer, voice torn. "They are all gone."

Ravena clutches my elbow. "What do you mean they're all

gone?" She plucks at the front of my shirt and I flex my abs. "Where did all this blood come from? Are you hurt?"

I shrug off Ravena with a grunt. She rolls her grey eyes, all four-foot-eleven of her persistent in helping me stand upright. I don't bother shrugging her off again.

"Was it the fae? Explain yourself," Darius demands, his arms crossed over his chest. Trained and stoic as he is, his worry is palpable.

"It was dragons. General Solbourne, the soldiers, Malek..." I pause, my eyes heating. "They're all gone."

"All of them?" a guard asks.

"Where did they go?" probes another.

With a tick of his jaw, Darius seems to realize it right then. My power is lethal, and I am the Legacy Legion's most deadly weapon. With but a thought, I can annihilate almost any foe so long as my eterì stores are full. But the others, numbering so few, didn't stand a chance against the dragons.

"And the beasts?" Darius manages, his shoulders tense.

"I obliterated the ones that stayed behind."

"Alone?" He is dumbfounded.

My sisters stand on either side of me now, their support evident.

"Alone," I reiterate.

"How did this happen?" Darius demands, reaching out a hand to grab me before thinking better of it. I am, after all, his new general—and most people are terrified of me.

"We arrived in Dieppe early," I explain, "and General Solbourne insisted we camp along the Alabaster Coast. I advised against it, but the soldiers accompanying us were tired, and the general wouldn't force them to stay in the boat. Malek suggested we set up camp on the cliffs. He thought it'd be best to have higher ground, and Solbourne agreed."

"And what transpired?" Darius asks.

"Though we didn't see the dragons immediately," I went on, "they had a sort of safeguard around them that I could *feel*, capable of incapacitating my eterì. When my power left me, I informed the general, who ordered us to rush down the hill to find shelter. We didn't see the beasts until it was too late. Without my eterì, I was caught off guard. I had to fight by hand, leaving the others to fend for themselves. Some dragons were immune to fire, so Solbourne was the first they took out." I shake my head. "I think the dragons planned it, coordinated with one another. They seemed to know exactly where we'd be and what Solbourne had ordered. They're smart, Darius. They must be."

A loud murmuring fills the courtyard.

"What do you mean, Lieutenant-General? They're beasts."

I scowl at Darius. Obviously, they're beasts. Of everyone here, I know it most. It's a divergent theory; some legacies whisper it among themselves when they think no one is listening. I'd laughed at the mere suggestion, but now I find more truth in their eccentric notions.

A cool, dark voice cuts in: "She's *general* now, Darius. You know the protocol."

I groan, slapping a hand over my dirty face.

Asher Aidos descends the steps, one lethal foot after the other. Everyone turns their attention to the seven-foot-tall icy blond fae, his teal half-buttoned shirt billowing, revealing his heavily tattooed neck. He smirks, causing some legacies to swoon and others to cower.

"My apologies, General," Darius quickly bows, his tusks almost scraping me. "The shock deceived my tongue. It won't happen again."

I nod curtly, turning my attention to the fae king. The last time I was (stuck) in his presence he was needling me about squeezing more fae into my training regimen. I countered that my schedule was already bursting at the seams with training the legacy soldiers, leaving no room for additional burdens. In response, he suggested he join me, collaborating to incorporate more troops into the mix. I retorted with a few choice words that were far from polite, but he deflected them with infuriating ease. Our argument stretched on endlessly, neither of us willing to back down.

It wasn't until nightfall that the tension finally lessened so that we might sleep. So now, as I catch sight of him, all smug with that nauseatingly handsome face, my irritation flares up once more.

"Why is it that you only appear when there's trouble, Asher?" I ask. He doesn't appear to be affected by the authority in my voice.

"That's *King* Asher, General," he corrects me. "King Asher *Trouble* Aidos."

I sneer down at him, my cheeks reddening as some of the murmurs become chuckling. "I am not in the mood for your shit today, King Trouble. If you'll excuse me, I have some debriefing to do and a shower to take."

"Happy to come along," he returns, his eyes darkening.

I lift a swollen middle finger at Trouble and walk with my sisters up the stairs and into the Intelligence Division's head-quarters to file an official incident report. I ignore the fae king who trails behind us.

We lost a lot of good people on the unforeseen battlefield.

I wonder if Malek is dead.

For his sake, I hope he is.

CHAPTER 3
ASHER

If I hadn't been tied up at the Fae Capitol, busy assigning roles for my departure, I'd have gotten to the Legacy Compound sooner. Be as it may, I wouldn't have been at the docks when the dragons had come to attack on the other side of the English Channel.

I planned to accompany Jade—the fae Minister of International Development and Trade—to oversee the trade, then travel back to the Compound with Astraea's group. When they didn't show, I instantly hopped on a boat and fled down the Seine River to visit the legacies. I had a suspicion something had gone wrong. I hadn't expected it to be this bad.

They were to complete a simple assignment: getting seed for the greenery and a few extra weaponries. They shouldn't have disembarked their boat, but as Astraea explained the situation, it was clear their group was tired and so requested a short rest before coming to my territory. Astraea had been right to try convincing General Solbourne otherwise, even if she hadn't been successful. Solbourne was too concerned with the feelings of others, with making them comfortable instead of doing what was best for their safety. His mistake had cost them their lives—all their lives, save for Astraea and perhaps Malek.

As I listen to the newly appointed general explain their exact movements from hour to hour, it becomes clear she'd done everything she could to protect those around her. Even if she couldn't save the lives of the few soldiers that had gone on assignment, she'd slain as many dragons as possible before they evacuated.

Astraea, the deadliest legacy alive, is a power to behold. She is a rarity with her spirit eterì, something seldom heard of. She is born of power—as am I. Though only the legacies are assured the gift of eterì, some other species receive the gift too, but it is uncommon. I, king of the fae, am also born with spirit eterì. Perhaps that's why Astraea hates me. Maybe it bothers her that she shares this trait with me and no other.

Though she'd torn through beasts and trekked back alone, burdened with grief, she wears her chin high in upholding her duties to the Compound. She even has enough energy to send me stormy looks with her fox-sharp eyes when the Intelligence Agents are busy typing in their processers, updating their system, marking the brave soldiers as deceased. There will be a funeral next eve, and though that wasn't why I'd necessitated a week away from the Fae Court, it was all the same in the end.

Aspen, my sibling and Regent, is governing in my absence. I completely trust Aspen, and know the Fae Court is safe under their and our Council's rule. Aspen is not only kind and fair, but can also be strict when necessary, ensuring every member of the Council and our people stay in line. Although I miss them, I am confident they will be fine each time I depart to join the Legacy Legion.

I completely trust my sibling, and know the Fae Court is safe under their and our Council's rule. Aspen is not only kind and fair, but can also be strict when necessary, ensuring every member of the Council and our people stay in line. Although I miss them, I am confident they will be fine each time I depart to join the Legacy Legion.

The legacies and the fae have an accord clarifying our alliance in the war against the dragons and any other creatures who go against the celestials' rules. As king, I can often be found beside General Solbourne and Lieutenant-General Astraea, which seems to madden her.

I smirk at the woman still glaring at me with the most impressive scowl. I cock a brow at her when she crosses her arms. *Is it me, or did she wince?* Aside from her auto-immune diseases, Astraea's pain rarely lasts, as anything that isn't biological can be healed with eterì. Surely, she would have healed herself if she'd been injured.

"If that is all, you may leave, General Astraea," says the Intelligence Agent, noting all that Astraea reported. I am always pleased with the reminder that no one knows her purposely buried surname—no one but me. She likely assumes her name is lost to everyone, but I found it.

"That is all," Astraea replies, then hastily leaves the chamber. My attention snaps in her direction.

Astraea glides through the building, leaving a trail of wind behind her as I shadow her through the Compound. Being fae has its perks. We are the fastest in the world—likely. I wonder who would win in a race between us.

As we slow, I ask, "Do you need any assistance?"

"I don't want anything from you, *Asher*." She hisses my name like an insult.

"One of these days, you'll see that I am only here to help."

She grumbles, displeased. "You are only ever here when I've fucked up, or to try to show me up." She turns on me as we reach her apartment, somehow looking down at me though I am much taller than the legacy. "I don't want you around. When are you going to get that through your thick skull?"

Ouch.

"It is my duty to aid the Legacy Legion, thus making it my duty to help you, *General.*"

Astraea winces as if I've burned her. I can tell what she is thinking. She has always wanted the promotion to General, but this was a poor way to achieve it. Not because she is only twenty-nine—and would replace the eighty-year-old late-General—but because lives were lost for her to take his place. Solbourne was getting soft with the years. I still can't believe how he handled his last assignment, which cost him and the Legacy Legion more soldiers than they could afford.

"Then go find someone else who needs your *help*," Astraea snaps, crafting air quotes around the word *help.*

My eyes darken with a not-so-subtle warning. She knows I'm a king, yet she never shows me the respect my title deserves. I'm getting tired of her hatred for me, especially since, try as I might, I can't make myself hate her.

"Goodnight, Astraea."

She scowls before opening her door and shutting it in my face. "It's General," she mumbles from inside her apartment.

I shake my head. *General, indeed.*

CHAPTER 4
RAVENA

"Seriously, Raea," I say. "Let me help you! You must have been injured somewhere."

It's absolutely no use. My stubborn, unyielding sister won't budge.

Her eyes narrow. "Are you calling me weak?"

"Gods, no, Raea. Even if you didn't get wounded in battle, your body must be tired, and your joints must be aching." Though Astraea's resilient, she was born with limitations—autoimmune diseases. She was diagnosed with rheumatoid arthritis when she was very young, which affects her joints with stiffness, pain and swelling.

When she was twenty-one, she was diagnosed with lupus. Despite these challenges, Astraea's resilience is a beacon of inspiration. She never shows it more than she must, but it causes her many troubles in her daily life. It makes her heart race, leading to premature ventricular contractions. It also gives her the shakes, makes her intolerant to heat, gives her immense trouble sleeping, causes hair loss—which she detests—and makes her feel weak, one reason why she works tirelessly to keep her strength.

"I just need to take a shower and sleep it off." Astraea motions impassively, shouldering her way through her bathroom door and shutting it closed.

My sister Aurelia nudges me, hard enough to remove me from my spot in front of the bathroom door. "She'll be okay, Vena. Don't worry,"

"We don't know that." I sigh, defeated, flopping onto Astraea's bed with a humph.

"This isn't her first battle. She's tough."

I eye her, unconvinced. "She's never been through something like this." I shudder in thinking of all the people who lost their lives on a day when no one had even expected to see battle. "Astraea killed a horde of dragons on her own. She's powerful as hell, but *that*... She's not supposed to be able to do that. She shouldn't have had to, either."

"We've always known she was strong. Who says she wasn't supposed to be able to wipe out a horde of beasts? If Urðra deemed it, it was destined."

"Our mother had nothing to do with today, and you know it. At the very least, she would've warned Raea," I reason. "Just because she is the Celestial of Fate, it doesn't mean she creates it. She gives hints about paths to choose from."

"She doesn't inform me about my paths like with Raea," Aurelia answers bitterly. I chuck a pillow at her form, and she lifts her shoulders at me. "What? It's true." She folds her arms and joins me on the bed.

"The only reason she gets so much help from Mother is because she's one of her eterìan rulers. If Mother's sector ruled us, she'd do the same for us. Just because you don't get divinatory guidance from her like Raea does, it doesn't mean she's not looking out for you."

"Still, it would be nice to—"

I cut her off with a glare. This is not meant to be an Aurelia pity party. We are here to support our sister, who just survived an entire battle on her own. Oasòs above, that poor girl. Day and night, she takes on such enormous weight in climbing toward this leadership position. I can't imagine this is how she thought she'd receive the title.

"Astraea needs us, Rel." My determination to support my sisters is unwavering.

Aurelia deflates, understanding. Sometimes, she can be a little daydreamy, a little absent-minded, but Aurelia cares and loves us just as dearly as we love her. Astraea would never admit such a thing, but we know what we mean to each other.

As Relie and I wait for Astraea to come out of her bathroom, my mind wanders to our beginnings, wondering how we got here. Our mother raised me and Astraea together until Raea was five years old. Mother sent her from Oasòs to learn and train at the Compound. She never told me what it was like for her when she was alone here, saying only she was glad our mother had sent me and Relie to her. When my sister turned six, she swore to protect and care for me like a mother should. I was five then, crying like a babe, snotting all over my sister's hug. Our bond, forged in tears and mirth, has only deepened over the years.

We grew up together and went to the academy, only one grade apart. We were inseparable, especially in our early years. When Aurelia came into the picture, Astraea was eleven and already starting combat training. I was ten, excited for my first year of introductory botany. Aurelia was five and the sauciest child known to man, far braver than I when I was sent down. I giggle to myself, remembering her tiny finger pointing in the face of the guard who'd brought her from Oasòs to the Compound, as she swore up and down that she'd repay him the favor of taking everything he loved dearly.

Who'd have thought that feisty little blue-eyed girl would turn out to be a healer, just like her big sister? Though she didn't continue her studies to become a botanist like me, Aurelia is happy to be a routine healer since her eterì is air.

"What are you smiling about?" Astraea says, startling me out of my memories.

"Sorry, Rae Rae," I say, trying to elicit a grin with her most hated nickname. I am rarely successful, so seeing her fake smile is hard. She doesn't need to hide her pain from us. We're her sisters.

Raea pokes at my forehead. "Stop fretting. I'm fine."

"But—"

Aurelia stops me with a slight tug on my sleeve. I watch Astraea take her nightly medication and decide not to push her. I heave a heavy sigh, then ask, "Can we sleep on your couch tonight? Just for our own peace of mind."

Astraea's usual frown deepens, but she agrees with a slight nod.

"Speak for yourself, Vena. That couch is not sleep-friendly." Aurelia juts her chin, standing from the bed and striding through the room. "I'm going to get a cot from the infirmary."

"Suit yourself, sassy pants."

"Please don't make a mess in here," Astraea groans. "I'm too tired to clean up after you slobs tonight."

"Yes, Your Majesty." Aurelia tosses her hair over her shoulder, where it hangs down her back. I don't know how she carries that blonde mass on her head every day. I watch her leave the room before turning to find Astraea in bed.

"Can you turn out the lights, Ravena?" Astraea asks from under her chunky knit black blanket. When had she climbed into bed? Poor thing must be so worn.

"Not in the mood to spook me with your magical lights-out trick?" I laugh, making my way to the lamp.

"Depleted."

It is one word, muffled into her pillow, but it says it all. My stomach churns at the thought of Astraea—the strongest soldier in the Legacy Legion—depleted of her eterì. I silently shut the light off, softly tuck the blankets around my sister, and let her drift to sleep.

CHAPTER 5
AURELIA

When I return to Astraea's room, the lights are out, and Ravena quiets me with a soft shush. I brought two folding cots, not caring what Vena said about the hard leather couch, over which I knew she'd prefer a semi-soft mattress.

Ravena thanks me with a hand on my shoulder and helps me with the blankets and pillows.

"Is she asleep?" I whisper.

Ravena nods.

"I take first watch?"

She nods again.

"Okay." I remove my hearing aids, place them in their case, then wrap myself in the blanket.

Before returning to the room, I'd gone down to the liquor stores and loosened myself up a bit. There's a long night ahead, and I always get tense when things like this happen. It was when Astraea went through trauma that her celestial rulers would shove their divinatory guidance down her throat. I wonder what she might see tonight.

Ravena and I settle in our cots, facing each other. Her worried expression matches how I feel. Ravena slides her small hand and reaches out to me.

"Night, Sis," she whispers.

I squeeze her hand firmly before letting go. "Night."

As Vena starts snoring, it begins raining. It's almost symbolic, like the celestials of Oasòs are mourning their dead. I hear Astraea shift and turn to face her, watching silently to see if she's awoken. Her brow is pinched tight, her frown heavy with sorrow. I sense a pang in my chest as I imagine all she'd seen tonight. Knowing her, what she did now followed her into the dream realm.

My eldest sister is the strongest of them all. The world doesn't call her Reaper for nothing. Known for her slaying skills and lethal determination, she is a force to be reckoned with. Every species in every territory knows who she is, and fears what she represents: death.

Ravena and I take to the other side of nature, wanting to heal the world rather than destroy it. I am sure Astraea's motivations are good-willed, but she so readily follows the celestial's guidance that I sometimes wonder if she wouldn't benefit from questioning their judgement more often. Even just *once* might make a change. She is a devotee to their every command. Astraea doesn't need to fight in the war. She doesn't need to kill. She is told to, and so does so. Deep down, she must enjoy it. There are moments I've seen a disturbing gleam in her eye while she trains, knocking down every opponent. She is good at her craft, sure. But at what cost?

"Malek," my sister murmurs in her sleep.

A chill runs up my spine. Is she having a divinatory guidance, dream, or nightmare? Worse yet, is she being tormented by her atrocious memories?

I let a soft breeze flow from my palm toward my sister,

aiming to soothe her. My air eterì stirs her hair, lessening her frown, if faintly. With the swelling thud of rain, I relax into my pillow, promising not to fall asleep to ensure, in any way, that I can comfort Raea.

CHAPTER 6
ASTRAEA

I almost ignore the sun when it shines through my window, debating whether to shove my face into my pillow. I don't want to die, per se, but I do want to skip this day. There will be a group funeral at twenty hundred hours, where I will be speaking as newly appointed general.

Last night, I dreamt of Malek, a memory of him and I sparring on the mat. He wore a happy grin, while I remained stoic.

"Oh, loosen up, Lieutenant-General," he teased me. "Your face won't crack if you smile occasionally."

"Are you telling me to smile, Malek Azadiron? Surely you wouldn't be so foolish." I lunged forward, bending low to swipe out my leg and knock him swiftly on his back.

"Not fair!" he groaned. "I wasn't ready."

"And is that my fault?" I asked, peering down at him.

"Maybe." He shrugged. "You are responsible for my training."

I snorted, giving him my hand to help him up. "You are responsible for your damn self. If you let your mind wander, that's on you."

Malek laughed, patting me on the shoulder. "But I know you've always got my back, Raea. What do I need to worry my mind for?"

The dream ended there, haunting me with the memory of his words. I wasn't able to protect him yesterday, and that unforgettable black dragon had fled with him in its clutches.

I have to let that go, to focus on today. I stretch, immediately wincing as my bones, muscles, nerves all object, not to mention my stomach injury. I forgot about that hindrance.

I'd come dangerously close to being dragon meat myself. This wound just reminds me how sharp their claws are. I didn't even realize how severely I'd been struck before entering the washroom last night and undressing in front of the mirror. Only after the adrenaline faded did I notice the burn, which had torn through muscle and flesh and pierced my shirt. Thankfully, legacies heal quickly from injuries, and I even quicker, with the help of my spirit eterì. Manipulating energy, life, and death has its perks. Unfortunately, I spent most of my eterì last night in wiping out the rest of the dragons. I don't have enough in my stores to fully heal myself.

I had to reopen the wound to clean it—nothing unusual. My sisters were in my room, though, so I turned the shower on and bit down on a hand towel to mask my pain. Pain makes me most uncomfortable of all, less from the experience of it than from the attention it attracts. Legacies don't typically get auto-immune diseases, so my having two stirs enough notice on its own. It isn't necessary to go around limping because of a wound that will eventually heal.

I never allow myself to display my limitations, not even around my sisters. I am the fiercest legacy, whether I get hurt or not. There is no need to scare those I'm responsible for protecting. I can handle the scrapes and bruises. The last run I did, I broke two ribs fighting a vampire. I didn't even wince when my sister Ravena poked me teasingly in the side. She would be none the wiser.

"You're awake," Ravena says. It's like she knows I'm thinking of her. I wince and turn onto my back, staring up at the ceiling as I let my hips and shoulder blades set. My muscles are tender, and my stiff joints grind until they stabilize.

"Yup."

"Good," Aurelia grumbles. "I'm going to sleep now."

From the corner of my eye, I watch Ravena smack our baby sister with her pillow. I almost crack a smile.

"It's not my fault you didn't wake me to take over watch," says Vena.

"You were snoring like a trucker," Aurelia argues. "There was no waking you."

Ravena gasps in mock embarrassment. "A trucker? A lady would never." She fans her face and puts her round glasses on the tip of her nose.

"Exactly," Relie snarks. "A *lady* never would."

I laugh. Ravena walked right into that trap. "Would you two knock it off? Neither of you had to take watch. I am the general of this entire Compound. I don't need either of you two bickering about responsibilities that aren't even real." I stretch once more, testing the ache in my stomach—how acceptable enough for me to get up. "I've got shit to do and no time to waste." I stand on my shaky morning legs, mentally preparing myself for today.

"Want me to run down to the kitchens to grab some food?" Ravena offers. Gods, why was she always so nice? I didn't deserve it. "I've volunteered to set up the service," she adds.

"That would be great." I rummage through my seamlessly organized dresser and grab a pair of heavy-duty leggings, a long-sleeved shirt, and underthings. I decide to be ridiculous and wear my favorite lingerie. Feeling put together always boosts my confidence, and though no one will see my matching ice blue lace set with all the straps, I know I'll look hot under my training attire.

"Are you really going to train today?" Ravena asks, with an accusing eye toward my clothes.

"I've got to stay sharp."

"One day off won't hurt," she tries. She knows she's wasting her breath.

No days off, no exceptions.

"Let her train, V," Aurelia whines from under her blanket. "She will do it no matter what you say. The quicker you let her take a piss, the quicker I get to sleep." Her long blonde hair falls over the sides of her cot, sure to knot up in ways she'll hate brushing out later.

I snort. "Touchy."

Ravena shakes her head at Relie's grumpy form. "Make sure you pick up after yourself when you get up," she warns her. "You know how Raea is about having a clean space."

"Shh..." Aurelia turns onto her stomach, shutting us out.

"Come on," I say. "I'll join you in the assembly hall for breakfast in an hour."

Ravena cheers and I take that chance to tend to my stomach, showering off last night's nightmare and preparing for another day—my first actual day as general.

As the water rinses last night's death, my divinatory guidance comes roaring back to life, repeating itself in my head:

Embrace not death. Seek instead solace in knowledge. Let wisdom be your guiding light as you navigate the challenges ahead. Have faith in your instincts, for they will lead you to greatness.

What were the celestials trying to tell me? Which one of them had reached out to me?

It couldn't have been Mother. She usually shows me a selection of choices, leading me down paths potentially open to me. Though she isn't supposed to hint at which is best, she has a habit of breaking those rules to help me.

It wasn't Aegliðs, Celestial of Volition. He's never commanding.

I'd been warned against death, so it would be odd for Ahemì to have spoken against himself.

Had it been C'tarð? She's the Celestial of Wisdom. Am I meant to follow her in battle? She rarely gives advice when it comes to the bloodshed I sow.

The rulers of my eterìan sector often give me necessary signs of aid. I can't figure out who gave me this new indication, or why.

Let wisdom be your guiding light.

I will certainly try.

CHAPTER 7
ASTRAEA

I walk fast down the corridor, ignoring the burn in my abdomen and trying to focus on reinvigorating my muscles. Despite yesterday's disaster, I am treating this day as an ordinary one at the Compound. My training is important, as is keeping my soldiers fit.

"You look like a woman on a mission," says a voice.

I jump, whirling on my adversary, grabbing him by the throat and pinning him against the brick wall.

"Ugh," I groan, hissing as I release the fae king, whose wild eyes are filled with excitement.

Of course, it's Asher.

"That's an entertaining way to be greeted in the morning," he says. "It isn't typical, but I'm not opposed to it." He smirks, knowing his words will burrow under my skin.

I inhale harshly through my nose and turn away from him, resuming my path down the hall.

"No apology?" he teases, easily striding alongside me, as though my fast pace is a leisurely stroll for him.

I snort. "The day you hear an apology from me is the day I die."

"Oh, Reaper. You wound me," he drawls.

I look at him from the corner of my eye, catching him watching me. A blond strand of hair curls over his ice-blue eyes.

"Are you following me?" I question.

He dramatically rolls his striking eyes. "Yes. Because I have nothing better to do than follow you around." He looks ahead, his smirk still plastered on his smug face. It doesn't reach his eyes, though, which tells me I've successfully irked him.

Good.

"You're still following me," I taunt as we march tightly down the spiral staircase, side by side. I am all-too-aware of his arm brushing mine, and it sends a revolting shiver through my skin.

"For your information," he says, "I was called to the Intelligence Division. Believe it or not, I have better things to do than irritate you."

"Doubt it," I mutter under my breath as we reach the entryway.

Asher stops, blocking my path with an arm across the door. His eyes narrow into slits. "What was that?" he asks, voice low.

"Move, Aidos. Before I make you." I stand my ground, fists clenched and at the ready.

He laughs darkly, looming over me. "I'd like to see you try."

I grin, a wicked expression settling over my features. "Don't tempt me."

We stare at each other for a long while before he lowers his arm and admits defeat.

I clap my hands and stroll past the tall fae. "That's more like it."

We split in separate directions, him heading to the Intelligence Division, and I eagerly stepping on the field for weapons training to release my frustrations.

"Astraea," Asher calls.

I slowly turn on my heel, eyes closed and breathing steadily.

"What?" I demand between clenched teeth, opening my sights to stare up at him. Apparently, he changed his mind, and decided to follow me after all.

He casts his gaze down at our feet, his brows furrowed. "Last night..." he begins, his lips tight. He lifts his gaze to me again, and it baffles me to see a troubled expression on his face. "Are you all right?"

The question catches me off guard. After our lovely chat in the corridor, it feels out of place. I nod slowly, my regard inquisitive.

He nods back, and I catch the moment he swallows. "Good."

"Good," I reiterate, mouth dry.

He licks his lips, and suddenly the worry on his face dissipates, replaced with his usual complacency. "Right then. I'll leave you to your morning brooding."

I grumble, and punch his shoulder. "I was not brooding."

Asher chuckles as he backs away. "You could've fooled me."

CHAPTER 8

RAVENA

Astraea tried to sit with me to eat our breakfast earlier this morning, but too many people needed her aid in preparing for today. She gave me an apologetic look before leaving me to work. I understood, though it still made my heart ache. I busied myself throughout the day, making myself as useful as I could.

The kitchens are packed with volunteers and the customary culinary personnel. With so many lost in last night's battle, there are many families to feed for the upcoming service. Legacies mill about, helping one another with various tasks. It's good to see my people come together, but hurtful, too, knowing it's under heartrending circumstances.

"Ravena! Good. You're here." Emir ushers me in and hands me a large tray of sandwiches.

"Isn't it a little early to send out the food? The service is only at eight tonight." I look closer, chuckling at the heart-shaped sandwiches on the platter. The head cook at the Compound is an older gentleman whose laugh lines are a permanent reminder of his soft soul.

"It's for the children," he replies, a grim smile on his face. "Many are mourning. I thought I would send them something with a little extra love for supper."

I return his smile. "That was very thoughtful of you. I'll take it to them now."

Emir pats the top of my head, sending me away.

I stride through the halls, down one corridor and into the next. On the first floor of the Compound's dormitory is a daycare center for young children whose parents work during the day. Though I am a botanist by night, working in research labs and creating potions for the Legion, I spend the day as a healer, helping wherever needed. The daycare is actually my favorite place—I love being surrounded by the children, healing their minor scrapes and hugging them till they feel better. I've always had a soft spot for kids. I would have twenty if I could, though I'd need a willing counterpart. I laugh internally, picturing twenty little curly-haired kids running amuck.

Okay, maybe not *twenty*.

As I enter the daycare, I'm startled by trembling underfoot. I brace myself for more, but thankfully, this aftershock is a light one. We've been getting them more often now that the Outer Edge is expanding. Because we can't enter said Outer Edge, no legacy—or any other being— knows what's causing the tremors. Many have tried and failed to enter the Outer Edge, winding up either wounded or killed in the process. The dragons inside are strong, their domain impenetrable.

I wipe the concern from my face as I enter the room full of bright-eyed kiddies who greet me with big hellos. Most of them are oblivious to today's sorrow. That's good. They're so young. They don't need to understand just yet. Let them keep their innocence for as long as possible.

"Hey, Ravena." Juniper, the daycare teacher, salutes me with a slight wave.

"Hey, Juniper. Do you need a little break before I return to the kitchens?"

"Yes, please!" they reply enthusiastically. "I have been holding my bladder for too long. It was getting risky."

I snort, shooing them away. "Please don't make a mess I wouldn't want to clean up."

They laugh. "No promises." Juniper winks before spinning on their heel and running for the restroom.

"Miss Avena!" Adorable little red-haired Valentina lifts her tiny fists, pointing at the tray I carry. She's still unable to pronounce her Rs, making her even more endearing. "Are those sandwiches for us?"

"Why, yes, they are, honey. Will you help me share these with your friends?"

Valentina stretches up, swiping a ham and mustard delight from the tray and shoveling it in her mouth. She garbles heartily around the sandwich, crumbs stippling her chubby cheeks. I set the tray down and watch the kids eat, enjoying my time playing with them and listening to their interactions. They count adventurous stories around mouthfuls of food, swinging foam swords at invisible monsters.

"Miss Avena," Valentina says, tugging on my shirt. "There's a dragon in the hall."

"Oh, honey." I laugh, patting her on the head. "There's no dragon."

Valentina grumbles, raising her weapon of choice behind me.

"Avena," she whines. "Look!" I smile at the silly girl and turn to play the game. Except, *holy gods,* this isn't a game!

"Oh, my gods! Kids!" I shriek. "Go hide in the back room! Now!" The children scream for their lives, their tiny feet taking far too long. I suddenly feel like Juniper wasn't the only one playing chicken with their bladder.

What am I going to do? I can't let the dragon reach the

distance of the kids. I'll have to distract it, somehow, to get it away from the daycare. On shaky limbs, I step into the hall and quietly shut the door behind my back, chilled by the decisive click of the passage bolt.

The dangerous beast eyes me warily, motionless, save for its coal-black eyes which track me.

"H-h—hey, there," I croak, my voice quieter than a mouse.

The beast huffs.

I wave. "Um, nice dragon."

It follows my hand gesture, and I jump. "N-n-n—no," I try, my voice so wobbly. "Stay."

The dragon grumbles, angling its head and prowling toward me.

I cling to the wall, inching my way down the hall, trying my best not to panic. I need to convince the dragon to retreat. Without thinking, I thrust my arm out, pointing to the window. "Look!" I scream. "A flying monkey!"

To my vast surprise, a deep indigo dragon soars across the yard, faster than the speed of light.

"Shit," I groan. "That's not a monkey."

"Avena?" Valentina asks, stealing the breath out of me.

What the hell is she doing out of the room?

"I don't think that dragon is nice," she says.

I want to laugh, but I can only muster a watery smile.

"Go back inside, Valentina. Lock the door behind you."

"No!" she yells, her tiny little voice earsplitting in the cramped hallway.

It's too late. The dragon set its sights on her.

I bolt toward the beast, with no plan beyond desperation to keep the children safe. "Come get me, you big-toothed bitch!" I taunt, throwing all my weight into the dragon. It rears its head at me, throwing me against the wall. My body throbs under the impact, but I have no time to waste on me.

"Avena!" Valentina screams. I look in horror as she raises her ridiculous foam weapon, facing the beast alone. I stand, inhaling, mindful of my asthma as I grind my teeth.

"You will not hurt that child!" I order.

The dragon turns back to me. Before I can blink, it lunges, tail whipping up and slamming into Valentina who, for some unblessed reason, decides to cling to the vicious thing.

"Run, Valentina! Let go and get out of here!" I shout as the dragon closes its talons around me and spreads its wings. I watch in terror as the rest of the children run toward the door, looking far too brave as they peek their heads out.

"Valentina!" bellows Theo, the mightiest-looking brother I've ever seen. He bolts, pushing his friends out of his path with harsh determination set in his eyes. He grabs hold of the dragon's tail, joining Valentina.

"Theo, no!" I scream as he shoves Valentina off the beast. The dragon whips its tail again, hurling Theo into the air and swallowing him in one bite. "No!" My voice shreds, my heart splintering to pieces.

The dragon lifts into the air.

CHAPTER 9
AURELIA

A catastrophic detonation propels me out of my bed—sharp and full of agony. I'm stunned by a burst of vivid light. As the smolder fades, I gape in shock at the giant monstrosity who'd burst through Raea's bedroom wall. I'm covered in rubble, and the cots are burnt to a crisp. The massive black beast searches the room with glowing gold eyes, able to fit only its head through the hole it made. It grunts, then, surprisingly, abandons me.

I have but a second to compose myself before another dragon, smaller than the first, lands in the bedroom. It lowers to the ground, preparing for attack.

"So, uh," I choke, looking around the room for some type of weapon. "You come here often?"

A small bout of relief finds me as I spot some of Astraea's knives hung on the wall just a few tormenting feet away. I eye them as I carefully walk backward. The dragon huffs, hot smoke billowing out and fanning me. I do the first thing I can think of and seize a heavy vase, chucking it at the beast. It blasts its fire, incinerating the makeshift weapon without a thought.

One second, I stand in Astraea's bedroom, eyes locked with a monster. The next thing I know, I'm upside-down as the beast snatches me up in its great claws and swoops me into the sky. Everything in me seems to fall into my throat, and I scream.

"Aurelia!"

"Ravena?" I cry, whipping my head this way and that as my hair tries to strangle me. Why, oh, gods, why had I let it grow this long?

"Relie!" my sister screams again.

I clutch tightly to the dragon's claw, righting myself to find Ravena in the grasp of a violet dragon. Disturbingly, she and the dragon are all I can see in the oblivion of the clouds.

We're going to join that oblivion.

We're going to die.

CHAPTER 10
ASTRAEA

I'm about to retire my sword to join in on strength training when suddenly the ground quakes. At first, the soldiers around me ignore the shock. We're accustomed to it. But after the sound of an explosion comes from the west wing of the Compound, it's clear something isn't right.

What the fuck?

I did not just see that.

I'm losing my mind.

Fire sweeps overhead, shaking me out of my stupor. I glimpse my sisters above me, screaming in the clutches of dragons.

"Those who can't fight, get to safety!" I cry. "The rest of you, give them hell!"

My soldiers roar at my decree, already strapped and ready to go.

"Never look back 'cause what?" I add, running toward the fire.

"Carnage awaits no matter the direction!" we all shout, armour clanging with every step. I have no protection, but don't have time to load up. I have a sword, my mostly replenished eterì, and a fury like none other.

No one messes with what's mine.

"Attack!" I scream, my spirit awakening, eyes going white.

At least a dozen dragons burn their way through unlucky passersby, the Compound taking the brunt of the damage. Though the dragon's fire can't breach the repellent placed on the buildings, their massive bodies easily bust through. How did they find us? The dragons were never able to see past the Compound's disguise.

I centre myself, allowing my strong eterì to guide me, trusting I'll make it out the other end. Three heavy beasts burst through the windowed ceiling in the atrium, landing at my feet. I use my eterì to shield me from the glass, then smile sharply.

"Looking for me?" I taunt, voice low and deadly. I tuck my sword in its sheath, wanting to save my physical energy as a last resort. Without a blink, my eterì lashes out, stealing their souls for my reaping. I always sense an increase in drive when my eterì does this, even if it means I'm depleting my power. I don't enjoy taking life, but it's either kill or be killed, and I bow to no one.

A loud tremor rocks the walls around me, and I surge through the opening before any mouth can swallow me whole. To my surprise, a giant beast with golden eyes sits still, watching me.

"Oh, you've got to be kidding me." Its scales, black as pitch, glimmer under the moonlight. It's a memorable enemy: the dragon who'd almost found me—the one who'd taken Malek.

"It's you," I say.

The dragon cocks its head at me, unmoving. He shadowed me here. There's no other explanation for how the dragons found the Compound.

"Come on, asshole. Let's do this."

My eterì springs to life, the black haze reaching for the beast.

I smile as I wait for it to drop dead, but the power doesn't do what I expect. It just... hovers around the monster as it grins.

Oh shit.

The black eterì leaps toward me, and I brace myself for impact. The pain never comes. The dragon's grin drops, and we eye each other warily. I might not survive if I can't use my magic in this fight. This dragon is enormous, bigger than any I've ever seen before. The look in its eye says it knows precisely what I'm thinking. I don't even have the chance to breathe before the beast is on me.

Unsheathing my sword, I take my stance, lifting my weapon to block my opponent. My blade meets unbreakable scales, each blow a burst of gold. Giant talons reach for me, and I evade them.

"Oh, no, you don't," I grunt, grabbing its tail as it thrashes toward me. I dig in, climbing higher, trying to find an advantage. Colossal spines protrude from its back. I claw my way over its haunches, relying on my physical strength to pull myself up. If I can find its Achilles heel, this will be over with.

Sitting astride the shifting, wrenching beast, I weigh my options. I can try piercing its neck just beneath the jaw, though its scales are so large they may be just as durable there as its stomach. I can jump onto its wing and slice through to incapacitate it, but that would still leave me with a dragon at the Compound I may not be able to vanquish. Or I can try my eterì again, though it hadn't worked the first time. Basically, I'm royally screwed.

Fuck it. I'm going for the neck.

I ascend its neck as it continues thrashing about. Raising my sword with both hands on the pommel, I thrust downward as the monster jostles me. The dragon screeches its anger as my weapon pierces through flesh, my wrists screaming at the shock. To my chagrin, the blade doesn't hit its mark.

The dragon lifts into the air too quickly for me to do anything but grab at the pommel of my flesh-stuck sword and hold on for dear life. At a ninety-degree angle, we hurtle into the sky, ripping through clouds toward darkness broken only by the moon and the stars.

This isn't good. It could be worse—it could have eaten me.

My heart thunders as the wind blows my face apart, tearing the remnants of my sweater from my body. Terror sweeps through me as I watch it flutter in the sky, picturing how I might look if I let go of the sword as the dragon finally levels.

We're flying toward a group of airborne dragons who were undoubtedly at the Compound.

"Raea!"

My sisters.

"Hold on!" I scream back at them.

My dragon flies closer to the others now staggered in a group, and all heading directly for the Outer Edge.

"Guys!" yells Aurelia, struggling in the dragon's grip, her legs dangling above nothing. "I think they're aiming for the—"

"No shit!" I yell in frustration, still clinging to my sword. *Think. Think. Think.* How am I going to get us out of this?

"Don't yell at me!" my sister cries, bawling her face off.

"I'm trying to think!" I retort.

"It—" Ravena sniffles. "It. Ate. A. Kid!" She sobs uncontrollably.

At this, the dragon holding Ravena shakes her, and she cries out.

"Hey, stop that!" I scold it. "You're hurting her!"

The dragon huffs, smoke billowing from its nostrils.

Okay then.

"Raea, we're closing in," Aurelia warns, her eyes wide in horror.

"Just brace yourselves," I command in my most authoritative voice. "You can do this. You're both strong. I know it's dangerous, but you'll have to use your eterì to heal yourselves. Don't overdo it."

Hopelessly ensnared in those great claws, my sisters stare up at me with wide, wet eyes.

"Do you understand me?" I ask sternly.

They both nod, and I'm satisfied with the tiny bit of hope that they'll at least survive the impact and the fall when the wall shuts us out and the dragons drop them. My eterì is gone again because of my captor, so I can't use it to shield myself. No matter. My sisters will live.

"Focus! Almost there, girls. Get ready!" I take in their lovely, terrified faces, bracing myself for impact and hoping this won't be the last time I ever see them again.

"Til Oasòs greets us among the stars," I whisper, as the Outer Edge engulfs us.

CHAPTER II
ASHER

The Intelligence Division building shakes apocalyptically. The floor beneath my feet crumbles apart, the walls collapsing as legacies run for safety. White-hot fire blows in from outside the window. It's clear we are under attack—by dragons, no less.

Fuck.

This is going to be catastrophic. How have they found the Compound?

Astraea.

They must have followed her here. But how did they see through the ward? It should be impossible, unless Astraea was affected by them in some way. Perhaps the dragons have magic potent enough to put a tracker on her. But if that's one of their abilities, why didn't they ever use it before? It's been almost two hundred years since the Compound was founded by the Celestials, and the dragons have never been able to find it until now—until Astraea.

Where is she? She must be in her room by now, getting ready for this evening. The legacies plan to hold a funeral for the departed, and as newly appointed general, Astraea would have to prepare a speech for the fallen.

Dodging bits and pieces of rubble, I sprint as fast as my fae legs will take me, zipping through halls and finding Astraea's room. Grey smoke seeps at the foot of the entrance. Not taking any chances, I barge through the door into a war-torn dormitory, empty and demolished.

A loud cry pierces the sky, and I hurry to the giant opening in the wall, astonished to find Aurelia and Ravena screaming in the grasp of two enormous creatures. Astraea, the fierce general, surely won't be far behind. She would never allow those beasts to take her sisters without a fight.

As if I've summoned her, a giant black monster swoops past her window, its eyes burning into me, carrying Astraea on its back. She sits atop the beast like she's in charge, her shining sword speared through the dragon's scales, her hair whipping in the wind as they ascend to the clouds.

Give them hell, Astraea. I'll be close behind you.

CHAPTER 12
AURELIA

There is no pain as we pass, the Outer Edge brightly flickering as if eterì is in use. One minute, we find ourselves in the brisk night skies of Paris. The next, we're flying into humid clouds above rocky terrain. How can this be? We're in another region of the world.

Every time we dip, I expect my abductor to drop me to my death. At least I'd die on impact. I don't want to die. I turn around to see that Astraea, with her dragon also made it out the other side. Her shocked expression scares me. Is she hurt, or is she surprisingly relieved?

"Are you guys all right?" Astraea bellows over the whistling sound of the wind. Though she's screaming at the top of her lungs, I can barely hear her. With the wind thrashing and my hearing aids out, focusing on anything is a real struggle. I watch Ravena, who's closer to me, sigh in relief.

"Not hurt! Are you?"

"Fine!" Astraea replies. My sisters are okay. I can focus on my impending doom now.

I've always loved clouds, and cloud watching. As an air eterì wielder, it's only natural. So this feels like cruel mockery.

"Relie, you good?" Ravena asks. Her beast glides to my left, a dragon's height below my own dragon's claws. I dip my head. Ravena smiles up at me through her tears.

"The mountain!" Astraea hollers, daring to lift a hand to point ahead. "I think that's where they're headed!"

I gulp at the massive peak.

"How do you know?" Ravena asks.

"A hunch," Raea answers.

I hope for our sake they aren't taking us there for lunch.

Just then, the dragons plunge in unison, their speed increasing as we descend. "Hold tight!" Astraea shouts, as the wind whooshes around me on our cloud-slashing plummet toward the mountain.

Ravena screeches. Raea prepares by squaring her shoulders, never moving her eyes from the dragon's target. My body seizes, my head whipping back as my dragon suddenly pulls back and whips me toward the rocks.

"Eterì ka'aìh mììyre, cõh'ìde mììyre sù'võq!" Astraea screams as she soars through the air, her arms outstretched and shielding us from the impact. Her spirit eterì hugs us tightly, cushioning our fall as we tumble into a cave's entrance. I roll onto my back, the hard ground harsh on my shoulders. The dragons shriek, the ground rumbling as they launch back into the skies.

"Are you guys okay? Are you hurt?" Astraea checks us over, turning our heads back and forth. I stare up at her bloody face, unable to speak. Ravena sobs into my shoulder, her tears soaking my nightgown. "Come on, answer me. You can do this. Are you hurt anywhere?"

I shake my head. Vena does the same. I curl into her, hugging my trembling knees to my chest and clinging to my sister.

"Um, I'm a little bit injured," says a voice, startling us all at once.

"Agent Lightcrest?" Astraea asks, all of us bewildered by his presence.

"Uh, yeah. Hi." He waves, then winces, his shoulder jutting at the wrong angle. "Ow." He groans.

Ravena lifts her head from my arm and scuttles toward Calix, trembling all the way. She's braver than me. I want to haul her back to my side.

"Need help?" Astraea offers.

Sitting at Calix's side, Ravena sniffs. "I've got this," she responds, moving the legacy's auburn hair from his sticky pale face. "Is it just your arm?"

He nods.

"Okay, just sit up real straight for me, all right, Calix? You won't feel a thing."

I watch as Ravena works her eterì, Calix's gaze fixed on her hands that work the healing. His shoulder pops back into place, and a look of relief fills him.

"Thank you, Ravena. I owe you." She gives him a wobbly smile, then turns to me. That's when I see *him* huddled in a darkened corner, looking distraught. I point a shaky finger in his direction, and my sisters follow alertly.

"Holy shit, Malek!" Astraea rushes to his side, collapsing at his feet. "Are you okay? Say something."

She jostles his shoulders, snapping her fingers in his face, and would've slapped him had Ravena not intervened.

Calix sighs heavily. "I found him like that when I was tossed in here. He's not right..."

"No shit, he isn't right. What's wrong with him?" Astraea presses.

Ravena lowers to his level on unsteady limbs, pressing a hand to his forehead. "Malek, honey? Are you feeling well?"

"The voices," he whispers harshly, brown eyes erratically darting from side to side. He holds an arrow to his chest like it's a comfort. Ravena attempts to pry it from him, but he won't let go. "The voices. The voices. The voices!" Malek's rocking only worsens the more he speaks.

"Okay, Malek. It's okay. You're safe." Ravena tugs on the loose sweater around his waist and tucks it behind his head. She always thinks of others first, ensuring they are cared for. I feel guilty for standing by, but I honestly can't move.

"The fire will catch," Malek mutters. "Claim, claim, claim, cl—" Malek suddenly stops, slumping back into the wall.

"What's wrong with him?" Astraea demands, fists clenched tight at her sides. "This *isn't* Malek. I've never seen him like this before."

Ravena grimaces. "He doesn't have a fever, but his behaviour is... concerning."

"You don't say," Raea snaps.

"General, everyone's upset right now. This isn't Ravena's doing." I gawk at the bold legacy, unsure if I've heard him correctly. *Go Calix.*

"I know, I know," Astraea admits, still on edge and irritable. "Fuck. What is happening?"

Calix clears his throat. "Um, well, I think given the circumstances... Given that we're alive and well, the Outer Edge didn't keep us out, I think..."

"Oh, just spit it out already!" Astraea is fuming. She isn't known for her patience.

"Raea," Ravena cautions.

Astraea squares her shoulders, unmoving. "We don't have time for apologies or hurt feelings. We don't know how long we have 'til the beasts come back for us."

"We likely have the night," Calix interjects, earning himself a chilling glare. "Assuming the dragons expended their energy, they will likely sleep through the night."

"Okay," Raea murmurs, seemingly agreeing. "Now, what of our situation? Why did they take us? Why are we still alive and inside the Outer Edge? It should be impossible."

"It didn't hurt at all," Vena states.

I nod, agreeing, though I don't believe they're paying me any mind.

Ravena wrings her hands nervously before adding, "Something that concerns me is that when you told us to focus on our eterì, I couldn't feel mine."

"Wait—you too?" Astraea's eyes widen, her jaw flexing. "I couldn't use mine against the beast who took me. I tried to kill it, but my eterì seemed to deflect. It almost looked like the dragon had control over it. It was like it threw my own eterì at me."

"It likely did," Calix confirms with a grimace. "I tried to use my water eterì against the dragon that took me, but it malfunctioned and turned back on me. I dodged it by a fraction of time. That's when the dragon caught me and took me into the skies. It was so fast; I didn't even see it coming. I didn't know there were others, either. My dragon swooped me up and threw me in here with Malek."

"Where were you when it attacked?" Ravena asks gently.

"I was in the lab doing overtime. I was alone, thank Oasòs. I don't think anyone else got hurt. Well, certainly not during my timeframe. I imagine there was a mess in the aftermath. Did you get a good look, General?"

"Not good enough," Astraea answers glumly. "Though the dragon who took me was their leader. I am almost certain of it. I think the rest of the dragons followed his leave."

"You'd be correct," Calix approves, his posture surer of himself. "Our observations have established that the dragons work similarly to the Legacy Legion—there is one leader, or general, if you will." Calix smiles shyly, but Astraea only scowls further. "Anyhow, the giant beast, the black one with the gold eyes, is the strongest of its horde. I don't know if they're completely intelligent, but from our feeds, we've seen it give a command with but a look toward its warrior. We're told not to read into things. They're creatures—killing machines with a one-track mind."

"What do you believe, Calix?" Ravena probes.

"I think they're just like us. And I think they've claimed us, so to speak." The word *claimed* rings through my mind, Malek's disturbing mutterings a warning.

"Claimed how?" Astraea wonders, arms crossed, chin tilted.

"I think we were able to pass through the Outer Edge because the dragons allowed us to, and I think they can control our eterì. How, or to what extent, I don't know. But that is my theory."

"Agreed," says Astraea.

"Really?" Ravena questions, a brow cocked. "You're not going to interrogate him further?"

Astraea takes a step forward, and the pair cower just a little. Even I swallow apprehensively.

"Would you like me to?" Raea inquires, her eyes lighting.

"No, thank you," Ravena retorts quickly, giving Calix a warning look before sitting next to him again. Jealousy pricks me. Why hadn't she come to me? I almost go to take my place at her side, but her eyes drift shut, her head falling atop Calix's shoulder. She's worn out.

I decide not to worry her and stay put in my spot in the dimly lit cave, surprised to realize Astraea is missing. My heart thunders rapidly, and I might start to hyperventilate. Though she is terrifying at times, Astraea is our protector. The thought of her missing chills me deeply.

My eyes snap up at the sound of crunching gravel. Raea carries a small pile of wood and a rock, not gone after all. *Thank the stars.*

CHAPTER 13

RAVENA

Venture through the depths of the woodland and receive the wonders which unfold afore your eyes. Embrace nature, for within its comfort lies the key to unlocking all you require.

My eyes shoot open, and I sit up quickly, wiping the drool from my mouth. My heart drops when I realize we're still in a dusty old cave, awaiting our destiny to be dragon food.

"Calix?" I blink at my acquaintance, my glasses crooked on my nose. He lifts a hand and fixes them for me, his cheeks reddening.

"You fell asleep. Didn't want to wake you."

"Oh," I respond, unsure of what to say or do. I look around, searching for my sisters. Aurelia, usually spirited, rests in the same spot I'd last seen her, her knees wrapped tight against her chest. She's always been fair, but now she appears paler than a ghost. Astraea paces back and forth by a fire I hadn't known was there, repeatedly cracking her knuckles.

"Everyone's all right. General Astraea made a fire for us just as you fell asleep."

I incline my head in thanks, feeling a little dazed. "How's Malek holding up?"

Calix frowns and shakes his head sorrowfully.

"I'll try again. There must be something I can do."

"If there is, I'm sure you'll be the one to figure it out," he reassures me.

I smile, squeeze his hand, and get to my feet. My back is achy after sleeping against a cave wall, but all things considered, I am healthy, and so are my sisters. *We'll be all right*, I try to convince myself.

I kneel in front of Malek, who, sadly, looks no better than he did last night.

"Hi, Malek. How are you feeling today?" I ask him gently.

He rocks back and forth, mumbling.

"Can you tell me your name?" I continue, trying to get him to come back to himself.

"Listening, listening…" he murmurs.

"You're listening to me?" I try again. "That's good, honey. Can you tell me your name?"

"They'll hear you," he whispers, rocking more harshly. "They'll know!"

"Okay, okay, Malek," I say. "You rest up. We'll try again later."

I rearrange Malek's sweater, ensuring it cushions his head generously, then return to the fire, sitting an equal distance between Calix and Aurelia.

"Poor guy." Calix sighs. "He hasn't stopped rocking since I got here."

"We need to heal him before the next full moon. I don't want to chance him turning while he's like this." Lycanthropes always turn during a full moon, the change sapping every bit of their strength. We have roughly two weeks to cure him. If Malek turns like this, he likely won't make it. "Gods, I wonder how long he's been like this. I mean, has he eaten? When's the last time he drank water?"

"Likely since that beast took him from the battlefield," Astraea comments impassively. Her lips are pressed into a firm line, and I know she's doing her best not to show any emotion.

"I'm sorry you had to endure that, Raea," I offer, though I know she doesn't want to discuss it. What I don't say is, *I'm so glad you didn't end up like him.* That would only hurt her. I am a healer—I don't hurt people.

"I've been through worse," Astraea says faintly.

"Doesn't make it okay."

"Whatever."

There's a sharp pang in my heart as my sister patches up her walls, shutting me out. Calix reaches out a hand, and I lace my fingers with his. He squeezes mine gently, returning my earlier gesture, and I sigh into his comfort.

Comfort.

What was it I was supposed to remember about comfort?

CHAPTER 14
ASTRAEA

"I'm going to look for food," I tell the group. They're exhausted from their recent terror. If I stay in the cave any longer, staring at my wide-eyed sisters, Calix, and Malek, I will lose my stability. My legs already tremble from over-exertion, and my pulse still races like I've been running ceaselessly. I am on high alert, taking in my surroundings and counting all the exits.

The dragons dropped us in a cave at the bottom of a giant mountain that seems made for Olympian Gods. It's massive, taking over most visible terrain. I wonder where we are and if I can distinguish any of the landscapes. If I can determine where we are, maybe I can find someplace nearby to escape.

"Don't leave us, Raea." Ravena's eyes grow wet again. The poor thing is shaken to her core, her red-rimmed stare pleading.

"You'll be okay. I'll be just outside that opening," I tell her. "I won't go far."

"Be careful." Aurelia whispers, the first words she's spoken since our imprisonment. Her teeth chatter.

"I've got this. Just sit by the fire and warm yourselves. I'll be back before you know it."

I hurry out of the cave, not daring to turn back. If I do, it may tip me over the edge. I must get us out of here, and I have to protect them at all costs. They aren't cut out for this kind of danger. Those dragons are monsters—deadly killers. My sisters are saints, natural healers with caring hearts.

As I peek around the corner and into the woodlands, I scan for any signs of danger. The dragons are nowhere in sight. Unfortunately, as I glance above, the mountain's peak rises into clouds —likely where the dragons are perched.

Stealthily, I traverse through the trees and begin a brisk jog, ignoring the fatigue in my thighs as I search high and low for anything useful. By the looks of it, we're stranded at the bottom of a large mountain, walled by various trees. The dragons took over so much of Earth, it's anyone's guess where they dropped us.

Turn back.

I pause. That's the second time I've heard that grating voice in my head. I must be losing my mind, the Outer Edge playing tricks on me. I need to find a way out of here.

I'm not going far, I fight back.

I spot bright orange stone fruit, high in the leafy branches. The apricots sit in twenty-foot-tall trees, taunting me. With my sword still stuck in the dragon's back, I'll have to climb up and pick the fruit myself. Beyond weary, I adjust my leggings on my hips. I'm about to start climbing when a cool breeze catches my attention.

I am not alone.

My heart halts for a moment before I steady myself. I can't hear anyone approaching, but can smell them—mulled berries and ash trees.

"Hello, little Reaper." I nearly jump out of my skin at the

sound of his voice, his breath barely a whisper but rattling none-theless. My habitually fast heart rate pounds ever faster, pulsing at the base of my neck. I turn rigidly, my face brushing against his chest. I gawk at the sweaty, shirtless, hard-muscled fae who leers down at me.

"What are *you* doing here?" I hiss, punching him in the chest. It hurts my knuckles, but it's worth it.

The corner of Asher's mouth dips roguishly as he leans toward me. He takes a long pause, sweeping his gaze over my hourglass figure. I'm not oblivious to how I appear. Some might find me alluring. I exude strength, and my physique is a testa-ment to the countless hours I dedicate to rigorous training. Though I maintain a disciplined routine, I really love cake, and cake adores my hips.

"Chivalry isn't dead." He chuckles, then tugs on my messy hair. "You're delightful when you're angry."

I grumble, irritated, whirling back toward the tree.

"Hey, that's not how to treat your knight in shining armour."

"Please." I snort, hauling my weight up the tree with expert precision. I ignore the ache in my joints and concentrate on the fruit above. "You're a jester, at best." I scowl down at the fae king, pluck fruit after fruit, and toss them to the ground. I chuck the last one at his head for good measure.

"Nice try," he purrs, snatching the offending apricot midair.

I jump from the tree, landing in a crouch, looking up at him through my lashes. My knees scream, but I command the strength in my muscles to hold me steady. "Next one won't miss." I stand swiftly, gather the fruit, carrying them in the crook of my arms, and leave the fae king. Though his steps are silent, I know by the *tsk*-ing behind me that he's following.

"Don't you have something better to do than annoy the shit out of me?" I say, eyes pointing at the cave's entrance a few yards away.

"Are you always this grumpy?"

"Leave, Asher."

"You wound me." His mocking tone says otherwise. He enjoys seeing me tense. It's his favorite game.

"If it weren't for the treaty between our people, I gladly would," I throw over my shoulder. I'm close to the cave's entrance, nearly rid of the nuisance, but Asher grips the back of my long-sleeved shirt, ignoring the small tear he makes while turning me to face him.

"What is your problem, woman? I came to save you, and all I get is a cold shoulder?"

I can tell he's truly upset now, no longer just teasing. I widen my stance, preparing for a fight. This could get ugly fast. I don't want to alert anyone to Asher's presence by making a spectacle, so I swallow my pride, look him in the eye and exhale defeatedly.

"The dragons have claimed us, Asher. We're linked, some-how. I don't believe they'll just let us go. I'm not asking you to leave. I'm telling you to because if you don't, you may never get the chance again."

Asher searches my gaze, his chest puffed out. I realize he was also preparing for a brawl. He releases the breath he'd been holding and shakes his head. "I'm not leaving without you," he declares. "Or the others. Besides—" his typical smug grin returns over his lips—"I'm pretty sure the dragons want me, too. I walked into the Outer Edge without a scratch. I imagine that has something to do with the beasts."

My brows raise. "Holy shit."

"Yeah." He chuckles. "I guess you're stuck with me."

I curse, lowering my gaze. That's when I spot the large ruck-sack at his feet. "You packed?" I look from the bag to him, confused. "When did you have time to get that?"

Asher bends to retrieve the bag and passes it to me, opening the top so I can peer inside. He slides his hands nonchalantly into his pants pockets.

"You brought a first aid kit, socks..." I gawk up at him. "Are those my meds?"

"Did you think I'd come ill-prepared?" Asher scoffs.

"I didn't think you'd come at all," I respond frankly.

I watch his jaw tick, the movement visible among his sharp features. "Well, I saw the first few dragons swoop up your two sisters and figured you wouldn't be far behind them. I mean, I didn't expect to see you riding that giant creature like a horse."

"I was not riding it like a damn horse." I cross my arms.

He sneers. "Oh, yes, yes you were."

"How would you know? Better yet, where the hell were you when the Compound was under attack?"

He stiffens, not meeting my gaze. "I went to your room."

My heart does a funky thump in my chest, and I wordlessly scold the errant organ. "Why?"

"Oh, to have a peek in your dresser drawers. Nice lace, by the way. Love the red."

"You dirty creep!" I chuck the fruit into the rucksack and slap Asher's shoulder a little harder than intended.

Asher grabs my hand and holds it in his own much larger hand. "I needed to know you were safe, Astraea. The room was empty, so I was going to leave to find you. Couldn't have the Compound under attack without the legendary Reaper on the front lines." He smirks, though it doesn't reach his eyes. "That's when I spotted your sisters, soon after spying you riding atop that ridiculous monstrosity through your window. I grabbed some of you and your sisters' belongings, stopped by storage for a rucksack, and tracked your scent."

I want to nag at him for stopping to pack things, but he is obnoxiously fast on his feet. I know his packing likely took less than a minute. He proved oddly considerate.

We stand in silence for a moment, Asher's thumb delicately tracing a vein in my wrist.

Cautiously, I meet his eyes. "You went into the Outer Edge, knowing it could harm you, even possibly kill you. Why?"

His thumb slows, and he exhales before releasing my hand. "Not only did I come with the intention of saving your ass, but I know Aurelia needs her hearing aids, Ravena needs her inhaler, and you definitely need your medication. I wasn't sure if we'd be leaving this place, so I didn't take any chances and grabbed some necessities, too."

He knew we could be stuck here, and still, he came.

"I didn't need you to do that. I would have found a way to get us—" He stays me with a look, stalking forward until my back hits the cave wall. Admittedly, I am trying my best to come up with an excuse not to thank him, when really I should be groveling at his feet. My sisters and I do need those items if we are stuck here. Stopping my medication would severely impact my health.

"I didn't hear a *thank you* in there." Asher growls, his fae fangs a little longer than usual.

"Because I didn't say thank you."

He smirks, resting his right arm against the wall, grazing the point of my ear. "You're welcome."

I tilt my chin, our breaths mingling for a dangerous second. "You could leave. You could try."

I can't help myself from offering the out again. Whether I like him or not, I don't want his death on my hands because he feels like the need to be a hero. I am perfectly capable of taking care of myself and my sisters.

Asher frowns and closes his eyes pensively. His brows pinch, and he appears almost vulnerable, but before I can read too much into it, his face hardens, and he stares at me once more with that devilish grin.

"Can't let you have all the fun, now, can I?" Asher casually straightens, picks up the backpack, and hands it to me just as I was about to leave. "You'll be needing this."

I take it just before he lets it go. My fingers ache as the bag bends them as far as they'll go. I'm steadily losing mobility in my hands, but I won't allow that to compromise me against Asher Aidos. I grumble, and drag the heavy rucksack behind me as I enter the cave.

It's a relief to have these items—but Oasòs *beyond*, did it have to be him who gave them to me? He will never let this go.

CHAPTER 15
ASHER

She is safe, and naturally bitter that I've come to her rescue. I smile to myself as I watch her struggle to carry the giant pack that I'd so graciously prepared for her and her sisters. I'd gladly carry it for her, but I know Astraea—she is resilient, and even when she isn't, she wishes to keep up appearances. So, I observe her flawless body lug that bag, her long legs taking it in stride, her back flexing beneath her shirt. Her ample hips swish with each step, her long braided hair swinging left and right. In the cave light, it almost looks black, but I know it is the prettiest shade of ash.

"King Asher?" Aurelia blinks, seemingly out of a daze.

"In the flesh," I announce, raising my arms in a sweeping gesture.

"What in Oasòs?" Ravena mutters, tucking her hair behind her ears.

Astraea's sisters and the two unexpected cellmates look worse for wear. They're jittery, covered in sweat and filth, their eyes darting back and forth. Shockingly, one of their companions is Malek, who I'd heard was missing. I guess they found him, but he doesn't look so good. I can hardly tell if the smudges on his brown skin are mud or blood.

On the other hand, Astraea looks far too good for someone just kidnapped by a dragon. The rigid muscles in her shoulders seem to be the only signs of her distress. I watch as she feeds the fire, undoubtedly having built it herself. She is a warrior in every sense of the word, a survivor all her life.

"What are you doing here?" Ravena asks me, sniffling.

I smile kindly, trying to put her at ease.

"He's here to get on my last nerve," Astraea grumbles violently.

I pretend not to hear the moody legacy. "Figured you lot could use some help." I gesture to the rucksack I'd packed with them in mind. The girls lunge for the bag, squealing enthusiastically as they retrieve their necessities.

"Our hero!" Aurelia rejoices, quickly removing her hearing aids from their case and placing them in her ears. "Hearing loss and abduction-by-dragon do not mix. I was really starting to freak out without these. Thank you!"

Aurelia jumps up and squeezes the life out of me. I cough, on guard, unsure what to do.

"Down, Relie," Astraea orders.

Aurelia blushes, laughing it off. "Sorry, King Asher. I'm just very grateful."

"It was nothing," I respond.

"It was everything," Ravena cuts in, looking braver and even healthier now that she's taken her blue puffer. The celestials must have been watching over her if she hadn't had an asthma attack after all she'd been through. "Thank you."

"See?" I point, pinning Astraea with my gaze. "That's how you thank someone when they help you."

Astraea mutters profanities under her breath, and I shake my head. I'll never get a thanks from that dragon slayer. I don't need one, but it would feel so good to rub it in. My cock twitches in my pants as I consider rubbing things into her. *Fuck.* This is going to be a long day. My adrenaline is elevated, and I must calm down. I grunt, deciding now would be a good time to empty the rest of the pack and set things up before my mind drifts into dangerous territories.

Astraea is my hamartia. That damn woman left a mark on me the minute I'd laid eyes on her. She'd been single-handedly fighting off a group of lycanthropes, protecting a small family of orcs from the wolves' ravenous bite. Blood spurted from throat after throat, Astraea sporting a wicked gleam in her eye. I stepped out of the shadows to help her, but she lifted her sword to me instead of the enemy. The way she'd been about to pounce had sent a rush of heat through my groin, something I'm sure scientists would love to dissect. I wasn't usually turned on by violence, but she was something out of this world.

When she spotted the crown atop my head, she knocked it off with her silver sword, the one crafted by *my* people, and warned me to stay out of her way. Even then, she wanted to keep me far away. She can try.

"H—hey."

"Gah!" I yelp, taking a step back from the terrified legacy who cowers at my feet. I hadn't realized I'd been about to step on him. "Oasòs above. Don't startle a man in thought like that."

"S—Sorry, King Asher. I didn't mean to."

I chuckle, offering him a hand up. He tentatively accepts, trying his best to look brave. "Don't worry about it, uh?" I scratch my head, trying to remember his name. It doesn't really matter to me. All the legacies are the same except *her.*

"Calix Lightcrest, sir. Of the Intelligence Division."

"Intelligence, you say?" I grin, knowing my impressive teeth are on display. He gulps audibly. "You wouldn't happen to be in charge of spying on my territory, would you?"

"N—No, sir. I assess information. I'm no undercover agent." He snorts, laughing at his own expense.

"Hmm," I hum, making him squirm.

"Quit bugging Calix, Asher. We have more important things to do than boost your colossally large ego."

"Says who?" I question, Calix still at my side. I wonder what he sees when he assesses the general and the king.

"She's right, you know?" Calix dares intervene. "Statistically speaking, the first twenty-four hours of kidnapping offer the greatest chance for escape. Since they've already taken us to a hidden location, I imagine the chance of a positive outcome is significantly lowered."

"You don't say?" Astraea deadpans. I laugh inwardly. Astraea snaps her eyes to me, squinting like there's something strange on my face, then shivers. I angle a brow at her, and her expression mirrors mine.

"Okay, let's put our minds to good use," Ravena suggests, and she and Aurelia come stand in the circle we formed reflexively. "What parts of the world does the Outer Edge encompass?" *Good. Someone is thinking with their head on straight.*

"Asia," Astraea and I state simultaneously. We glare at one another, but I let her take the floor with a mocking bow. Her frown deepens.

"It includes all of Asia, Oceania, and plenty more. It'd be easier to say which countries are *not* inside the Outer Edge—parts of Portugal, Spain, France, the Netherlands, the United Kingdom, Norway, Ireland, Iceland, Greenland, and North America."

"And, of course," I add, "as we all know, Canada and the United States are a wasteland."

"It's so bad, even the dragons don't want it," Calix remarks.

"With the Outer Edge so massive, that's going to make for a lot of guessing where we are," Aurelia chimes in a whiny voice.

"Not necessarily," Ravena reacts. "I can go outside and check the earth. Look at the plants and trees, check out the soil, see if I can pinpoint a general location."

"Excellent," says Astraea, authority taking over her voice. "Let's go."

I smirk. "Aye, aye, General."

CHAPTER 16

RAVENA

"Holy flora!" I gasp, taking my first step out of the cave since being tossed into it. "This is incredible!"

I spin around, unable to choose where to begin. This is paradise—aside from the fact that there are literal dragons just out of sight.

"Do you see anything resourceful?" Calix asks, following my every step. I push my glasses up the bridge of my nose and study the cave's entrance. The dragons had thrown us into that giant mountain we'd seen while flying to our early graves.

The mountain is made of sedimentary rock, reaching high above the clouds. Had I not seen its tip myself, I could swear it reaches Oasòs. Among the limestone are precious blue perennials, omphalodes luciliae, growing through the cracks. Breathtaking… This is a brilliant clue. Just by the sense of our surroundings, my eterì detects a Mediterranean climate, or as some might call it, a dry summer heat. I walk closer to the trees, noting the many wildflowers underfoot. I beam at a rare Balkan plant in full bloom. With this, and the omphalodes luciliae—which are commonly found growing in the shady cracks of limestone cliffs on certain mountains in Greece—I'm guessing that's where we are. Or, at the very least, nearby.

"We must be somewhere near Greece," I tell the group. "Maybe Turkey, but I think we're in Greece." I lower to the ground, allowing my eterì to flow through the soil, trying to gauge our location.

"Well, shit," my sister swears.

I turn to look at Astraea, who appears baffled, her ghostly white eyes searching the sky. She's searching with her eterì, too. She must've found something.

"I was right. We are at Mount Olympus."

CHAPTER 17
AURELIA

My sisters, Calix and King Asher continue examining the plants nearby while I study the clouds overhead. I steal a moment for myself, closing my eyes and feeling the air around me. It's warm and dry, and the sky is pale blue. I open my senses, allowing my eterì to search the atmosphere, feeling for any disturbances in the air.

I don't have to hunt for long to know the dragons are at the top of the mountain. I can feel the snow lying atop the caps, chilling my spine. It's hot and cold, a sure sign there's fire amid the winter-like climate. I probe further, but am met with resistance. *Why can't I feel the air any longer?*

"Raea," I whisper, the cold seeping into my bones.

Astraea walks to my side and places a hand on my shoulder. "Get Vena and Calix back into the cave."

I gulp, about to question why, but her eyes turn white again.

"Aurelia, do as she says." It's King Asher's turn to command me.

"What's going on?" Calix asks, Ravena to his left.

"They're awake," the king states. "They know we're planning to escape."

A thunderous roar splits the clouds as a large group of flying beasts shoot down from the sky.

"Go! Now!" the fae insists. He doesn't need to tell me twice.

"I can help!" Ravena protests, trying to withdraw from my grasp.

"You'll only be a liability," King Asher asserts harshly. Ravena's lip trembles as she looks between us and Astraea, who chants with her white eyes aglow, palms out and leaching shadowy haze.

"Come on," Calix ushers us. "She'll be fine. This is what she does."

Ravena accepts defeat, and the three of us bolt for the cave, entering just as the first dragon lands, quaking the ground around us.

CHAPTER 18

ASTRAEA

"Go, Asher," I command.

Though my eyes are white, I see his figure with the power of my eterì. Wherever the smoke blows, I can see and feel—my eterì is an extension of myself. The fae king stands with me, back-to-back, his teeth glinting. Asher's eterì springs to life, his white fog blending with my dark haze.

"And miss out on kicking ass?" His eyes turn black. "I think not."

"Last chance," I growl, getting in position.

Five brutish dragons crouch at the ready, their commander's head low, almost grazing the forest ground. Their bodies crush the giant trees, pulping everything into a pasture.

"On your right!" Asher announces, just as the purple dragon who'd stolen Vena swings its tail at me. I grin, then push off the ground and leap onto its feral appendage. I grapple with the slippery tail, trying to get a good hold. The moment I get my feet to grip, I launch myself further up its body, grab onto its horn and wrench my eterì forward. The dragon cries out, whipping its head to throw me off. My hand slips and I sail across the space, my lungs catching as Asher plucks me from the sky and lands in a crouch, where he cradles me to his chest.

"Put me down, you big oaf!" I hiss, pushing at his shoulders. He releases me, laughing darkly.

"Big oaf? Gee, I'm flattered."

Another dragon swipes its tail at us, and we both duck in time.

"In case you haven't noticed, Asher," I grumble, dodging another attack while fueling my eterì stores. "I'm kind of in the middle of something."

"Looked to me like you were in trouble just a second ago." He throws out a hand to block the blow of the iridescent green monster.

"Where there is Asher, there is trouble," I mutter to myself, empowered and ready to strike at the entire assembly of beasts.

A sudden *thwack* catches me in the ribs, and I groan, clutching my side. A white, red-eyed dragon sneers at me with satisfaction, proud to have struck me with its tail.

"Don't touch her!" Asher roars, pushing me out of the way and taking the second hit meant to knock me down. Asher's eterì strengthens, his power seeping out his soul, ready to attack.

"Enough!" A thunderous voice pierces my ears, startling me briefly and giving my dark rival sufficient time to swipe my feet from under me with its large, leathery wing—eradicating my and Asher's eterì.

"Astraea!" Asher says, lifting me to my feet in seconds before whirling to face our foe. I'm in such shock that I don't even brush him off. "Did that thing just talk?"

"You can hear it too?" I gasp, looking between the black dragon and the fae king. I notice offhandedly that the other dragons have retreated a few steps back, boldly leaving their leader with me and the king. I dare a greater glance at the dragon

—its golden eyes point down at me like I'm an annoying little bug it'd love to squash.

"Can you understand me?" I ask, feeling like a fool. "What am I thinking?" I curse under my breath. Of course, the fucking creature of nightmares can't understand me. The notion is absurd.

"Absurd? I think not."

My gaze snaps back up to the dragon.

"Has she lost her ever-loving mind?"

I turn to Asher, whose mouth isn't moving, though I can hear him *thinking* things at me.

"No, I haven't lost my mind," I retort.

"Did she just?"

"Wait a damn minute." I inhale sharply, and so does he. *"Can you hear what I'm thinking?"*

"Can you *hear what* I'm *thinking?"* he thinks.

I nod, grimacing.

"Fuck me," we swear in unison, paling.

I catch an intriguing train of carnal thoughts from Asher's mind, but brush them off.

"Shit. She can hear that?"

I huff with disdain. "Yes."

"Nauseating," remarks the dragon.

"It can hear our thoughts, too," Asher verbalizes in horror.

Never mind the problem between the fae king and me. We can hear the thoughts of a damn dragon.

"How is this possible?" I venture. "Why can I only hear you? Do the others not speak?"

Its nostrils flare, emitting a puff of smoke. **"They are not your bonded, Legacy. I am."**

"Bonded?" I repeat.

"Who's mine?" Asher wonders aloud.

The dragon chortles, lowering its shoulders to the ground and reaching its snout closer to us. ***"Disappointingly, also me."***

"This is ridiculous!" I throw my hands in the air in frustration. "Why the hell am I mind-talking with a dragon? Let's get this fucking show on the road."

I crouch in a fighting position again and raise my swollen hands. *My eterì. Gods!* I'd forgotten that it doesn't work around this dragon. With an absurdly unsatisfying breath, I scream out my frustration.

The dragon snorts.

"Are you laughing at me?" I grit between clenched teeth. I glare at Asher, daring him to join in.

His eyes widen, his mouth tipping up at the corners. *"Delightful."* Asher's mind says it all. He's enjoying this.

"What a piece of work you are."

Asher scrunches his nose at me. *"She loves me."*

I groan in frustration, turning my attention to the dragon. "Why haven't you eaten us yet?"

"Why would I do that?" it asks, tilting its head to the side as if examining me for a head injury.

"Because that's what you do. You eat people," I reply dryly, clenching my fists. The screams of my allies being chomped to bits will haunt my memories even in the afterlife.

"I cannot eat you," it responds pragmatically.

"Fine." I grunt. "Then *I'll* eat *you*."

"Lucky dragon..."

I growl at Asher in warning. His cheeks flush a bright red.

"Why in Freìre would you do that?" the dragon questions, its expression almost curious.

"You are my nemesis. If I can't kill you with my eterì, then I will resort to more horrid solutions."

"I do not belong to you," it snarls, standing at full height, its chest proud.

"What?"

"You said I am yours."

"No, I said you are my nemesis."

"Exactly," it snaps irritably.

"Huh?" I rub my brow, my headache growing stronger by the minute.

"I am Nemesis. I belong to no one."

Head craned to the sky, Asher suddenly laughs out loud. The unreserved radiant sound stuns me momentarily, my frown wavering.

Naturally, its name is Nemesis. Why wouldn't it be?

"I think it's fitting," Asher decides, coming down from the apparent absurdity. This is not a laughing matter. We are talking to dragons! Living, breathing, people-eating dragons.

"Not surprising," I snap at the fae king.

"Feisty," Asher thinks. "What's that supposed to mean, little Reaper?"

"Do you two ever quiet?" The dragon groans in annoyance.

"No," we reply in harmony.

Asher grins, which only deepens my scowl.

"How did you find us, and why did you take us?" I ask the beast.

The Compound has a protection ward that prohibits outsiders from seeing in. The dragons haven't found our home in all these years. I can't trust that Nemesis won't change his mind about making a meal out of me, but I approach cautiously anyway. I need answers. Asher follows my stride, our shadows twisting at our feet.

"We are bonded. It transpired during our first encounter. Though eterì bonds have not occurred in almost two centuries, I do remember the legends—I've lived them myself. Was I to leave you with the weaklings of your race to fend for yourself? I think not."

"I was doing just fine without your big scaly ass in my way."

"The war has just begun, little one. It is high time you learn what is good for you."

"And what is that?" I huff.

"Learning when to shut up, for starters." Asher grunts.

I whip my head at the grinning fae fool and punch his chest for good measure. He woundedly rubs over his heart, feigning woe.

The dragon blows a hot, temperamental breath at us. **"Come,"** it insists. **"Let us find your companions and converse."**

"Over my dead body." I stand tall, my eterì trying its best to surface but failing.

"It'll be all right, Astraea," Asher reassures me, though he doesn't look even half as convinced as he sounds.

"I will not let my sisters or my friends come to harm," I tell them. "Speaking of which, what did you do to Malek?"

"Your companions are bonded to my horde. They will not come to harm," says Nemesis. **"As for your companion, I did not cause his condition. I took him from the cliffs, because he was a danger to himself and to you."**

"First of all, what are the odds that my sisters *and* Calix and Malek are bonded to your horde? Secondly, I call bullshit. I have never seen Malek act that way in my life. It didn't start until you abducted him."

"I swear on my life I did not harm your friend," the dragon says in its rumbling voice. **"As for the bonding between your companions and my horde, it is factual. I am their leader. My bonding to you was a causal nexus."**

"And your horde just happened to choose both my sisters, and our friends? You expect me to believe that?"

"I expect you to listen. It is the least you owe my kind."

"What did you just say?" I hiss.

"Okay, let's just all take a breath," Asher suggests.

"You know what? No. Why aren't you a little more concerned? This is so fucked up!"

"Again, with the profanities," the dragon grumbles, appearing to roll its gilded eyes. ***"Let us go. I tire of this conversation."***

I gape at the beast. No one would chance a snide comment like that around me and live to see the next sunrise. I'm going to wring that beast's neck until its head pops off.

Nemesis snorts and points its attention to Asher. ***"Is her mind always so wicked?"***

"Want to find out?" I taunt, standing my ground.

Asher chuckles, shaking his head at me. "Come on, Reaper. You can think your wicked thoughts while we walk."

CHAPTER 19

ASHER

I can tell Astraea is in shock by the way she reaches out and grabs my hand like I am her anchor in this world. I thought she was about to attack me. I walk by her side, dumbfounded.

"*Don't read into it,*" she says, "*or I'll feed you to the creepy one with the red eyes.*" She's reading my mind again. I am reading hers. She's... singing? The same words repeat over and over, her mind-voice chanting a tune that sounds oddly familiar.

"*You look at me like an enemy. You take a bite just to see if I'll bleed.*"

"What the hell is that song?" I ask in thought.

"None of your business."

"Hey," I tease. "Not nice." We're almost at the cave's entrance when I remember where I'd heard those lyrics before. I chuckle, looking at her proud, sharp angles.

"Careful, Asher," Astraea quips. "You're looking for trouble again."

"*Take a good look at what you see. I'll give it right back, 'cause I've got teeth,*" I reply smoothly, showcasing my sharp fangs.

The little Reaper blushes.

How charming.

"Tell me you're not a fan of that album right now, so I don't have to stop listening to it." Her hand flexes in mine, perhaps wanting to let go. I hold tighter for good measure.

"It's the only album you listen to while training. I figured I'd give it a listen to see what all the fuss was about." Her hand grows warmer in my palm.

"And how would you know that?" Her voice is cross, even in her mind.

I gesture to my pointed ears and grin.

"I wonder if he's heard me take a piss," she thinks. Her eyes widen. I burst into genuine laughter and her hand slips from mine. "Oh, my gods, I hate this!"

"No more than I, Starlight." I stiffen, waiting for her to mock me for the secret endearment I've kept from her, but she is so lost in her anger that she must not have heard me.

"But I did," Nemesis chimes in.

"You shut your big mouth, or I'll sic that feisty woman on you."

"Oh, but I do so enjoy your banter. I cannot fathom living without hearing your stories filled with bleeding, pissing, and teeth."

"Boy, are you ever sarcastic?"

The dragon chuckles. Outside our minds, it sounds like an ungodly growl.

"Holy smokes, it's true?" Ravena's voice interrupts us, her head peeking around the corner. "Ah!" She jumps back, staring wide-eyed at the purple dragon who lowers its haunches. "She just... but she... What in Oasòs?"

Ahh. Ravena's bonded dragon must be speaking to her in her mind. That explains the jumping.

"Um, hi, Orion," Calix speaks quietly, waving a hand at a

sizeable indigo dragon. Its black eyes stare back at him, and Calix's smile broadens.

"It's okay, Rel," Astraea assures her youngest sister. She stands at Aurelia's side, encouraging her to seek out the dragon who'd bonded to her.

An impressive jade-green dragon slithers forward, its pearlescent scales shining under the sunlight.

"You didn't call me impressive," Nemesis complains, his nose blowing smoke my way.

Astraea laughs, her wicked eyes watching my interaction with our dragon.

"I am not yours," Nemesis barks.

"You kind of are, buddy." I grin.

Nemesis returns it menacingly, baring all his vulturine teeth. *"You are mine, Fae. You cannot control my magic. I have control over yours. Only I have this power. Not you. Therefore, you both belong to me."*

"In your dreams, you overgrown turkey." Astraea wipes her nails on her shoulder.

"Careful, turkey," I say. "They don't call that one Reaper for nothing." I point to an irritated Astraea, who admittedly was right. "How about no one belongs to anyone? We're all our own people, just trying to work things out."

"Fine," Astraea agrees, quicker than I would have assumed.

"Hmph," is all that comes from Nemesis.

"Now back to controlling our eterì. Can you please return my power? It feels strange not being able to call on it."

The dragon eyes me intimidatingly. *"Can I trust that you will not wield it against my horde?"*

"If they don't attack us, yes."

Nemesis grumbles. *"Very well."*

"What about me?" Astraea jeers, cocking a brow at the beast.

"You, I fear, are a menace. Though I will return your eterì so long as you agree to the same terms."

Astraea's lips form a tight line, but she nods, giving in.

"Good. I've restored it to its full potential."

"We appreciate it," I tell him, my body relaxing as I feel the wisps of magic return to me. I sigh heavily. "So, we're bonded. What does that mean?"

CHAPTER 20

ASTRAEA

"In the makings of time, celestials and dragons were bonded together, ruling their creations in harmony."

"Really?" Calix asks Nemesis.

I eye the black dragon. "Wait, you can hear him too?"

"If I choose, I can speak with them through my horde. Their bonded dragon can permit me to speak through their minds."

"Weird."

The dragon grumbles in irritation.

"This is just a lot to take in, mister dragon sir," Ravena says suddenly, shyly. "Excuse my sister's interruption."

I snort. Leave it to Ravena to make peace between me and a monster.

Asher shakes his head at me. I eye him, willing his thoughts toward me.

He raises his brow. *"Curious?"*

"Shut up."

"Carrying on," Nemesis interposes. His horde sits at attention, listening intently. **"Each celestial was bonded to a dragon; each mirroring their eterìan power. For example, the Celestial of War, Zephrðn was bonded to Ulrich, the pair sharing their fire eterì."**

"How do dragons share their eterì?" asks Calix.

"Dragons are like syphons, able to strengthen your eterì without costing our energy."

"You can give us more power?" Asher queries, unconvinced but biting.

"The act of syphoning involves the transfer of energy from a higher being to its weaker component. We can do that with our bonded."

I huff, incredulous. I am not weaker than a dragon. If Nemesis would stop shutting my eterì off, I could give him and his entire horde a run for their money.

"Why would you want to strengthen our eterì?" I ask, skeptical. This is all a little too good to be true. There has to be a catch —like, perhaps we're tastiest to the monstrous dragons when we're most powerful. Nemesis glares at me, and I match his stare.

"Because the bond between a dragon and its rider is created to fight together. Your strength is our strength, and vice versa," he explains. ***"We are not unlike other species', little legacy. Perhaps we are large, and you may be repulsed by our appearance, but we are wise and kind, with families, hopes, and dreams, like most. Let go of your prejudices,"*** he adds, only for me to hear.

"You have to understand that you're attempting to erase everything I thought I knew," I respond. However, the more I reflect, the more I see that I was right about one thing. The dragons are intelligent. In fact, Nemesis is even well-spoken, and for a beast, his temperament is unexpectedly relaxed. That could have something to do with being the biggest predator around.

"How is it possible to share strength?" asks Calix, bringing my mind back to the main conversation. Calix seems to be soaking up this experience, getting his hands on all possible knowledge.

"As dragons, our very essence is made of eterì, and we do not rely on external sources to strengthen it. To tap into your eterì, you must be willing to sacrifice a part of your being, whether physical, mental, or spiritual strength. Then you must rest before your stores replenish. We, the dragons, do not harbor such reservations."

"So, you're saying you can make it so that our reserve is always full and doesn't drain your own eterì?" Calix ponders.

"The opposite, in fact. The more you use eterì while bonded, the stronger we get."

I narrow my eyes at the dragon. "And what happens when you're stronger? You kill us? Or, wait. Let me guess." I sneer, pointing a finger at the group. "You'll use us against our own people, and *then* you eat us."

"That depends on who you consider your people to be, Reaper," Nemesis challenges.

I laugh, scrutinizing his words for what they are. "There's that catch I was looking for." I purse my lips. "Who do you want us to kill and why?"

"We do not wish to kill anyone." Nemesis growls in frustration. **"The only people we've ever killed were those who attacked us."**

"That's a lie, and you know it!" I'm shocked to hear the words leave Ravena's mouth. She's rarely confrontational. My sister points at the purplish dragon, who watches her with studying eyes. "She ate a child!"

"Nyx tells me the child attacked her," Nemesis rebuts.

Ravena's eyes water. I almost go to comfort her, but Calix

surprisingly does so for me, putting an arm around her shoulders. My sister huddles into him, her red-rimmed eyes biting.

"Theo didn't hurt Nyx one bit," Ravena argues. "He was unarmed and only trying to save his little sister." She rubs at her eyes, her glasses fogging. Then she snaps her head up to her dragon and pouts. "Sorry, doesn't cut it! That boy was only eight years old. He had a life, a family, things to live for."

Nyx whimpers, dropping her head.

My sister lowers her gaze, defeated. "You'd better never do something like that again. You'd be amazed to find I'm not as sweet as I look when it comes to protecting the ones I love."

"It's okay, Vena," Aurelia murmurs.

Ravena gives her a look of incredulity but doesn't comment.

"She's young," Nemesis supplies. **"It was her first time leaving Freìre. She did not know what she'd done was wrong."**

Ravena sniffs. "Prove you're better than your mistake, and I might find it in my heart to forgive you."

Nyx whines again, and it almost compels me toward pity.

It's Asher's turn to speak. "So, what's the motive behind your capturing these legacies?" I've been watching him closely, seeing the wheels turning in his head. He's been analyzing every bit of information as much as Calix.

"The truth," Nemesis replies, standing tall. **"We want to get a message to the creatures of the world and the celestials of Oasòs. It is due time they know about the traitor in their midst."**

CHAPTER 21

ASHER

"A traitor? In Oasòs?" Astraea's breath hitches, her spine going rigid.

This is not good.

"One traitorous act spawned the Asherian War. Had the celestial understood and admitted her mistake and dealt with the consequences, we'd never have seen the destruction of our world."

"What do you mean? What happened?" asks Calix.

"There used to be seventeen celestials. Phaðs, the god of all gods, was the initial entity to arise during the inception of our existence. Phaðs, in all their magnificence, created the realms and ruled over the space that bridged Oasòs and Earth. Moreover, Phaðs's nature was intertwined with the threads of destiny, much like their illustrious daughter, Urðra."

"We have a grandparent?" Aurelia asks.

Urðra is their mother? Astraea, Aurelia, and Ravena are direct descendants of Fate. This is even more complicated than I'd initially thought. If their celestial parent is the ruler of Fate, doesn't she know that dragons took her children? Though the celestials can't interfere with life, Urðra crafts destiny. Surely, she hadn't put her children on this path. Or had she? Perhaps the Celestial of Volition had kept her from trying.

Crossing her arms, Astraea asks, "What did Phaðs do to trigger the Asherian War?" Her golden skin is still streaked with the dirt and blood from her fight.

"Phaðs did not do anything. Urðra destroyed Phaðs."

"What?" Astraea hisses, her eyes bulging from her lids. She laughs unreservedly, her hands on her knees, braid falling over her shoulder. "Okay," she declares, wheezing. "You almost had me there." Her laughter fades, and she dries hysterical tears from her cheeks.

Is it just me, or has she become paler?

"I do not jest, little legacy. I will provide proof," says Nemesis.

Astraea stands ramrod straight, her pulse visible at the base of her neck.

"Look into my memories. See the truth with your eyes."

My vision blurs, and soon I find myself in a dark fog. To my shock, I can see a large black snout protruding from my face. I'm seeing through Nemesis's eyes, watching a memory unfold. My thoughts become his, our minds connecting as one.

"You are far too childish to rule over fate alone, Urðra. Let me guide you. It is not too late."

"It is far too late, guardian," Urðra spits, her hands aglow in red. She holds thousands of sparkling strings which wrap around Aegliðs, her twin. "I am tired of watching from above while innocents die from disease and tyrants thrive. I have the power to change fate. It is my decision. I can do what I please."

"There must be a balance, Urðra," my rider pleads. Phaðs is

bleeding out, their silver blood soaking the floor, making a slopping noise every time they move. Phaðs cautiously slides nearer to her children, trying to reason with a fool. I am incapacitated, dying in the middle of the mess. As Urðra had avowed, it is too late.

"If you kill your brother, take away volition from the people," says Phaðs, "the world will burn."

"It will burn whether Aegliðs dies or not," Urðra hisses. "Don't you see? I am going to rid the world of its worries."

"If Aegliðs falls, so will you."

"That's where you're wrong, Phaðs. I will thrive, and—"

We're floating in some kind of chaotic, unstable substance, my broken wings aching as the air jostles me.

"Take care of our world, Nemesis," Phaðs speaks in my mind.

No. They wouldn't.

"Do not do this, Phaðs. Do not surrender your life for hers. She is not worth saving."

My rider looks upon me with sympathy, silver blood leaking from their eyes as they cry. "The world is worth it. Remember..."

A bright light bursts from Phaðs' chest. With Phaðs' last surge of eterì, my body heals instantly, and I jump up, snarling at Urðra's wilted form.

"What? What's going on?" she asks. "Where am I?"

I blink.

"Urðra?" It is Aegliðs. He's finally roused from unconsciousness. "What's going on?"

Urðra lifts a shaking finger at me, gulping for air.

"Dragon," she whispers.

It is then I realize what Phaðs did. The first-risen Celestial of Creation had gone into Oblivion, wiping the world of its memories, leaving me to pick up the pieces. No being would ever remember that dragons were from Oasòs.

"Don't move, Urðra," her twin brother orders, though I am unsure of what he could do against me. He rises hurriedly, though his legs *buckle beneath him. He peers around, confused— and that is when we find ourselves at the gates of Oasòs.*

"Remember..." Phaðs' voice carries on the wind. "A new dawn awaits."

Phaðs will no longer be remembered by anyone but me.

CHAPTER 22
ASTRAEA

The visuals of Nemesis's memories stop, and the dragons and those bonded come back into view. My body temperature is at an all-time high, my heart pounding in my chest, skipping beats wherever it pleases. I can hardly believe it, and yet, I can't deny the truth: my mother is a monster.

Nausea climbs my throat. I rest against the cave, using it to support my trembling limbs. Asher steps closer to me, joining me against the cave, pretending not to watch me from the corner of his eye.

From a young age, I held a deep conviction that my mother, the Celestial of Fate, would eventually find me deserving enough to stand by her side, aiding the inhabitants of Earth from above. She would guide me in her ways, and when the time was right, I would step into her role, allowing her to find peace among the stars. To find that she is the reason behind the wars, behind the famine and struggle of the people I fight for, sends me reeling.

"Is it really true? What we saw?" I breathe unevenly, leveling a hopeless look at the horde of dragons, and their solemn, confirming looks.

"It is. Everything I've shown you is a direct memory."

Asher moves closer, allowing me to lean against his side, though I barely notice.

I swallow thickly. "What did you do?"

"I left Oasòs immediately, wanting to find solace on Earth," Nemesis explains. **"That is when I discovered that the other dragons had been sent away from the celestials, making sure no being had any recollection of their bonds. The people of Earth were unwelcoming to our kind, as the celestials, not knowing the truth, created the legacies to destroy us. It did not take long for all creatures to band against us. Thus, forcing me to create Freìre to protect my species."**

"Freìre, as you call it, is taking over Earth and wiping us out." I swallow down bile, trying my best to ignore my shortness of breath. It doesn't escape me that Nemesis calls the Outer Edge *Freìre*, which translates to *freedom* in the celestial language.

"That's the downfall of our having to protect ourselves. The longer time passes, the more dragons couple and have hatchlings, needing more space. We are also limited in sustenance."

"And how is that our fault?" I know my anger is misplaced, yet I'm unable to control it.

"If our safety was not in question, there would be no Freìre needed."

They want to be free.

"You're saying you want true freedom," Asher points, reaching the same conclusion as I have.

"Yes."

Ravena steps forward. "But, you eat people."

"Not to mention, you're enormous," Aurelia adds. "You'd crush every village you stand in."

"Firstly, we prefer animals for nourishment. Even so, I ask you, do all other creatures of Earth refrain from eating and killing people? What would you say of your Reaper?"

Nemesis angles his head at me, daring me to argue. Though I don't like it, he does have a point. Legacies, fae, vampires, orcs, nymphs, and lycanthropes can be persuaded to kill, some even feasting on people.

"Okay, so besides murder, what about the villages?" asks Aurelia.

"We can manage fine," Nemesis replies blandly. **"The biggest problem lies with the celestials. They think we are swine, mindless creatures out to kill. We need to show them who we are, who we were before Urðra's cataclysmic tirade."**

"You want them to punish her," I assume. My own mother is a corrupt, selfish, world destroyer. Though Phaðs was the incendiary detonation, Urðra had been the trigger, causing the Asherian War, the very one Asher's father, Endyr, had led and won. We'd lost thousands of soldiers in that war, and our kind had celebrated the win, nonetheless, thanking Urðra for the guidance and blaming the death on the dragons.

"They blamed the celestials' bonded, in fact," Nemesis clarifies via our mind-link, as I'm seemingly the only one to hear him.

"Are they still alive?" I wonder.

"Some."

"Do they know about your plan?"

"Indeed. I am their leader. My horde works with me, not against me like Urðra did the celestials. We are a team, our mission a search for peace."

"So, we rally up the legacies and tell them about your memory. Who's to say they'll believe us?"

Nemesis seems to grin. **"Because you are their general, and the fae king is at your side, spreading the same message among the other creatures."**

"*Aside from my court, most territory leaders won't make this easy,*" Asher warns, apparently having been listening in on our conversation. "*But I think it's worth a shot. It could work.*"

"If it doesn't," says Nemesis. **"The world will burn."**

CHAPTER 23

AURELIA

"**He's not always this irritable,**" Idris defends, connecting with me through my mind. He'd introduced himself briefly before Nemesis began his lecture. **"All right. Perhaps he is."**

I raise my brows at the polished jade dragon. *"He's perfect for Astraea,"* I retort. Though we had a rocky start, I like my bonded just fine. He's funny, for a dragon.

"You're charming, for a tiny human." He laughs, though in the outside world, it sounds like a hum.

"I am a legacy, Idris. I'm not as weak as I appear." I'm sure two hundred-and-thirty pounds of woman looks like a harmless fly to him. Idris is huge.

His giant dragon mouth twitches into a smile. **"Thank goodness. I thought I was going to have to do all the heavy lifting."**

I roll my eyes.

"Are you sassing a dragon?" Ravena asks, gawking.

"Don't worry, V. He's just as sassy as me."

Ravena looks at me like I've grown another head. "You're a

little comfortable," she mutters under her breath, as if Idris can't pull her words from out of my brain.

"She's scared," Idris tells me. **"Her reaction is reasonable."**

"Yeah, but this is just so cool."

"You didn't watch me eat a child upon our introduction," Idris contends.

"I suppose you're right."

"Get used to it."

I chuckle, facing my sister. "I was wrong," I tell her. "He's even sassier than me."

Vena raises a questioning brow at me, and I hug her. She takes the love gladly, and I squeeze her tight.

"Gods, you reek, Relie!" Ravena coughs into her sleeve, beyond dramatic.

"So do you." I hate that nickname, almost as much as Astraea hates us calling her Rae Rae. "And stop calling me that. I'm not a kid anymore."

Ravena smiles up at me. "You'll always be my little Relie, even if you're taller than me."

"What do you prefer to be called?" Idris asks me.

Pride warms my heart. My sisters have never bothered to ask. *"Aurelia is fine. But as a nickname, I like Lia,"* I tell him.

He lifts his head in approval. **"It suits you."**

"Thanks," I respond, positive I'm blushing.

"You two are really chatting, huh?" Ravena notes, hauling me from my thoughts.

"It's so cool, isn't it?" I beam.

"More like a nuisance," Astraea cuts in, glaring at the giant black dragon who towers over everyone. It bares its teeth at her, and too-brave-for-her-own-good Raea returns the favor. Asher snickers in the distance.

"I like my dragon," I tell my sisters. They both stare at me, Ravena looking weary, Astraea displeased.

Idris huffs blithely.

"Lucky for you, you don't have to share yours with a pest," declares King Asher, looking calm and cool with his hands in his pockets.

"Oh, bite me." Astraea's eyes dart to the fae king, her cheeks showing the barest hint of flush.

That's new.

Astraea gruffly turns to Nemesis. "When do we leave?"

It's difficult to believe my sister is willing to put aside her faith so easily and follow the dragons. Astraea worships our mother, aspires to be her. What's going on in her head? She's either in denial, or so angry she feels she must act swiftly. Unfortunately for Raea, there are two others riffling through her thoughts. *Poor Rae Rae.*

"Why wait?" Asher asks. I notice he's conversing with the dragon leader. "You want your freedom. Let's go tonight."

There is a pause.

"We'd survive just fine," Astraea refutes, a hand on her hip.

There is another pause.

"Agreed," she settles, on what, I'm uncertain. "But only because of them. And you will take me first so I can see for myself that it's safe."

Nemesis snorts, smoke puffing from his nose.

"I'm going, too," says King Asher.

The dragon bows its head, turning on its heel, its long black tail swooping low.

Astraea jogs over to me and Ravena with hardened features.

"What's wrong?" I ask.

"The dragons want to take us to a tavern to replenish our eterì and health. Nemesis says there's food and shelter."

"Is it far?" Ravena asks.

Astraea's lips purse, her eyes darting. "He wants us to fly."

My heart races in my chest. Just like that? I do like Idris, but I don't know that I can trust him.

"I promise to keep you safe," he assures me.

Astraea speaks up. "Asher and I have agreed to go alone with Nemesis first, to ensure it's safe. You guys should go keep an eye on Malek until we get back."

"You're going without us? What if he hurts you?" Ravena questions. I can tell by the wobble in her voice that she's close to crying again.

Astraea smirks, crossing her arms. "I'll be fine. It's the dragon you need to worry about."

"Let us go!" Nemesis bellows.

My sister tosses her head. "I'll be back before you know it. Stay safe in the meantime."

Before I can object, she spins on her heel and joins the king as the pair climbs up the giant black dragon.

CHAPTER 24

ASTRAEA

"There is no way I am putting my ass in your crotch, Trouble."

Asher lifts his hands in surrender. "Fine, fine." He settles a little further behind me as we sit astride Nemesis. "It's your funeral."

"I don't need you adhering yourself to me to ride a dragon," I hiss. "I've done it before."

"So, you admit it then," he states.

"Admit what?"

He leans down, his lips brushing the tip of my pointed ear. "You were riding him like a horse."

I elbow him in the ribs hard. He groans, his hot breath on my neck. A shiver dances up my spine, but I quickly shake it off.

Asher chuckles. "So wicked."

"Ready, dragon?" I ask, changing the subject. My favorite sword is still lodged in the dragon's back, and it is high time I retrieve it. Putting both hands around the pommel, I test the pull. This is definitely going to hurt.

Nemesis growls. **"You are enjoying this far too much."**

I smirk. "Wicked is my middle name."

Asher laughs. "Wicked and Trouble." To the dragon he says, "What's *your* middle name? Grouch?"

With one thrust, I pull the sword out, its blade coated in silver blood. I wipe it on my leggings just as Nemesis shifts, throwing his weight onto his haunches. I dizzy at the memorable takeoff I'd experienced at the Compound. Wasting no time, I hurriedly sheathe my blade at my back.

"Hold on," I warn the fae behind me, grabbing onto the dragon's scales for dear life.

"To what?" Asher asks—just as Nemesis launches us into the sky.

His arms wrap around my waist, drawing me tight to his chest as I grip the dragon's scales for both of us. My head is thrown back, slamming hard against Asher's chest as we rocket through the clouds.

"Why is he going so fast?" Asher yells, my braid undoubtedly slapping him in the face. "We're just going around to the other side of the mountain!"

I chuckle inwardly, aware of Nemesis' glee. "He's giving you the same welcome I received!" I yell back.

Nemesis' wings slant, caught in the wind. The clouds dissipate around us. I laugh, throwing my head to Oasòs, and howl with elation. Asher joins in, his large palm flattening against my stomach. I wince, having forgotten about that injury in the mayhem. His hand stills, gentling. His fingers graze the thick, raised scar through my shirt, and I hold my breath.

"You're hurt." His voice is a low growl in my head, accusatory.

"It's nothing," I tell him, trying to remove his hand, but his arm won't budge.

"Who hurt you?" Asher's muscles flex beneath my back as he closes the space between us. I can sense his rage as I plunge in his mind. *"Tell me, and I will end them."*

My stomach flutters in response. *"They are no longer breathing."*

My eyes shut for the briefest moment. Every time they close, I see the flashes of violence I'd both witnessed and carried out. The crimson beast who'd cut me was also the one who'd slaughtered Solbourne. I consider his execution an eye for an eye.

"It was a dragon," Nemesis fills in the blanks.

I grunt, neither confirming nor denying.

"Which one?" Asher asks, all-encompassing violence on his tongue.

"Malek's bonded."

My heart stops, the cool breeze in the sky no longer feeling like air.

"Fuck," Asher swears.

"It's my fault."

"No, Astraea," Asher tries.

I inhale sharply. Asher's hand remains in its place as I shut down and store away my emotions. I can't allow myself to spiral now. There are more pressing things to do than wallow in my shame. As a legacy—as a general, nothing is worth my tears. I must remain focused. I can't afford another mistake. After all, I am the one who led the horde to the Compound. My sisters wouldn't be in this mess if it weren't for me. If I had just died on those cliffs in Dieppe, I'd have saved many people.

"We have a chance at saving the world because you didn't die." Asher holds me nearer, and though I stiffen, I let him.

"The world needs saving from me."

"Perhaps," he muses. "But only because of your grumpiness."

"I am not grumpy," I say, rather grumpily.

"Exhibit A." I can hear Asher's smirk.

"I've just been told I am both the cause for Malek's condition and the reason my sisters—my only family—were taken by dragons into the Outer Edge. I have a right to be *grumpy*, as you kindly put it."

"Now, yes," Asher agrees. "Outside of this particular situation, you could work on your personality."

"Wow." I laugh bitterly.

"What?" he asks. I appreciate that he's trying to divert my thoughts. Admittedly, it *is* working.

"My personality outshines yours on any given day," I sneer, leaning my head further against his chest, my back and sword slowly resting against him, too. Asher relaxes, a sign I shouldn't be so close to him. But he feels strong, and I am tired of being the tough one. If he wants to be my pillar for a moment's reprieve, I'll allow it. These are unusual circumstances. Besides, we're far from prying eyes. No one would be the wiser if I yield.

"You don't have to be strong all the time, Astraea," Asher murmurs, his voice soft on the wind. He's reading my mind again. I am too exhausted to care.

"I do if I want to make a difference in this world." I swallow thickly. "Since the day my mother sent me to the Compound, my life has been about being the best at everything—the strongest fighter, the best leader, a decent sister, the smartest, the fiercest, the bravest. All these things are all I have ever been, and for what? Was it to take a place at my mother's side in Oasòs? How much longer would it have taken for me to become her?"

"You are not your mother, Astraea," Asher says, his rough hands lowering, moving to wrap around my lower stomach to avoid my injury. His warmth is like a balm to my aching heart. Why is he being so kind all of a sudden?

"Because you need it," Asher answers my thoughts. "And if I'm being honest, I do too."

I exhale heavily. "What if I become the monster she is, Asher? I was oblivious to the truth. I've killed too many dragons. I've taught so many others to do the same. I believed uncritically, never stopping to ask myself why the dragons had created the Outer Edge in the first place. Freìre was necessary for their survival, yet the celestials, especially Urðra, convinced us all that it was to take over the Earth. Why didn't we look further? Why didn't we see?"

There are so many questions that will never be answered. *What if I'd done better? What if our Intelligence had dug deeper?*

"You cannot be judged for doing what you were taught was right," Nemesis tells me. **"That you are willing to rewrite your wrongs is the real marker of your courage."**

"He's right," says Asher. "You know that my father led the Asherian War. He was the weapon the celestials used against the dragons when they'd been cast out of Oasòs all those years ago. Is he completely to blame for all that death? Don't the celestials deserve most of that blame? You and I, of all people, know that the celestials do not merely suggest paths—they tell us what we must do, and make us feel disrespectful if we dare question them. It's unfair to judge yourself for the things you didn't know."

I exhale shakily. "Neither was it fair of me to obey the celestials' commands so thoughtlessly."

Asher's arms tighten around me, as if insisting I relax. I hadn't realized I'd gone so tense.

"You know the truth, now, Astraea," he says. "Do right by it."

CHAPTER 25
ASHER

Even the brightest stars have their limits, and Astraea is burning out. It is strange to see the fiery general of the legacies so defeated. Empathy eats at my insides, scoring an Astraea-sized hollow in my heart—I can hear her thoughts in her mind, after all, vividly painting how she feels. She's shredding herself apart for the things she's done. I know she is altruistic in nature, but with this mind-link, and an exterior as hardened as hers, I never before understood how deep is her concern for others' well-being. The world weighs heavily on her, burdensome, and yet she welcomes it, believing she deserves it.

"Stop reading my mind." Astraea's grumbling voice rings in my head.

I don't bother answering. She knows I can't stop it from happening, just as she can't prevent hearing my thoughts either.

"I'm going to start singing another song if you don't watch yourself," she barks, smug satisfaction evident in her tone.

"Careful with that voice of yours," I warn. *"It's a weapon all on its own."*

Astraea gasps aloud. "You know?"

"Of course, I know, *Sirenstar*."

"How in Oasòs do you know who my father was?"

"Sirius was my father's best friend. How could you possibly think there wouldn't be records connecting the two of you?"

Astraea's father was a noble siren fae, making him high fae. He was gifted with the rare ability to enchant and charm anyone by the sound of his song, which is incredibly uncommon. The siren fae were revered in their time, which is what led to many being targeted for death. It is believed they are extinct now, but I know for a fact that their descendants live on.

"You would have had to have done some intensive digging," she says. "Since you know everything, you must know I'm a triple threat: a high fae, siren fae, and a spirit celestial descendant. That makes my voice, in fact, all of me, deadly."

"I've got bigger fish to worry about."

"Hey!" She slaps my knee, which is pressed snuggly against her leg. "I am not a fish. That is a myth."

"I'm teasing you, Astraea. You should know it is one of my favorite pastimes." It isn't a lie. I regularly claim every mission regarding the Legacy Compound. Though I am king of the fae, I am also a fighter—the Commander of the Fae Force. Astraea and I have this occupation in common.

As Commander, I work directly with the other leaders of armies worldwide. I help make decisions that impact the various armed branches on Earth. Each species has a distinct leader, and collectively, we collaborate to ensure the safety of our planet.

It isn't anomalous for me to take up training or join battles with the Legacy Legion. It's easy to find reasons I might be discovered at the Compound or found fighting at Astraea's side, maddening the life out of her.

"*Lucky me,*" she mutters.

I sigh with contentment, staring down at the top of her

soiled head. Dirt and blood cakes her ash-colored braid. I pluck an offensive twig from its snare and toss it below. I'd almost forgotten we were flying.

Nemesis suddenly banks right, swooping around the last bit of mountain before plunging lower. I clutch tight at Astraea's waist.

"This tavern is one of the only buildings left standing in this region," Nemesis explains, angling us so that we can see everything below. *"It has rooms on the top floor. We've peered inside a time or two, hoping to find dinner."*

"I hope you mean birds," Astraea quips.

"In the beginning, there were wolves and wild cats. Now, they are few and far between. We are lucky if we find birds."

I hold onto Astraea a bit tighter as Nemesis lands.

"Scout as you wish. You will find it is safe here. We like to rest in the field just past the building."

"Why?" Astraea wonders aloud.

"The breeze is nice. If we are stuck in Freìre, why not choose a mountain?"

I blow a rapt breath, absorbing the breathtaking view.

Yes—a mountain fit for the gods.

CHAPTER 26

AURELIA

"**H**ow do you fair with the news of your mother's betrayal?" Idris asks as we wait for Nemesis, Astraea, and Asher to return.

I can sense Idris' concern—more, and odder still, I can hear all his thoughts. He worries I've not accepted the truth, and is concerned for my well-being. He thinks Astraea will make things difficult, and he's worried the plan will fail. So many thoughts, all of which are difficult to cling to, but the most prominent is that he seems to care deeply for his horde. Surprisingly, he also cares for me.

"It's a lot to accept," I admit. *"I might not be feeling the full effect of it, to be honest. It seems absurd, but I know it's true. I saw it."*

"I understand. It will take time to process," says my dragon.

"I guess so. But I don't want you to worry about me and my sisters. We're on your side. We'll help you."

"It is my honor to worry for you and your kin."

I smirk. *"This magical bond thing has its perks."*

Idris huffs, smoke billowing from his nose.

When my sister and King Asher return, relief washes over

me, and my heart resumes its normal rhythm. They are all right. My sister returns unscathed.

"Come, Lia," Idris says, lowering his entire body to the ground. **"We ride."**

"Am I going to ride on your back?"

"Of course," he answers, as if this were an ordinary thing.

"What about Malek?" I remember the poor shattered man left in the cave, wondering how he'll handle the dragons.

"His dragon is departed," Idris responds grimly.

It seems Nemesis has already informed Astraea and Asher about Malek, the three of them going through options, Astraea appearing on edge.

"Malek can ride with us," I offer, drawing my sisters' attention. "I can hold onto him."

Astraea snorts. "With what? Your five-foot-barely-two frame? I think not."

I pout at her. Part fae, Astraea stands at five-foot-nine, and never allows me and Ravena to forget her height advantage.

"Orion and I will take him," Calix offers, standing tall and proud. He appears just as motivated as I am about getting to ride a dragon. Flying in their sharp-taloned grip was hardly the same. This is going to be fun.

"Excellent," Asher announces, and he and Calix enter the cave to collect Malek. Though he issues strange utterances, his mind seems to war with him, and the men manage to make him cooperate.

I watch my sisters talk a while, and wonder what they're chatting about. I make questioning eyes at Ravena, who soon comes to relay the message.

"Malek's sick because his bonded died," Ravena whispers solemnly. "Nemesis told Astraea what happened, and she told me let you know."

"How is his bonded's death affecting him? How did this all happen?"

A few paces away, Raea's normally golden face is pale, and it makes me nervous.

Ravena leans in covertly. "Malek's bonded was killed during the fight in Dieppe, and that's why Nemesis took Malek into Freìre. It was to protect him. Apparently, when a rider or dragon loses their bonded, it alters their brain chemistry, causing the condition of their mental health to worsen for a short period. They try to hurt themselves, and some don't make it out alive."

"It happened to Nemesis with his first bonded, Phaðs, and he persisted. Surely, Malek will make it through this." I certainly didn't want Malek to meet his end because of this. He never even got to know his dragon. My heart wrenches for Astraea's friend. He is charismatic, driven, and kind. Seeing him in that cave tore at my heartstrings. I wonder if he'll recover. Will he survive if the bonding has altered him, forever feeling like a piece of him is missing?

Ravena's lips rise hopefully. "If Nemesis survived, then there's hope that Malek will recover too."

"We'll help him," I assure her. "It's what we do."

CHAPTER 27
RAVENA

"I am sorry, but I cannot ride with you," I tell Nyx.

The dragon I am bonded to whines. ***"I swear on my life that I will not harm you,"*** she promises. She lies flat on her stomach, her head at my feet. I presume she's doing her best to look docile.

"You ate Theo," I say plainly, the hurt still aching and cold in the pit of my stomach.

Nyx whimpers hard, even huffs repeatedly. *Is she crying?*

"I am sorry, my bonded." Nyx's onyx eyes shut tight. A large tear falls down her cheek.

Oasòs above, this is so messed up. I groan. *"Do you regret your actions?"* I ask, my own eyes watering. This is so difficult. I understand that she's young, and it was her first time out of Freìre. She was scared and didn't realize that Theo was harmless. She didn't recognize he was a child, like her.

"With all of my soul," she replies solemnly.

I clutch at my chest, rubbing where it hurts. *"Oh, honey. Don't cry."*

"But he is in my belly," she wails, her chest rumbling and tears flowing freely.

"He'll be gone soon enough. It will be okay." The words like ash in my mouth. "You didn't know better." Carefully, I move closer to Nyx. "If I'm being honest, I am most angry with myself for not protecting Theo. It was up to me to protect all the children. Had I done my job, none of this would have happened."

"It's not fair to put that on yourself, Ravena." Aurelia approaches from behind and puts a comforting hand on my shoulder. "You both need to forgive yourselves. It was a mistake."

I sniffle, pulling myself together for the sake of Nyx. *She is also a child that needs protecting.*

With shaking limbs, I step up to the violet dragon and pat her shoulder. "It's going to be all right," I murmur, trying to reassure the both of us.

"I will do better."

"As will I, Nyx."

"Will you ride with me?"

I shake my head, apologetic. "No. I'm sorry, but I'm just not comfortable with that yet." Nyx whines, but I continue, "I'm going to ride with my sister. It will give us time to reflect."

"I understand," says Nyx. **"I am deeply sorry."**

"Thank you."

CHAPTER 28

ASTRAEA

The flight back to the tavern has me on edge, my feet tingling and numb and anxieties nipping at my every end. I keep looking past Nemesis's head to watch my sisters now astride the green dragon. I worry for them, wondering how greatly we can tempt fate before it smites us.

"They are safe with Idris," says Nemesis.

"I'll believe it when I see it."

Asher clutches my hips, his hands soft, yet firm. "They're okay, Astraea," he almost whispers, his voice soothing. "We are almost there. Breathe."

"I will breathe when we land, and my sisters are found unharmed."

Nemesis huffs. **"You are stubborn."**

"I'm realistic. Could you hurry? The others are touching down and we're still among the clouds."

Nemesis grunts before nose-diving toward the tavern. The wind threatens to carry us away and my back slams into Asher as he clings tighter.

The dragon slows, his wings out and gradually lowering us to the ground. ***"Idris tells me they are all well. They only wish to sleep."***

"Is it safe?" I question.

Nemesis chortles. ***"They are in a tiny building surrounded by dragons who'll guard them with their lives. Does that sound safe to you?"***

"That depends whether I trust you and your horde," I tell him. No point in skirting the truth when he can see into my mind.

"It is good that you have a strong shield. But I assure you, you do not need to protect yourself from me. I will protect you. This I swear."

"Why? As far as I'm concerned, you should hate me. I am the reason so many of your horde are dead."

Nemesis growls, lowering his head. My and Asher's bodies dip with the movement, but I steady us with a firm grip on the dragon's scales.

"I am filled with rage on their behalf, but I do not fault you. We cannot view life dichotomously. Certainly not in this world."

I raise my brows, surprised. "That's big of you."

"I am an ancient, greatly evolved being. You should consider this next you reduce my ability to be understanding."

"I didn't mean—" he cuts me off.

"Go. Be with your companions. We shall continue this conversation once you've rested. Though your eterì is returned, I can sense your fatigue."

He isn't wrong. I am spent. "You'll truly protect us?" I ask, listening to his thoughts and trying to catch anything amiss.

"You are our bonded, thus our connection is sacred. We will protect you, little legacy."

"I guess time will tell." I am still uneasy.

"Thank you, Nemesis," says the fae king. He tugs on my braid before hopping off the dragon and reaching up toward me.

I jump down, ignoring Asher's outstretched hand and stumbling when my knees protest. The fae king rights me, and I huff, "That wasn't necessary."

"Sure." Asher smiles. "You're welcome."

CHAPTER 29
RAVENA

I can hardly believe it. We're in Litochoro, the gateway to Mount Olympus—one of my dream destinations. Litochoro, a unique small Greek town, is something of an oddity, receiving sea breezes from one side and fresh mountain air from the other. As a botanist and an earth eterì wielder, I've always wanted to climb Mount Olympus to study its plant life. This is where I'd planned to stay all those years ago when the Outer Edge hadn't taken any part of Europe yet. Litochoro is considered the perfect base to set out on an adventure.

Now, the town itself is a muted representation of what it once was. At least the tavern is still intact—not to mention the outhouse.

"Vena!" Aurelia exclaims, popping her head out of the tavern's doorway. "They've got booze!"

I snicker, following my sister's excited hoots as Calix and King Asher help Malek up the stairs. Malek hadn't been frightened by the dragons when he flew with Calix, which proves he's still not himself, and I'm unsure of what to do. I will spend more time with him tonight to see if I can get through to him. Aurelia and I are healers. Though we've never seen a case like this, I believe that, with a little determination and hard work, we'll be able to help Malek—at least a little bit. But I can't guess how he'll feel after snapping out of the fog.

"Ravena!" Aurelia hollers from upstairs.

"Coming!" I answer, climbing up the stone staircase, years of dust billowing around me. I cough, covering my nose with the crook of my arm. I don't need to encourage my asthma.

The hall isn't very long, though the tavern is a generous size for a drinking place. The building hasn't been modified, and so has kept its picturesque Grecian architecture. It's a pity the Outer Edge devastated such a beautiful place. I hope that, one day, the people of Greece and all the other countries will make it home again once we're finished saving the world. Those who've survived the Asherian War have found new homes within the untainted countries around the world. Unfortunately, they're growing fewer, which makes for many conflicts. People need homes, food, and clean air to breathe.

In the aftermath of an apocalyptic era, all manner of species—we legacies included—find ourselves navigating a desolate world, desperately clinging to survival amid the ruins left behind by the catastrophic war. Nemesis's memories unveiled the bitter truth, revealing our foolish mother as its true adversary.

As I enter the hall's first room, shame hangs on me like a heavy shroud. I can hear Malek muttering incoherently. Everything that happened, including Malek's condition, is because of our mother. Urðra was the driving force that pushed Phaðs to act.

Putting an end to the Celestial of Volition would have undoubtedly accelerated the world's destruction. Still, I wonder if Aegliðs' death would have been worse than the erasure of memories regarding the bonded. Had Phaðs made the right call? They'd killed themself to ensure Urðra failed. It had to mean something. All this destruction wasn't for nothing. It couldn't be.

"In here!" Aurelia calls, waving at me through the doorway. "I put all our stuff from the king on our dresser. There're only three rooms. I picked this one for us." She beams as I enter the room. Although it's dusty, as well, it's also quaint, and there's a double bed that'll surely fit Aurelia and me. The room adjacent to ours has two single beds, both of which are occupied by Malek and Calix.

"What about Astraea?" I question, raising a brow.

"She'll have to fight King Asher for the bed in the other room." Aurelia quirks her mouth, making her look, appropriately, like a sly fox.

"She's not going to be happy," I say, fighting my own smirk. "Knowing her, she might choose to sleep in a booth downstairs over sharing a room with him."

"Are you kidding me? Twenty bucks she takes the room for herself and makes *him* sleep in a booth."

I laugh. "Yeah. You're right."

"Usually am."

"Right about what, pray tell?" asks Astraea, striding into the bedroom with a broody glare on her too-pretty face.

"Oh, nothing," I say, extending the word coyly.

"Have you seen your room yet?" Relie snickers.

Astraea slowly turns on her heel, annoyance radiating off her in waves. "What did you do?"

"The real question is, what will you do?" asks Aurelia, twirling her finger down her long, tangled hair. She innocently skips over to Astraea, far braver than I, and hands her the half-empty rucksack.

Astraea huffs, thoroughly irritated, before snatching the bag and stalking out of our room and down the hallway.

CHAPTER 30
ASTRAEA

Tired and sore, I groan, wholeheartedly dispassionate about sharing a bed with Trouble. "You've got to be kidding me."

Asher chuckles, seemingly having picked up on my thoughts. "Don't worry. I'll be good."

I roll my eyes and chuck my sword to the ground.

"Is that all? No arguing who gets which side?" He goads me, stealing the rucksack before I can chuck it at his face.

I curse, crossing the room, leaving shoeprints along the dusty floor. "So long as you keep your hands to yourself, you'll get to keep your fingers."

The fae king follows me, digs in the bag, and pulls out my medication. He sets it on the nightstand.

I blink at him, confused by the gesture. Asher huffs, shaking his head, his blond hair curling over his brow.

Why does that one piece of untamed hair have more charm than I do in my entire body?

"And to think I believed we were getting past our reservations," Asher says, voice low as he places the rucksack on his side of the bed.

I eye him, trying to impart an obvious warning. "Don't think that things changed just because I accepted a bit of help today."

"Wouldn't dream of it," he says. *"All I do is dream of her."*

A shiver runs down my spine at the inadvertent confession. *Does he really dream of me?*

"Don't let it get to your head, Reaper. They usually take place on a battlefield."

He probably dreams of all the ways he'd enjoy torturing me.

My mind flickers with images of a tall woman sporting ashy-colored hair with whip-like strands. It's me, through Asher's point of view. I'm grinning, stalking toward him. The king's mind is full of sultry thoughts. My stomach dips. I breathe harshly, staggered by the mirage.

"Don't pry if you don't want to know." I'm startled by Asher's flat voice. His dreams are not torturesome, but carnal and enticing.

I run a hand down my face and exhale heavily, then flop onto the bed. "Apologies. It won't happen again." I fling my arm out toward the nightstand, nab my pills, and swallow them dry.

Asher chuckles, shucking his boots and sitting on the edge of the bed. He looks over his shoulder at me, one corner of his mouth sinking into a grin. "Unlikely."

I stick my tongue out at him, earning myself a more handsome smile from his striking fae face. He appears more relaxed like this, just us in an empty room, our minds connected whether we wish it or not.

"It's not so bad, is it?"

I shrug. "Could be worse." I peer down at my feet and nearly groan at the prospect of getting up to remove my boots.

Asher tilts his head toward them, apparently offering to

remove them for me. That I don't refute becomes sign enough, and he begins untying the laces.

"I rather enjoy the mind-link," Asher says as he makes work of pulling off my boots. With the removal of each, my feet seem to sigh with gratitude.

"You enjoy reading my mind?" I watch him curiously as he sets my boots on the floor next to his. "Aren't you bothered by my hearing your every waking thought in return?"

"Well," he begins, voice quiet and pondering, "at the very least, now, when you look at me, you're actually *seeing* me."

My brow furrows. "What's that supposed to mean?"

Asher's look heats, the corners of his eyes sharp. "That you don't know only further proves my point."

My muscles tighten, my skin prickling under his gaze. It's easy to ignore the discomfort in my breast when it's eclipsed by a rush of yearning. I hastily try tampering my nerves by scrambling up the bed and climbing into the covers, turning my back so as not to see Asher's earnest face.

He sighs forcefully before I feel the blanket lift when he slides in next to me. His warmth radiates beneath the covers, announcing his presence with every second. It wouldn't take much to reach him, only the slight stretch of a limb or simply turning over to lie on my back. He felt so good embracing me while we rode the dragon, so warm and sure, giving me strength when I needed it. Though I don't wish to admit it, Asher Aidos feels good—*is* good.

My heart patters faster the more I acknowledge his proximity. I haven't shared a bed with anyone in ages. Is it wise to do so now? Perhaps I should have kept my sword closer.

The bed moves—he seems to be getting up. I jump out of bed, eyes wide and snatch my sword. I raise it, ready for a fight— only to find the king coolly standing at the edge of the bed with a gesture of surrender.

"What are you doing?" I demand, my heart racing while I mark the exits and listen for sounds of distress.

"Relax, Astraea. You're safe with me." With grace, Asher lowers himself to the floor. I peer down at him over the bed, able to see him only from the chest up.

I swallow, my brain taking a long time to comprehend what's happening. "Again, I ask: what are you doing?"

"If sharing a bed with me is truly so taxing, I'll sleep on the floor."

He'd been reading my thoughts.

"The floor's disgusting." I grimace, eyeing the space. The room is chock-full of dust, and gods only know what else.

"Yeah, well, it beats hearing your mind conjure the many ways you could kill me if you'd kept your sword closer."

"Hey, I wasn't thinking—"

Asher just glares at me, then glances at my sword, which I'm still holding.

I stomp back to my side of the bed and lean my sword against the nightstand. When I turn to look at Asher, his brow is cocked, as if waiting for me to apologize. I snort, crossing my arms over my chest. "When you make an unexpected move around a killer, said killer tends to act. I'm just playing my part."

"You're not the only killer in this room, and yet somehow, I have the capability of trusting you won't slit my throat when I close my eyes. But if you can't extend the same courtesy, I'm not going to fight to convince you I won't try anything. So, the floor for me it is. Goodnight, Astraea."

I groan, then climb back into bed and press the back of my head against the headboard. "What is your problem? I didn't ask you to sleep on the floor. You jumped to conclusions and went on your merry way."

"I heard your thoughts."

"Well, stop."

"Stop talking to me, and I will."

"Fine."

"Fine."

"I'll take first watch. You rest," I command, crossing one leg over the other, getting as comfortable as feasible for the long night ahead.

"Mm, I think not. *I'll* take first watch. *You* rest," Asher argues.

I pinch the bridge of my nose, maddened by the fae so eager to quarrel with me. "Are you being serious right now?"

"Deadly."

"Well, that's too bad. I'm taking first watch."

"What makes you think you get to order me around?" he says.

"I'm the leader of an entire army."

"And I'm the king of an entire kingdom."

"Ugh! Fine. You stay awake. Procure more ways to fight with me while I get my beauty sleep."

"Good. You could use it."

I whip my gaze at him, hoping to convey my resentment, but not before his thought reaches me:

"She's never been more beautiful than when enraged."

"You have strange tastes."

"Oh, bite me, little Reaper." He growls spiritlessly, though his fangs glint in the darkness.

A certain, pleasurable heat stirs in me at the mere mention of sinking my teeth into him.

I wonder what his teeth would feel like pressed against my throat.

If Asher heard my thoughts, he doesn't say anything. There's a long moment of silence. I lay back down, covering myself with the old blanket that used to belong to someone else. The quiet should be peaceful, the room dark and inviting rest, but I can't yield to it. Not while knowing the king of the fae lies on the dirty, old floor. He should get back in bed. Not because I want him to sleep at my side. I would never want that. I like my solitude. Although, with him constantly in my mind, I'll likely never know solitude again. Besides, he was quite warm...

"Astraea."

I gasp, his voice piercing in the night. "Huh?"

"You're overthinking things."

I lick my lips, a battle warring within me. I *know* I'm over-thinking. The only way I can live with my selfish, wayward thoughts is for me to overrun them with more practical, sheltered ones.

"Is it selfish if I want it, too?" Asher asks, a sound of hope in his tone.

"Want?" I echo. Why are we like this?

"Do you want me to lay with you, Astraea?" he asks.

Lay with me. Like, *beside* me, or *with* me?

"A yes or no would suffice."

I snort, my cheeks heating as I bite my lip, trying to quell the jump in my heart and curve of my smile. "You're such an imp."

Asher sits, leaning his arms over the bed and resting his chin on his forearm. "I get the sense you like that about me."

I swallow. "I sense you might be onto something."

A lock of ice-blond hair curls over his darkened eyes as he tilts his head. "What do you want, Astraea?"

You, I unexpectedly think. *To be less alone. To not be responsible for the safety of our world. To not be in this fucking mess we're in.* I think of all the things I wish for and then some, but instead of confessing them aloud, I reply, "I want to sleep."

Asher smiles, his eyes gentling. The look threatens to ruin me. "Can I lay next to you? To sleep?"

I nod, tentatively peeling the blankets down and inviting him in. He lays at my side, his hair like silk against his pillow as he regards me. I hope, for both our sakes, that we aren't making a mistake by giving in to whatever this is. Asher's fingers brush mine, testing, reaching to see if I'll allow it. Spinelessly, I do.

"I don't want to push you, but when you're ready," he whispers, "if you want to talk, I'm here."

Why does he show me this kindness? I don't deserve it, but I accept it, anyway. I close my eyes and settle into the comfort of the bed, casually nearing the warm presence beside me.

"What if I'm never ready?" I dare murmur.

Asher twines his fingers with mine, the gesture feeling bold yet tender. "I'll wait for as long as you let me."

CHAPTER 31

RAVENA

As soon as morning breaks, I wake Aurelia. She and I had spent the night talking, worrying about the future and saddened by the truth of the past. We laughed, we cried, and fell asleep with the promise that we'd make sure to right our mother's wrong.

We head downstairs, ready for the day. To our surprise, we're the only ones awake, save for the dragons.

"Good morning, my bonded."

"Good morning, Nyx."

"Idris tells me Aurelia would like to bathe. Shall I take you both, or would you like to fly with Idris again?"

"We're going out?" I turn to Aurelia in question.

"Idris says there's a waterfall nearby. It's small, but it's fresh. I think we should go. Afterward, we could work on helping Malek."

"Do you really think it's wise to leave without Raea?"

"The mountainside and waterfall are much too small for a large group," says Nyx. **"Two humans and one dragon at a time. That's what Nemesis told us."**

"I don't want you and Aurelia out of my sight, Ravena."

I jump at Astraea's harsh voice. "Gods, Raea. Warn a girl when you're stalking the shadows."

Astraea frowns. "And that's exactly why you're coming with me to bathe, and the men are staying here."

I throw my hands on my hips, looking up at my bossy sister. "You may be general of the Legion, Raea, but you are not my commander."

Astraea raises a cocky brow at me, daring me to continue.

Relie frowns. "I hate to break it to you, Sis, but aside from Malek, you look the worst right now."

"Besides," I continue, "Aurelia and I didn't fight our way through a horde of dragons two nights in a row. Knowing you, you probably didn't even sleep last night."

She looks away sheepishly, but her scowl stays in place. "Are you saying I stink?" Raea's mouth twitches.

"Yes. And so does Smelly McGee upstairs." I pinch my nose, and she tries to hide her grin.

"Fine. But I'm going first to verify that it's safe."

"Okay," I tell her. Aurelia complains, but begrudgingly agrees.

"What's the real reason you want me to leave you?" Astraea asks, leaning against the tavern doorframe. "Is it because of Calix? You two seem a little cushy..."

"No! No," I interrupt her. "It's not that. Well, there isn't really a *that*, but never mind," I stammer. I can feel my cheeks going red. Had Raea caught me ogling Calix?

Astraea reaches out a hand and pokes me between the brows. "You're doing it again," she snickers. "You're thinking too hard."

"Oh, shut up, Raea," I blow, swatting her finger. "Aurelia and I want to try to work some magic with Malek now that our eterì is almost at full strength. The poor guy's been suffering long enough. He needs to bathe too, at some point, and we'd all prefer not to do it for him," I explain, coming up with an excuse on the spot. Quickly I add, "Though I will if I have to."

"That doesn't explain why I need to leave you two alone with him," Raea states.

"Nyx explained that where the water drops, the pool is relatively small, and no matter what, they'll only be dropping people off two at a time. They can't even fly more than one dragon into the mountainside cavity, which is why I'm going to go with Aurelia after we work on Malek. You can protect yourself. Relie and I should stick together. I don't trust the guys enough to go with them and bathe. You, on the other hand, can give any of them a single look, and they'll wither away. You catch my drift?"

Everything I say is true, but trying to convince Astraea to leave me and Aurelia alone leaves a sour taste in my mouth. I'm not worried, however, about her being alone with King Asher. Whether they realize it or not, I can tell he has her back, and if my guess is correct, he'd lay his life down to protect her—if it came to that.

"Are you sure you'll be fine alone?" she asks, with a firm yet pensive face.

"Calix will be with us when we work with Malek. We won't be alone until you get back from bathing and give us a turn."

Footsteps sound on the stairs as King Asher approaches.

"That's my cue!" I announce as cheerfully as possible. "Don't fret, Raea." I throw her my most encouraging smile.

"Keep an eye on each other, and Malek," Astraea warns me, before turning out the door.

"She's only worried," King Asher utters. I catch his intense regard. "Don't give her a reason to regret leaving you two."

I bow, unsure what to say. I watch the fae king run to catch up with Astraea, a rucksack on his shoulder and two empty jugs and clothes held securely in his arms, presumably for them both.

CHAPTER 32

AURELIA

"How's he doing?" asks Ravena. My sister looks blue, a sign that her mind is wandering a dark space. If Astraea is the strongest of us, Ravena is the weakest, but only in that she is so extremely full of love and compassion that the pain of others wounds her. I'm glad to have some good news for her, even if it means I'm drained.

I'd almost given too much.

"He's talking," I tell her mid-yawn.

"Still muttering about someone listening?" she asks.

"They *are* listening," Malek says, making Ravena gasp.

"Malek?" she whispers. She hurries toward him, but his eyes close just as she places her hand above his brow. "Did he just…?"

"Yup," I reply, sleepy but feeling fulfilled.

"You're amazing, Relie." Ravena sniffs, looking awed.

"Thanks, Sis." I smile, warmed by her compliment.

I am never the sister people seek for help. Ravena is the best healer at the Compound, and Astraea is a force to be reckoned with. I'm always falling short, never quite good enough. I am the sassy one. I am the bratty one. I'm the flirt. I'm never called the smart one, brave, nor valuable. Not until now.

"I can't believe you did it." Ravena continues.

"Secrets, secrets, secrets," Malek mutters, back to his ramblings. He must have fallen asleep again.

I feel defeated. "It isn't done. All I did was bring his consciousness forward, but it keeps drifting in and out. When he falls asleep, the muttering continues. His body is also still fragile. You'll have to take over in that department. Getting him back took everything out of me."

And it did. I'm positive I'd wither to the floor if I tried to stand right now. I don't want to scare Ravena, so I remain seated at Malek's feet.

I am not going to tell my sister that I've done the one thing all legacies are warned against. If we are to heal others, so we're taught, we're to use eterì in unification with the wounded's eterì, coaxing it to function independently and to heal its proprietor. I've broken the one rule we are never supposed to break: I'd given Malek *my* eterì—nearly all of it.

"I'll do everything I can," Ravena vows. "You did all the heavy lifting. Wow, I can't believe it. My baby sister might have saved a life."

I shrug, feeling the early flow of embarrassment and guilt. Calix gently pulls Ravena from me and Malek, offering her a handkerchief.

"Thanks," she mumbles, blowing her nose into the material before sneezing. "Where did you find this?"

Calix smiles down at my sister as if she holds the moon in her palm instead of a snotty rag. There is definitely something sparking between them, whether Vena sees it or not. Good. She deserves to receive love (beyond myself and Astraea) after all this time of giving it.

"There are closets and dressers full of clothes," Calix tells her.

I've already seen its contents, and am incredibly relieved to have found a few dresses that will fit my plus-sized curves. I imagine only dresses will fit Ravena, too, as she's almost as short as I, and all the pants seem built for fae legs. The fae are all tall, like Astraea, whereas Vena and I take after our nymph fathers.

"Are you okay to sit with Malek while I go looking for clothes for us?" Ravena asks.

"I already got some for me," I tell her, pointing to the wooden chair in the corner that sits next to a parched washroom.

"Oh, good," she replies. "I'll be right back."

I nod groggily, unsurprised to see Calix linger behind my sister.

"Looks like it's just you and me, buddy," I declare to Malek, who kicks me in his sleep. "Hey," I say, forebodingly. "That wasn't nice."

His eyes blink open, and he looks down at his feet before meeting my gaze. He looks perplexed.

"You're okay," I speak softly, inelegantly patting his foot beneath the blanket.

"Where?" he asks, voice dry.

"In Greece, apparently." I chuckle, shaking my head at the universe.

"Outer Edge..."

I sigh. "Yeah. They call it Freìre."

CHAPTER 33

ASTRAEA

The dragon was right about the pool being small, but holy Oasòs, the waterfall is breathtaking. Nemesis hovers above a person-sized opening in a craggy mountain. Asher leaps off the dragon, landing on the ledge. He offers me a hand, and I accept.

"Seek me out through the bond when you're finished. I'll not be far," Nemesis insists, flying out of sight and leaving Asher and me alone.

"Alone at last," Asher remarks, following my line of thought. "How long until another misfortune arises?"

I glower, searching for danger, then for passages of escape. I descend, jumping from ledge to ledge until I reach the water's edge.

"I brought you something to wear," Asher tells me, chucking the attire at my feet, which stand just out of water's reach. "Your undergarments are in the bag."

I look at him unimpressed, raising the amber-colored silk to examine it. "A dress?" I snort. "This is entirely impractical."

Asher smirks. "Would you like to trade?" He shakes the black cotton pants in my direction. It seems that both the dress and pants are tailored for tall fae. Though I am five-foot-nine, I'm nowhere near Asher's height. He is *so* tall.

"Seven-foot-one, if you're asking."

"I wasn't." I wonder how it feels for him to look down at me from up there.

Asher chuckles. "Do you want my pants?"

I balk. "Definitely not."

He raises a brow. "Then the dress it is," he declares, tossing his newfound clothes on a large boulder. *"Difficult little enchantress...."*

"I heard that."

"Insufferable, testy—" I cut him a warning glare.

Asher only grins. His eyes darken. Slowly, his fingers trail the edge of his shirt, challenging me as he flashes me a peek at the dark ornamental ink on his skin. Without leaving my gaze, Asher lifts his shirt over his head and tosses it to the ground. Every ripple of his firm, defined abs commands my attention, as does the tantalizing mystery of that area at the bottom of his V-shaped muscles, below his pants. The gothic lines of his tattoos adorn every inch of his flesh, continuing below his waist. Asher flexes under my attention.

I meet his gaze once more. He smirks, knowing I've been caught looking.

I harden my jaw. "Turn around," I demand, twirling my finger in a circular motion.

Asher grimaces. "What for?" he questions, placing a hand on his muscled hip. "You can't possibly be too modest."

"I certainly am," I say. "Now turn."

"I won't gawk at you like you did me," he teases, coming closer. "Believe it or not, you really are safe with me. Always."

He's more serious now, and it makes me squirm. It forces me to face the reality of our situation. The fact is, I know I'm safe with him. Even if I weren't able to read his mind and hear his every thought, I've always recognized him as safe. Maddening, but safe. Yet this mind-link, however new, allows me to hear every unspoken word, and I'm not sure I'm ready to hear those words.

"Just fucking turn, Asher," I huff apprehensively.

He raises his hands in defeat. "Okay," he settles. "Just don't stab me in the back while I'm giving it to you."

"No promises," I chuff, grudgingly unstrapping my sword and laying it on the ground.

Asher spins to face the mountain rocks. I sense him laugh internally. *"You have witchcraft in your lips."*

"Shakespeare? Really?"

"I saw you reading it on your off time. Thought I'd give it a try."

I hadn't realized just how much he'd been paying attention to me. How much had gone unnoticed while I wasn't actively heedful?

"I'm attentive. Arrest me."

I laugh, shaking my head. "Stalker."

"Witch," Asher growls playfully.

Without wasting too much time thinking about all the things Asher had spied me doing, I strip off the sweaty, blood-soaked leggings, peel my lacy, strappy underthings from my skin, then rip away my blue top, flexing my muscles as it burns my wound. I look down at the scar it's leaving. Malek's dragon had really done a number on me for the injury to be still healing.

I quickly step into the water, careful not to slip on any rocks. The water is shocking at first, colder than expected. My bones instantly feel lighter, my swollen joints thankful for the reprieve. The salt of the water is harsh on my many wounds, especially irritating the one slashed down between my breasts all the way to my hip. It's nearly two inches thick, curving like a C across my waist. I don't go too deep into the water, stalling the sting that's sure to come. I should try to heal it now that my eterì is replenished.

"Astraea," Asher says, his voice choked.

I am frozen, my back to him. I was so focused on the scar on my stomach that I didn't think to take down my braid and hide the eyesore of my back. I quickly unravel my braid with stiff fingers, the water not deep enough to conceal me. I've only gone in past my hips. I flinch as the water laps higher at the wound. Asher moves steadily toward me.

"Don't, Asher," I implore, as I feel his fingers brush against my hand.

"Don't hide away your fire."

"My fire?" I laugh, spent. "There is barely an ember left in me."

"Astraea," he tries, his voice unsteady.

"*Please.*"

"Hey," he speaks softly. "Look at me, Starlight."

Goosebumps cover my skin, and my eyes widen at the unexpected endearment. Asher closes the distance between us, his hands brushing aside my hair and over my shoulder. I lower my head, my brows pinched and shoulders tight, not bothering to try hiding myself. After what he just saw, there is no pretending, no forgetting the mess on my body.

Asher emits a rumbling noise from deep within his chest, then reaches out to grab my chin. "You are made of fire and light, Astraea. Just like your namesake, you burn bright."

I was named Astraea as a nod to my ancestors' patronymic, as was my father Sirius. I'd never met the fae, and I've always wondered what inspired my mother to respect a patriarchal tradition.

I shudder as Asher draws nearer, resting his chest against my back.

"How much longer will I go on until I burn out?" I dare ask, turning around to face him, my chin still resting in his hand.

"I won't let that happen."

CHAPTER 34

ASHER

Astraea sighs gently, closing her eyes in this rare moment of vulnerability. Gods, she is so strong. Scars mar her honey-gold skin from head to toe, healed, likely, by only her, and her alone, and that's why they left a mark. She's always been unyielding, never showing weakness. Yet here she is, her long black lashes fanning over her cheeks, her small, sharp chin resting in my hand. She looks...defeated. The large gouge in her stomach almost causes me to sway. Only hours ago, she fought dragons under that pain. How on Earth is she still standing?

"Would you let me help heal this one?" I ask hesitantly. Her tiny nose scrunches, and I smile at her pretty face.

"Why would you want to do that?"

I scoff playfully, brushing my hand down her jaw, coasting down her neck until I hold the back of her head, her hair flowing through my fingers. "Why would I want to help heal you? Really, Astraea? I thought we'd gotten past that misperception."

She frowns, her eyes questioning, her tongue unwilling to ask what she wants to know. *"Stop reading my mind."*

I laugh, fondly capturing the image of the brooding legacy in my arms. I note every place our skin touches, committing each one to memory. *"I care for you, Astraea."*

Her lips part, and I watch her flounder. My heart skips a beat as her thoughts race. *"Care for me? What does he mean? Like, he doesn't want me to become dragon food? What the hell does* care *mean?"*

I tug on her hair, grinning when she gives me an irritated look. "I care for you," I say aloud. "I care when you're hurt, I care when you're upset, and I especially care that you're rarely happy. I care when you're training, when you're sleeping, and even when you hate me."

"I don't hate you," she snaps.

I narrow my eyes at her, and she closes her lips tightly.

"I care that you hide your pain and never share burdens with anyone," I say. "And I am astonished that you've decided to entrust me with them. I care when you tell me how you feel. Hell, I even care for you when you don't have the energy to care for yourself. I *care*."

"Well, okay then," she replies frustratedly, blinking self-consciously. "Care all you want, Asher. No one's stopping you."

I pull her even closer, holding her face between my hands. Astraea's breath catches and I can feel it against my lips as I watch her mouth with hunger. I hear her heart thundering— even louder are her lecherous thoughts.

"Stop me, Astraea. Stop me now because I don't want to stop myself."

She stares up at me, her bright eyes searching. *"You care about me?"*

As I watch her, a tortured laugh escapes me. *"Desperately."* Even my mental voice sounds hoarse.

Astraea pants breathlessly, and I am all too eager to consume her. *"It's about time you show me."*

One minute, I'm looking into her fiery eyes, and the next, our mouths collide. Her lips are soft as petals, delicious in all their glory. She tastes even better than I expected.

"Keep thinking those filthy thoughts, and I'll give you something else to taste, Trouble."

"Gods, I cannot believe you just threatened me with that," I say. *"If your wound were healed, I'd gladly take you up on that offer and thank you for it."*

"Kiss me harder," she demands.

"Make me."

Astraea's hands curl around my neck, drawing me closer. I eagerly obey her every command. I bend down to make it easier on her, loving the feel of her fingers in my hair. Astraea's heart thumps so loudly I initially mistake it as my own.

"Ash," she breathes, the endearment like a song, our breaths mingling in the space between us.

"Yes." My chest swells. No one calls me Ash. My name carries a weight of painful history, as my father chose to honor his son with the memory of war. Yet now that Astraea's uttered the nickname, I find myself yearning to hear it again.

With some hesitation, she asks, "Ash, will you help me heal this thing?"

I'm almost giddy with pride. "Of course. Thank you for asking."

"Thanks for offering." She smiles sweetly. I've never seen her face glow like this before. She is deific.

CHAPTER 35
RAVENA

The rooms above the tavern are all very similar, and each one has its own bathroom though the water isn't working. Nevertheless, they are stocked with towels, toilet paper, and even some unopened travel-sized toiletries. My curls will be glad for the conditioner. The rooms are furnished the same way: one bed, one dresser, and one chair set between the bedroom and bathroom door. Some of the rooms have clothes left for us to use. It's unlikely someone will return for them any time soon.

Aurelia and I wait in our bedroom across from Calix and Malek's, keeping them in ears' reach in case Malek needs our help. Calix assured us he'd let us know if Malek wakes up, suggesting we take this time to grab some items to bathe with once Astraea and King Asher arrive.

The dragons rest in a giant field, having told us to ask if we should require anything. Before joining the horde, Idris informed Aurelia that he'd come and get us once Astraea and King Asher were back, but that didn't help ease our tension as we waited.

We're alone in a tavern with two men and a horde of dragons just outside, and our eldest sister is gone.

Aurelia and I keep ourselves occupied by dusting the bedroom as best as possible. We each choose several dresses and hang them in the closet, eager for Astraea to return and give us the chance to bathe. We refrain from picking anything out for our sister, since she'll only scowl at us if we offer dresses. We couldn't find any pants that would fit her, so Aurelia suggested we let Astraea pick out her own clothes when she returns.

"She's back," Aurelia says from her station by the bedroom window.

A giant black dragon swoops in and touches down noisily.

"Thank goodness," I murmur, grabbing a pretty lilac colored dress from the closet. It's a lovely cotton fabric, flowy enough to stay comfortable in this humidity. Aurelia, who's been dragging her feet, has a little more pep in her step at the prospect of getting clean again. And, of course, to see that Astraea is all right.

As we round the doorway and start down the stairs, my eyes catch on something orange, and I do a doubletake. My jaw drops as Astraea, intimidating, tough Astraea, dismounts her giant beast in a long silk dress made for a goddess.

Aurelia whistles, making Astraea stiffen.

King Asher bows, grinning with sharp teeth. "Oh, please. There's no need to make a fuss about me."

Aurelia giggles. "Oh, no, mister. That whistle was all for her!" she says, waving at Raea. "Look at you!"

Astraea glares irritably. "It's just a dress, Rel. Cut it out."

I can tell all the attention makes her uncomfortable. The fae king seems to notice, too, stepping before her almost protectively.

I snort. *As if.*

"You're all right, then?" I ask, looking over my sister. This is the most skin she's ever shown outside of the dark. Though the dress is long with billowing chiffon sleeves, it plunges low on her chest, her assets barely hidden. As if she can tell I'm examining her, she folds her arms across her chest, rigid.

"I'm fine," she responds. She is always just *fine.*

I sigh. "Malek is resting upstairs."

Aurelia jumps in excitedly. "I woke him up!"

I smile at my little sister, proud of who she's growing up to be. Though she's twenty-three years old, she's still learning.

"Explain." Astraea's words are curt, but I understand where her terseness comes from. She doesn't dare to hope.

"I sort of gave him my eterì," Aurelia admits sheepishly.

"Aurelia!" Astraea and I scold her in unison.

Our little sister flinches, looking elsewhere. "Well, I got the idea from Raea when she told us to use our eterì when we were entering the Outer Edge. If doing it for myself just once was okay, I assumed it would be okay to do it for Malek instead. Since we didn't have to do it when we entered Freìre, I figured, what's the harm in giving it to Malek?"

"You didn't tell me, that's what you did!" I hiss. She knows how dangerous it is to do that. "I thought you'd coaxed his eterì out with yours. I didn't think you'd give over your eterì. You could have lost control and depleted yourself entirely, Rel."

"But I didn't," she replies, annoyed. "And Malek is going to be okay now."

"That was extraordinarily irresponsible, Aurelia Nox."

Ouch. Full name.

When Astraea turns guardian on us, she never seizes the opportunity to make us feel like our name is a failure.

Astraea's anger and worry are unmistakable as she continues, "You could have died during a transfer of that magnitude. Do you understand? And for what? Malek might not even survive without his bonded; sickness or no. Gods, Aurelia, you can't do shit like that."

"I'm sorry that I've worried you, but I am not sorry for doing it." Aurelia lifts her chin defiantly at Astraea, who in turn gifts her a venomous look all should rightly fear.

"You'll be sorry when you're six feet under, and we're the ones having to bury you because of some foolish choice you made."

"Raea," I interrupt delicately. "That was a little harsh."

She closes her eyes, breathes in sharply through her nose. I watch her fists clench, then notice the fae king doing the same. "Don't do it again. Understood?"

Aurelia mutters a string of curses under her breath, stomping toward her green dragon. Astraea suddenly whips out her spirit eterì, the dark clouds of spirit swarming Aurelia and stopping her in her tracks. Idris stands on guard, his wings pulled back and ready for flight.

"Did I make myself clear, Aurelia Nox?" Astraea's voice is low and deadly. It only ever sounds like this when she wields her eterì.

Relie's lip quivers, but she bows her head.

Astraea releases her hold and gives me a warning look that says I might listen well, unless I also wish to find myself in the clutches of her eterì. "You shouldn't have let her do that," she says.

"I didn't know she did, Raea."

She nods rigidly, her scowl so deep it's going to leave a trace on her tired face. "Don't let it happen again."

CHAPTER 36

ASHER

"Don't," Astraea hisses, her eyes so close to turning white on me.

"I'm not going to say anything." If Astraea—reserved, stoic, tough Astraea—is losing control, it's best I keep quiet.

"I can literally hear your thoughts, Asher. Don't even try to pretend you don't have anything to say."

I cross my arms. "That is not the same as talking, Astraea. By all means, if you don't want to hear what I'm thinking, then step out of my head."

Astraea groans, turning from me and marching up the tavern stairs. "I'm not trying to hear your thoughts. You're just terrible at keeping them to yourself."

I shadow the fiery legacy up the stairs, watching her hips sway beneath the amber silk dress, remembering how perfectly they'd felt in my grasp just moments ago.

"Stop staring at my ass," Astraea says.

This only makes me chuckle. *Gods, she is a sight to behold when angered.*

Astraea strides right past the first two rooms, then stalks toward the furthest room of the hall and pushes the door open. I follow her inside and watch her check for safety and exits. When she finally faces me again, shedding her sword and anger and breaking down her walls, I pause to let her have her moment.

She exhales dramatically. "I'm not angry. I'm just so exhausted, you know?" She looks at me with desperate eyes, so blue and clear I can almost see every suppressed emotion swimming there.

"I know," I tell her.

She bites her lip, but I can still see it trembling. "I'm scared." Her voice breaks on each word, like they physically pain her to say them aloud.

I close the distance between us in two easy strides and wait for permission. Her gaze searches mine.

"Look as much as you want, Astraea. You will never find me judging you for having feelings. I truly do understand. I am exhausted and scared, too." My thoughts are all the confirmation she needs. She burrows her cheek against my chest and I wrap her snugly in my arms, holding on for the both of us.

"What happens when you let go?" Astraea asks.

My chest rattles, a growl climbing up my throat. "So long as I am still breathing, I will never let you go." The words are jolting, ringing true in the deepest parts of my soul. I recognize my primal side taking over, but I do my best to compose myself. I don't want to frighten her.

Astraea caught my attention the moment I laid eyes on her. Her strength, her courage, her wicked, sharp tongue—everything that makes her so uniquely *her* is entrancing. If she'll allow, I'll hold her just like I am now, forever.

I feel warm dampness on my skin, and look down to find Astraea crying. My heart sinks. Never once have I seen her weep. "Astraea," I whisper, feeling haunted. Did I cause this? With a trembling hand, I brush her hair out of her face and lift her chin to peer into her gaze.

"I thought you hated me." She sniffs, hiccupping on a laugh.

This both shatters and intrigues me. "Why on Earth would you think that?"

She playfully swats my chest, making my heart want to leap out and hold her hand. "You always seem to find me at the worst of times. I assumed you intentionally did it to rub my nose in my failures."

"Astraea," I speak, voice low, making sure she's listening. "I was only ever there to ensure you were all right."

Her breath catches at my admission. I run my thumb under her eye, admiring the fawn-colored freckles on the apples of her cheeks as I wipe her tears.

"I wish I could say I don't believe you, but being able to watch your memories and hear your inner monologues makes it pointless." Her voice is quieter, and from the thoughts I hear, I surmise that she's going through hurdles trying to find a time where I've done something with malicious intent toward her. She will never find one.

"You're a fool," she thinks with purpose, frowning her pouty lips.

I laugh, grinning down at her. I cup her face tenderly, looking into her shining blue eyes. *"For many reasons, I am. But not for loving you."*

Astraea's eyes widen, her spine stiff. I can hear her heartbeat pounding wildly, as if racing mine.

Fuck. I'm being too reckless. I shouldn't have told her that. Not so soon, and not while she's upset and worrying over her sisters' safety.

"Ash," she snaps, interrupting my thoughts.

Don't make me let go.

"Shut up," she demands, that wicked gleam on her perfect face. I have but a second to blink before she reaches up, twining her fingers in my hair and hauling me down for a kiss so hot it could scorch the Earth.

CHAPTER 37
ASTRAEA

Asher's lips are my salvation. We find ourselves in the Outer Edge, a lifeless confinement, and yet, unexpectedly, I am alive for the first time in his embrace. This kiss is nothing like I've ever experienced before. It is slow, passionate, and full of all the truth that I am not, after all, alone.

He *loves* me.

He shouldn't.

"*Stop,*" he rasps, his lips still pressed to mine. His hands lower to my waist, trailing their way down to my hips. "*You deserve love, Astraea.*"

My knees weaken, and Asher lifts me up and pushes me toward the bed. My legs meet the mattress and my stomach dips as Asher lowers himself onto me as I lay down, hovering mere inches above.

I stare at him. "You barely know me." He is far too striking to be real. Tall, powerful, and marked to perfection. His ice-blue eyes darken as he stares at my mouth, and I lick my lips under his attention.

"I know exactly who you are and who you pretend to be," his

voice rings, deep and heavy. "You are the most caring of your sisters, though you pretend you have no heart. You keep everyone an arm's length away because you don't want to be the reason others get hurt. You keep no friends. Malek and your sisters must work just to breathe the same air as you, and it's all because you can't stand the thought of losing someone you care about. You are not responsible for the actions of others, Astraea. If someone harms them, it is not on you. But you take that on and multiply it by every single being on the Earth because that's what you do. You take the weight of the world on your shoulders and look to Oasòs for more to carry. You are not soulless like you tell yourself every minute of every day. You care so much that you pretend it doesn't exist.

"I see you. I commend you for your bravery and strength, but I also don't want you to have to go through this life thinking you're alone. You are not. Your sisters aren't as weak as you think. They can take care of themselves without you worrying about their every thought and move. And though you've never wanted my help before, I have offered at every turn. Time and time again, I have given you support, even when you hated me for it. You are not alone, Astraea. You have your sisters, and you have me."

"I don't *have* you," I reply quietly. I'm not sure why I say it, but I am knotted up at the sudden realization that he could abandon me. It is a sour, soul-curdling thought.

"Whether or not you want me, I have been yours since you knocked my crown to the ground with your sword." Asher's eyes are alive as he looks down at me. He is handsome, with a face both angelic and sinful. His ice-blond hair falls forward, framing his features as he looms over me, his chiseled jawline exuding power, his eyes full of anticipation. That his throat, and the rest of his physique, is marked with fae ink lends to his air of danger I'm drawn to.

He bends to press a sweet kiss to my lips, which vanquishes the bitterness for absolute and unexpected delight.

My hands bunch in the blankets as I suck in breath. Slowly, I let go, reaching up to brush the backs of my fingers along his jaw. My fingers tremble against his skin. For all that I am brave, for all that I am strong, I now find myself vulnerable in ways I never thought I would.

"I always knew I'd never be rid of you," I tell him, grinning then biting my lip to keep the grin from spreading.

Asher growls, stealing my lip for himself and snagging it between his teeth. I inhale as his canines sharpen, a small trickle of blood pooling in his mouth. His eyes widen, and he releases my lip, arms trembling.

"Ash?"

He begins hyperventilating, his chest moving in quick bursts. He's panicking.

"Ash? What's wrong?" I cup his face, holding him still, shocked to see his eyes turning black. "Oh, shit!"

He suddenly scoops me up and rolls us over so that I straddle his hips, his hands tightly gripping my ass. "Astraea," he says, deep and guttural. My core clenches as his stomach vibrates against my legs. "Tell me you didn't know."

"Know what?" Confused and anxious, I try but fail to read his mind through the haze.

Asher bites his finger and thrusts it toward my mouth, imploring me to taste him.

I eye him wearily. *"Is this some kind of kink?"*

"Do it," he demands, his eyes black as night. "Do it, Astraea."

I swallow hard before tentatively licking the droplet of blood from his fingertip. The taste of him explodes in my mouth, my body heating to treacherous heights as his eterì surges forward, filling me with the fiercest, most desperate desire. Power stems from blood, and his magic flourishes on my tongue. My eyes turn white, my body overtaken by the demand to claim him, a need so palpable I feel my eterì leeching out of me and reaching for Asher, who struggles to keep from doing the same. I slide his finger into my mouth, drawing his essence across my tongue and my body demands more with every lecherous suck. My blood chants to his, and his to mine.

"Astraea," Asher thunders as he shoots up, bringing us chest to chest in the fusion of our spirit eterì. My power—a black smoke—snakes around us, keeping us locked in place. His white eterì, a fog pale as spirit, caresses mine. It smells like mulled berries and ash trees.

"This is—" I inhale shakily, trying to get a hold of myself. "Is this real?" I am barely able to focus on words, the sensations paramount and divinely overpowering.

"Real?" Asher laughs, his nails sharp but never piercing on my back. "It better fucking be. *Nothing else will be enough for me now.*"

"*Your soul calls to me. We're connected.*" The words resonate perfectly, bringing to life the monster inside. The power in our blood pushes the truth to the surface. I cling to Asher like he is my lifeline, my chest almost rattling from the force of my pulse. "*You're mine.*"

"*And you are mine, my Starlight.*" My heart nearly explodes as he pronounces it so.

I breathe heavily, unable to stop myself from rolling my hips against him. It feels as if my soul is trying to escape my body to join his.

Holy shit. This must be a dream.

"It's real," he assures me.

"If I am truly yours, then claim me, Ash."

Asher moans, bucking his hips into mine. "Now? You're certain?" he asks, his gaze aflame. I can feel him flipping through my thoughts, looking for any sign of reluctance. "I don't want any regrets between us. Tell me you want this. I need to hear it."

He's barely in control of himself, but he has enough sense to leave no room for uncertainty.

"Yes." I gasp as another surge of hot need courses through me. How could I not want this? This is a gift from the universe, one never to disregard. Why didn't we realize it sooner?

"Because you wouldn't give me the time of day to get this close to you before now," Asher taunts, kissing my shoulder, my neck, and underneath my jaw. He holds me tighter, grabbing my face in both of his rough hands. His smile illuminates his perfect features as his hopeful eyes search mine.

My brows crease. "I didn't know."

"You know now. And so, I ask you, Astraea, do you claim me?" His tone is more of a command than a request. "We can wait." He chuckles. "I have been waiting for you for years. What's a few more?"

"You'd really wait?" I ask.

"I would wait for you endlessly."

I laugh, still breathy. I appreciate he's making sure I have the chance to decide for myself before giving me his vow. All this will take are words, and he doesn't want me to regret accepting him. He's a fool for thinking I'd ever refuse this. There are few good things in this world, and I am selfish enough to take what is mine. My body thrums, barely able to wait any longer. I smile up at Asher, a warm tear streaking my face.

"I claim you, my soulmate."

CHAPTER 38

ASHER

My soulmate.

Oasòs above, Astraea is my mate, and she is accepting me. I can hardly believe it. Of all the people on this planet, I am destined to have a soulmate in my lifetime, and she's been right under my nose all these years.

"I claim you, Astraea Sirenstar, in every lifetime, for eternity." Warmth spreads in my chest as I declare it so.

"I claim you, Asher Aidos, in every lifetime, for eternity," she answers breathily.

"*Bokontaì,*" we say in unison, the ancient word a divine decree.

Our eterì blooms, becoming one as our vows solidify in our souls. It is a legends-old affair, the oath simple yet sacred.

We are soul-bound.

I smile broadly, unable, and unwilling to suppress my joy. Tears sting my eyes and I blink them away. This is everything I never knew I needed. That my soul chose her as my mate feels *so right.*

"Ash," Astraea whispers, trailing a delicate, curved finger down my cheek and wiping my tears.

Though the touch is soft, it wakes every part of me, and my mind, body, and soul hunger for more. I take her hand and kiss her wet fingertip, tasting the salt of my tear on her skin.

Astraea moans, the heat of our soul-bond coursing through her veins just as it does mine.

"Astraea," I moan into her mouth, relishing the feel of her body pressed to mine. I grab her silky dress and tear it in half. She gasps. To my utter delight, she's wearing the red lace set I'd packed for her before coming to Freìre. Her perfect breasts fill the transparent cups as if made for them, and the lacey strings over her hips threaten to send me into a frenzy.

Carefully, I peel off her undergarments, savoring the heat of her honey-gold flesh under my fingers. I gaze upon her like she is my salvation. Eyes burning with lust, she clutches my shirt and rips the sleeves clean off.

Though the claiming amplifies our emotions, they must exist to begin with: Astraea wants me, and she wanted me even before this revelation. With her guard down, I no longer need to read her mind to know she cares for me. But I can also sense that she's scared.

"Off, now," Astraea demands, tugging on the hem of my shirt.

I obey her command, stripping my torn shirt off and chucking it to the floor. She ravishes me with her stare and I shiver, gripping her hips.

"Never in my thirty years of life," I say, "have I seen someone look at me the way you do."

"How do you feel about it?" she asks cautiously, dropping her gaze.

"Look at me, love," I plead. I don't want to leave room for any doubt. Not about this. Her magnificent Aegean blue eyes glow bright like the star she is. "I would tear the world in two for the chance to be looked at like this by you. You are awe-striking in every sense of the word. I vow that I'll spend an eternity showing you just how incredible you are, until I am able to convince you of it."

"Asher..." she murmurs.

"Read my mind. Look at me. Just, fucking see your worth," I implore, cradling her face in my hands. "I love you. Let me love you, Astraea."

Her lip quivers as she lowers her forehead to mine. "Love me, and I will grow to love you endlessly."

With fervor, I bridge the gap between our lips and lift her high into the air. She squeaks, an unbearably delightful sound. Astraea beats on my chest until I finally lay her back on the bed.

"Big oaf," she teases, kissing down my jaw before lavishing my neck as if committing the tattooed lines to memory.

I am in Oasòs.

"Beautiful, vicious, little witch."

She groans, arching into me as I cover her skin with passionate kisses. "More," she moans, pulling me closer with the backs of her feet.

"Be sure, Astraea," I say, still searching for any signs of uncertainty. We're moving quite fast, and though I'm glad for it, I won't take this any further than she wants. I'll wait a lifetime for her if I must.

"Good Gods, please don't," she says.

I laugh, loving how demanding and needy my mate has become with me.

"Tell me exactly what you want, Astraea, and it is yours."

Astraea lifts her hips, grinding against my aching cock that's still trapped beneath my trousers. Her mouth quirks, and I see that wicked flash in her eyes that I adore.

"There's that look I fell in love with."

Astraea pierces me with a meaningful look. "If you don't stop teasing me now, I will come before we get to the good part."

Holy fuck. Is she that turned on?

"Want to find out?" She smirks, lowering her hand to the apex of her thighs, and I can do nothing to keep my eyes from wandering. "Look your fill, Asher Aidos. It's all yours."

I pull away just enough so I can watch her tease her clit, which makes my balls grow impossibly tighter. "Look at you play with your pretty pussy."

I clutch my cock over my pants, give it one hard rub. "I can't wait to feel you clenching around me."

Astraea gasps, her intoxicating scent bringing me closer and closer to just grabbing her and thrusting deep.

"Do it," she demands, voice sultry and irresistible.

"Not until I taste you."

CHAPTER 39

ASTRAEA

I gasp sharply as Asher throws my legs over his shoulders, and I cling to his hair as if I can pull him into me.

"*May I?*" he asks, peering over my sex with the most decadent look I've ever seen.

"Please," I beg.

His hot breath fans over me, making me clench around nothing and leaving an insatiable ache wherever it heats.

Asher chuckles, his voice deliciously low. "I love hearing you beg."

"Fuck!" I cry, as Asher's tongue strokes my entrance. I am getting wetter and wetter, Asher happy to drink me up.

"Gods, the taste of you," he growls heartily. "I will never get enough."

I throw my head back as he flicks my clit with impassioned precision. "Your tongue is sinful."

"*You love it.*"

I pull him closer, grinding against his face, taking control as I hiss, "Lucky you."

"Careful, Starlight. If you keep throwing quips my way, I'll find a way to busy your mouth."

Fuck, yes.

Asher grunts, drawing from my wet cunt and leaving me wanting.

"Are you going to fuck my mouth now?" I tease, heavy-lidded and dazed beyond belief. Who knew this pleasure could be *so good?*

Asher smirks pridefully. "That good, huh?" he teases, wiping my slick from his mouth with the back of his hand.

I roll my eyes, unable to stop my widening smile. "Shut up."

"Admit it," he demands, climbing over me with his large, muscled body. His muscles flex beneath the impressive markings all over his skin. I feel along each ridge of his abs, constantly impressed with his physique. He is strong and powerful.

"Admit what?" I ask.

"Though you're always telling me to shut up, you love my mouth."

I bite my lip, watching his gaze snag there. "I might."

Asher laughs darkly, then lifts his hand to cup my jaw as he bends down tenderly to kiss me. "Knew it."

A loud *bang* sounds on our wall, and we jolt upright.

"Calix." My heart pounds. We didn't hear a dragon land, so surely it isn't my sisters. They have, however, been gone longer than expected.

Asher lets his head fall, forehead resting on mine. "Let's go wash up so we can wait for them to return."

My heart performs a funny little jump at the thought of him caring enough to know that I'd want to do just that. I bury the thrill, his command not escaping my notice.

I fold my arms over my chest, annoyed my skin is starting to itch. *Gods damned disease.* I scoot to the end of the bed and gently lower my legs over the edge. No matter how much I train and take care to strengthen my body, I will always find flaws.

"Come on, let me help you up," Asher insists, holding his arm out for me to take.

I sniff derisively. "Don't think just because we're all lovey now, it gives you the right to boss me around."

Asher grins, shaking his head. "Don't worry. I was never under the impression that *I* was in charge of *you*." He kisses me fiercely before getting up from the bed. *"I am a man possessed."*

I unenthusiastically take his offered arm and follow him into the washroom, my weak legs trembling and my mind whirling.

"I don't want to tell the others yet," I say hesitantly.

Asher grabs a washcloth and one of the large jugs of water he filled when we went to the waterfall. I can see its usefulness now.

He frowns. "Why?"

He pours water onto the cloth and approaches me, looking concerned as he cleans my mouth and down my neck. I hadn't realized how heated I had become until the cool soothing press of the wet cloth.

"Am I not good enough for the almighty Queen Astraea?" Asher asks timidly, lowering to his knees and kneeling to wash the rest of me.

More like I'm *not good enough for* you.

His tattooed hand splays out possessively on my waist as he glares at me from under his lashes. "You are exactly what I want and need, Astraea."

"Surely not as your *queen*," I try, unsure how I feel about the new title. New titles are being thrown at me too quickly lately.

General.

Bonded.

Soulmate.

Queen of the Fae Court.

"They suit you," Asher states, so much surer than I. His pride assures me he is being honest.

"Says who?" I poke his hard abs, his muscles flexing under my touch. My stomach dips at the glorious sight.

He chuckles and draws me into his warm chest. "You are always so quick to argue, my wicked, little mate."

I scrunch my nose, looking down at him. "Will the Fae Court be angry with us? We didn't even bring it up with the Fae Council. We just..." I trail, exhilaration and fear warring with my heart. *The king of the fae is mine.*

"It is our right to claim our soul bond, Astraea." He exhales slowly. "I am the luckiest male alive to have found you. It's so rare."

He's entirely right. Soulmates are a gift, and after the Asherian War, it's practically unheard of.

"Anyone would be a fool to try to stop us from claiming one another." Asher's expression is stern, and I quickly become aware of his slip into suppositional rage. "Besides. It is done. You are mine forever, Astraea. There's no escaping me now. We vowed it so."

I'm not trying to escape you, you fool. I'm afraid I'll lose you.

"Never," he swears.

I take a deep breath, inhaling his honied scent—mulled berries, ash trees, and, now, a heady musk from our earlier passions.

"Keep thinking those delicious thoughts, and I'll never let you leave this room."

I swallow, heat coming off me in waves. *Will I ever get enough of him?*

He hums, sinfully sweet. "I hope not." He stands and wraps me in his arms.

"But alas..." I sigh heavily. "My sisters will be back soon. I need to be sure they're all right."

Asher nods, stealing one more kiss before letting me go. "You're sure you want to keep us a secret, love?"

Love?

Asher grins victoriously, playfully tugging at my hair. "It's going to be hard resisting me for the sake of a secret, now that you've had a taste."

I smirk and lick my lips. "Is that a challenge, Ash?"

CHAPTER 40

ASHER

"Malek?" I hear Astraea's surprised voice as I round the door.

When I emerge through the doorway, I spot Malek, Astraea's sweaty, sickly friend, stumbling in the hallway. I hurriedly take one of his arms and loop it over my shoulder to hold him up.

Malek smiles weakly, giving me a weak thumbs up. "Thanks, man."

"Don't mention it."

"Malek, what are you doing out of bed?" Astraea scolds him with a stern finger. "Are you okay? What's going on with you?" She steps forward, pressing the back of her hand to his forehead. She frowns, her lips tight as she regards him.

"I'll be fine, Raea," Malek assures her, though I know just how difficult it is for him to stand. I carry most of his weight.

"Bullshit," she huffs, crossing her arms in front of her chest. Either she sees through his libels, or she can hear my thoughts.

Malek blows her a raspberry. My gut clenches at the camaraderie. Not only am I a little envious, but Astraea's friend is hurt, and it hurts her in turn to see him like this.

"I'm just not used to seeing him weakened," she says.

"I understand."

"Relie made me better," Malek explains, as if Astraea doesn't already know about the dangerous situation in which her little sister put herself.

I hear Astraea's angry thoughts, though she doesn't let her sour sentiments appear fully in her expression.

"I just wanted some air," Malek says mid-yawn. He's still tired. Whatever happened to him clearly drained him.

"Well, open a window next time, or else you might break your neck." Astraea points to the staircase just two feet from where we stand.

"Yes, *Mom*," he quips.

Astraea rubs her temples. "Go back to bed. I'll get you whatever it is you need."

Malek yawns again, his head slumping a bit. "Mm-kay, Rae Rae...."

"Is he?" I gawk at the now-snoring form that tries to weigh me down.

Astraea snorts, shaking her head. "Help me take him back to bed?"

"Of course." Lifting the rest of Malek's body, I stride into his and Calix's bedroom, following Astraea's lead. The blankets are already drawn back, so Astraea instructs me to lay him down. I do as I'm told and watch her carefully pull the covers over Malek. She touches his forehead again, her lips pursed.

"Still no fever."

"That is good," I reply.

"Do you think it's done? The sickness?"

As if stirring it back to life, Malek begins mumbling anew.

Astraea deflates, and I gently coax her from her friend.

"When?" Malek murmurs. "When? When?"

"Let's go," Astraea insists.

I kiss the top of her head, wishing I could ease her pain.

CHAPTER 41
AURELIA

I can't believe Astraea threatened me with her eterì. My heart aches at her total disregard for my life. I know she only did it to prove me wrong, to show me that I'd played with my life and how quickly I could have lost it. Still, it doesn't justify her exposing me to her power.

"It wasn't fair of her to do that," Ravena mumbles, trying to apologize on Raea's behalf.

"Damn right, it wasn't." I wring out my long, finger-combed hair. The water was refreshing, but I still find myself exhausted from feeding Malek my eterì. Thankfully, Idris replenished my stores, but my body is still tired.

Now that my hair is no longer soaked, I put my hearing aids back in place, thankful Asher grabbed them before coming to find us in the Outer Edge.

"You know what you did was dangerous," Ravena counters, plopping her hair.

I know she's right. But gods, would it kill my sister to just be on my side without evaluating logic?

"It was reckless and just plain foolish on your part, Aurelia,"

Ravena continues. "You could have given him all your eterì. You know this. When you give over your eterì, you can lose control and only realize it too late."

She sighs, grabbing my hand. I tear it from her, then feel guilty for the look it puts on her face.

"We are healers, but we do not sacrifice our health for the benefit of others. It's the number one rule," she reminds me, as if I don't already know this.

"Idris, we're done." It's starting to get dark out, anyway. Calix will want a turn to wash before the sunset. Maybe Malek will be able to go with him. Or perhaps he'll be too tired or, reasonably, too afraid.

"Coming," Idris calls.

"I'm talking to you, Aurelia," Ravena interrupts. "I am worried about you. You look so drained."

"Gee, thanks, Sis," I scoff.

"You know what I mean," she answers dryly. "You may not see it now, but you put yourself in harm's way."

"She is worried for you. Be grateful," Idris supplies.

I exhale, my nostrils flaring with irritation. "I know I fucked up, Vena," I admit. It's evident in the way my body sways as I wait for Idris. "I know it could have ended differently, but it didn't. And I'm glad it worked because, for once, I made a positive difference in someone's life." I pace along the rocks, shame making tears come to the surface. "I'm not like Raea." I laugh, shaking my head. "Hell, no one's as good as Raea when protecting people. But I'm not like you either. I heal minor cuts and bruises. I hand out acetaminophen for headaches. I am an assistant healer. I am only ever the sidekick, and never the one to save the day. You two being out of my way gave me the chance to try. And I know it was irresponsible. To be honest, it was an impulsive decision."

Ravena rolls her eyes. "No kidding."

"V." I sigh, annoyed. "I am trying to apologize. Don't make it worse on me."

Ravena gives me a pitying look and shrugs just as Idris swoops down to the waterfall's edge. "You don't need to apologize, Relie. I just want you to be safe."

I embrace her, relieved to get that off my chest. Still, I feel ashamed for what I put my sisters through. But I can't feel guilty for helping Malek. My life isn't worth any more than his.

"Come, Lia," says Idris. **"You'll have plenty of time to prove your worth safely. Your friends at the tavern await your return."**

"Is Raea still mad?" I ask.

"It is not my place to pry in Nemesis' bonded's affairs."

"Meaning?" I question further.

"Meaning I inquired, and he suggested I worry for my own bonded."

I laugh. *"Yeah. I was right. They are the perfect pair."*

"Trio," he corrects.

"Right," I answer thoughtfully. *"Isn't it strange that Astraea and King Asher share the same dragon?"*

Idris is quiet for a moment before deciding to explain. **"They share the same spirit eterì, and Nemesis is the most powerful of dragons. It is strange, but not surprising."**

"I suppose that makes sense."

Idris *hmphs* as we climb aboard.

"Are you two ready to go, or do you need a minute to yourselves?" Ravena goads me.

"Oh, shush. It's not my fault. My dragon's the coolest."

Idris raises his head with pride. **"Please tell Nemesis you think so,"** he teases. **"It is time someone else enlightens him."**

"Who else has said that?" I raise an eyebrow.

"Me."

I laugh out loud. My sister studies me questioningly.

"Dragon mind-talking is going to take a lot of getting used to," Ravena chides. "You look like you've lost your marbles."

Idris launches us into the air, gently gliding out of the mountainside and taking us back toward the tavern.

"I'm not so sure I haven't," I confess to Ravena over my shoulder as she clings to the back of my shirt.

She snickers. "You wouldn't be the only one."

Idris lands softly, and we disembark.

"Incoming," Ravena warns.

In seconds, Astraea sprints toward us, fury in her eyes. "What took you so long?" she demands, hitting me on the shoulder. The action is light, but Astraea packs a punch no matter the restraint.

"Ow." I grimace, rubbing at her target.

"We're okay, Astraea," Ravena assures her, stepping between us, arms outstretched like a barrier.

"How was I supposed to know that?" Raea clenches and unclenches her fists. "Aurelia gave Malek a lot of eterì—an ungodly amount. I just saw him for myself." She points, her body rigid. I can sense she's keeping big emotions back. "He was up and walking, Relie. How much are you weakened because of it? Do I have to give you some of my eterì? Tell me. I have enough to spare." Her shoulders are tight as she looks me over. She is scared.

"So, you can give me yours, but I can't give mine to Malek?" I push. I know I shouldn't, but I can't help myself. She's being hypocritical.

"You know it's different, Rel. I have more to give," Astraea argues. She's right, but it doesn't mean I need to like it.

"I don't need you to fix me, Astraea." My voice is quieter than I'd intended, but at least I managed to say it. "I am fine. I need rest, and I'll be good as new in the morning."

"Are you making light of it?" Astraea continues, calming as she assesses me.

What does she see when she looks upon me? I feel powerless under her stare.

"I'm sleepy and dizzy. Aside from that, I'm perfectly well."

"See?" Ravena says, eyeing the two of us. "All's good."

Astraea laughs, though it lacks energy. "All's good? Are you really that dense?"

"Don't vent your anger at her," I snap, pulling Ravena out from between Raea and me. "If you're upset with me, say what you have to say, but leave Ravena out of it."

Astraea's frown intensifies. "She was supposed to be looking out for you," she says, shutting her eyes and thrusting out her hands in frustration. "We're in the fucking Outer Edge. We're bonded to dragons, for crying out loud. Who knows what else will come for us?" She drops her head in her hands. "I can't have eyes on you all the time. I must know you'll look out for yourselves when I'm not around."

Gods, I hate her anger, but I understand where it's come from.

"It was a mistake, Raea," I confess. "It won't happen again."

"It better not." She looks away, toward the trees. I watch her jaw tick before she admits, "I can't lose you."

My heart thumps heavily. It seems my sister's overwhelmed —even more than she is cross, she is terrified. "Well, then you won't."

She looks back at Ravena and me for a while before accepting. "We're good."

"Yes, boss," I say.

Astraea's lips twitch. "Let's go get you two something to eat."

My eyes widen. "There's food?"

Ravena jumps, acting like she'll trample Raea to go find it.

Astraea chuckles. "Follow me."

CHAPTER 42

RAVENA

Beans. Astraea had promised canned vegetables, most of them beans. Calix doesn't seem too perturbed, gratefully eating kidney beans straight out of the jar.

"What?" he asks. "Do I have something on my face?"

I smile, ignoring the jar's wet sloshing sound when he shakes them. "Nope. You're good."

He beams back at me with the kindest brown eyes I've ever seen.

He is so adorable.

"Do you want some?" he offers. At least a hundred other jars are available, yet he's offering me some of his. My heart flutters a little at the prospect of sharing food with Calix. It likely doesn't mean anything to him. He's naturally kind-hearted, and simply offering food. That's all it is.

This doesn't stop me from imagining him feeding me from his fork. His eyes focus on my mouth, a soft moan leaving my lips.

A moan over beans?

Get a grip, Vena.

"Ravena," Aurelia hisses, elbowing me in the ribs.

"What?" I shout, waking from the daydream.

"Do you want his beans?" she asks, giggling.

I facepalm, feeling the heat settle in my cheeks. "Go away, Relie."

"Not likely," she replies, waggling her eyebrows.

"I can get you your own," says Calix, not catching onto my sister's dirty innuendo.

"I'll do it," Aurelia jumps in excitedly. "She doesn't like beans, anyway. I'll get us some carrots." I give her a thankful look, but she leans in conspiratorially. "Enjoy your time alone with Calix's beans."

I swipe her long blonde hair out of my face, and she snickers at me. Some help she is.

"You two seem to have a really close relationship," Calix remarks. He finishes eating his dinner, and I silently thank Oasòs for the relief.

"We do," I tell him. "Though she gets on my nerves, she's my baby sister. I love her to pieces."

Calix smiles. "I can tell." He looks away, and I track his gaze to the booth that houses my eldest sister and the fae king. More cautiously, he says, "Her, on the other hand...there seems to be a different relationship going on between you. Astraea's..."

I pat his knee, *tsk*-ing. "Don't go down that road, honey. Those fae ears hear everything."

Calix blanches. When he turns his attention to the hand I placed on him, I watch him tentatively lower his hand closer to mine. My stomach flutters, and I feel dizzy. He reaches out his pinky, and when I look up, he is regarding me with a longing in his eyes. My pulse races as I link my pinky with his.

"Do you often call people honey?" he asks, his voice lower.

"Y-yes," I stammer.

He tilts his head. "That's a pity. I was hoping I was special."

My mouth falls open as he leans in. Calix lets his head fall forward, returning to his shy self. "We've got company."

"Huh?" I am utterly flustered.

"Hello, you two." Aurelia smirks devilishly. "Hungry?"

"Starving," I mutter under my breath. Calix's finger flexes against mine, and my heart flips. I have to stop my overexcited indulgence. I'm only fooling myself, doing some rather rousing wishful thinking. He's messing with me, that is all. A man like Calix doesn't fall for a woman like me. He's an impressive member of the Compound, an Intelligence Agent who often leads research teams.

Though I hold a high position within the Healer's Division, I'm not a high authority in the general aspect of the Compound. I'm okay with that, since I've never sought the spotlight. I genuinely enjoy caring for others, and helping heal their bodies and minds. I have a talent for understanding precisely what people require when unwell. My knowledge of plants and their medicinal—and harmful—properties is vast. I dedicate all my time to crafting remedial concoctions or aiding in the Healer's Division at the Compound. It is my calling, and I am good at it. But I am nowhere near as impressive as Calix. He is the brains behind so many of our findings, helping navigate this ruined world one analysis at a time.

"Want to go for a walk with me after you've had dinner?" Calix asks, wrenching me out of my thoughts.

"I, uh—"

"She'd love to," Aurelia answers for me.

I blink rapidly before answering for myself. "Sure."

Calix beams. "See you later."

I dip my head, my eyes wide as I watch him head upstairs.

Aurelia elbows me. "Vena," she whispers, "he's obsessed with you."

I cringe, batting her away. "Stop, Rel. He's not into me like that."

Aurelia gives me a 'you kidding?' look, full of attitude.

"Oh, come on, Relie. He's Calix. I'm just a botanist with a knack for healing. He's important."

Aurelia looks disgusted, pushing my canned carrots toward me. "I don't care what he is. He is into you. And you're a catch, V. Calix would be lucky to have you on his arm." Relie waggles her eyebrows suggestively. "Or on…"

"Rel!" I shriek, covering her mouth with my hand.

Her laugh is muffled against my palm as I sink into my seat. "What if he had heard you?"

Aurelia plucks my hand and grins knowingly. "You like him."

"Of course I freaking like him. He's so cute and nerdy. But he's an Intelligence Agent, Rel. He's got bigger and better things to do than—"

"You?" she cuts in, throwing her head back in laughter.

I can physically feel how red my cheeks are.

"What's so funny?" Astraea asks, scaring both of us with her surprise approach.

Aurelia chuckles, pointing to me with her thumb. "This one's got a crush." She beams.

Astraea raises a curious eyebrow. "Knew it."

I balk at my sisters, the carrots I ate now churning in my stomach. I push my glasses up the bridge of my nose. "Is it that obvious?"

"Definitely," Aurelia replies haughtily.

I turn my attention to Astraea, trying my very best to lose my blush. "What about you, huh?" I ask, stammering more than I care to. "Mrs. Too-Good-For-Company sure has been spending a lot of time with the fae king."

Astraea's face doesn't budge from her usual scowl, not deepening, not lessening. She shrugs her shoulder as if she doesn't have anything to say.

"Mrs. Fae King," Aurelia adds teasingly.

That gets a reaction out of Raea. Her irises succumb, her eterì coming to the surface.

"Woah," I gasp, grabbing her arm. "Settle down, Raea. We were only teasing."

Astraea's eyes return to their blue, narrowing at me and Relie. "Be careful of the things you say."

I scrutinize her. "You were just doing the same to me!"

Raea's shoulders tense before she finally takes a calming breath.

"You good?" Aurelia asks.

Astraea nods. "Being bonded to the same dragon as the fae king comes with... complications. No matter how innocent, a snide comment will be loudly broadcast to him through my thoughts."

Shit. I forgot about that.

"Oh, my gods," Aurelia says, throwing a hand over her mouth. "I hadn't thought of that."

Astraea's lips purse. "It's fine. Just be wary of what you say. The wrong thing could start a war we don't have time for."

Does she think us calling her the fae king's bride would be her demise? I guess times are worse than I thought.

"We'll be careful, Raea," I promise.

"Cool." Then her lips twitch in the faintest form of a smile. "Now, tell me about that Intelligence Agent."

CHAPTER 43
AURELIA

Ravena's eyes glow when she talks about Calix Lightcrest, explaining how they've apparently had a quiet comradery going for a while. She and Calix often work late nights in the labs. She studies plant properties while he studies the terrain that has yet to be overthrown by the Outer Edge. The pair was exchanging small conversations regularly, albeit reservedly.

Ravena is a sucker for love, and though she has all the time in the world to spread hers, she never gives herself the same courtesy. She is typically introverted, only sharing her bubbly side when comfortable. If she put herself out there, there would be flocks lining up to date her. She's intelligent, courageous, kind and, while only four-foot-eleven, absolutely gorgeous. Her grey eyes and rich brown hair contrast nicely with her warm tawny face, making her a sight to behold.

"It sounds like you genuinely like him, V," I note as she spills her emotions to Astraea and me.

"I think I do," she admits, blushing like a rose.

"I think you owe it to yourself to see if something is there," I tell her, looking to Astraea for her opinion.

Raea nods tentatively, thinking. "You know how I am about... feelings." She swallows heavily, angular brows raised. "However, I think you'd be a fool to overlook what destiny suggests. We were put on this path for a reason. That you and he were smitten before we were all captured and taken to Freìre is a sign that the stars have aligned."

Ravena and I blink up at Astraea.

"Wow, Raea," Ravena sputters. "That was deep."

Astraea grunts. "Don't get used to it."

I chuckle. "I don't think we could if we tried."

Ravena stands and reaches out, grabbing Astraea and my hand. "Thanks, girls. I needed the boost of confidence."

Astraea nods.

"Any time, Sis," I tell Vena. "Now, go get your man!" I whack her hip and she giggles, shooing me away.

"All right, all right." She lifts her hands in surrender. "This conversation never happened. Got it?" She points a tiny, stern finger at us.

"Whatever you say."

Without a reply, Raea crosses her arms and struts back over to the king's booth, where she sits with her back straight. When she looks up at him, her lips lift into what Raea would consider a smile, and King Asher returns it.

There is unquestionably something going on there, but if Astraea is worried my prying will endanger her, I won't bring it up again. Perhaps one day, she'll feel comfortable telling us what's going on, like Ravena has.

It's too bad my companions aren't here to distract me. Now, that would be entertaining.

Maybe I'll find fun at the bottom of a rum bottle.

CHAPTER 44
RAVENA

I hear mumbling from the other side of Calix and Malek's bedroom door, and decide to listen. I don't want to pry, but can't help my curiosity. Though Malek was awake, and we got him to begrudgingly eat, he still mumbled mostly incoherent phrases.

Sometimes, it seems like he's coming out of it, but he quickly returns to babbling before we can make something of his words. It's odd, seeing as how I am almost certain Aurelia succeeded in bringing his mind back during the time he was awake. It's sad to see him reverting.

Understanding none of the mumblings from the other side, I knock on the door, giving up on eavesdropping. I'm nervous to see Calix, but wholeheartedly excited for our date—if this is a date.

Calix steps out of the room and closes the door behind him. "Hi, Ravena."

He's shirtless.

I slowly raise my gaze, meeting his eyes. "Hi."

He smiles, pulling his shirt on. "You still up for that walk?"

I bob my head, my mouth dry. "Sure," I manage, backing up and almost tripping over my feet. Calix rights me, and my stomach flutters. "Thanks," I murmur, accepting that I won't be hiding my blush any time soon.

"After you," he bows.

I tentatively take the stairs, doing my best not to fall. "Where are we going?" I ask over my shoulder.

"I thought perhaps we'd ask Orion to take us for a flight," he says.

I'm unsure of how I feel about that idea. Going out alone with a guy and his dragon isn't exactly safe, but Calix does seem like a good guy.

"That would be fine," I answer nervously.

Calix looks at me with compassion. "Don't agree to something you don't want to do, Ravena. I wouldn't ask that of you."

I exhale, feeling relieved but also trapped by my people-pleasing condition. "If it's all right with you, I prefer we stay on land. It's been a long couple of days, and I'm not cut out for adventure."

Calix smiles softly, placing a hand at the small of my back. My heart leaps at the comforting gesture. "I wouldn't be so sure."

"What makes you say that?" My arm itches to wrap around his waist, but I can't find the courage.

Calix draws nearer, whispering, "Because of your passion for life, Ravena."

I shiver, gulping audibly. "Oh."

Calix removes his hand, and I immediately miss its warmth. "You're a healer. You take care of others who need you. And you are very connected with your earth eterì, studying plants and gaining knowledge of their uses. Figuring out how best they grow or thrive. You cannot possibly lack a want for adventure."

He has me there. "It was a long-lost dream of mine to come here," I admit. "Before, when the Outer Edge hadn't taken so much of the world, I'd wanted to explore. This place was high on my bucket list."

"Ahh," he murmurs, intent on listening.

I silently thank him. It's been years since anyone asked me what I lost because of the Outer Edge. I've always felt selfish for even thinking about my dead dreams. People died fighting to keep the dragons at bay, and now I know that dragons have killed and died to protect their own. My silly dreams of staying in Litochoro seem trivial at best. My being here now makes me feel even more ridiculous. I made it, didn't I?

"Now that you're here," Calix says in a thoughtful tone, "I imagine it doesn't feel as good as you'd expected it to."

"Mount Olympus, Litochoro, it is all achingly beautiful, but..." I trail, examining the tall trees that surround the trail the tavern occupies.

"But it is uninhabited," he says, gazing out at the scenery.

I nod. "I worry that if it stays like this for much longer, its history will vanish with its people."

Calix twines his fingers in mine, and I lean into him. I rest my head against his arm, taking in this quiet moment.

"We won't let it get to that, Ravena," Calix promises.

"Do you think the celestials will give us the chance to explain our presence with the dragons?" I ask. "Not just the celestials, but the others? I worry they won't give us and the dragons a chance."

Calix exhales deeply, his eyes lowering to the ground.

I watch tentatively, knowing that he specializes in analyzing situations as an Intelligence Agent. He's excellent at prediction, and even better at solving puzzles. If anyone can presume what is to come, it's him.

"I believe it will take much convincing, but success is achievable," he tells me. "There are many variants which will affect the outcome. The biggest problem is that your mother, the Celestial of Fate, is the traitor among the others. Though her memory is wiped, and she cannot remember a time before the dragons were on Earth, I don't imagine she'll react positively to being accused of attempted siblicide.

"I wonder how the other celestials will react to this. Will they believe us? Will they take Urðra's side? What if they turn on her, and we can do nothing to stop them from putting an end to Fate? What will happen to the world?

"Like I said, there are many variants."

"So, we go to the legacies first, as Nemesis implied." This is a lot to accept and even more to contemplate. "If we can get the legacies to agree to a course of action, then perhaps we'll be able to sway the celestials into rational thinking. Without our worship, what would the celestials be?"

"That is an excellent observation," Calix responds, idly rubbing the back of his neck. "Perhaps with enough incentive, the celestials will consider our judgements."

"So, we band the legacies together and explain the truth behind the Asherian War. Then, we take it up with the celestials."

Calix ponders a while longer, seeming far away.

Aurelia's dragon swoops low, landing in front of the tavern. Is Relie okay? I shake my head. She probably just wants to have a chat with her new friend.

"I have a concern that I don't know what to do with," Calix admits, drawing my attention. His dark brown eyes appear tired, as if something's been weighing on him.

"Can I help?" I ask.

He reflects a while longer, before tentatively accepting. "We cannot kill Fate, but what shall we do with her?"

I shiver, though the air is thick and balmy. I feel sick to my stomach when I think of my mother. I can hardly believe what she did, and yet, I know it to be true. "My mother can't be trusted."

Calix nods. "There is the possibility of a transfer in ruling."

"But—" I sputter, my mind frantic. "That's only supposed to happen when a celestial turns to the stars. That's not supposed to happen for eons, Calix. That's *not* supposed to happen." My chest heaves, and I fall to my knees, grabbing fistfuls of rocks in my palms to bring myself back to Earth.

"Ravena," Calix gasps, joining me on the ground and holding me up by my shoulders. "How can I help?" He probes me with his wild eyes. "Should I get Astraea?"

"No!" I wheeze, coughing on nothing.

Calix's regard is alarmed until relief settles on his brow. "Aurelia!" he shouts.

No, no, no.

I cling to my chest, tilt my face to the sky, and beg for the air to return to my lungs.

"Inhaler!" Aurelia says, panting and handing me the blue inhaler. She must have run fast. I grab it with my dirty hands and inspire the medicine, holding my breath as long as I can. I exhale shakily, before taking a second puff.

"Better?" Calix asks, rubbing my shoulders with care.

I just stare wide-eyed. Aurelia looks spooked, waiting for me to tell them I'm all right.

"I'm okay," I mumble, coughing a little. My lungs have found relief, but my heart hasn't. Thankfully, one meaningful look in Calix's direction is enough to keep him quiet about our earlier discussion.

Aurelia can't know. She'd try to stop us from doing the right thing.

Astraea can't know. She would sacrifice herself too early to save us from a fight.

CHAPTER 45

ASHER

"What?" I grin across the table at Astraea, who sits with me in a restaurant-style booth.

She kicks my foot under the table, her pretty lashes darkening. "You know what," she hisses, crossing her arms.

My tongue darts out to wet my lip, as I appreciate her curves. "Mrs. Fae King?" I cock an eyebrow at my overheated mate, taunting her.

"Shut up," she snaps, with a rather haughty air.

I lean in, practically taking up all the space in our secluded booth. "What did we say about my mouth, little Reaper?" I ask in a lowered tone. I watch her through my narrowed gaze, enjoying how she squirms before crossing a leg over the other. I smirk.

"I don't recall." She tilts her sharp chin, acting as if moments ago I hadn't been worshiping her between those legs she'd just crossed.

"You love it."

Her smile is full of mischief. "You love *me*."

My hand rubs at my chest, watching Astraea's eyes light up.

"That I do." I can hardly believe I've said it aloud, never mind the fact that she seems to like it.

Astraea's gaze softens; her divine features even lovelier when she looks at me like this.

"Are you sure you're fine, V?" I hear Aurelia questioning her sister from a far-off distance, their footsteps sounding as they near the tavern. Astraea and I shoot up instantly, running for the entrance. Aurelia steps in before we reach the door, followed by Ravena, who clings to Calix's arm.

"What happened?" Astraea demands, waiting for a report with the tap of her imposing foot. Her eyes spark white as she clenches her fists, her eterì on high alert, coiling around her arms like venomous snakes.

Such fire.

"Asthma," Ravena answers quietly, avoiding Astraea's impenetrable gaze.

"Did you have your inhaler on you?" Astraea asks.

Ravena lifts it with a tired hand, shaking it before her sister.

"I got it for her," Aurelia explains. "She hadn't been having an attack for long."

Astraea nods, seeming pleased with that answer. "Good. Do you need anything? Water?" she suggests.

"Just some rest," her sister replies.

"I can help you upstairs," Calix offers.

Astraea and Aurelia take a step forward, about to argue, but Ravena smiles happily at Calix, accepting the offer. "Thanks."

Calix takes that as his cue, and the pair saunter off upstairs.

"I'm going to go check on Malek," Aurelia tells us, following Ravena and Calix to the rooms.

Our companions will likely stay in their rooms for the night. Twilight approaches, and they've been through hurdles as of late.

"Just you and me again, Starlight." I sigh, contented.

"You, me, and Nemesis," she replies sourly. "We should talk to him about strategy."

"Fine," I grunt, not wanting to waste my time and energy on anything but Astraea.

I observe her every move as we traverse a rocky trail to where the dragons landed. They lie only a few yards from the tavern, so it doesn't take long to reach them.

Nemesis expects for us, anticipating our arrival—no doubt reading our minds.

"You may rest for a while longer if it is needed," says Nemesis.

Astraea throws a hand on her hip. "Gee, thanks, master."

Nemesis huffs. **"Very well, my petulant bonded."**

Astraea rolls her eyes so hard I almost believe the blue might never return. I chuckle, placing my hand on the small of her back. At first, she freezes, looking from me to Nemesis and the group of sleeping dragons just out of reach.

"He probably already knows." Astraea curses under her breath.

"Undoubtedly." I rub her back.

"It was high time for both of you to accept your soul-bond. I was growing tired of your ongoing arguments, which stemmed from carnal frustration."

"You knew before?" I take a furious step forward, while towing Astraea closer to my side.

Astraea's jaw tightens, wisps of eterì seeping through the cracks of her flexed fingers. *"He didn't tell us."*

Nemesis huffs in displeasure. **"I did not realize you were unaware. You both felt the pull, did you not?"**

I was drawn to Astraea since the moment I met her. There was no question—the pull had always been there for me. My pulse quickens as I wait to know if Astraea felt it, too.

She grunts, sharpening her eyes, which soften when she

looks at me. *"Of course, I felt it, Trouble. Why do you think I kept telling you to go away?"*

"Because of how charmingly annoying I was?"

"That and your smug face, and your alluring scent, were all driving me mad."

I fist a hand in her shirt, and she gasps. *"My scent?"*

"Your banter is sickening," Nemesis cuts in.

"Save it, dragon," I say. "You could have avoided plenty of banter if you had told us that we were soulmates."

We should have known sooner. If Nemesis would have told us, we could have claimed our soul- bond earlier. So much time has gone by, and I feel guilty for how much of it was wasted.

"Nothing was wasted, Ash," Astraea calms me, her voice gentling in my mind, only ever for me. I wrap my arm around her shoulders and kiss her forehead, inhaling her like it is my last breath.

"Apologies," Nemesis responds. **"No one should be kept from their soulmate. It is a sacred bond one should cherish. I would have informed you had I known you were oblivious."**

Astraea serves him a warning glare but seems to incline her head in acceptance. I embrace her tenderly and pull her down to sit with me. The ground is wet from the humidity, and I gladly let it dampen my pants as I sit cross-legged with Astraea in my lap. She's permitting me to hold her in the presence of others. I am decidedly elated.

"Don't get all mushy on me, Mate," she teases. That she calls me *Mate* is her way of saying she feels mushy right back. I grin, drawing her closer. She tucks herself into me, her head resting on my chest.

"Regarding our quest," I begin. There is no time like the present, and with Astraea in my arms and the night stars shining above, I feel readier than I've ever been to end a war.

"We will seek out your legacy allies and enlighten them on

the true past. Assuming they believe us, we then include other species, inviting leaders of each to the Compound to inform them."

"Why at the Compound?" Astraea asks. "Couldn't we just go visit them in their respective regions?"

"And risk their thinking we plan to attack?" Nemesis questions.

"Right," Astraea hums, imagining all the ways that this could go badly. I see each imagined scenario as they flash in her mind.

"The Compound also gives us the upper hand if things go poorly," I add. "A controlled environment is best."

Astraea smirks. *"Okay, smarty pants."*

"I know things," I say, tugging on her hair for good measure.

"What if the legacies refuse to listen?" Astraea continues.

I frown, very much afraid of what might happen.

"It cannot come to that," Nemesis responds. *"Without the legacies, there is no hope with the celestials. It would mean an unavoidable battle."*

Astraea's mind goes through the consequences before stopping for one. *"If I could communicate strictly to Ahemì, C'tarð, and Aegliðs, we'd have a chance. They've guided me my whole life."*

"But there is no guarantee that they aren't working with your mother, or that Urðra won't receive the message either," I remind her. I, too, am guided by the four spirit rulers. I know it would be a risk as much as she does.

"It also creates possible conflict within Oasòs, allowing rash decisions to be made. We cannot allow Urðra to be killed. There is power in numbers. The more people who know before the celestials are involved, the better control we have of the outcome."

Nemesis is right about having better luck with more people on our side, but something about this concerns me. What will we do with Urðra if we do not kill her?

"Ahh," Nemesis drones, reading the direction my mind has wandered. I perceive flashes in my mind—images projected from Nemesis. Astraea's hands fist against my chest. Our hearts hammer as one, our thoughts wild and turbulent in the silence of the night.

"What happens?" I say, not wanting to believe it.

Astraea breathes erratically, defeated and looking so very small in my arms. "I do."

CHAPTER 46
ASTRAEA

I've always known I'd eventually find myself in Oasòs. I've always believed my mother, the Celestial of Fate, would one day deem me worthy of working at her side, helping the people of Earth. She would teach me to be like her, and when she was ready, I would take her place so that she could rest among the stars. I hadn't imagined I'd find myself among the celestials, replacing her so soon—and against her will.

"No," Asher growls. "No. Fuck that. I will not allow it." He rises swiftly, picking me up in his arms as if I weigh nothing.

I am resigned, knowing there is no other option. What are we against the fate of the world? Nothing.

"No!" Asher roars. I curl further into him, a single tear streaking down my face as I hear all his thoughts. This will break him, yet I still must complete my task.

"This does not mean the end for you both," Nemesis assures us, steam blowing from his nose. His golden eyes are piercing in the dark night, all-seeing.

"If she goes to Oasòs, we'll be torn apart!" Asher hisses,

holding me so tight it becomes a kind of painful bearhug. I push at his arms and he loosens his hold, if slightly.

"That is for you to decide, Fae King."

My body goes cold at Nemesis' words. He can't mean...

"I do not suggest his death, Reaper."

I cringe at the moniker coming from the dragon.

"Then what?" Asher's eyes begin to darken, his eterì trembling beneath his skin. "The only thing that will bring me anywhere near Oasòs is if I haunt the stars."

No. He can't die.

"Or you can rule united," Nemesis declares. **"You are soulbound, and you are bonded to me. No matter where either of you are, I can follow."**

"Are you saying...?"

"I was first bonded to the god of all gods. I can come and go from Oasòs as my bonded can." Nemesis chuffs, seemingly proud of his announcement.

It can't be... My heart leaps out of my chest until I catch Asher's contemplations.

"My sibling... My court..."

I sense everything Asher feels, and it's painful. Obviously, he can't follow me into Oasòs. Ash has a court to rule, and he can't leave Aspen behind. He *wouldn't*.

"I would, my love. I would."

"N-no, no, you wouldn't. No, Asher, you can't." When had I begun sobbing?

Asher smiles sadly as he looks down at me, his brows knitting. I can barely see him through my tears. I've just found him, and now I am going to lose him.

Asher caresses my cheek, his warmth bitter-sweet. "You will never lose me, Astraea, my heart."

"But your sibling—"

"Is strong and happy to rule in my stead," he interrupts.

"But you'll miss them," I cry, wiping my tears. "No, I can't make you leave your sibling. I won't."

"You're not making me do anything, Astraea. I would choose you over everything in every lifetime."

"You can't choose me over your family," I argue.

Asher pulls me closer until our foreheads touch, and I cling to his neck, searching his gaze.

"You are my family," he tells me. "When the time comes for us to leave, we will look out for our siblings from Oasòs."

My sisters. I hadn't even thought about them. No. I can't leave them.

Ash draws my head to his chest, where I weep in his embrace.

"Take your mate to rest, Fae King. Come tomorrow, we will discuss strategies with your companions. We will decide on a course of action then."

CHAPTER 47

AURELIA

Ravena rolls out of bed. "I think I'll go check on Calix and Malek to see if they need anything."

"Want me to come?" I ask.

"It's fine, Relie. I'll be quick."

That means, *I don't want you near Malek after what you did.* I don't want to give my sisters a reason not to trust me, so I don't argue.

"Keep an eye out for when Raea gets back," she tells me.

"You got it," I reply, removing my hearing aids and placing them in their case on the nightstand. With a forceful sigh, I promptly fall back on the bed.

I count the seconds as they pass agonizingly slowly. I don't appreciate being cooped up—I always find distractions to keep me occupied. I love celebrations, being social, and drinking, things that liberate.

I nearly give in to find the liquor again when Ravena comes back into the room, frowning.

Springing up into a seated position, I ask, "What's wrong?"

"Nothing, at least, I think...." She muses for a moment, then sits next to me. "It's just Calix. He wouldn't let me in the room to see Malek. Told me he was sleeping, and I should leave him be."

That's odd.

"He never had a problem with us checking in on him before, whether Malek was sleeping or not."

Ravena fixes her glasses on her scrunched nose. "I under-stand wanting some privacy, but—" She sighs. "Oh, I don't know. He was just acting really strange. He wouldn't let me look in the room."

"You don't think he would hurt Malek, would he?" I ask hesitantly.

Ravena's eyes widen. "Oh, gosh, no!" She shakes her head. "That hadn't even crossed my mind."

"Then why was he being weird about you going in to see him?"

Ravena's face is weary. "I don't know."

"Maybe Malek's gotten worse, and Calix didn't want to worry you." That is a possibility. It would make some sense.

"You would think he'd want me in there helping if that were the case."

I grimace, trying to solve the puzzle but coming up empty-handed. Vena and I then jump at a scuttling noise downstairs.

"Do you think it's Astraea?" Ravena asks, getting up and sliding her shoes on.

"Do you want to talk to your sisters?" King Asher's muffled voice asks from just outside the door. Ravena reaches for the handle but pauses when Astraea's soft voice sounds.

"They are likely asleep, and I don't want to wake them. Besides, you and I have unfinished business."

Ravena's eyes widen as she shoots me a surprised look, mirroring my thoughts. Asher's footsteps fade, and Vena raises a hand to her mouth, trying not to snicker. I'm the first to blow it.

"Oh, my gods!" Ravena gushes. "You don't think?"

"I certainly do," I reply, trying my best to conceal my giggles. "It's about time she gets laid."

"Hey!" Ravena swats me with a pillow and flops back onto the bed with me.

"What?" I say. "It's true."

"Says you, the party animal."

I smirk, remembering all the good times I've had since I came of age. "You two could take a few pointers from me about letting go."

"We're simply not as cool as you," she says sarcastically.

"To each their own."

"I wish I were a little more like you," Ravena admits, rolling onto her stomach and facing me. "I spent so much of my life with my nose in a book. Think of all the things I've missed out on."

I smile sympathetically, patting her shoulder. "You're only twenty-eight, V. You've got a hundred years, and maybe more, to change that. I mean, look at the adventure you're on now. And with Calix at your side, no less." I waggle my brows for emphasis.

Ravena tries to hide her excitement and fails miserably. "You're right. I think it's time I make the most of things. Though we are in a crisis, and we're definitely in denial, seeing as how we aren't panicking nearly as much as we ought to be, I'm glad we get to be on this side of history. And I'm glad we're doing this together, even if it is dangerous."

"Me too, Sis," I agree.

None of us are panicking like we should be, but perhaps that's working to our benefit. The more you panic, the less control you have over a situation. That we were able to see Nemesis's memories and hear the dragons and their plea was a blessing and a curse. We're on the right side of history, yes, but surely, it will come at a cost. No war was ever won without casualties. I just hope to Oasòs that my sisters and I make it out alive.

"Do you think Raea is okay?" Ravena asks softly, breaking the silence of the night.

"I think she has to be," I exhale mournfully. "She was born for this, I know. But do you ever wonder what life would have been like if Astraea had chosen a life like ours? Or, what if she'd have worked in Intelligence, or taught lessons on history instead of becoming a soldier?"

Ravena scoots closer, the two of us sharing a pillow as we stare up at the dark ceiling. "Then she wouldn't have been Astraea."

I chuckle morosely. "You're probably right."

"She's a fighter, Rel. Being anything but a brilliant warrior would have run her mind to the ground."

"I only wish she weren't such a trailblazer. She's the one everyone looks to for protection. It was bad enough that she had the highest-ranking record of eterì. Why did she have to become the general of the biggest army on Earth?"

"Because that is what she does—she fights for others when they cannot do it for themselves," says Ravena. "She's done it for us all our lives, and she worked hard to be able to do it for the rest of the world."

"I know, but I wish she wouldn't take on the responsibility on her own," I respond, only imagining the weight Astraea must carry on her shoulders.

"You know she's not alone. She's got an entire Legion at her disposal."

I groan, irritated. "You know that's not what I mean. Even if she has hundreds of soldiers fighting the good fight with her, in Astraea's world, she is alone."

"Because she prefers it that way," Ravena says.

I frown. "I think there's more to it than that."

"Maybe one day she'll feel safe enough to share her burdens with us."

Maybe we should try reaching out to her before it's too late.

CHAPTER 48
ASHER

Astraea and I are spiraling, but at least we're doing it together.

"I don't want you to be spiraling with me, Asher. You shouldn't have to make a choice like that." Astraea still clings to me with all the strength she can muster. *"I want you to choose me, but I am afraid the cost will be our undoing."*

With one arm wrapped around her waist, I carry her to the bed, where I withdraw the sheets before tucking us both in, not daring to take my hands off her.

"You will have to pry my cold, dead hands off of you if you think you're going to become a fucking celestial and live out your days in Oasòs alone."

"But, Ash—"

"No buts. Fuck that, Astraea. We're supposed to be together."

Her perfect lip quivers, and I try my best to wipe every tear that streaks her face. They fall faster, and it shatters my soul to see her so anguished.

"Aspen has been preparing for the day I might leave the Fae

Court to them. It will be far sooner than we'd hoped, but they can handle it."

"Ash, we're going to have to leave our siblings behind," she mutters, her voice garbled from crying. "We'll never see them again."

My heart desperately wants to console hers. Astraea will lose so much of herself by leaving her sisters. I will lose my only sibling and my court. It will be difficult to bear, but I have no doubt it will be worth it. It'll be the most trying thing I do, but I will follow Astraea to the ends of the Earth and into Oblivion if it means I get to spend eternity with her.

"Ash…" My name breaks on a sob as she buries her face in my chest.

"Come here, love," I soothe, smoothing a hand down her hair. "I've got you."

"I can't leave my sisters and worry about how coming with me will tear you apart. It's too much. You have to stay here."

Her words sting like no others. I have been enamored with her far longer than she. Does she not want me as I want her?

"Gods, Ash. You were made for me! I want you so much it hurts. It's not something I ever imagined I'd get to experience. I am not as heartless as I wish I were. You were right when you said that I keep away everyone an arm's length because I don't want to be the reason others get hurt. I am desperate to keep you safe. I want to be selfish and keep you at my side, but it would hurt me more to see you suffering because you followed me into Oasòs." She sniffles before releasing a ragged breath. "I was always going to go, you know. The circumstances have changed vastly, but this has always been my destiny."

"And we were destined to be soul-bound forever," I remind her, holding her close and running my hands through her soft hair. "What more can I tell you that will make you understand how miserable I would be without you, now that I have you?"

Astraea draws small circles over my heart as her mind whirls. I can hear everything she thinks, can feel her every emotion as though it were my own. She's relieved I want her, ashamed for wanting me to choose her over everything, guilty for keeping this from her sisters, scared for our future, and determined to save the world.

"Ash?" she whispers.

"Hmm?"

"I can't keep trying to convince you to stay. I am selfish, and it's taken everything in me to ask this of you." Astraea swallows hard. "I will try once more, but if you still cannot see reason, I will keep you."

I laugh, my heart tightening around the spot made solely for loving my soulmate. "I've said it before, and I'll say it again, Astraea. You're stuck with me."

She smiles solemnly, caressing my jaw. As she looks into my eyes, I recognize everything that she is to me. I am the luckiest soul alive. I will never let her go.

"I love you, Ash, I do," she whispers.

My brows lift, awed at the sheer truth in her words. I bend down and gently kiss her lips. So much is said in this kiss: everything we've ever feared, wanted, and needed hanging between us. "I love you, Starlight. Always have, always will."

Her lashes lower, her brow puckers, contemplating.

"What is it?" I ask.

She exhales, finding my gaze again. *"Will you still hold me like this when you've lost everything else?"*

I cup the nape of her neck, encouraging her to see everything in my mind. "Aspen will not be lost to me. They'll always be in my heart, and we'll do our best to look out for them from Oasòs. I'm sure of it. Ruling my court has been a duty, one I upheld with pride, but it has never been a love of mine. Why do you think I was shadowing you around the Compound so much?"

She rolls her eyes. "Because you were looking for trouble," she says thoughtfully.

"I was looking for you, you wicked little thing."

Astraea's grin widens as she hits me flirtatiously. "You're sure?" Her smile fades, vulnerability shining through the blue of her eyes.

"Yes. There is nothing I am surer of than you."

I hear a loud thump, my gaze lowering to the pulse in her neck.

Astraea groans, punching herself in the chest. "This damn thing has been going wild since you professed your undying love."

I grin, lowering my lips to the sensitive hollow on her neck. Astraea gasps, clinging to me like her life depends on it.

"Yes," I purr, provoking a shiver from Astraea. I chuckle darkly, lifting my gaze to hers so that we are eye to eye, our lips barely touching. "It is beating violently," I declare. *"You are breathtaking when you're flushed."*

"You're always annoyingly breathtaking."

I lick my lips and watch her eyes dart to the spot.

"Careful, Reaper. That gaze will be the death of me."

CHAPTER 49

AURELIA

When morning breaks, I'm surprised to find that Ravena already left our bedroom. The sun still hasn't fully settled in the sky, and though she is a morning bird, I hadn't expected her to wake so soon. These past few days have taken a toll on all of us, and I assumed she would have savored the sleep like I did. Who knows if this will be the last good rest we get?

There's a creaking sound as Ravena tries creeping back in. She startles when she sees me, and I give her a questioning look.

"Where might you have slipped off to?" I ask, still groggy.

Ravena flushes, her brows pinching so tight they might blend.

"V? What's wrong?"

"It's Calix." She wraps her arms around her torso, fretful.

"Come closer. I can barely hear you."

"Sorry," she murmurs a little louder as she steps closer. "I went to check on Calix and Malek, but again, Calix wouldn't let me go inside." She tosses her hands in the air in frustration. "I don't know what's wrong, and it's turning me inside out!"

"Well, why don't I go with you to see what's up?" I offer.

Ravena tuts disapprovingly. "I don't want to make something out of nothing."

"He's being weird. It's not nothing."

She contemplates for a while, her face contorting as she considers my offer. "I think I'll give him the benefit of the doubt, at least for today. If he doesn't let me see Malek by tonight, I'll go to Astraea about it."

"Why? Am I not scary enough?" I toss my head with attitude.

She huffs a sorry laugh. "Not even close."

"Gee, thanks." I stretch, hauling myself out of bed. "Well, since you woke me up at the butt crack of dawn, I'm going to go steal the outhouse before the others get up."

Ravena chuckles. "You know what liquor does to you, Rel. It's your own damn fault."

"Hey," I say, raising a hand. "At least it was rum and not milk."

Ravena's chuckle turns into a rounded laugh. "Can you imagine the state of the milk here?"

"Ew!" My stomach sours at the thought of terribly spoiled milk hidden in this tavern. It's best not to go searching.

After turning my hearing aids on, I change into clean clothes, choosing a black billowy knee-length dress and the underwear Asher had brought us. I don't even want to think about how and why he'd gotten them. I am grateful, and that is all that matters.

"Do you need anything from downstairs?" I ask Vena.

"I'm good for now, thanks."

"See you in a bit then," I tell her. Before leaving, I add, "Don't give up on either of those guys yet, V."

"I won't," she promises as I close the door.

I stand in the hall staring at Calix and Malek's bedroom door, my feet unwilling to go down the stairs just yet. I don't want to worry Ravena, but I'm starting to question Calix's conduct. I hadn't seen any of the interactions, but it bothers me, the way Ravena's portraying it. Is Ravena making more out of things, or is there something to Calix's strange behavior?

Deciding on a whim to find out for myself, I gently knock on their door. I hear a jostling noise before footfall, and then the door quietly opens, revealing an apprehensive Calix.

"Oh, um, hi Aurelia," Calix greets me quietly. "Did you need something? Ravena told me she was heading back to your room. Did she not go?" He fidgets with his hands, his eyes darting to my and Ravena's door.

"No, she's in our room," I tell him, acting as casually as possible. "I just wanted to check on Malek before I go downstairs."

"Oh," he responds, his back straight. He is acting out of the ordinary, as if he's nervous. "He's sleeping, and he seems to be getting better. I asked Ravena to let me keep an eye on him since he's only resting."

I offer him a smile, hoping it doesn't appear forced. "It's good of you to want to help, but I'd really like to check on him to see if I can help him with anything."

Calix's features tighten as he blocks the doorway with his arm. "I think that would prove unwise, seeing how you endangered yourself the last time you helped him."

I wince. *Yeah, he's got me there.*

"Fine," I grumble. "Just tell us if he wakes. Find Ravena."

Calix purses his lips before he answers, "Will do." Then he silently backs away and shuts the door in my face.

Ravena is right. He's acting like a child, trying his best not to get caught doing something wrong. And Malek is stuck in there with him. I have a bad feeling about this. His behavior doesn't sit right with me. He's unquestionably hiding something.

Perhaps Ravena's correct. Astraea will know what to do.

CHAPTER 50

ASTRAEA

"You're up early." I'm surprised as Aurelia comes in from outdoors. She has a look of determination on her face, and something about the way she eyes Asher has my suspicions running. "What's wrong?" I ask, a hand on my hip, waiting for her to spill.

Her gaze darts between me and Ash before she whispers, "I'm not sure if you'd prefer to be alone to have this conversation."

"He can read my mind, Rel. Whatever you have to say, you can say in front of Asher."

"Love your vote of confidence, darling," Asher thinks at me.

I pinch his arm, and he yelps, making me smirk.

"Astraea Wicked Aidos, indeed."

"Aidos?"

"Yes, my queen?"

"We haven't been married yet, Asher. Are you proposing?"

Ash meets my smirk, coming closer. *"We are soul-bound, Queen Aidos. We are beyond married."*

My lip twitches. *"I suppose it has a nice ring to it."*

Aurelia stomps her foot in annoyance. "Would you two quit having a silent conversation without me while I'm standing right here?"

I can't help the grin that widens my face. "He's safe to speak to."

Aurelia gawks up at me, with her remarkably round, blue eyes. "Who the hell are you, and what did you do with my sister?"

I frown. "Shut up and tell me what's bothering you."

"Fine, but let's go outside." Aurelia tosses her long blonde hair over her shoulder.

I cock a brow at her, but Asher nods, accepting for the both of us. We trail outside after my sister, the rich, humid air seeping into my clothes and hair. I can already tell it's going to be another hot day.

Aurelia takes unwavering steps as far from the tavern as possible, without entering the field in which the dragons lay. She turns, chewing on her lip.

"Are you well?" Asher asks her.

Her eyes widen. "Who, me? Yeah, I'm good. It's not me I'm worried about."

"Then who? Is Ravena all right?" I wonder, taking a step toward her.

"Put away your menacing hellhound pose and let me tell you." She throws up her hands.

"Sorry," I mutter grouchily, doing my best to act cool.

"An apology? Why do I never get any?" Asher says pointedly, though the tease in his eyes reflect his mischief.

"Ash," I grit between clenched teeth, a warning not to test me. I hear his laughter echoing in my mind.

"It's Calix," Aurelia tells us, drawing us out of our regular banter.

"What of him?" asks Asher.

Aurelia's face contorts into puzzlement as she looks down at her feet. "I don't know what's got him acting up, but his behavior has changed drastically."

"How so?"

"Ravena went to their room several times to see if she could check on Malek, but Calix refused to let her in," she explains.

I scowl, suspicion flaring to life. "That is odd. He never had a problem with this before."

"Perhaps he was doing something rather private and didn't want her to see?" Asher tries.

"Unlikely."

"I thought maybe Vena was making a bigger deal of things than they were," Aurelia rationalizes. "You know how she is. A drop of rain is a hurricane."

I must agree. Ravena has a flair for the theatrics, especially when anxious.

"But I went to see Calix just a few minutes ago, you know, to see for myself," Aurelia continues.

"And?" I prod.

"And I think he's hiding something, Raea."

Ice runs through my veins at the proposition. "Like what?" My nails dig into my palms as I consider what this could mean. Is he hurting Malek? Fuck, is he a *spy*, somehow?

"I don't know, and neither does V, so that's why I'm telling you. Ravena doesn't know about this conversation, and I don't think she needs to."

"She is rather fond of Calix." I pinch the bridge of my nose. "Rose-colored glasses and all. I agree. Keep this between us for now. She doesn't need to know that we know."

Aurelia exhales a relieved breath, scratching at the back of her neck. "So, are you going to look into it?"

"Certainly," Asher answers. My sister and I swing our heads

in his direction. He cocks his brow in question. "What? Did you think I was sitting out on this quest?"

"Wouldn't dream of it," I reply dryly.

"That's my girl."

My core heats at the teasing praise. Ignoring Asher's seductive thoughts, I focus on formulating a plan.

"Tonight, the dragons wish to convene with all of us to discuss what's to come. We will all be expected to attend. We'll include Malek, whether he understands us or not. I'll take a moment's reprieve and check out their room. If Calix is hiding something, I'll find it."

Asher bows, fully on board. "I'll keep my eyes on the rest of us. If someone leaves the group, I'll tell you through the bond so you can get out of there with time to spare."

"I suppose that bond was good for one thing."

"I suspect it has plenty of worthwhile advantages, Mate."

I shiver. "Okay," I say, exhaling a tense breath. "The plan's made. Let's go get something to eat and get our shit together."

"Ever the eloquent speaker," Asher goads.

I lift a hardened fist and punch him square in the chest. His eyes darken, and his body grows taller before my very eyes.

"Careful, Reaper," Asher says. "You wouldn't want me to have to tie up those fists."

My stomach flutters at the thought, and I envision giving him all control. *"Maybe one day I'll let you try."* I wink.

"All right," Aurelia interrupts, coughing into her fist. "I'm just going to back away and pretend I was never here."

"Smart," I reply, red-faced for having forgotten she was ever here in the first place.

Aurelia bolts for the tavern while I stay pinned under Asher's searing gaze.

"What to do with that rebellious mouth of yours?" Asher asks, circling me.

"Careful, Trouble," I warn, taking a defensive stance, fists at the ready. "I do so enjoy a challenge."

Asher grins, his impressive fangs glinting in the sunlight. *"Tempt me, I beg you,"* he sings, *"detain me, I dare you."* His voice sends a warm shiver through me. He's teasing me with that damnable song that's forever repeating in my head. The song is ancient, but it feels novel when he sings it.

Why does his voice sound so tormented?

He laughs darkly, knowing precisely what he's doing. "Because you have been tormenting me for ages," he enlightens me.

I laugh, beaming from ear to ear. "You're a fool, you know that?"

"Come on, Astraea," he taunts, flexing two fingers in a 'come at me' motion. My gaze sharpens on his digits, carnal images flashing through my mind.

"Fuck," Asher pants. "If you don't stop looking at me like that, this sparring session will turn into something far more pleasurable."

I roll my eyes, then spot his prominent arousal through his trousers. *This is going to be rough.*

"I don't mind it rough, darling. Whatever you're willing to give, I will gladly take."

I groan, gritting my teeth. "Just shut up and hit me already."

Asher chuckles, then braces himself for an attack. "Ladies first."

My eyes darken, sharpening on him. "I am no lady."

CHAPTER 51

ASHER

Sparring with Astraea is like walking into a tornado and trying to punch a wall. She is as fast as lightning and deadly strong. We've decided to omit use of our eterì to condition our physical strength. I am tough as hell, but where my movements are hard and sharp, she is lithe and quick, making for a slippery opponent. She's exceptional—made for this.

"That's high praise coming from the fae king," Astraea shouts after hearing my thoughts, her breaths coming in short, focused pants. Her body glistens in the sunlight, the sweat on her chest an alluring view.

"*High praise for his deserving queen,*" I answer, my chest heaving from all the chasing.

Astraea flinches at my response, and my heart wrenches at her discomfort. "*I am not deserving of a title like that. Especially when I'll be the one taking the king from his court.*"

I let my fists fall to my sides, dropping my longsword and closing the distance between us. She raises her sword, dangerously close to cutting my throat. Her teeth grit, and her fox-shaped eyes glare at me with a whirlwind of emotion.

I tilt her chin to meet my gaze, and though we are panting like wolves on a hunt, all I see is the most beautiful creature in existence.

"Creature, huh?" She licks her lips, pressing the blade further.

"Of course, that's what you fixate on out of that entire sentence," I tease.

"Ah, so the most important part was when you called me a dog," she says, leaning in.

I grab her fists, forcing the blade to meet my flesh, the slight bite of the metal adrenaline-charged. "Firstly, I said *we*, not *you*. Secondly, shut up."

Astraea smirks at me, that wicked look I've come to know and love ever-present in her eyes. "Make me."

I growl, then pounce, devouring her on the spot. She drops her sword just before it can hurt me, and it falls between our feet. When our lips meet, I'm convinced we are among the stars. She tastes like sweat, sunshine, and wrath. I will never get enough.

"You taste like you want more," Astraea moans into our kiss, clinging to me with all her might.

"Make no mistake, Astraea," I blow, resting my forehead against hers. "I want *all* of you."

"Then have me," she dares, almost imploring with the energy thickening between us.

My heart thunders, my body so hot and aching to do just that, but unfortunately, the tavern door closes with a loud *bang*, stealing the opportunity for my sweetest fantasy to come true.

"How much longer are we keeping us a secret?" I ask as I grudgingly let her go.

Astraea exhales. "I'll tell them before we leave for the Compound."

I kiss her quickly before telling her, "You don't have to do anything for my sake, Starlight. I'm with you, no matter what you decide."

She smiles softly. "I know."

"Have you two been fighting all day?" Aurelia bellows as she jogs steadily toward us.

"Has it been so long?" Astraea inquires, checking the wristwatch I had given her. "Hmph. Four hours. Not bad."

I shake my head at her. "Not bad," I grumble under my breath.

"*You want to go another hour?*" she goads me, a cocky brow raised.

"*In another room, gladly.*"

Astraea clicks her tongue. "*Good things come to those who wait.*"

I bite down on my lip, turning from the women and heading toward the tavern. Astraea's laughter follows me all the way to the door.

"*Little minx.*"

CHAPTER 52

RAVENA

"Oh, hey, King Asher," I stammer, my fork of asparagus halfway to my mouth. He seems ridiculously tense. I push a few cans of food down the table. "You hungry?"

The king scratches the back of his head before sighing harshly, apparently annoyed to have to eat in my presence.

"Um, I can leave if you need some space, King Asher," I offer.

His eyes widen. "Oh, no. That won't be necessary," he assures me as he takes a seat across from me. "And please, drop the king nonsense. It's just Asher to you."

I chuckle. "Cause you're going to be my brother-in-law?" I joke, pointing my asparagus at him. His shoulders grow even more rigid, and I snicker. "Don't worry. I won't pry."

He appears to relax at that. "What's best?" he asks, pointing to the jars.

"Anything but the beans," I warn him. "Those things are nasty."

He chuckles. "Astraea hates them as well."

"Yup."

There's an awkward bout of silence for a moment. I don't dare take a bite and just fill the silence with chewing.

Asher finally grabs a can. Before he can open it, though, I reach out and snatch it from his startled grasp.

"No cucumbers!" I shout.

Asher's eyes go wide as saucers. I likely sound bizarre, and I've just stolen goods from a king.

"She's allergic," I stammer, pulling the can even further from his reach. "No eating Cucurbitaceae."

The king is still silent, and I hiss out a frustrated breath.

"Melons," I explain. "No melons."

King Asher only stares at me, his face unreadable.

"You can't kiss her if you eat this," I whisper harshly.

"Oh," he responds.

That's it? Oh?

"Do you want the cucumbers?" I ask, slowly pushing the jar toward him.

"No, thank you," he grunts.

Ha! I thought so. There's no hiding your secrets from me, Rae Rae.

"I would advise against telling her that I am forgoing the cucumbers," he finally speaks again.

"Mm-hmm." I can't help the smile that spreads across my face.

His lips purse. "She has enough to worry about."

I shoo away his worries with my hand, then shove a can of beets toward him. "Eat up, Asher. Your secret's safe with me."

He grumbles before opening the jar and tentatively eating the red root vegetable.

"Couldn't you grow something fresh with your earth eterì, if you hate beans so much?" Asher asks.

"I wish." I snort, staring at the jars. "I'd need seeds. If vegetation was already growing somewhere, I could grow more of it, but we're on a mountain, where most things we'll find are flowers."

"It's too bad the fruit your sister got from the bottom of Mount Olympus ran out so quickly," he replies.

"It's too bad I didn't think to keep the seeds." I chuckle, inwardly scolding myself. "So," I begin, looking out the window to watch Raea and Relie bathing under the sun as they lie on the ground.

"So?" Asher repeats.

"How's she doing?" I inquire shyly, my sights never straying from my sisters.

"I'm not sure that I am supposed to disclose that with you," he answers, his tone clear of any judgment.

"I'm her sister," I tell him. "I'm concerned about her."

The king sighs, and I hear him close the lid of his jar. I turn my gaze back to him and find his shoulders are tight again.

"Is it that bad?" I worry, fear swallowing my voice.

"She is doing better than most would in her situation," he considers. He runs a hand through his hair, cursing under his breath. "She's stronger than she should be."

"That's Raea for you."

"Yes, I suppose so."

"Will you let her know she doesn't need to be strong for us?" I request hesitantly, looking back through the window. "We're here for her if she needs us."

"She knows," he answers quietly. "The problem lies with her proficiency at taking on the responsibility of the world without asking for help."

I grunt. "Don't I know it?"

Asher sits straighter, reaching his hand across the table and kindly laying it atop mine. "Offer help," he insists. "Offer it, even when you think she'll say no. She might surprise you." The fae king stands from his seat and bows.

I snicker at his gesture. "If I'm calling you Asher, then you don't need to do the kingly things like bowing."

His lips twitch. "Noted."

I give him an awkward thumbs-up, and he returns the gesture.

"I'll be getting bathing necessities for Astraea and me. Once we're done, perhaps you and your sister should go. I believe our nights here are running out. Best to be prepared."

I nod. *That's ominous.*

"If you have clothes you prefer to wear back to the Compound, I suggest washing them."

Even more so.

"Will do."

The king grunts and heads up the stairs. Perhaps the conversation we're going to have this evening will shed light on what's to come. Likely, Asher and Astraea already know what the dragons have planned. The leader of the horde is their bonded dragon. I, on the other hand, am stuck with Nyx.

I still can't shake the horrors of little Theo's death, but I understand that what happened was a mistake. Nyx is young and new to this world. She left Freìre with the instructions to kill anyone she thought would harm her. She didn't know that Theo was just a child and couldn't hurt a fly if he tried.

I wonder where all the other dragons are, if Nyx is so young. Where are her parents? I have a sullen impression that they are gone. Had Astraea killed them too, like she'd killed Malek's bonded? Does it matter if it had been my sister? War is a disheartening villain. No one can escape its darkness.

I truly, desperately hope we'll return the light.

CHAPTER 53
AURELIA

As the hot sun rises in the sky, the dragons persist, busy preparing for a bonfire. Even those who haven't bonded to riders have stuck around, habitually resting with one another. I am shocked to see them breaking down trees, and ask Idris what they are doing.

"I suggested we arrange seating for our bonded," he informs me.

"That was kind of you."

Idris huffs. **"I am always kind, Lia."**

"I didn't mean otherwise," I assure him, approaching his side. He is strikingly tall, his green scales glittering as the sun sets.

"Do you think your sister will overcome her aversion to Nyx?" asks Idris. He and I watch Ravena and Calix, who help Malek sit on the tree trunk that Orion had set up. Nyx quietly observes her bonded, her head low and body language inquisitive. I can sense she wants to approach Ravena, but she's nervous.

"She will come around," I believe. "Nyx is young, which gives her a leg up at winning over Ravena's heart."

"How so?"

I chuckle. "Ravena is obsessed with children. She loves every kid she meets, and I'm sure she'd have many of her own if she could."

"Can she not produce children?" Idris questions.

"Oh, I am not really sure, but that isn't what I meant."

"Hmm." He lets out a breath. **"Explain, please."**

I pat Idris' neck, then lean against his leg. "She hasn't found love yet to try."

"But she and Orion's bonded seem close, do they not? Perhaps this will be her chance."

I frown. "I don't know."

"You do not like him," Idris states.

"No, well, I don't know what to think of him." I exhale, frustrated. "He's very hot and cold. One minute, he's sweet and shy. The next, he's fidgety and guarded."

"You believe he is keeping something from your sister."

So much for hiding secrets.

Idris snorts, his nostrils flaring. **"There is nothing to hide from me, bonded. We are a team. You can trust me with your thoughts."**

I angle my brow at him. "You won't go telling your leader about all my dirty secrets?"

Idris shakes his head. **"I will not."** He pauses momentarily before adding, **"Unless it directly endangers you or his bonded."**

I purse my lips. "I'm not sure if what's going on with Calix endangers us."

"Have you asked him if he is troubled?"

I roll my eyes. "Things aren't as simple as asking someone if they're troubled, Idris. We need to be careful in case..."

"In case?" he prods.

"In case he's dangerous."

"Hmm." Idris ponders that statement, his mind showing me he understands and agrees.

"We'll find out shortly," I assure him.

Idris's wings raise protectively. **"Do not put yourself in harm's way, Lia. You are strong-willed, but your flesh is soft."**

I laugh. "I'm not planning on doing anything of the sort." I pat his neck again, which seems to bring him comfort. "Astraea knows about everything, and she's going to look into it."

"Nemesis would want to know in case of a threat," Idris says.

"He likely already knows. He can read her and King Asher's minds, and they're both in on it."

"I see," says Idris. **"If her partner is protecting her, she should be safe."**

Partner. Is that what they are?

"They are both bonded to Nemesis. Does that not make them so?"

I shrug. "I guess."

"What distresses you?"

"Astraea's never had a partner before."

"Hmm. And you are concerned for her."

"The opposite. She could use a partner."

"He is good for her," Idris decides.

I chuckle, turning my gaze from Ravena over to Astraea, who wears her usual scowl and crossed arms, staring down the fae king. "He knows how to push her buttons, that's for sure."

Idris huffs in agreement.

"Horde," Nemesis booms, the air growing cold as we all turn to face him. The massive black dragon stares at everyone over the fire, his golden eyes aglow. **"It is time."**

CHAPTER 54

ASTRAEA

As we sit around the fire, dusk at its peak, Nemesis stands tall and proud, ready to command his horde.

The tree beneath me is rough, making my tailbone ache. I try crossing one leg over the other but give up, deciding I can ignore it. It isn't anything I'm not used to.

"You could sit in my lap again," Asher offers.

"Nice try."

Asher frowns, appearing genuinely concerned.

"I'm fine, Ash," I assure him.

"You're always fine," he retorts, lowering himself to the ground and leaning against the tree trunk. *"Sit next to me."*

I flick his pointed ear for good measure but reluctantly elect to join him. I am aware of the gazes of my peers, following my every move. I glare up at them all, each one flinching back just a little. *Good.* I smirk. *I've still got my charm.*

"Yes, charm. That's what we'll call it."

I chuck my shoulder into Asher's, causing him to grin down at me. I want to melt under that look for an eternity. *"You look like a lovesick fool.*" I purse my lips, trying not to match his expression.

"*Oh, bite me.*"

I swallow thickly, heat coursing through me at the thought of my half-fae fangs piercing his hard muscles.

"If you would all pay attention," Nemesis bellows, throwing Ash and me a pointed stare.

Aurelia snickers next to Idris. I slowly turn my head and pin her with a brilliant look of caution, a warning not to piss me off. Everyone is on edge tonight, and I am ready to crawl out of my skin.

"It is time we explain our course of action so that we might all be prepared for what's to come."

"*Don't tell them about me,*" I tell Nemesis. Although it comes out as a command, it's a plea. Odd coming from me, I know, but I don't need my sisters to worry about something they can't change. They don't need to know I'll be replacing our mother so soon.

Nemesis chuffs, his golden eyes serious. **"*Of course,*"** he responds, his tone understanding as it rings in my mind.

Asher leans into me, offering his warmth. I steel my spine, but pitifully accept his comforting touch.

"*It is not a weakness to feel comfort, Starlight.*"

"*Then why does it feel like if I accept it, I'll get burned?*"

"*You cannot burn what is already on fire.*"

"Please refrain from your banter. It is splitting my head," Nemesis grumbles.

The group of riders and dragons all laugh, and I feel the heat rush to my cheeks.

"*Couldn't have kept that comment to yourself, huh?*" I complain.

"*You do not keep your comments from me,*" he retorts, huffing hot smoke from his nostrils. His eyes gleam eerily in the night.

"You have our attention, Nemesis," Asher states, ever the king. "The floor is yours."

Nemesis puffs out his chest. **"Horde and respected riders, the time has come to decide on a course of action. I will explain our mission, and invite you to join me and my bonded riders, but know that you have the choice.**

"We aim to locate your legacy allies and educate them on the history of dragons, celestials, and the Asherian War that ensued after the tragic loss of Phaðs. If the legacies are properly convinced, we will extend our outreach to include representatives from all species, inviting their leaders to the Compound. Operating from the Compound provides a controlled setting to foster positive relationships with the other species.

"Our goal is to reveal the truth to them and gain their support. We are to make it clear that we only wish to have freedom, as is the right of every species. We will also explain that Urðra was traitorous and should be dealt with accordingly. We want to work with the celestials to come to a fair treaty. Without the legacies on our side, we are unlikely to reach an agreement with the celestials."

Nemesis outstretches his wings, occluding the stars, symbolic of the journey ahead.

Asher stands, his broad shoulders impressive. "We are with you," he declares, reaching for my hand. I accept, lacing my fingers with his and letting him help me up. I nod, taking a small moment to look him in the eye to acknowledge what lies ahead of us. That we are doing this together is a blessing from the universe.

"We will fight for justice," I affirm at Asher's side. "I won't ask any of you to come along. It could be dangerous, and the legacies may not be reasoned with as we hope."

Aurelia rises from her perch, looking up at Idris before bowing her head. "We will fight for peace," she announces, firelight warming her features.

A deep sense of pride fills my heart, though it is tainted by an even stronger fear.

"I'm not letting you do this without me," Ravena says. "Nyx, are you in?"

The purple dragon huffs excitedly, her head bobbing up and down.

"Looks like you've got yourself another teammate," says Vena, smiling quietly at her dragon.

"Clearly, I am coming, too," Calix states.

I refrain from frowning more than usual at his words. I haven't forgotten what Aurelia had told me about his strange behavior.

"Malek can ride with me and Orion," he continues. "We can't leave him here alone."

Asher claps his hands together approvingly. "Perfect. Then it is settled."

"Very well. The horde will replenish your eterì, and then we shall discuss our approach in detail," Nemesis begins. This is my cue.

"If you'll excuse me, I'm going to go get a blanket from my room. Anyone else need something?" I ask.

"I'm good," Aurelia replies.

"Don't you need to hear what Nemesis has to say?" Ravena questions, a look of puzzlement on her face.

"Ash and I already talked to him about everything last night." I redden, caught using his nickname.

Ravena beams knowingly. "All right," she croons. "Hurry back."

"I love it when you blush," Ash purrs into my mind.

"Oh, baby, oh, baby."

"Hurry back," he says, parroting Ravena.

"Hush up and focus, Trouble."

He chuckles. *"Yes, my queen."*

CHAPTER 55
ASHER

My mind is divided in two.

I sit in front of a fire, listening to Nemesis explain the rankings of his horde. He explains he will not invite the other dragons to join us on this mission, so as not to scare the legacies any more than necessary. We are to fly only with the dragons who have bonded riders. I am entirely on board with that strategy—no need to invite provocation.

The other part of my mind follows Astraea through her thoughts. She mumbles a sling of curses as she searches Calix and Malek's room.

"Do you see anything out of place?" I ask cautiously.

"No," she says. *"Perhaps I would if you'd stop badgering me and let me think."*

"Badgering. That's a new way to tell me I'm annoying."

She sighs irritably. *"Help me or get out of my head."*

I chuckle. *"Fine, fine. Did you check the bathroom? Any knives or medication bottles?"*

"Do you think he'd hurt Malek?"

"We can't rule it out."

Astraea rummages through the cupboards, checks behind the shower curtain and even behind the toilet but comes out empty.

"Check the dresser drawers."

"I already did."

"Closet?"

"Yup."

"Under the bed?"

"Of course. It's the first place I looked."

"Did you check under the sheets and pillows?"

"Yes, dearest." She's growing more frustrated by the minute.

"I'm only trying to help."

She exhales forcefully. *"I know. Keep going."*

I think for a moment, going over the bedroom in my mind. *"How about between the mattress and the box spring?"*

Excitement flares to life in Astraea's mind.

"Shit," I hiss. *"You've got incoming, Astraea."*

"Stall."

I groan. *"How long?"* I make to get up from my spot, but am halted by Astraea's triumphant exclamation.

"Got it! I'll put it in our room and be back in a minute."

Our room.

"Yes, our room."

"I like the sound of that."

Astraea hums darkly. I release a frustrated breath, then plop back on my ass and wait for Astraea to get out.

Just as Calix readies to hoist Malek up, Aurelia cuts in and grabs his arm.

"I've got him, Calix," she avows, giving him her best winning smile.

"I'd really rather bring him up myself. It's no problem."

"Oh, it's no problem for me either," she responds. Damn, she was a decent thespian. One would never know she was scheming against him by looking at her.

"Really, I'll bring him up and be back out momentarily." Calix attempts to pull Malek out of Aurelia's grip, but she holds firm.

She leans in conspiratorially, whispering, "Ravena wanted some time alone with you tonight. Please give her that. She deserves it."

Calix stiffens, returning to the shy agent I'd first met. "Oh, um—that would be lovely. Thank you, Aurelia. I owe you one."

Nice save, I think.

"That's Relie for you. She's skilled at persuasion," Astraea says, catching the exchange as she exits the tavern.

Gods, she is stunning.

"And you look like you're starving," she says.

"I am absolutely famished, and you look delicious."

"Want to go for a walk?" she asks, a bit of tension lingering in her words.

"Wherever you go, I shall follow."

CHAPTER 56
AURELIA

As I lead Malek up the stairs toward his room, his mutterings appear to worsen, a cold sweat shining above his brow.

"I'm so sorry I wasn't able to heal you fully, Malek," I tell him.

"Where am I?" he asks, a little more coherent than usual.

"You're in Freìre, Malek. Do you remember what I told you about Freìre?"

"Outer Edge..." he murmurs. His eyes glaze over again, and he grinds his teeth together.

"Okay. Let's get you into bed so you can rest. Tomorrow will be a big day with lots of travelling. You'll need your energy."

"Not here..." he mutters, and I help him get under the covers. His eyelids fight to stay open, but his lethargy wins.

"Why won't your eterì save you when you need it most?" I ask aloud, mostly to myself.

A strong breeze enters the room and my hair sweeps up, blonde locks floating around me. A divinatory guidance? I haven't had one of these in ages.

The wind flourishes, growing stronger, my dress billowing as the room around me turns to a vast field of white clouds. I grow dizzy.

Time, time, ticks by; now is the time for you to fly. Time, time, ticks by;
you cannot stop it;
he shall die.

THE CLOUDS DISSIPATE, leaving me in the dim room with Malek's sleeping form. A single tear trails down my cheek, and I wipe it away, at a loss for words.

Malek is going to die.

There is nothing I can do about it. No way to save him. The Celestial of Time Sybìron declared it so.

CHAPTER 57

RAVENA

"**How old are you?**" Nyx asks her millionth question, causing a pulsing ache in my temples.

"Twenty-eight," I answer. "How old are you?"

Nyx wags her tail excitedly. **"I am seventeen years old. Idris says I'm just a babe, but growing fast."**

"What is the age of maturity for a dragon?" I ask, increasingly curious about dragonkind.

"We do not have one, but most dragons who are joined have reached fifty years of life."

"Oh, I see." Intriguing.

"What age do other species join?" Nyx asks, causing me to cough on my surprise.

"Um, I'm not sure." I try my best to reign in the coughing. I clear my throat before adding, "Most species reach the age of maturity between twenty and twenty-five, but it is different for each. I heard that when humans existed, their age of maturity was eighteen, so, not far off from you."

"Oh!" Nyx exclaims. **"I like that! I want to be mature when I am eighteen."**

I giggle. "I am sure you will be."

"Have you joined with anyone yet, Ravena?" asks Nyx.

I blanch. "That's not really an appropriate question to ask."

She huffs. ***"Why not? I ask this of everyone."***

"Do you hear other dragons asking this of others?" I ask.

She nods, her big purple head bobbing up and down. ***"Oh, yes. It is all we speak of. The dragons worry our race will perish. Our greatest wish is to see our loved ones coupled so they may have children."***

"The dragon species is only growing in population, Nyx. There's no reason to fear extinction."

"That is not what Nemesis tells us," she says solemnly. ***"The humans were billions, and with but one war, they were all gone. Does that not frighten you?"***

"I suppose it does."

"Do you have any children, Ravena?"

"No." *I wish.*

"Hey, Ravena," Calix calls as he jogs over to where I sit on a giant tree trunk. Nyx stays at my back, trying to get my attention back on her.

"Hey, Calix," I greet him, rubbing at my temples.

"Would you like some company?" he offers, gesturing to the trunk.

I snort. "I've got plenty already."

Calix flinches back, lowering his gaze. "I—I'm sorry for how I've been acting lately."

"Sure," I respond humorously.

"Is everything all right, Ravena?" he continues, quieter.

I shrug my shoulders in defeat. "No, not really. But it mostly has to do with this whole dragon war thing. Not so much with how you've been pushing me away."

Nyx cuts in: ***"What is wrong, Ravena? Are you sad?"***

"Don't worry about me, Nyx. Why don't you go find Idris and Aurelia and see how they are doing?"

Nyx shakes her tail. **"Okay. Goodbye, for now, my bonded."**

"Bye, Nyx," I say, waving her off.

Calix scratches the back of his neck, kicking the dirt at his feet. "I am really sorry if I made it seem like I want space from you."

"It's okay, Calix. You don't have to explain yourself. If you're not interested, it's fine. Please spare me this awkward conversation."

"N-no, Ravena," he stammers, taking a step forward. He kneels in front of me, and we are now eye to eye. The firelight casts a glow behind him as he stares at me with a fretful expression. "I am very much interested." He licks his lips, his brow creased as if pondering. "In fact, being here in this daunting situation has given me the push to admit it to myself truly. I have been extremely interested in you for a while now. I do not want space from you. Not at all."

"Oh," I breathe.

Calix smiles, reaches out, and takes my hand in his. "I have been feeling many things as of late. Scared, worried, exhausted, confused, but none of that has to do with you."

"Then why wouldn't you let me see you and Malek? I tried several times."

He exhales heavily. "It's complicated, but I assure you it has nothing to do with you and everything to do with me."

I snicker, rolling my eyes. "It's not you, it's me? Really?"

He shakes head with a small smile. "Cliché, but true, nonetheless."

"What have you been doing, Calix? What are you afraid I will find?"

Calix swallows thickly, averting his gaze.

"What is it?" A pit forms in my stomach as I watch him war with himself. "What has you feeling like this?"

"I've merely been using my time to the best of my abilities," he says. "That's all."

I furrow my brow. "That's vague."

"I know. I just don't want to say or do the wrong thing. I am trying to use my skills to analyze our situation. I have been tearing apart the information and trying to piece things together."

"And you couldn't tell me this? I would have respected your privacy."

"I know," he assures me. "But I didn't want to frighten you."

"As if your odd behavior was doing anything but frighten me."

"I'm sorry," he replies. "I'm not very good with people."

I squeeze his hand. "You are doing just fine right now, Calix. Just be honest with me. That's all I ask."

Calix raises my hand to his lips and presses a light kiss there. A sweet, honeyed sensation flows through me.

"Thank you for understanding." He rises gracefully, pulling me with him.

I gasp as he draws me close, holding my hand so that it lies against his chest. His other hand wraps around my waist, holding me in place as I behold him. His brown eyes are full of questions. Every time Calix Lightcrest looks at me, I wonder what he sees. Now, it's almost written on his fair face.

"You have such a beautiful soul, Ravena Ruinoak."

My heart hammers in my chest. That he seems to savor me so is still surreal.

"Th—thank you," I whisper.

His eyes are trained on my mouth, and I lick my lips in anticipation. He smiles, an adorable dimple adorning his cheek. "May I kiss you?"

Holy flying dragons. He wants to kiss *me.*

"Yes." I tremble, but Calix holds me safely in his arms.

Calix lowers his lips to mine, a featherlight touch as warm as a thousand suns. I part my lips invitingly, causing Calix to hold me tighter as he accepts the encouragement. His perfectly plump lips are unyielding, taking and giving all at once. My head spins, dizzy from the growing exhilaration.

When Calix withdraws, panting as heavily as I, he lowers his lips to my forehead, and I close my eyes.

"I have wanted to do that for a very long time," he says.

"Me too," I whisper, my heart pounding louder than my voice.

Calix pulls away, beaming down at me, causing my stomach to flip. "Will you lay with me under the stars?"

I gulp. "What?"

Calix chuckles and pokes my nose. "Not like *that*," he drawls. "I prefer not to have an audience for that." Blushing, he glances toward the remaining party.

"Right," I giggle, feeling silly and happy about everything.

"Just for a while, let's watch the night stars. Perhaps they will give us guidance."

I smile, allowing him to help me to the grass. "Maybe we'll catch a shooting star and get a wish."

Calix lies beside me, gazing up at the vast galaxy above. He tugs on my sleeve, and I scoot closer, resting my head on his shoulder. "I already got mine."

CHAPTER 58
ASTRAEA

Asher and I walk hand in hand, a childlike giddiness in my veins. Though I haven't told my sisters yet, I am certain they know by now. Try as I might, I can't keep myself from Asher's side. It just feels *right*.

Asher draws closer, humming as he breathes me in. "It does feel right, doesn't it?"

I chuckle as he grazes my ear, sending shivers down my spine. "You don't know how long I've wanted your affections, Astraea."

I nuzzle into him, breathing in his mulled berry and ash tree scent. "This probably sounds horrible but, I'm glad you came for me when a dragon napped me."

"Not horrible at all," he responds, beaming.

"Well, it was foolish and dangerous, but it gave us a chance. We likely would have never realized we were soulmates had all this never happened."

Asher kisses my cheek, then lowers to my jaw, where he places an even tenderer kiss. "I've said it before, and I'll say it again: where you go, I follow. I mean that, Starlight."

I grin. "Just days ago, I would have hated that fact."

Asher winks. I turn and he wraps his strong arms around me as we gaze out over the mountains. "I would have loved you, anyway," Asher whispers, his voice low and full of meaning. The air stirs in the night, the stars glowing around us.

"How long did you, um…"

He laughs. "How long did I pine over you?" I can hear the teasing in his tone, and I grin coyly at the night sky. "You already know, Astraea." He holds me tighter, his warmth a caress on its own. "From the moment you knocked my crown off, I knew you were special. Then I got to see how you worked, and how dedicated you were to the people of Earth. I've always wondered what it would feel like to be cared for by you. Nothing could have prepared me for you and *this*." He points between us, his brows lifting. "What we have is divine, and I am both fearful and in awe of you."

"Fearful?"

Asher kisses the top of my head, then rests his chin there. "I fear you are too brave, powerful, and caring, and that will take you from me."

"Ash." My heart swells at the sheer, unadorned depth of his love. I turn in his arms to face him. I glide my hands up his chest and caress his sharp jaw, which has begun growing stubble. I let myself feel him, familiarize myself with the structure and textures of his perfect face, looking deeply into his crystal blue eyes. "You know who I am, more than I even know myself. This means you understand why I am the way I am and why I do things. I cannot change that. Not for anyone."

Ash narrows his gaze. "I never want you to change, Astraea. I adore you—the *real* you. Always have, always will."

"Then why would you say that you fear that who I am will take me from you?"

Asher's eyes grow dark. "Because it's true. I know you'll

never give up fighting for what's right, and you would gladly fight till you're dead."

"I'm not going anywhere," I assure him, bunching my fists in his shirt for emphasis.

He raises an eyebrow, his warm hand clutching the back of my head. "Except, of course, to Oasòs."

I roll my eyes. "You know what I meant."

He sighs, running his fingers through my hair. "Yeah," he settles. "Just promise me something, okay?"

I melt into his touch. "What is it?"

Asher raises his hands to cup my face, his palms searingly warm. He moves closer, every part of our bodies aligning as he leans down. "Promise you'll let me carry some of the weight," he demands, voice serious. "I know you're used to doing things on your own, but I am here, and you've claimed and accepted me as your soulmate. We are *soul-bound*. That means letting me share your burdens. I will never ask you to change who you are, but I need you to let me help you be the fierce woman I know and love."

Every inch of me feels electric. "I can't promise I won't put up a fight, if it means keeping you out of harm's way."

"You will accept my help, Astraea Aidos." His command is bold, and my name change amplifies its significance. "I am yours, and you are mine. We will share in the responsibility, the fight, and everything in between."

"Okay," I murmur, unsure when my eyes had filled with tears. I've never wept so much in my life.

"Okay."

CHAPTER 59
ASHER

I lift my mate into my arms and savor this moment. Who knows when we'll get another chance once we leave for the Compound?

"Oh, I'm sure we'll find the time," Astraea thinks, wrapping her legs around me.

I chuckle. *"I suppose the mind-reading will help."*

Astraea nods into my chest, making my laugh sincere. My wicked little Reaper is adorably soft when she wants to be.

"Don't push your luck, Trouble. The reaper in me is very easily motivated."

I grin roguishly, gripping her ass appreciatively, causing her to gasp. Her legs tighten around my waist. I gently pull on her hair with my other hand, making the little minx look up. She pins me with her fiery eyes—my undoing. I growl, the rumble deep in my chest.

"I *like* trouble," I say, "and you're tantalizing when you're motivated."

Astraea bites her lip with an outstanding sparkle in her eyes. "I've come to realize I quite like trouble, too."

"Ahem." Aurelia coughs, startling Astraea out of my grasp as she spins to face the danger. I tut at my feisty mate, who'd raised her smoky fists, ready to attack.

"Shit, Aurelia!" Astraea blows, tamping down her eterì. "Don't you know better than to sneak up on me?"

"You don't usually allow yourself to be snuck up on," Aurelia snorts, full of snark.

I bridge the gap between me and Astraea and slowly force her fists to her sides. She gives me a snarl, and it takes all my strength to hold back my elation.

Aurelia stands with a hand on her hip, tapping her foot like she has somewhere better to be. "I just finished helping Malek get back to bed," she tells us. "I only came back out to ask about..." She pauses, leaning closer before whispering, "The situation."

"Not here," Astraea hisses, looking around to see if anyone had caught our conversation. We stand on the edge of a mountain cliff, and the others remain by the fire. The only thing to catch our words is the wind.

"Did you find anything?" Aurelia presses.

Astraea crosses her arms defiantly. "It's been handled."

Aurelia stomps her foot, her mass of blonde hair waving behind her like it's angry. "Do *not* exclude me, Astraea."

Astraea squints. "I wouldn't dream of it, dear sister. Just wait till we're alone."

Aurelia grunts, but seems to agree.

"If you'll excuse us, we have some things to do in our bedroom," I announce pointedly at Astraea.

"Ugh! Gross!" Aurelia boos us, giving me a disgusted look.

I tip my head back and laugh, towing Astraea from her sickened sister.

"Not that kind of something." Astraea grunts. "Come find us in fifteen minutes."

"I mean, I wouldn't be opposed—"

Astraea cuts me off with a warning glare.

Aurelia looks affronted. "Fifteen minutes is all it takes? Gosh, Raea. Where are your standards?"

Astraea pinches her sister's arm. "Use your head, Relie. Come find me when you've figured it out."

I laugh as I become the one who gets towed, pursuing my wicked mate who tugs me by the rope around my heart.

"You did that on purpose," Astraea hisses.

I shrug, pleased as she glares at me over her shoulder.

"Was that really necessary?" she asks, her eyes catching on my smile.

"You love me," I reply, pressing my tongue into my fang.

Astraea holds her grin back with effort. "Shut up."

"That's it." I shoot forward, grabbing Astraea around the waist and effortlessly hoisting her over my shoulder.

"Put me down, oaf!" she shrieks as she pounds on my stomach with her fists. I smack her ass, and she gasps.

"Not a chance."

"You will pay for this," she says.

"Can't wait," I assure her, my voice so low I barely recognize myself.

Astraea gulps audibly, and the sound makes me flush with desire. "Asher," she warns. "Clear those filthy thoughts from your mind."

I look down at where she hangs upside down, her hair billowing over my legs. "It's proving difficult, what with your ass in my face and your mouth so close to my—"

"Ash!" she hisses.

I chuckle darkly. "Good to see I still irritate you."

"Let me down," she demands.

I purse my lips. "I think not."

Astraea softly smacks me, making me laugh as we enter the tavern.

"Fine." Arm hooked around her waist, I lift her off my shoulder and cradle her in my arms, where I wish she would stay forever.

"I wanted you to put me down, Asher." Yet her mind and body tell another story.

"Call it a compromise," I say.

Astraea grits her teeth, then punches my chest with a huff. I smile down at my violent, fierce mate, thanking the stars for her.

"I can't keep fighting you when you're thinking things like that," Astraea murmurs, curling her fist into my shirt.

"As long as you let me hold you, we can do whatever you want."

"Take me upstairs," she demands, then reaches up to wrap her arms around my neck. I lift her higher, making sure she is comfortable, and comforted.

As we ascend the shadowy hall, I take us to our bedroom and close the door. The room is dark, save for the few candles we keep lit.

"So, what did you find?" I ask.

"A journal," she responds, trying to leave my hold.

I hug her tighter, closing my eyes and inhaling these last seconds of bliss.

"Fine." Astraea exhales. "If it makes you happy, you can keep me a while longer."

My heart does a loud thump of appreciation.

"He feels like home."

"Astraea..." my voice is hoarse at the effect of her thoughts. *I feel like home?*

"Damn mind-link." There's a spark in her eye that hadn't been there before.

"You mean it?" I ask, hopeful.

"I do."

"Gods, Astraea. I fucking love you." I crush her to me, cradling her head in the crook of my neck as she once again wraps her legs around my waist. "You are my home, too."

"Don't ever let go."

My heart aches with bliss. "You either."

She dips her head against my shoulder, and I press her closer. She chuckles, playing with my hair at the nape of my neck. "Okay." She huffs. "Bring me to the dresser so I can get the journal."

I kiss her perfect ash-colored hair and carry her where she leads me. After she removes the journal, I close the drawer and make my way to the edge of the bed. I unwind her legs from me and sit her in my lap as we look at the journal together, Astraea holding it and me looking over her shoulder with my arms wrapped snug around her belly.

Astraea carefully opens the leatherbound book and flips to the first page. "I can barely read it."

I kiss her cheek, reaching down to draw the book nearer. "Would you like me to read it to you?"

"You and your perfect fae eyes."

I smirk. "Perfect, you say? Was that a compliment, Starlight?"

Astraea nudges me in the ribs. "Just read it already."

"You know, you also have perfect fae eyes," I note, brushing a kiss to the corner of her lashes. "They are the prettiest, most vibrant shade of blue." I gently pull her hair from her face, tucking it behind her ear. "You know, they've always reminded me of the Aegean Sea. It cannot be a coincidence that we've found ourselves in Greece, when I've always seen a part of it in you."

"Asher," she speaks warningly, though she relaxes in my arms. "If we don't stay on track, this will all have been for nothing."

I hug her closer, Astraea lays her head back against my chest, under which my heart beats rapidly.

"Read, Ash."

I can do nothing but oblige. I would give her all the stars in the sky if she asked.

BELIEVE I AM NOT IMPORTANT.

Yes, I am.

My duty to know everything.

They trust me.

I pretend.

On their side.

Fools.

Can't know what I know. (Secrets... All along?)

Knew she'd do this.

They told me.

Must kill her.

They're waiting.

Wait to strike.

Time.

I won't let them in.

CHAPTER 60
AURELIA

"Fuck," my sister says.

Astraea's curse almost stops me from knocking until I hear King Asher trying to calm her.

"It's okay. It's going to be okay."

"How the hell is this okay?" she hisses.

I decide knocking is no longer critical, so I enter their room and close the door behind me.

"Aurelia," Astraea exhales sharply, eyes wide with panic. "Ever heard of knocking?"

"What's wrong?" I ask, cutting to the chase. I hurry to their bed and grab a pillow, stuffing it in the crack between the floor and the door, hoping it will muffle some of the sound.

"Could you hear us?" asks the fae king.

"Barely, but enough."

"Shit," Astraea groans. "Did anyone else come in?"

"No," I assure them. "The others are all outside. Only Malek is in his room, but he's several doors down. Even if he wasn't sleeping, there's no way he'd have heard you."

"Good. We've got trouble," Astraea updates me. I can almost see the fear coming off her, like waves.

"Oh?" I approach cautiously. My eyes do a double take as I fully regard my sister, who I now realize is seated in King Asher's lap, his arms wrapped around her waist. My eyes must bug out of my head because Astraea snaps her fingers in my face.

"Quit gawking and sit down," she orders.

Ever the bossy queen.

"Read this," Raea continues, shoving a book in my hands.

"What's this?"

"A journal," she snaps.

King Asher runs a hand over Astraea's arm before adding, "Astraea found this between Calix's mattress and box spring."

"Oh..." I whistle, flipping it open to read the contents.

Astraea and the king wait until I am finished. I can hardly believe my eyes. I blink, confused and terribly worried, as Raea recovers the book.

"We think Calix is planning to kill someone," Astraea informs me. "A woman."

"Yeah," I murmur, my mouth dry. "Got that part."

Asher nods, his expression grim. "Now to figure out who he's after."

I swallow hard, my head going dizzy as the room darkens. Black spots blur my vision, and I realize my hands are trembling as I still pretend to hold the book.

"Aurelia?" Astraea calls, shaking my shoulder. "Hey, take a few breaths, Rel."

"Ravena," I whisper, my voice barely there. "We have to go get her. She can't be left alone with him."

"I agree, but I don't think we can tell her that."

"What do you mean?" I shout, turning to face my sister. "We can't keep something like this from her."

"We must," Astraea insists, her jaw set.

"It isn't that we don't want to, Aurelia," King Asher interrupts. "We've reason to think Ravena wouldn't believe us if we told her. She has grown quite fond of Calix, and we're afraid she'll go to him about it."

"Why shouldn't she?" I ask, baffled.

"Because if we're ever going to figure out what he's up to, we need to stay quiet and pretend we don't know anything about this."

"You mean you want to give him the chance to kill someone potentially?" I gawk at the pair.

"Of course not!" Astraea says, filled with fury and terror. "We're going to watch him closely to find more evidence."

The king nods, the pair decidedly in accord. "There's more to the story than we know, and because Calix mentions there being a group of people who are prepared and willing to kill someone, we need to wait this out to see if we can discover more."

"Okay, fine, yes. But what about Ravena?" I point.

"You do everything in your power to keep her at your side," Astraea maintains. "Calix has been doing most of that work for us by pushing her away and spending his nights cooped up with Malek."

"He's outside alone with her right now!" Celestials above, are they not worried at all?

"Ash told Nemesis about everything through our mind-link. He is watching over Ravena right now."

"What about Idris?" I ask, feeling slightly better about having Nemesis protecting my sister.

"I leave it up to you to decide if you'd like to involve him—on the condition that he is not to tell anyone else. The less anyone knows that we're spying, the better."

"Spying on an Intelligence Agent, of all people," I mutter, cursing our predicament.

"We've got this," Astraea assures me. "Just focus on keeping Ravena safe, and we'll take care of the rest."

I swallow hard, uncertain of what I am agreeing to. How messy will this get? How long will they play this out?

"Trust us, Aurelia," King Asher implores. "No one wants to ensure your and Ravena's safety more than Astraea. She will keep you safe, and find more information."

"And you?" I question, tapping my foot against the bed in agitation.

"I will help her do it all," he says assuredly, not missing a beat.

I watch them, hesitating before finally asking, "Why are you two so cozy?" I can't keep the curiosity at bay any longer.

Astraea's eyes narrow, but the king only laughs and squeezes her tighter.

"Hey, I'm not judging!" I say, hands up in surrender. "It's just that Astraea has never even held someone's hand in front of me, let alone sat in someone's lap. I had to ask."

Astraea clenches her fists as she slings curse after curse under her breath. "I might as well tell you since I don't foresee you letting this go." She looks elsewhere, her hands flexing more rigidly.

"What is it, Raea?" I ask cautiously.

King Asher pulls the hair from her face and watches her tentatively. His eyes almost glow with anticipation.

"Asher and I," Astraea begins, exhaling a long breath. "We're mates."

"What?!" I shriek, jumping off the bed and standing before them.

"We're soulmates," she answers again, her voice deadly serious. "Soul-bound, in fact."

"Astraea, tell me you're not joking."

King Asher kisses her cheek. Even more shockingly, Astraea lets him.

"Holy shit!"

"Rel!" Astraea swipes the air between us. "Cut it out, all right?"

I laugh, jumping up and down, uncaring of how foolish I must look. "My sister is soul-bound!"

"Relie!" she scolds me, grabbing my arm and dragging me back to the ground. "Be quiet, else someone might hear you."

I shake my head at her, beaming. "You two should be shouting it from the mountaintops. My big sister is blessed with a soulmate!"

"It is *I* who is blessed," the king responds, drawing my antsy sister in for a giant hug.

"Would you two quit it already?" Astraea says, though she cannot hide the smirk playing on her lips.

"I'm so happy for you both." I reach out a hand for each. Both take mine, and I squeeze their fingers. "You deserve this."

"Rel," My sister begins, her words—oddly—stuck in her throat.

"I love you, Raea. I am happy for you. You should be, too."

"Yeah, yeah," she replies, shrugging me off. In Astraea terms, that was thanks.

"Well, I thank you on behalf of us both," says the fae king, smiling down at my sister.

"You're very welcome, King Asher."

He laughs. "Just Asher, little sister."

I beam wide and, without warning, throw myself at them and pull them into the biggest hug.

"Down, Relie," Astraea orders, though she's laughing, too.

"Okay, okay." I surrender, reluctantly letting them go. "So, the journal?"

"Will be brought back and placed exactly where I found it," Astraea confirms.

"And we tell no one?"

They both nod grimly, each with a look of determination in their eyes.

"All right," I agree, sighing heavily. I am so elated for Astraea and Asher yet grossly weighed down by the contents of Calix's book. It's a lot to digest in one night.

"Go get Vena and go rest," Astraea insists. "Tomorrow's a big day."

"That it is." I whirl on my heel and head for the door. I remove the pillow and throw it at my sister's head. To my disappointment, Asher catches it before it can hit her, and I stick my tongue out at him.

"You are a child," Astraea says dramatically.

Asher and I chuckle.

I waggle my brows at her. "Night, Rae Rae."

"Goodnight, Aurelia."

CHAPTER 61

RAVENA

When Aurelia comes to find me, insisting we all need to return to the tavern to sleep, I am reluctant to say goodnight to Calix. Tomorrow, we will embark on our newest journey, taking the first step toward global peace. Though no one wants to say it, we recognize that things might not go our way. I hope to the stars that everything will work out, and that no one will get hurt.

I usher Aurelia inside our room, asking her to give Calix and me a moment. She argues briefly, but ultimately caves. Calix holds my hand gently as we stand in the dark hall, his eyes fixed on mine.

"Don't look so glum, Ravena," Calix says with kindness. "We've yet to see the last of the stars."

I smile softly, still high on happiness from having star-gazed at his side. "I just worry that tomorrow will bring change."

His brows furrow. "That is exactly what we need, Ravena. It's what we're fighting for. It's why we've joined the dragon horde in the first place."

I exhale dejectedly, a sense of foreboding ahead. "I under-stand that. I only worry it will be more than we bargained for."

Calix thinks for a moment, lowering his regard to our woven hands. "No matter the outcome, I hope you always fight for what's right."

I gulp before agreeing. "Absolutely. It will be a difficult task to get all the legacies to listen and understand. But I am sure as hell going to do my best to make it happen. Astraea will lead, and I will help her to the best of my abilities."

Calix smiles affectionately, his dimple making an appear-ance. "I'm pleased to hear that." Why does it feel like he's saying goodbye, and not goodnight?

"Calix?" I look at his apprehensive expression.

"Yeah, Ravena?"

"You'll fight too, right?"

He exhales, drawing me in for a gentle hug. "Unquestionably. I'll be right by your side."

"Good," I tell him. "I'll see you tomorrow, Calix."

He lowers his face to mine, then kisses the tip of my nose. I giggle at the sweet gesture.

"Goodnight, Ravena."

"Sweet dreams," I whisper, touching my fingers to the tip of my nose as I watch him retreat toward his and Malek's room.

I turn around and creep inside my and Aurelia's room, finding my way to the bed in the candlelit space.

"You okay?" Aurelia asks, nearly shaking my skeleton from my skin.

"Goodness gracious, you scared me!"

"I didn't mean to. You're just easy to spook."

I shrug. "Maybe."

Aurelia moves the blankets back for me, and I hop into bed. I hand her my glasses, and she places them next to her hearing aids on the nightstand. I throw my arms above my head and settle into the pillow, wishing it were softer on my hair.

"You really like him, huh?" Aurelia asks quietly.

I exhale dreamily. "He's very kind. He's the sweetest, nerdiest man I've ever known." I hold my breath, unable to contain my elation. "I think I'm falling for him."

"Don't you think you're moving fast?" she questions. I turn to face her, her mass of blonde hair taking up most of the space between us.

"We've known each other for a while now, Rel. The interest isn't new."

"I just worry you'll get hurt," she explains, looking away. "That's all."

"I know, I know. I appreciate your concern for me, but I promise I'll be careful with my heart."

Aurelia frowns. "I'm not worried about how you'll care for your heart. I worry what Calix could do with it."

"I mean, I haven't quite given it to him yet. There's not much he can do." However, it was his if he wanted it.

"Just be careful, okay?"

I chuckle, angling a brow at my baby sister. "That's my line."

Aurelia quirks her lips. "I'm sure you'll get your chance to say it sometime soon. I'm due for another misfortune."

I swat her arm, jokingly. "Don't say that. We don't need you jinxing tomorrow."

"I take it back," she replies swiftly, knocking on the bed's wooden headboard three times. I join her, knocking thrice as well. Jinxing is a superstition we firmly believe in, and we've learned from our nymph heritage to knock thrice on wood to reverse it. Some call it silly, but we know it works.

I wonder aloud: "Do you ever think about what it would be like if we'd have chosen to leave the Compound after graduation, to live with our folks?" I think about the family I'd been offered upon graduation. All celestial children are obligated to attend the Compound until completion. Then, they are given the choice to live among their blood species if they can't provide for the Compound. Though no one is ever forced from the legacies, those who aren't cut out for the military, labs, or Intelligence typically feel swayed to leave.

"If I had gone with my grandparents when they offered, I'd have no one now," Aurelia answers glumly.

"You would have still had me and Raea," I tell her. "You know that."

She shrugs. "Do you ever think about what your life would have been like if you'd gone to live with the dryads?"

"Often, actually," I admit. Though my father is gone, I do have other relatives. I often reminisce on our time together. Uncle Remi looks so much like my father did. Dark brown skin with brawn to boot, and a smile that lights up a room. The only difference between the two is that my father sported his natural afro, while Uncle Remi prefers to keep his head clean-shaven.

"I would have liked living with my uncle Remi and my cousins," I finally tell Aurelia. "I mourn the time I lost with them. They grew up so fast, and I wish I could have been there to see it. I sometimes imagine what it would have been like to help them run the inn."

"That's understandable," Relie considers. "You know, you can change your mind any time, V. You can live a normal life within the Nymph Wilds."

"Oh, no," I say. "I love my job at the Compound, and if I have to choose between my sisters and my uncle's family, there's no choosing at all."

"I don't want you to leave us, but I want you to know that neither Raea nor I would resent you for it."

"I know," I say. "Same goes for you and her."

"You never know," Relie chuckles. "Asher might convince Raea to choose the Fae Court now that they're together."

"You know?" I gasp, kicking my feet. "Gods, I've been holding it in all day long! Asher hinted to me that they were kissing."

"What?" she balks. "Why in Oasòs would he be talking to you about kissing our sister?"

"The melons!" I announce, laughing into the darkness.

"Melons?" Relie groans. "Dear stars, please tell me he wasn't talking about Raea's melons."

"No, no." I snort. *That would have been worse.* "He was going to eat cucumbers, and I told him about Raea's allergy."

"And that led you to believe they were kissing?"

I smirk. "I told him if he was considering kissing her, he couldn't if he ate those cucumbers."

Aurelia giggles, her eyes wide with mischief. "What did he say?"

"I asked him if he wanted the cucumbers, and he awkwardly declined."

Aurelia bursts out laughing, surely waking anyone who might be asleep. I join in, remembering King Asher's reluctance to admit what he wasn't quite confessing.

"I would have paid good money to see that interaction," Aurelia says.

"It was uncomfortable in the moment, but it's hilarious to look back on."

Aurelia snorts. "I can only imagine."

"What about you?" I ask. "Have you got a special someone waiting at home for you?"

Aurelia cackles, shaking her head. "I've got a couple."

"Rel! Why didn't you tell me?"

"Oh, as if you want to hear anything about my sexcapades."

"Well, maybe not the actual sex part, but I do want to know about you. Do you have feelings for them, or is it more of a fling?"

"I'm not sure," she reflects, seeming to think about it. "They were unexpected, let's just say that."

"Unexpected, how?" I question.

Aurelia shoves me playfully. "Nope. Not tonight."

"Aw, come on! You get to interrogate me about my maybe relationship, but I don't get to do the same with you?"

"If, and I mean *if*, something romantic evolves, you'll be the first to hear about it. Deal?"

I sigh theatrically, grabbing the blankets and bunching them up to my chin. "Fine."

"Fine."

"All right. Enough gossip. We should try to get some sleep."

Aurelia grumbles as she turns on her side to face the window. "Tomorrow awaits."

"See you when the sun's up."

Aurelia yawns, hogging the blankets. I yank them back, and she grunts.

"Night, Relie Bean."

"Night, V."

CHAPTER 62
ASTRAEA

When the sun wakes me, lighting my lids, my body stiffens in pain, alert and aware of the heavy limbs atop me. I flex my feet, my legs caught between someone else's.

Ash.

He takes up the entire bed, like the royal he is. I exhale, releasing the tension, melting as I realize I'm wrapped in his embrace. "Good morning, my king."

"Fuck," he groans, hauling me up until I straddle his hips. I gasp, feeling every part of his hardness pressing into me. All that separates us is a pair of lace underwear, courtesy of Asher's packing.

"You're in a good mood this morning." I run my fingers down his ornamented sides, watching him flex beneath my touch.

"Hard not to be when I've woken with the girl of my dreams sprawled atop me."

I roll my eyes, then begin grinding against his length. He moans, his eyes flickering black for the briefest moment. I relish the storm inside him.

"Astraea," he says, deep and guttural. He grabs my hips, his nails digging into my flesh as he rocks me against him.

"Yes, Ash?" I ask innocently, batting my lashes in a suggestive taunt.

Asher grins, grabs me and rolls us on the bed until he hovers above me. "The things you do to me." He flashes his fangs, leaning down to kiss my neck. "You drive me wild."

He licks up my throat, hot and slow, drawing a shiver from me.

I arch from his touch. "You haven't seen anything yet."

He exhales breathily. "I wish we had more time."

I throw my head back, exasperated by the sun peeking through the window.

Asher rests on his elbows, one hand cupping my jaw with tenderness. I look up into his ice-blue eyes, wishing I could swim in them forever.

"Kiss me, Ash. Forget about the world with me for one small moment."

His smile is awing and full of adoration. Leisurely, delicately, Ash bends down, pressing his soft lips against mine. Lightning strikes in my chest, my body alight with energy. I open for him, and he delves deeper, still soft in his touch.

Ash pulls away, sweeping my hair out of my face. *"Whenever you need rest from your hardships, I'll be but a thought away. Just reach out, Starlight."*

"Promise?"

"I promise, Astraea."

"Okay," I reply, beaming up at him.

Sudden fog fills my vision, and I bite back a cry of alarm as my world turns dark.

"Astraea?!" I hear someone call me, but I am already gone. I can feel a strong presence around me—*a celestial.* I can't decipher which it is, even though I search my mind for an answer.

· · ·

Never trust fire, for your fate is to be consumed by its destructive flames. The vast expanse of Oblivion eagerly awaits your arrival, beckoning you to claim your rightful position amidst the tapestry. You, Astraea the Star, Spirit of my Spirit, shall forge your own path and shape your destiny, transcending the limitations imposed by mere Earthly existence.

Be prepared.

"Astraea?"

My eyes are wide, the fog dissipating as Ash appears afore me.

"Astraea, come back to me, love."

My brow creases as I persuade the divinatory guidance to remain in the forefront of my mind.

"Are you with me?" Asher asks, pulling on my shoulders until I sit upright.

In a hoarse voice, I tell him, "Oblivion awaits." I rub at my crown, easing the tension as best as I can.

"What the hell, Astraea? You were out for so long. I thought..." He draws me to him, wrapping me in his embrace. "You scared the life out of me. Are you well?"

I close my eyes against his shoulder, playing back the message I'd received. "One of the celestials gave me a warning," I explain, once I've caught my bearings. Goosebumps stipple my skin at the remembrance of how eerie it had been inside the fog.

"What did they say?" he asks.

Keeping my eyes closed, I recite the message word for word. Asher rubs gentle circles between my shoulder blades, releasing some of the tension.

"What do you think it means?" he asks.

"I think whoever it is knows I plan to usurp Urðra's rule. They were warning me that fire and Oblivion await, but what does that mean? Do they mean the dragon's fire? Is it figurative? Oasòs above, I wish these guides were more straightforward, especially about my potential to enter the void."

Asher nods gravely. "I understand, but it wouldn't be right for the celestials to sway you in any direction. Speaking in riddles is the only way they can meddle."

"I don't want to become nothing," I whisper, growing numb with terror. "Even if I don't take my mother's place in Oasòs, I'd much rather exist among the stars than just... vanish."

As far as we know, there are four realms: Earth, where the living reside; Oasòs, where the celestials rule; and the stars, where all beings go to rest after death. Now, we know there's another option—Oblivion, a place where nothing exists, thanks to Phaðs.

Asher hugs me tighter, and runs his hands down my hair. "It'll be all right, Astraea. I won't let that happen to you. We'll get through this."

A smile twitches on my lips. It is so bizarre to share a problem, committedly, with someone else.

"Get used to it, love. I'm not going anywhere."

"You'd better not," I quip. *"I'm just starting to enjoy it."*

Ash chuckles, the reverberation transferring to me. He continues stroking my hair, and I contentedly huddle into his warmth. "Thank you for being so open with me and choosing us," he murmurs.

My heart beats heavily in its cage. "I'm not a complete monster. I have... feelings."

Ash tugs my hair gently, asking me to look up. I oblige, gazing through my lashes at the perfectly sculpted fae king who holds me like I'm the most precious gem on Earth. "You are more precious than any gem in any realm," he assures me in his steady voice. "And I know you aren't a monster."

I cock a brow at him. "Most would disagree. I am the infamous Reaper, after all."

Ash leans down and kisses my cheek, then moves to the other to do the same. "You are powerful and swift, but you always fight for what's right. You don't go out of your way to reap the world's souls. You obliterate those who would do harm. It is not the same as being a soulless monster, as you tell yourself you are."

"But how many people did I kill who weren't entirely evil? What makes me any better than my enemies?"

Ash exhales gravely. "There's no way to know for certain, but when you're faced with only the choice to kill or be killed, you do what you have to do."

"I killed so many dragons, Ash...."

"And they killed so many other species. Until there is true peace, you cannot carry the *what-ifs* that come with their deaths. Every dragon you reaped has killed or was trying to kill someone you were trying to protect."

"How do you know?" I ask dubiously.

"For one, the first time I happened upon you was when you were defending a helpless group of orcs. You are always working to protect others. Secondly, every time we've been on a battlefield together, I've been able to do nothing but watch you. I have always seen your heart and how heavily it burdens you to take a life."

"That's just it, Ash. It doesn't bother me to take the lives of others. That is why I feel so empty."

"That it empties you is the surest sign that the death is wearing you down. You *do* care."

"I can't afford to care," I confess. "It is my duty to protect others, and with that responsibility comes hard choices. The choices have become less difficult for me over the years."

"That's the effect of war, Astraea. It has nothing to do with your soul."

I shrug defeatedly, drawing from Asher's embrace to stand in the room and face the window. I stretch out my limbs, taking a deep breath. "Let's hope this war is finished soon," I tell him over my shoulder. "I don't know how much more our people can take."

I gaze out at the dragons there in the sunlight.

I don't know how much more I can take.

CHAPTER 63
ASHER

After packing the rucksack, strapping my sword to my back, and heading downstairs, I join my mate and our group to have a quick breakfast before leaving. Most of them have finished already, so I quickly grab a jar of carrots and swallow them down.

"Not in the mood for cucumber?" Aurelia jeers, pointedly looking at the jar I'd pushed away.

I cock a brow at her as she and Ravena snicker. The pair sit on either side of Malek, working to get him to eat his last bit of beans. Astraea is perched on the table's edge, arms crossed under her bust, watching me and waiting for me to answer.

"They've proven rather unappealing as of late," I say, sending Astraea a wink.

She looks me up and down, her eyes roving over me. *"How about me, Ash? Do you find me appealing?"*

I cough, knowing well that my face has likely gone red. *"Very,"* I manage to reply, desperately hoping my desire isn't showing on the outside.

Astraea smirks, her gaze heating my cock beneath my pants. *"I find you insatiably appealing."*

"You are playing with trouble, little Reaper."

She smirks. *"Of course."*

I watch her leave her spot and walk out the door, and I can do nothing but follow her. I promised I'd always do just that, after all.

As I round the door, searching for the temptress, her hands suddenly snatch me from the doorway, towing me to the side of the tavern porch. Her lips crash against mine, and I let go of the rucksack I was holding so that I might hoist her up.

Astraea bites my lip provokingly, her smaller half-fae fangs enticing me before she pulls away, our breaths mingling in the space between us.

"What was that for?" I growl, my nails pressing into her perfect ass. "The others could see us."

"Can I not claim my mate whenever I wish to?" she challenges, placing another heated kiss on my lips. "I do not care who sees."

I inhale her essence, clinging to her with my very soul. "Claim me anytime, anywhere, in every life, Astraea," I beg her, pressing her body into mine. "I would gladly shout my love for all to hear."

"You can."

My eyes widen. "Truly?" I ask, lowering her feet to the ground, though never letting go. "Only Aurelia knows that we're soul-bound. We can keep it that way if it would make you most comfortable."

"I told you I would tell everyone before we left for the Compound," she says. "I meant it. Who knows how this day will go? I don't want to waste another moment hiding us."

"You're certain?"

She nods, her gaze going soft. "Of course, Ash."

My smile grows, and I wrench her into my arms, spinning us around as I bellow my excitement. Astraea laughs, and our celebration attracts others to see what all the commotion is about.

Aurelia gives me a knowing look, and I'm happy to return it.

"Are you smiling?" Ravena asks Astraea. Her eyes practically bulge from her head as she stares at my beautiful soulmate.

"Yeah," she answers, her grumpy little voice a little brighter. She rises on her toes and kisses me in front of everyone. "I am." And her grin widens into the most exquistite smile I've ever seen.

"Raea!" Ravena shouts.

Aurelia jumps up and down, hooting at us with glee. "That's my sister! You get your man!"

Astraea giggles—*giggles*,—and places a hand on my chest. "That's my mate," she says lovingly, gazing up at me with a tenderness I never imagined I'd get to see from her.

I am all the realms and equally nothing as she beholds me, professing our love for all to hear.

"Oh, my goodness, Raea!" Ravena screeches, running toward us to clutch Astraea's hand in hers. "You're soulmates? Like, real soul-bound mates?"

Astraea dips her head in confirmation, and I smile happily. I am overjoyed, and the support of Astraea's sisters is precious.

Ravena pulls her hands away, wiping her tears of evident joy. "Oh, Raea," she mumbles, sniffling. "My sweet Raea."

"Sweet?" Aurelia chirps from behind, eliciting a laugh from all of us.

Ravena swats at Aurelia. "Oh, shush!" she maintains, chuckling. Her watery grey eyes meet mine, and her brows slant compassionately. "I've always known you cared for my sister." Her eyes glisten with unshed tears. "I've seen the way you are around her, how you've always looked out for her. Thank you for loving Astraea the way she deserves. I'm so glad she found you."

My heart melts at her exchange. Astraea is so very loved, and I am glad for it.

"It is I who is thankful," I tell Ravena.

Astraea grunts, her joy still plastered on her sharp face. "Okay, enough of the mushy talk. It's time we get this show on the road."

I take a deep breath, squeezing her hand as we all linger on the porch, envisaging what is to come.

Calix stands behind Ravena with one hand on her shoulder. Malek waits on the steps where Aurelia had helped him settle. As Astraea gazes upon them, I can feel nothing but contentment radiating from her. She leans into me, twining her left hand with mine.

"Ready?" she asks.

I bend down, watching as the sun illuminates her blue eyes, and kiss her flawless lips. *"With you at my side? Always."*

CHAPTER 64
RAVENA

"Are you sure you don't want extra help?" I ask Calix as we stand at his dragon Orion's side. He smiles down at me and squeezes my shoulder.

"I've got this, Ravena. Don't worry about me. Just take care of yourself, okay?" His look is reassuring, but my gut is full of warning.

"Okay," I agree hesitantly. "I will."

"It is time we depart," Nemesis announces. His guttural voice gives me the chills, and I shiver. If there is one thing that I'm glad for, it's that my bonded dragon has a kind, melodic voice. She's been growing on me the more I speak with her. She's just a youngling, eager to learn and be like her fellow dragons.

Asher and Aurelia join Calix and me at Orion's side, the pair helping Malek walk. He appears dazed as usual, still undisturbed by the sight of dragons. I'd thought it peculiar, but perhaps he really is so ill that the dragons are the least of his worries.

"Ready?" Asher asks Calix, who dips his head curtly.

I bite my lip, hesitating to say goodbye.

Calix wraps me in a hug, and I delight in his warmth.

"Be careful up there, Ravena."

"You be careful, too," I tell him. "Keep Malek safe."

Calix presses a light kiss to my cheek. "I promise."

Orion, who's already kneeling, helps Calix climb aboard. I watch as Calix reaches a hand down, and Asher hoists Malek up as if he weighs nothing. Calix wrenches him up and onto Orion, settling him upright where he straddles the dragon.

"Are you sure you've got him?" I ask Calix.

My nerves are still on edge as Calix sits atop his dragon. It wouldn't be Calix's first time flying with Malek, but it doesn't yet make me more comfortable with the situation. With Malek aboard, barely conscious, Calix will have to focus on keeping Malek steady. I'm scared. I don't want either of them to get hurt.

"I am sure, Ravena."

I look over at Orion, who's watching our exchange. "Please stay close to Nyx and me," I kindly request.

Orion bobs his head, and Calix pats the dragon's side.

"Thank you," Calix says to him. "He's agreed. We'll be at your side the whole time, Ravena."

I smile timidly. "Okay. See you up there." I wave, reluctantly turning from him to find Nyx.

"Do not worry, my bonded," she speaks, her head lowering to the ground as I approach. **"I will take great care of you, and Orion will care for your friends."**

"Thanks, Nyx."

Her tail flaps. **"You are welcome, Ravena."**

I gently pat her snout, and she releases a contented huff.

"Are you sure you're up to coming with us?" I ask. *"It could be dangerous, Nyx. I want to stress that things could go wrong."*

"Are you worried for me?" she asks quizzically, her head tilting to the side.

"Naturally, I am," I chuckle as she wags her tail enthusiastically.

"Do not worry, my bonded. I will be the bravest dragon there is! I will make you proud."

"Oh, Nyx," I coo, caressing her head. *"You are brilliant, and you care deeply. I am already proud of you."*

Nyx whines, but I can sense it stems from happiness. **"I sound just like you!"** she exclaims.

I giggle. *"I must be amazing."*

"Oh, yes," she agrees. **"Very."**

I smile, climbing aboard my adorable purple dragon. I settle atop her back, scooting closer to where her neck begins. I admire the silver sheen in her purple scales, lightly grabbing hold of them to stay steady.

"Have you forgiven me for the pain I caused upon our meeting, my bonded?" she asks hesitantly.

My heart swells with pain as the devastating memory flashes in my mind. I close my eyes, take a deep breath, and let it out, along with the shame and regret.

There was nothing more I could have done at that moment to save Theo, and Nyx couldn't have known not to kill him. It was neither one of our faults. Though I will always mourn the loss of that little boy and feel devastated for the family who lost their precious, brave child, I will also honor him by remembering who he was in life, rather than dwell on his death.

"We both need to forgive ourselves," I explain to Nyx, leaning down and embracing her neck. *"We cannot change what happened, but we can do better in the future and hold Theo dear in our hearts."*

"Yes, I should like that," Nyx replies softly.

"Now, no matter what happens today, please be careful," I warn her. *"If I or your leader tell you to do something, listen. Okay?"*

"Okay, my bonded. You can trust me."

"Then I will do just that," I promise her.

Nyx whickers, then soars to the sky, her wings outstretched, catching the sunlight.

"Stay safe, everyone," Astraea shouts from atop her dragon. "Here's to new beginnings."

"To new beginnings!" we sing.

CHAPTER 65
AURELIA

As we head through the skies, the warm, pleasant air blows through my hair, lifting it off my back. Though we fly determinedly toward the Outer Edge's wall, the flight is languid, as if the dragons are taking their time. I have to wonder if they're as worried as I am. I can't help thinking about the divinatory guidance I received last I tucked Malek into bed.

Time, time, ticks by; now is the time for you to fly. Time, time, ticks by; you cannot stop it; he shall die.

"There is nothing you can do against time, Lia," says Idris. **"Whether you were given this guidance regarding this particular flight or not, you can do nothing."**

"But Malek is going to die." I whimper, clinging to his scales.

"He *is* a rather loose description. It could be one of us male dragons."

I glower. *"I don't think so, Idris. It was given to me while I was alone with Malek and worrying about him. I don't see why I would have been given the divinatory guidance in that moment if it weren't about him."*

"I suppose your suspicions could be factual. Still, what can you possibly do?"

"I get it, okay?" I bark. "I can't do anything. I just... I feel helpless. Useless."

"You are anything but, Lia," Idris reassures me. **"You are always searching for a way to help those around you, even when they do not acknowledge your actions."**

"This isn't about me. Malek's going to die."

"Calm yourself, my bonded. I can feel your legs trembling astride me."

I grit my teeth, trying my best to clear my mind. The black, hazy wall of the Outer Edge is mere feet away, and my suspicion grows.

"I need to tell you something before we cross." I hesitate, weary, my skin prickling.

"Concerning Calix's journal?" Idris asks. **"Nemesis has already informed me. I am to guard Orion should the occasion arise."**

I smack Idris' neck. "Gee, thanks for warning a gal!"

Idris huffs. **"I am telling you now. I always planned to."**

"I sincerely hope so! What if something does happen? I could have caused worse problems if I wasn't aware."

"You were always going to know, Lia. I was going to tell you moments before, but your thoughts were sombre, and I considered giving you the time to grieve what is to come before informing you."

I search his thoughts to find that he's telling the truth. "Okay. What happens if something goes wrong?"

"I am to get you to safety, then help Malek."

"I could have flown with Vena if I'd known you were tasked with this."

"Ahh," Idris hums. **"But that could alert Calix to a concern, which we could not afford. It is best we all play casual."**

"*Why do I get the feeling you expect something bad to happen?*"

"You do not survive a war without understanding that there is always dread and loss."

"*That's not ominous at all.*" I worry my lip, the warm air cooling my clammy skin.

Idris studies me. **"It is the truth, Lia."**

CHAPTER 66

ASTRAEA

The black haze of the Outer Edge billows around Nemesis' snout. I clench my jaw tight, forcing myself to watch as we enter the mist.

"Never look back 'cause what?" Ash asks, using my motto.

"Carnage awaits no matter the direction," I respond, voice low.

Asher grabs my hips more firmly, pressing his fingers into my flesh like an anchor. "I've got your back, Starlight."

As we pass through, I notice wisps of white in the black fog.

"It kind of looks like our eterì," I remark, letting it flow over my outstretched palm.

"I am made of spirit eterì. My ward reflects such," says Nemesis.

"Why is mine only black and Ash's white, but you have both?"

"Because you are two halves of a whole. I am complete on my own."

"That's quite poetic," Ash muses, drawing me nearer.

My back stiffens as we pass through to the other side of the ward. A sense of foreboding, of wrongness, settles over me.

"Do you feel that?" I ask, trying to look over Nemesis's head to see the Compound. Since Nemesis is its creator, the Outer Edge allows him to choose where he wants to go in and out of the ward. He told us he's taking us straight to the Legacy Compound, but something feels innately corrupt. I can't see it. All that lay below us are fields of grass.

"It seems the legacies have built a new ward against us, and it now repels you, too," Nemesis's reverberating voice sends goosebumps along my skin.

"But I am their general. I am the one who is supposed to make those kinds of decisions, not be the one barred," I counter.

Asher's grip becomes firmer than ever. "You weren't around to give orders, darling. And I don't think we'll get a warm welcome back."

Nemesis pulls up, his wings spreading wide as he gently lowers us to the ground. His horde crouches at our sides, waiting for orders.

"General Astraea of the Legacy Legion," a loud voice rumbles from a loudspeaker. My heart beats a worried thump, and the voice continues, "You are in violation of section three-twelve of the Legacy Compound Accords." A violation of that degree indicated treachery of the highest order.

"What?" I hiss, ready to disembark Nemesis and show them a piece of my mind.

A sudden burst of flame reveals dozens of fire eterì wielders, lined up and armed.

"Calix," Asher growls, keeping me in place. We both snap our heads to the far right, where Calix and Malek sit atop Orion. This must be what Calix Lightcrest has been up to. But how had he managed to get the Compound on alert? They couldn't have possibly known we'd even be alive after the dragons had taken us. How do they know we've sided with them?

"It was you, Calix!" Aurelia shouts from my left astride Idris. "You did this!" The air around us howls, Aurelia's eterì blooming.

The fire wielders raise their hands, each stepping forward, ready to pounce.

"What?" Calix balks, eyes wide with horror.

"Air eterì detected!" one of the guards bellows. "Strike!"

"Fucks' sake." I grunt, hoisting myself up until I stand upon Nemesis, my feet firmly planted on his shoulders.

My eterì roars to life, my eyes going white and black mist seeping from my pores, eager to devour. "Stand down!" I bellow, raising my hands toward the Legion. I let my power slither toward them, the tendrils of smoke nipping at their feet. "I am your general! We mean you no harm. Let us discuss this peacefully."

They all halt, rightfully wary of my wrath. I could consume their souls in an instant.

"Did you plan this?" I test Calix, keeping the fire wielders in my line of vision.

"Why would you think that?" he squeaks, looking from me to Ravena, who also appears dumbfounded.

"We know all about your little secret!" Aurelia's girlish voice is shrill, incensed.

"What are you talking about, Rel?" Ravena demands.

Nyx seems caught, confused as to where she's meant to look. Her feet dart, agitated.

"Malek?" Calix murmurs, reaching for his shoulder. Malek mumbles profusely, his body shaking. Is that... Is he *laughing?*

"Calix! Watch out!" I yell, pointing to the fire building in Malek's hand, shaped like a weapon. My friend grins at me, then rapidly twists his body with a furious roar, launching a fire arrow toward Ravena. "No!"

Calix dashes off Orion's back, swift as lighting, beginning to coat himself with his water eterì.

"Calix!" Ravena screams as he hurtles toward her, racing against the arrow's speed.

With a sickening thud, he collides with Ravena, knocking her off Nyx's back. Thrashing about, Orion issues a thunderous howl. Calix lies atop Nyx, a smoking arrow jutting skyward from his back—the very one Malek had been cradling like a comfort toy since we discovered him in the cave.

"No!" Ravena wails in horror, grappling with the ground and trying her best to get up. Idris comes around swiftly, blocking Ravena from pursuing her path. Aurelia reaches down, grabs Ravena's arms and hoists her up, Ravena kicking and screaming all the while.

"Tried to learn... Malek..." Calix croaks, blood pouring from his mouth. "To protect... everyone..."

"Calix! Please don't leave me!" Ravena cries, her broken voice jarringly devasted.

Calix smiles weakly, reaching out his hand. "Keep wishing on stars. I—" he coughs raggedly. "I'll always answer your call." As Ravena's anguish detonates, Calix's head lulls forward, and his life force departs.

"Malek," I say, my eterì in overdrive as I watch the son of a bitch beam.

He laughs, the sound grating against my every atom. "Thanks for the air eterì, Relie Bean."

"You fucking prick! You did this!" Aurelia screams. That she still holds onto Ravena is surprising.

Orion swings his head around, snapping his teeth only inches from our enemy.

Malek jumps off the dragon's back, strutting toward me and my bonded. "Surprised, Astraea?" he jeers, his fire eterì flourishing.

All this time, he wasn't ill. It was a ruse.

How in Oasòs had he achieved this right under my nose?

"Why?" It is one paltry word, yet it holds much command.

Nemesis begins retreating, alerting me to the fire wielders approaching. The horde whines, trailing Nemesis' tracks.

"We've always known you would betray the Compound. Urðra prepared us for this day, and we will not fail our celestials."

"We must go, Astraea," Nemesis declares.

Asher stands behind me, hand on my shoulder.

"Astraea," my name rings through the Compound's loud-speaker. "Legacy of Urðra, you are hereby accused of violating section three-twelve of the Legacy Compound Accords. Surrender now."

"Your time is up, General," Malek spits, mocking my title with the most ugly, repulsive sneer.

The world around me tilts, my surroundings growing foggy as the ground trembles underfoot.

I've long foreseen when you would betray me, accompanied by dragons at your traitorous side. Should you persist in your defiance and refuse to yield, Fate shall be the harbinger of your demise. Vanquish the beasts. Respite is yours 'til the arrival of the next lunar cycle.

Consider this guidance as your lone warning.

CHAPTER 67
ASHER

"Get us out of here!" I order Nemesis, who gladly rises to the skies with haste. The rest of the horde follows, Ravena screaming and crying as Aurelia keeps her astride Idris, a dead Calix slumped over Nyx. Orion, whimpering and inconsolable, straggles behind. Malek, disturbing and aflame, shoots his eterì toward us, but Nemesis shields us from all attacks.

"Ash," Astraea rasps, coming out of her divinatory guidance.

"My mate." I crush her to me, shielding her eyes from the sight below. She desperately clings to me, tugging my hair so hard I think it might fall out. "I've got you."

"My mother," Astraea lashes out, her body shaking in my arms. Her voice breaks, and I feel her anguish in my very soul.

"I'm sorry, Starlight."

Astraea growls her frustrations, her shadowy eterì thrusting out of her, proving how wounded she is. "I should have fucking known. Fucking Fate!" Her screams tear from her throat, and I cling to her even tighter for fear she'll self-destruct. "Damn rotten celestial! I will end her!"

Astraea's roar is like none other, terrifying in what is to come. Her wrath knows no bounds, and she will stop at nothing to usurp Urðra from her position in Oasòs.

"We will end her reign, my bonded," says Nemesis. His agitation matches Astraea's, if not outshines it. He'd been burned by Urðra before, losing his first bonded to her those many years ago. **"I will not allow her to take more from me,"** Nemesis assures me, reading my thoughts. **"I will not lose either of you. We will defeat her."**

"She will beg for death whence my eterì lands upon her," Astraea snarls, her beautiful ashen hair blowing in the wind.

"We will gladly watch as you destroy her and take her throne," I tell her, gripping the back of her head as she rests against my chest.

"We will aid you," Nemesis corrects. **"She will burn at our hands."**

"Take us to Oasòs," Astraea demands.

"It is not yet time, little Reaper."

"It sure the fuck is, dragon!" Astraea's rage is tangible, her eterì billowing around us yet never causing harm.

"We need others at our side if we want the best outcome. We need numbers, devotees of the celestials, to convince them that Urðra must be stopped."

"I can kill her myself," Astraea argues. "Take me to her, and it will be done."

Nemesis huffs, smoke wafting over his head and curling around us. **"There will never be peace if we act with hard-hearted impatience. No one will follow you as the Celestial of Fate if you do not do this correctly and gather your own supporters. We must sway believers to worship you. There is power in devotion. It is the only way the celestials can survive —the only way you will."**

"Don't mistake his sense for disloyalty," I tell Astraea,

rubbing circles over her taut back. "You can hear his thoughts, see into his mind. You know he's right." Astraea's shoulders tighten, and my heart quakes. "Breathe, my love. We have to play the long game in order to win."

"We have until the next full moon, Asher," she jeers, shaking out of my arms to look up at me. Her eyes are still white, her eterì whispering as I try brushing the worry from the corner of her eyes.

"Then we'll use all that time to our advantage and make what we do count."

Her frown deepens. "What if it's not enough? Will you see it my way and let me end Urðra?"

Nemesis rumbles as we pass through a thicket of clouds. ***"Trust me, my ferocious bonded. Have faith in us. We will see victory by the next moon."***

Astraea turns to look behind us, her heart thundering wildly until she spots her sisters with Idris. Her gaze turns to Orion and Nyx, who, for her part, is trying her best not to cry as she carries Calix's lifeless form through the darkening clouds.

"He saved her," Astraea whispers, her brows knitting together in sorrow. I can feel the weight of her guilt. "We blamed him for conspiring against us, and he didn't even bat an eye before taking an arrow for my sister."

"We didn't know..." I try.

She laughs dryly. "Yeah. It seems every day we discover that we really know nothing."

"He was a good man," I say to the wind.

"And we killed him."

"Malek killed him, Astraea. You cannot take the blame for that."

She shakes her head, a solemn smile heavy on her lips. "Malek was my friend. We accused Calix. I saw Malek wield his eterì, and we weren't quick enough. Calix's death is on my hands just as much as Malek's."

"Then his death is on me, too," I tell her, taking her hands in mine and warming her palms.

She sighs heavily, twining her swollen fingers with mine. "Where are we going?" she asks. "We keep flying further and further from the Outer Edge."

"We're off to find our people. Starting with the Fae Court."

CHAPTER 68

RAVENA

Darkness shrouds me like a veil. I barely feel Aurelia's hands holding me, but I know she won't let me fall. She should let go. It would rid me of the dreadful heartache.

Calix," I sob, unseeing, my tears threatening to drown me.

"It's okay, V," Aurelia sniffles, swiping my wet hair from my face.

"He's dead!" I scream, blood coating my tongue from how raw my throat has become.

"I know, Sis."

I shriek and yank my arms from her, but she holds firm. "Let me go!" I howl, my body shuddering in despair.

"I have you," she soothes.

I've never loathed her more.

"I don't want you! I want Calix!" I cry unrelenting. My lungs heave, yearning for my inhaler. *Good. Let my body die so that I might join Calix among the stars.*

"Breathe, Vena," Aurelia begs me. "Please. I need you."

"Let... me..." I gasp, my throat strangling me. "Go." I fall as the blackness takes me.

CHAPTER 69
AURELIA

"*Hold on, Lia. Ravena cannot do it for herself. She needs you.*"

I sob as Idris instructs me to hold my sister tightly as he gently descends, shadowing his fellow dragons.

"*Good,*" he encourages. "*We're almost there, my bonded.*"

"She's not waking up!" I cry, my face wet and eyes blurry as I keep her upright.

"*Be strong,*" Idris instructs me, though his tone is sympathetic.

"She's my sister!" I cling to Ravena, who slumps far too close to the edge of my dragon's back.

"*She will survive,*" he reassures me, his wings lifting to catch in the wind as we lower, touching the ground.

"Raea!" I call to my eldest sister, who's already rushing forward.

She jumps into the air, barely using Idris's scales for support as she climbs aboard, where she grabs Ravena in her strong arms and shakes her. "V, wake up now."

I whimper when Ravena's head snaps back, her eyes still shut. "She passed out."

Astraea checks her pulse as she concentrates, her eyes growing white in seconds. She feels around with her eterì, shrouding Ravena in her power. "She's fine," Astraea respires, relieved. "She's just asleep. There are no wounds."

"Thank you," I sniffle, still clinging to Ravena by her shirt.

Asher arrives and lifts his arms out. Astraea lowers Ravena into his hold.

"V!" I shout.

Astraea puts an assuring hand on my shoulder and squeezes. "She's going to be all right, Rel."

I blink up at her. "But—"

"Come," Raea insists, holding out her hand to me. I grab it, scooting closer to the edge of Idris's back.

"Steady, Lia," says Idris, who leans his head down as I slide off his neck with Astraea at my side.

"Where's he taking her?" I ask, panicked, as Asher begins walking up a cobbled street I hadn't even noticed before. There are so many colors filtered here. Hundreds of murmuring fae crowd the castle yard in the Fae Court's Capitol, their curious eyes following the king and us and the dragons.

"It's going to be all right, Rel. Just keep your eyes forward and do whatever Ash tells you. Okay?"

I nod, words evading me as I listen to the fae converse in large groups.

"Dragons?!"

"Who is the person King Aidos holds?"

"They are filthy! Look at them!"

"Are they hurt? Perhaps I could offer my healing services."

"They walk with the king. It is unheard of! Only Aspen is seen at his side."

"Do you think that one is well?" a fae points to me. I gawk at their finger, astounded they are worried for me instead of Ravena and especially Calix, who lies still on Nyx's back. As if carting a dead man is normal.

"Fae Court," Asher booms as he makes it to the first step of the grand staircase which leads to the castle entrance. "I bring my companions, the dragons and legacies alike, to the Fae Court as our allies. I have much to reveal to you all, but seeing as my friends are suffering, I must ask that you give us time to heal. I bid you a good day with this message: The time has come for greatness, and we will be on the right side of history. We will protect the Fae Court and the world with our lives. Please give us grace as we establish our plans. We will share them with you promptly."

Those in the Fae Court cheer. Some of them even raise a respectful fist.

"Follow Ash and V," Astraea whispers.

I grab her wrist as she turns from me. "Where are you going? Don't leave me." My eyes are wide with panic.

Astraea's jaw ticks, and she darts her eyes toward a whimpering Nyx. "I'm going to collect Calix," she replies, lifting her chin. Grief shines in her blue eyes, but she won't let it deter her from carrying out her duty.

I let her go, putting one foot in front of the other as I trail the fae king up the grandiose staircase. A set of silver-armored guards step forth to greet their king, allowing us to enter the castle.

"I am going to help my horde care for Orion. We will be in the back courtyard," Idris informs me through our mind-link.

My heart pounds rapidly, cold sweat breaking out on my skin. "Will you be safe?"

"Always."

CHAPTER 70

ASTRAEA

The thunderous *whoosh* of dragon wings rises above the chatter of the fae as we march ahead. Nemesis and his horde are to rest in the back courtyard, and are to reach out through the bond if we are needed, and vice versa.

Calix's body is lighter than I'd expected as I carry him up the stairs, several feet behind my mate and sisters. With each of my steps, the arrow which juts from his back threatens to poke me as his limbs hang lifelessly in my arms. His head lolls over my elbow, facing the ground.

"Tell me you're okay, love," Asher probes, never turning to look for me. He is regal even as he carries my unconscious sister, commanding orders from his staff as he leads us through the halls of his giant castle.

"I am," I confirm. *"How's Ravena?"*

He sighs. *"She is still unconscious, but she doesn't feel like she has a fever. She should wake up."*

"Brother," I hear a shocked voice sound as we round another corner.

"Aspen," Asher breathes, a tiny flicker of relief lighting his mind. "Can you please prepare a room with two of our best healers for Ravena?"

They nod vigorously, their eyes wide. "Of course. I take it that's Ravena?" They point to my sister, flopped in Asher's arms.

"Yes," he says. "She's passed out, and I want to be sure she is all right."

"*Thank you,*" I tell him through our mind-link.

"Absolutely!" Aspen replies, directing their brother as they quickly enter one of the tall doors that line the hall. "We haven't any guests this night. Ravena and your companions can take any room they wish."

"I'm going with Ravena," Aurelia squeaks.

"That would be wise," I decide, holding Calix in my arms. "Thank you."

She steps closer to Ash and his sibling. "I'm not leaving her side."

"Okay," Aspen approves, inviting my sister through. "Come on in, then."

Asher swiftly approaches the four-postered bed bedecked in silver silk and gently lays Ravena down.

"Get those healers as soon as possible, Aspen," he orders.

"Right away, Brother," they answer. "Is there anything else before I go?"

"Please bring some food and water for us all," Asher requests. "I will escort my mate to the morgue, and we shall reconvene once we return."

"Mate?" Aspen gasps.

Ash smiles reluctantly, his eyes finding mine. "We have much to catch up on."

Their mouth falls open, entirely shocked as they stare at me and their brother. "That's an understatement."

Ash chuckles, shooing his sibling away. "Go, Aspen. Please."

They bow their head before hurrying out the door, sneaking one last glance at me before leaving.

"Come, love," Asher gestures for me to approach him, his arms outstretched as if to take Calix from my arms.

"I can do it," I assure him, pulling away, but he insists.

"That doesn't mean you have to." Asher gently takes the body from my grasp. I can finally breathe now that I no longer carry him, but the breath I take is soul-shattering. *Fuck, this is so messed up.*

"Please be quick," Aurelia says, startling me out of my thoughts.

I nod curtly. "Watch over our sister," I stress, following Ash out the door.

We walk hurriedly, stopping at a black wooden door, which Ash directs me to open so he can walk through. I trail him down a curved ramp, chilled by the coolness of our decent underground.

The last few steps in the castle's morgue are bitterly cold, and I can't stop my teeth from chattering. I silently shadow Asher to an empty room made of steel, our reflections distorted on every surface.

"Redmond," Asher speaks, greeting a fae wearing an apron and strange-looking goggles. They glance up, surprised.

"King Aidos! I would say it is a pleasure to see you, but I suppose we do not find ourselves in the right place for that."

Asher solemnly agrees. "I believe you are right, sir."

"Who might this young fellow be?"

"Calix Lightcrest," I proclaim, my voice sounding harsher than I'd desired. "Intelligence Agent of the Legacy Compound, and our friend."

"I am grieved for your loss," Redmond states, taking Calix from Asher's arms and lying him on a silver slab of metal.

"This is my mate," Asher tells him, gesturing toward me.

"Queen Aidos," he exclaims, bowing at the waist. "My sincerest apologies. I did not know you'd claimed a soulmate, my king."

Ash calms him with a wave of his hand. "Don't worry. It's all quite new."

"It must be, seeing as I hadn't even heard of a nuptial announcement."

"I'm so sorry to be rude, but my sister is unwell, and I'd like to check on her," I say, cutting their conversation short.

"Certainly," Asher replies. "Apologies, Redmond. We must go with haste."

"It is I who must apologize. Be well, my king and queen." Redmond bows again, turning to face his abundance of tools I don't wish to think about.

"Come, Astraea," Asher encourages me with a hand at the crook in my back. "Let's get you and your sisters taken care of."

"I'm fine," I quip over my shoulder as we ascend the ramp.

Asher leans past me and opens the door for me, ushering me into the hall.

I quicken my pace, my mind whirling and trying to swallow me until I can't think at all.

"Stay with me," Asher soothes. He takes my hand in his as we walk side by side.

"I'm with you," I respond, biting my lip nervously.

"We are all going to be all right."

"Just not Calix."

"Sorry, Starlight. I should be more careful with my words."

I sigh as we reach Aurelia and Ravena's door. *"Don't hide your thoughts for my sake, Ash. The stars know I've got plenty of questionable things floating around in my head."* I squeeze his hand reassuringly. *"I know you weren't thinking of Calix. Thank you for taking care of my sisters."*

"They are my family now. I will always take care of them and you."

My heart sinks in dismay. *"Until we leave them..."*

"Even then, they will be cared for. We'll make sure of it."

"Promise?" I ask, hopeful.

"Promise."

CHAPTER 71

ASHER

"I can't believe you're mated," Aspen squeals, clearly very excited about the newest addition to our family.

"I can hardly believe it myself," I admit, rubbing at the back of my neck.

Astraea and her sisters wait in their room adjacent to my office, the healers having already gone and confirmed that Ravena is healthy and sure to wake within the night.

"And Astraea?!" Aspen gasps, their eyes looking at me in disbelief. "What are the chances you are mated to the legacy you've been pining over for the last decade?"

I throw my hand at Aspen and roll my eyes. "It hasn't been that long."

"Oh, spare me. Since you turned twenty-one and set off on your first solo mission, all you've cared to speak of is Astraea the Star, the beautiful, wicked legacy you found in the woods. You'll be thirty-one soon enough, Brother. It's been a decade."

"What was that about a wicked legacy?" Astraea asks, strutting through the door to the office where Aspen and I sit.

My sibling snickers. "He's also described her as fierce, alluring, enchanting, wild…"

I kick Aspen's chair, scooting them a foot back.

Aspen only laughs harder.

"Please, do go on," Astraea coos, making her way to my desk and sitting on the edge like a feline poised to strike.

"Deadly, powerful, the only one capable of ruining his heart for all others… Shall I continue?"

I groan, letting my face fall into my hands.

"No," Astraea drawls. "I think I've got the gist of it."

Aspen laughs, a bright beam on their face as they clap at my expense. "I like her!"

"Of course, you do. She is, in fact, all those things and more," I say. "But she's especially fond of provoking me."

Aspen snorts. "Oh, and I'm sure you absolutely *hate* that."

Astraea chuckles, and I lift my hands from my face to find her wicked eyes on me. She is perfect.

"Glad to see you smiling, love."

Astraea's eyes soften imperceptibly. *"Thanks for being my reason."*

"Are you two doing that mind-talking thing again?" Aspen asks animatedly. "Wait!" They halt, both hands raised. "Please don't tell me you two were making googly eyes at each other because of inappropriate dialogue. I do not need to know about that."

Astraea's fantastic eyes turn on my sibling now, who unmistakably senses the heat of Astraea's might. "Don't ask questions you don't want answers to."

Aspen gulps. Astraea cracks a grin.

"Be nice," I tell her..

Astraea rolls her eyes. "I am teasing you, Aspen."

Aspen breathes a sigh of relief, rubbing at the back of their neck. "Thank Oasòs."

Astraea laughs, shaking her head. "You know, I think we're going to get along just fine, Sibling."

My heart swells in my chest at Astraea's acceptance of Aspen, my family.

Aspen smiles wide, their eyes crinkling with joy. "I am glad to know that, Sister." Aspen looks at me with delight. "I am so thrilled my brother found his soulmate." They turn back to Astraea, pure happiness written on their face. "And I am so glad it was you."

"Careful," Astraea warns. "Wait until you get to know me before you profess your love."

"I already know all there is to know about who you are to my brother," says Aspen. "He knows he's lucky."

Astraea raises her brow. "Is that so?"

I stand from my desk, drawn to her side. I tug her chin toward me. "Absolutely."

"Do you still think you're lucky when I'm being wicked?" she asks.

I bend down and press a gentle kiss to her lips. *"Especially then. I like your wickedness."*

"Ew!" Aspen steps out of their chair and scurries away from us.

"What?" I keep my sights on Astraea.

"I can see your nasty thoughts by the look in your eyes. I am out of here."

I chuckle darkly, then grab my mate by the waist and throw her across my desk. "Good idea," I say, just as the door to my office closes with a bang.

Astraea paws at my chest, dragging her nails through my shirt. "You'd better behave, Trouble. We have things to discuss."

"Mhmm." I dip low to kiss beneath her jaw.

She sighs, allowing us a small moment of respite.

"Ravena is still asleep," I remind her. "We have time before convening with the Fae Council."

She laughs, swatting my chest as I kiss her neck. "Be that as it may, you and I need to decide what we'll reveal before we discuss with them."

"I've already spoken to Nemesis about it. He's stated his opinion, and I must agree," I tell Astraea, slowly pulling away, my chin grazing her jaw before I meet her regard. "We tell them everything."

"And if they do not believe us, consequently, not siding with us?"

"They will be on our side, Astraea. My court believes in me. I've spent my entire life making sure I never failed them, and they respect me for it. They will surely listen to what the dragons have to say, and they will likely all choose to support us."

"And those who don't?" she pushes.

"I will ask them not to intervene. My court is not like most, Astraea. They are kind and follow my rule."

Astraea exhales heavily, biting her lip.

I reach down, tentatively rubbing her lower lip with my thumb. "Don't fret, my queen. There is not much I can guarantee regarding the other species' regions, but the Fae Court's support is something I can promise."

"Okay." She lifts her chin, asking me to accept her love.

I move my hand down her neck and close the distance, peacefully kissing her soft, warm lips.

"Ash," she whispers. I greedily savor the way she calls to me.

"Yes?" I look deep into her Aegean Sea eyes, watching them glimmer.

Her breath hitches as her inner brows lift, an unmistakable vulnerability in her gaze. "I love you," she says, the words lighting my soul on fire. I would never tire of hearing that—a long-held desire made real.

I hold her face between my palms, her warm, soft skin against my rough hands. "And I love you, my light. My darling, beautiful mate."

Astraea shivers, a glaring mirroring of how I feel. "I'm scared, Ash."

"I know." After some hesitation: "Me too."

She bows her head gravely. "We lost Calix in the blink of an eye. I am used to death, but this is getting more and more personal."

"I won't let anything happen to you or your sisters, Astraea. I will protect you."

She smiles sadly, a single tear falling from her lashes. "I'm scared I'll lose *you*."

"Never."

"You can't make a promise like that," she says.

I pull her into me, loving the way she fits perfectly in my embrace. "I would promise you all the realms if you so much as ask for them. Do not mistake me. I mean it when I vow to you that I will protect you and us. You will never lose me."

Astraea quivers, then wraps her arms around my waist and hugs me with all her might. "Okay," she murmurs into my chest.

"I vow to love you, protect you, and cherish you forever," I whisper atop her head. "*Forever*, Astraea."

"Forever," she repeats.

CHAPTER 72
AURELIA

"You're sure you'll be all right?" Astraea asks for the third time in a row.

I wave her away. "Raea, I'm fine."

She stands in the doorway, Asher just out of sight, as I hold onto the doorknob. "I can stay with you guys," she offers again.

"Astraea," I stress her name, giving her an incredulous look. "Ravena is passed the fuck out. I'm tired as hell and could use the rest, too. If she wakes, I promise I'll go get you."

My sister grunts, finally bowing her head in agreement. "We're just across the hall," she tells me, her brow furrowed in what I recognize is immense worry.

"I know," I assure her.

She moves to leave but hesitates. "You're positive you don't want me to stay?"

I sigh, smiling at her. "I am absolutely positive." I reach out and squeeze her shoulder. It's our thing, our way of reassuring one another. It seems to work a little, the tension in her posture easing.

"Okay," she says, looking down at our feet, avoiding eye contact.

"Go spend time with your mate," I say. "Things are unsettling right now. Take advantage of this time together. V and I are just going to snooze the night through."

Her mouth quirks half-heartedly. "Snooze well."

I titter, matching her grin with a teasing smirk of my own. "*Don't* snooze," I murmur suggestively, waggling my brows.

Astraea slaps my hand that clings the doorknob. I shake it out complainingly.

"Touchy."

Asher comes into view, tugging on the back of Astraea's shirt. "Let us go now," he insists, hauling my sister out of the doorframe.

I smile happily at the pair, so glad they've found a little light in these dark times. What they have is rare, and it's only the beginning.

"Goodnight," Astraea calls, before entering her and Asher's room.

"Night, Sis."

CHAPTER 73
ASHER

As I guide my mate into the bedroom, I walk around her and close our door. Astraea turns around, and I observe her usually stoic face animate in pure shock.

"This is your room?" Her mouth hangs open.

"This is *our* room." I take her hand, loving the way she laces her fingers with mine with effortlessness. She allows me to lead her into the foyer.

Astraea blows an impressed breath, outwardly stunned. "This isn't just a room. This is the size of a house. Just look at the bed!" She gestures at the overly large four-poster bed, the blue canopy shimmering around the silver bedding.

"I do live in a castle, darling. It comes with perks such as these." The smirk I wear is confident, one I know gets under her skin in a way that makes her warm.

"Is that a clawfoot tub in the middle of your sleeping area?" Astraea runs to it, tracing her fingers over the rim of the marble tub. "This is *huge*. Who on Earth needs a tub this big?"

I come up behind her, bending to press a kiss to her cheek as I clasp her between my arms. She turns her head to side-eye me. "I like nice things. I covet them." I give her a knowing look, and her eyes taper to dangerous slits.

"I am not known to be *nice*," she says. "Certainly not when referred to as an object to be coveted."

I laugh. "Astraea, you are everything to me."

She grumbles, darting her eyes gauchely before deciding to elbow me in the ribs.

I cough, laughing at her viciousness. I nip at her shoulder and she arches against me. "Wicked as ever."

"Troublesome, as always," she counters, turning in my arms to face me. She presses her hands against my chest which sends a bolt of lust through my veins. I delight in the sensations as her hands trail up and around my shoulders, stopping to rest with her arms wrapped around my neck.

I lean down, angling our faces so that we're only inches apart, our breaths mingling. I tug at the bottom of her shirt, desperate to skim my fingertips over her enticing skin.

"Like I said," she says, "very troublesome."

"Just shut up and kiss me already."

Astraea grins, slowly angling her face, her dark lashes fanning her high cheekbones. Her arms loosen and her hands lower. Just as I begin to close my eyes, Astraea reaches down, rips off my belt and tosses it to the floor.

I gape at her, not having seen all of her movements for how fast they were. "Well, that was hot."

Astraea tauntingly bites her lower lip and I nearly pass out. She is the most alluring temptress in all the realms.

"Take your pants off, Aidos," she orders.

My heart thunders wildly in my chest. She is fire-made flesh, and I burn for her. "Take off your shirt, Astraea Aidos." My voice is so low I barely recognize myself. Saying her name provokes the beast within me, a very prominent, very primal part of me that exhilarates in claiming this woman as mine.

She raises her arms above her head, and I realize I'm still holding on to the hem of her shirt when it rides up her midriff.

I gladly oblige, lifting the material over her head, stunned by the remarkable vision of this living goddess.

"You look like you want to devour me," Astraea whispers, stomach flexing visibly under my stare.

"I want to worship you." I tower over her, trailing the backs of my fingers against her collarbone. Astraea arches into my touch, making my blood thrum.

I reach down and twist the bath water on, never leaving my mate's gaze. Her eyes are heavy-lidded, and her lush lips wear a seductive promise.

"Let me take care of you." The words leave my mouth like a demand, but it is a plea.

Astraea accepts, her magnificent ash-colored hair falling forward, draping across her pert breasts.

I brush her hair back behind her shoulders, admiring her body for as long as she allows me. Her dusty pink nipples harden at my touch, and I find myself stroking them again, just to relish the response.

"Ash," she murmurs, her tone making me shiver.

"Yes, my love?" My voice is barely comprehensible.

"Touch me," she breathes in her melodic voice, a relief to my aching heart.

I run my hands down her breasts, trailing down her torso before grabbing her small waist. Gods, she has perfect curves. I squeeze her lightly, caressing her ample hips, loving the way her flesh yields to my touch here.

"Every time I think you're going to mention my scars, you surprise me by thinking fondly about the area."

"Astraea..." I draw my hand back to the large scar that marks the front of her sternum, curving down to her hip. It's the one she'd allowed me to heal for her. "You are extraordinary, the most beautiful, awe-striking being I've ever known. I've told you before, and I will tell you every time you need to hear it: your scars mark you as strong. I admire you. Believe me, I wish you'd never have to experience a minute of pain, but I know I can't change who you are. You're a fighter, a formidable one. Pain comes with the territory."

Astraea sighs, closing her eyes and leaning into my touch. "You're not so bad yourself."

My laugh tears from my soul, making me wrap my arms around Astraea, if only to squeeze the hurt from her. "Oh, Astraea... ever the romantic."

She grumbles against my chest, pushing me away with her tiny hands. "I remember you saying something about worshipping me," she remarks, raising a provocative brow, her blue eyes aglow.

I chuckle darkly, then remove my clothes and bare myself to her. I watch her jaw tick, and I smirk. I grab the waist of her pants, stretching them an inch from her skin. "Pants off, Mate."

CHAPTER 74

ASTRAEA

The steam from the bath is inviting, but even more so is my mate, who sits in the tub, waiting for me to join him. He sits with his back pressed against the tub wall, his inked chest glistening with water. One arm rests on the lip of the tub, the other outstretched to me. I take his offered hand, carefully stepping over the rim, the hot water surprising me at first. Asher helps me down between his legs, my back to him. His large palm flattens against my stomach as he pulls me to lay against his broad chest. I groan, reclining my head back as my muscles loosen in the warmth.

"Have I ever told you how much I like your tattoos?" I ask, lazily tracing the designs on his arms.

"Do you?"

"Very much," I tell him. I trail my fingers over him, my hand sinking below the water to slip over his muscular thigh, then up to his knee, which is raised above the water's surface. "I find that I quite like a lot about you."

"Lucky me," he murmurs in my ear.

The press of Asher's cock grows against my ass, sending a shiver up my spine—a promise of what is to come.

"Oh, you'll be coming," he purrs, and I gasp a little.

His hands glide against my skin, caressing every inch of me. I tilt my head back until I spy him, finding his lustrous eyes fixed on me. His ice-blond hair darkens when wet, artfully curling to frame his chiseled face.

Never leaving my gaze, Asher's hands glide lower, trailing over my hipbones and making me squirm.

I inhale shakily, arching up as he seizes my pussy, cupping it possessively.

He grins down at me, a fragment of shadows leaking into his eyes. "Mine," he whispers, and as if on command, my legs part that much wider.

I pant, my nipples cold as they surface, the water lapping over them only when I stir.

Asher's fingers slip further, causing me to moan as he strokes down my center. "Tell me what you like, Starlight."

I reach up behind me, grabbing the back of his neck and lifting myself up his chest. Our eyes meet, hot with need, our breaths intermingling. One of his arms clutches my waist as the other continues working my sex.

"You," I confess, my breath gone as his finger flicks my clit. My mouth parts, and Asher dives in, claiming my lips with his. He pushes against me, our noses brushing as he licks my tongue. I groan, using both arms to lift myself higher, my waist out of the water, my body clinging to Ash. My fingers tangle in his wet hair, tugging, greedy—needing, wanting more.

Asher's fingers dig into my hips as he twists me around. He grips my ass in each of his palms, pressing my core against his hardened cock. My hair is plastered against my face, my chest heaving, my breasts aching.

Asher's rough palms graze my nipples before pinching each between his fingers.

"Stop teasing me," I demand.

He groans, planting his lips on my neck, sucking feverishly, making me dizzy.

I grip his hair even harder, forcing his tongue from my skin. "Ash," I hiss, loving that his lips are swollen from my touch.

He grins at me. "Yes?"

"Are you going to fuck me, or what?"

Asher chuckles, biting his lip as he brushes the hair from my face. "Impatient little thing."

I grind against his cock, producing a rousing moan from deep within his chest.

"Are you sure you want that?" he asks. His voice carries a teasing tone, but his eyes shine with a sincerity that makes me pause.

"You want to make love," I say, interpreting his thoughts.

Asher's pulse races, his brows lifting in uncertainty. *"Desperately."* He swallows.

"You don't think I want that with you." It isn't a question. I can read it in his mind.

He looks away, staring at the water between us. "This is all still new, and I don't want our first time to be about lust. I want to *love* you, and I want to be sure that that is what you want from me."

My heart swells, and I release his hair. I cup his perfect face, gently coaxing him to look at me. "I already told you that I love you, Ash. What would make you think *this*," I say, pointing between us, "would be different?"

"This is important to me. I want to make sure both our hearts are in this. I don't want to fuck you. I want to cherish you," Asher professes, his ice-blue eyes soft. "Our souls were meant for each other. We've claimed each other, and yes, we've expressed our love for one another, which I thought I would only ever dream of. But I don't want to take your body, your heart, without your choice."

I smile gently, trying to keep my frustration at bay. "My heart is already yours, Ash. My soul, my heart, and even my body." I caress his jaw, feeling vulnerable, but knowing his mind helps me recognize that he needs this reassurance before taking this step with me. "If you're not ready, I completely understand. But I want you to know that I am. When I claimed you, I claimed all of you. I want to be connected to you in every way." I chuckle. "Even knowing how corny that sounds. I want it *all* with *you*."

Asher enfolds me in his strong embrace. "I don't know what I did to deserve you, but I thank the stars each day that I was made to love you."

I close my eyes, breathing in the moment, safe in Asher's arms.

"Let's get you dried off," he murmurs atop my head. *"And into bed."*

CHAPTER 75

ASHER

I cradle Astraea to my chest, my arms beneath her knees and back, loving that she trusts me enough to carry her. We stride toward the giant bed, passing through the billowy canopy.

Astraea raises a delicate hand, sifting through the soft material. "This is pretty." Her fingers study the wisp-like patterns detailed throughout.

"It's the most precious of colors," I insist, turning to sit on the bed with her in my lap. Astraea's mouth curves in puzzlement as she contemplates the fabric.

"Is blue your favorite color?" she wonders aloud.

I lift a finger, brushing it under her eye before tucking a loose strand of hair behind her flushed, pointed ear. I smile down at her, knowing I hold my whole world in my arms. "It's the most exquisite shade," I tell her, watching her inner brows curve upward. "Aegean Sea blue—like the eyes of my beautiful mate."

A small breath parts her lips as she stares at me with astonishment. "You purposefully commissioned a canopy to match the color of my eyes." She bites her lip, looking up to admire the fabric sheltering us. "When?"

"Does it matter?"

Astraea's sharp jaw flexes, still pointed up. "When, Ash?" Her voice is soft, almost broken.

I kiss her jaw before admitting, "A few years ago."

Astraea's eyes squint. "Are the patterns...?"

I drag her nearer. "Spirit eterì."

Astraea whistles. "That is dedication."

I laugh, kissing beneath her jaw yet again, because I *can*. "I've always known you were special to me," I whisper in her ear. "I didn't realize just how much until these past few days."

Her cheeks flush, making her fawn-colored freckles dance. "I'm sorry I didn't see it sooner."

I kiss her cheek, and she closes her eyes, her lashes brushing my skin. "I rather like our story," I affirm, climbing further onto the bed and taking her with me. "It's a lot like those books you read, but pretend you don't." I wink, earning myself a playful slap on my thigh.

"You really are a creep. You know that?"

I chuckle, lifting the offending hand and kissing its palm.

Astraea gasps, her chest heaving with her breath.

"I am smitten, darling." I kiss up her arm, trailing heated kisses all the way up to her shoulder.

"You were spying on me," she states, her voice hoarse as I lick up the column of her throat.

I nip at her golden skin. "I was keeping an eye on you to be sure you were always safe."

"You listened to the music I like, read the books I read... What else have you done that I don't know of? What do you know?" Astraea's heavy-lidded eyes burn me, achingly delicious, as thin whisps of eterì seep from her hair, making it hover around her.

"I know you train whenever you possibly can, but you give

yourself the night so that you might read and enjoy your favourite treat."

"Cake is everyone's weakness," she remarks, her brows tight as if affronted.

"But it is your little pleasure." I kiss her pulse.

"What else?" she tests me, her curious mind listening to my thoughts.

"You train others out of the goodness of your heart, not because you must. You're often off the clock and still on the mat."

Astraea huffs. "Old news."

I draw her petite hands to my chest. "Your lupus haunts you, and your arthritis is getting worse, but you ignore it all." I rub at her fingers, the joints there curved.

"So, I get ill, and my hands are crooked. It's no big deal," she replies, trying to retreat. "I've been dealing with this forever. I take my pills; things stay regulated. It's fine. I'm fine."

"I wish I could take your pain for you," I say. *"Though I know you wouldn't want me to. You're stronger than you need to be."*

"There is no such thing as being too strong," she responds quietly.

"You love your sisters, and you love your people, and now," I breathe. I press a light kiss to her pouty lips, savoring the taste of her. "You love me, and I will spend the rest of eternity at your side, ensuring I deserve it."

Astraea lowers her gaze. *"I am undeserving of you."*

"Ahh... Your first lie to me." I tsk, grinning. I kiss her again, wrapping my hand around her head, drawing her even closer.

Astraea drapes her arms around my neck, pulling herself up and giving in to my touch. "I'll do the same, Ash. I swear I will spend eternity making sure I deserve you."

Her vow is my undoing. I can do nothing to stop myself from lifting her and lightly tossing her into the mattress. The silver blankets cloud around her as her ash hair flows ubiquitously. She raises a delicate hand, cupping my jaw, and I soften under the touch, cherishing it.

"Love me," she murmurs tenderly.

"It is my greatest honor and pleasure," I tell her. It is the truest words I've ever spoken.

Astraea climbs into the blankets, inviting me in. I gladly settle into the warmth, pressing my skin to hers. I lay above her, holding my weight with my arms on either side of her head, admiring how she looks at me.

"Do you have?" she trails, looking at the dresser.

"I take the yearly tonic," I tell her. "And I haven't had a partner since I met you."

Her eyes widen, the blue in them sparkling. "Really?"

I nod. "And you?"

She shakes her head. "I was a teenager the last time. I had what you could barely call a girlfriend when I was eighteen. I haven't found the time or the need to partake since."

"It's kind of fitting," I muse.

Her lips quirk mischievously. "I hope the fuck it fits."

My laugh bursts from my lips, and my heart grows ten times its size when she joins me, tipping her head back and closing her eyes.

"I am the least romantic being on the planet. Nasty, nasty, Reaper."

I kiss Astraea's scrunched nose. "You are perfect."

"Only to you," she remarks, amused.

I stroke her cheek, running my hand down her neck. "I am in awe of you, Astraea Aidos."

Her soft lips part as she gazes up at me, still wearing the remnants of her lovely smile in her eyes. Her hands move, wrapping around my back. I feel the soft press of her nails on my shoulders, indulgent, clinging to me. I will love, protect, and worship her forever.

CHAPTER 76
ASTRAEA

Asher looks at me like I am made of the stars, his piercing blue eyes affectionately caressing me with just a glance. His hands stroke over my torso, giving me frissons with every touch. Though I'd first been reluctant to let my walls down, I can now die happily, knowing I am loved this fiercely.

Ash leans in, his tattooed chest against my breasts, making me tingle as he presses a delicate kiss to my lips. I open for him, greeting his needy tongue with mine. Asher moans, the hum vibrating down my throat. He grows more fervent in his groping, his hands claiming every inch of my skin as our passion ignites. His knee pushes against my thigh, and I gladly part my legs to let him in closer. The enticing press of his cock is at my center, my slick cunt happily toying with him.

"Fuck," Asher grunts, leaving my mouth swollen. "You're so wet." He breathes raggedly, thrusting his hips, making his cock glide up and down, stimulating my clit with each push.

"All for you," I pant, my voice barely recognizable.

He growls, plunging his hand beneath the blankets, finding my clit with his fingers.

I moan unashamedly, arching into his touch, making his cock move harder against me.

He lifts his hand, slowly raising it between us. His fingers glisten with my need. My heart races as I watch his eyes darken, his wicked tongue snaking out and wrapping around his fingers. He moans, closing his eyes and thrusting against me.

"Oh, Gods," I gasp. *I've never seen something more arousing.*

"Hmm..." Asher hums, drawing his fingers out with a sucking pop. "We'll see about that."

One second, he's grinning down at me. The next, he dives beneath the covers, his tongue finding my core.

"Fuck!" I cry, reaching down to grab his hair and drive him closer.

Asher groans and I feel it against my flesh, wetness pooling at my center as he rolls my clit beneath his tongue like it's the most precious jewel. *"You taste divine, Mate,"* he purrs into my mind, lighting my body aflame.

"You feel divine," I pant, my stomach hollowing when he pushes his tongue into my core. With each drive, I buck my hips, the friction causing a storm in my veins, and with every thrust of my hips his tongue reaches further, sending goosebumps along my flesh. When it hits a sweet spot, my toes curl in, and my hands fist in his locks. "Yes! Right there!" I exclaim, unapologetic for how rigorously I thrash beneath him.

"Come, Astraea," Asher demands between thrusts, his tongue plunging and curling, working diligently to make me come undone—quite literally.

"Make me," I insist, pushing into his face.

He growls, the sound more animalistic than fae. With his tongue pressed firm against the spot, the heat rising dangerously high, he commands, *"Fucking come for me, Astraea."*

I throw my head back and roar, submitting to his rule. Asher's tongue moves side to side and against that sensitive spot, wringing out the last of my pleasure as I pant wildly. I pull him up, finding his sharp fangs glistening, his perfect lips red from use. He grins from ear to ear, a wicked gleam in his lusty eyes.

"You cry so beautifully when you come," he proclaims, his voice guttural.

I lick my lips, grabbing his throbbing cock, giving it a tight squeeze.

Asher groans, tipping his head back, his chest heaving.

I stroke him languidly, cocking it at my entrance.

Asher's eyes pin me to the mattress, the ice blue fighting to stay alive against the black eterì that tries to cloud them. His gaze sweeps over me, and I watch with bated breaths as his stare lands where our bodies join. He shudders, and I feel it all the way to my bones. He looks back at me, a slow grin appearing. *"Next time you come, it will be with my name on your lips."*

I bite my lower lip, watching his eyes dart to the spot. *"Is that a challenge?"*

Asher swiftly plunges into me, stealing my breath in an instant. I stare down, finding that he's only pushed the tip in.

"Fuck, you're…" I gasp as he pulls out. "Big." I blow out a long, salacious breath.

Asher laughs darkly, pressing into me again, the stretch burning, but gods, does it ever feel *good*. "And you are so fucking tight, I just might lose myself in you."

I cling to his arms, the muscles rippling beneath my touch as he pushes in and out, getting my body ready for him. "Ash," I moan, hauling him closer.

"Yes, Astraea. Just like that." He clenches his jaw, lowering his body so that we're flush against each other.

I stretch up, kissing his sinful lips. He meets my kiss with fervor, intensifying my desire. His cock thrusts deeper, my core feeling achingly full.

"I don't know if you're going to fit," I exhale shakily, trying to look down between us.

Asher kisses me harder, causing me to melt into him further. "We were made for each other," he murmurs. "Let me in, Astraea."

My body shudders as I wrap my arms around him, relaxing my muscles and welcoming him in my embrace.

"Are you all right?" he asks softly, his hips moving a little more, though gently, for my sake.

"Mhmm," I breathe, finding that the more he moves, the better I feel.

Asher kisses me soothingly before moving my hair from my face. "Tell me what you want, and it is yours."

I smile up at him, placing a shaking hand on his sculpted cheek. "You, Ash. *All* of you."

His brows knit, his eyes filled with awe.

I wriggle my hips, showing him that I'm okay. I push until Ash is seated inside me, our breaths ragged between us. "Move, love. I'm all right now."

"*Love?* I like that." Asher kisses my cheek. He lifts himself so that I'm finally able to see between us. My eyes bulge as I suck in a huge breath. His cock is buried deep inside me, not an inch of it in sight, except for the visible imprint of it in my lower abdomen. *Fuck, he is incredible.*

"You are beautiful," Asher murmurs, then slowly, achingly, he withdraws. When his cock emerges, large and erect, the sight of it glistening, coated in my arousal, causes my chest to flutter. His tattoos wrap down his pelvis, the lined curves ending at the base of his cock. He is perfect, thick, long, and strong, made precisely for me.

Ash laughs, shaking his head at me. "I always knew we were made for one another."

I hug his body closer, inhaling deeply as his cock slides into me again, igniting my eterì. The wisps of black stir in my chest, flowing out to hold Ash. His white eterì surfaces in turn, soft and cool against my skin.

Asher moves inside of me, his lips finding mine in an instant.

I wrap my eterì around his limbs and torso, allowing it to flow through his ice-blond hair. The tension and heat build higher and higher as we cling to one another. I need to feel him, *all* of him, and I know he desires the same from me.

His eterì, cool and light, traces my skin like phantom fingers, pressing into my flesh and leaving memorable marks I'll delight in recalling. Asher's kisses grow fiercer, and I writhe beneath him.

"You're perfect," he growls. He thrusts an arm beneath my back and around my waist.

"Ash." I breathe his name like a prayer.

"Louder," he demands, his thrusts becoming wilder, the slap of our skin an echo in the room. He commands his power to pleasure me in ways I never thought imaginable. My neck, my breasts, my clit, all receive the attention given only to gods. My eyes roll in the back of my head as I give in to all the sensations.

"More," I moan into his mouth, and he takes that as an invitation.

Asher pounds into me so hard that I see stars glimmering in the canopy above. We pant wildly, desperately stealing every feeling offered. Ash's hand slips down, eliciting a gasp from me as he presses his thumb to my aching clit.

"Ash!" I howl, bucking frantically, my body in overdrive.

"That's right," he growls low, thrusting hard, stealing my mouth. *"Scream my name, Astraea. Claim me wholly. Tell the world that I am yours, and you are mine."*

"Fuck, Ash!" I exclaim as he pulls from my lips.

"Hmm," he purrs. "I think my mate can be a little louder." His thrusts are so hard that my body inches up toward the headboard with each push, and it thrills me. "Where's that wicked Reaper I know and love?"

My core spasms around his cock, my body lifting off the bed as my shadowy power bursts forth and my eyes go white. Where my eterì flows, I see and feel, and right now I'm gifted a vision worth worshipping. I can see us together, intertwined and fueled with power, lust, and most potent of all, a love so rare it could shatter realms. "Ash!" I scream, clawing his back with my nails. "Ash! Ash!" I gasp, my control vanishing.

"Fuck!" he roars, hauling me off the bed as he kneels, lifting me up and impaling me on his cock as we both unravel. He holds me so close my lungs are unable to expand for breath. His fingers dig into my scalp, his breath hot on my neck as he buries his face in my hair. "Astraea," he whispers, his voice choked and broken. The white fog of his eterì curls around us, playing with mine.

"I love you," I tell him, a single tear streaking down my hot cheek.

He shudders around me. "I love you—more than anything, more than life. You are my heart."

I cup a trembling palm around his neck, drawing him impossibly closer and breathe him in. "You are mine."

CHAPTER 77
RAVENA

When I wake, I almost let myself relax, curling into the soft, silky blanket around me. I bolt upright with a start, my eyes wide and adjusting to the strange place I find myself.

"It's okay, Vena," Aurelia murmurs, coming to my side with haste. She raises a glass of water out to me, but I can barely look at it. I want to vomit.

"Relie?" I ask, beholding our surroundings. "Where are we?"

"The Fae Capitol." She moves nearer, and I shrink back against the headboard of the unexpected bed I lay in, my legs getting caught in the blankets.

"How long have I been asleep?"

"It's the next morning, V."

I nod. "Where's Astraea?" I dart a look to all the darkened corners of the foreign bedroom.

"Just across the hall, with King Asher."

I swallow thickly, all of yesterday rushing back into my mind at full speed, cutting like razor blades down my dry throat. The terror, the betrayal, Calix… "No," I croak, scratching at my skin that bars me from tearing my broken heart out.

"Vena, please," Aurelia tries, setting the glass on a nightstand and sitting at my feet. "What can I do to make it better?"

My lungs wheeze, and I gape at her with incredulity. "You can't make it better! He's *dead!*" I gasp, feeling the lance of blood well under my nails. "Oh, my stars, he's really dead!"

"She's awake?" I hear Astraea's domineering voice echo through the room, a loud bang reverberating as the door swings to hit the wall.

"I don't know what to do!" Aurelia exclaims, and I only now realize she's trying to pry my hands from my flesh.

"Let me go!" I scream, my throat so raw I can barely get the words out.

"I will not!" Aurelia argues, but Astraea steals her from me. Finally, I think, but Astraea takes Aurelia's place, not as gentle as she pins my hands on either side of my body.

"Calm down, Ravena."

"Don't tell me what to do!" I yell, kicking my legs and struggling to get her off me. She pushes me into the mattress further, using all her strength to keep me down.

"Enough!" she spits. "Calix wouldn't want you to hurt yourself over his death. He was kind, and he cared for you."

"He is *gone.* You can't know what he wouldn't want because he can no longer want anything."

"I know damn well that he wouldn't want this, Ravena. Knowing that you were hurting yourself would be worse than his death."

"You can't say that!" I cry, feeling my body go weak beneath her.

"I can and I will," she grits between clenched teeth. "You can grieve, Sister. You can grieve with all your might, but you will not harm yourself."

"I just want it to end," I sob, feeling my heart splinter even further.

"I know," she says. "But you will avenge his death, instead. You will use this hurt to continue fighting like Calix would want you to do."

A memory flickers to life, the ceiling above me turning into the night sky. Calix said: *"No matter the outcome, I hope you always fight for what's right."*

I whimper, watching the stars disappear.

"Are you okay, my bonded?" It's Nyx. ***"I could hear your cries."***

"Nyx? Where are you?" I respond through our bond.

"I am with the horde, caring for Orion. He is very sad, Ravena."

I whine, having forgotten about Orion. What he must be going through...

"Do you need me?" she asks sweetly.

I inhale deeply, calming myself as best as possible. "No. That is all right. Thank you for taking care of Orion."

"Of course, my bonded."

"Come on, Ravena," Aurelia begs, drawing me out from Nyx's thoughts. Relie steps up beside Astraea, who's relinquished her grip on me. I look her in the eyes, my pain reflected in hers. "Please don't give up," she whispers.

Tears stain the silk I lie in, and the fire in my lungs pleads for relief.

Aurelia offers the glass of water again. I soberly accept, downing half of it in one go. I take ragged breaths, my chest heaving as my eyes dull.

"Let's get you cleaned up," Aurelia suggests. I nod blankly ahead, letting her guide me to a washroom and allowing her to care for me when I surely can't.

THOUGH MY SKIN hums with renewed warmth, my heart still aches —a bitter, unrelinquishing chill. The shower was steaming hot, and it felt good to cleanse the grime of these past few days. My curls finally coil again, and my lungs appreciate the soothing vapors

Astraea popped in to leave a few dresses for me to choose from, courtesy of King Asher. If I weren't still solemn, I might laugh at how our lives had changed. We officially live in a castle; we can ask for anything we want. King Asher is even more doting than Aurelia, and that is saying something. He continues checking in, asking us what we need and bringing us things even when we don't ask for them. There is always food and drink on a small, oval table in the bedroom, and he stocked our closets with tons of clothes and shoes, making sure we feel as comfortable as possible. He also sent assistants to take care of the cleaning, and he himself opened the windows to let in fresh air after carefully hanging each piece of clothing. If anything, I know for sure that my eldest sister will be thoroughly cared for now that they are soul-bound.

A sadness fills my chest that Calix is gone. Though I recognize we weren't destined soulmates, he became very important to me. He was so shy and adorable, and he made me feel so special when he looked at me with his beautiful, intelligent brown eyes. I miss him terribly.

"Ash?" I hear Astraea call, her voice apprehensive. "Ash!"

CHAPTER 78
ASTRAEA

"What is it?" Ravena gasps, finding the king unconscious in my arms.

I hoist him upright, letting his weight rest against my body with a grunt. "I think he's receiving a divinatory guidance."

Ravena's eyes widen as she notes the white wisps of eterì swirling around Asher's feet. "Do you want some help?"

"I'm okay. Just have to wait it out."

"Has he done this before?" Aurelia asks.

"Not in front of me," I blow out a tense breath, still holding onto Asher so he won't fall to the floor. "I've never seen someone lose their balance during. This is strange."

"I suppose I only ever get mine while I'm asleep, so I can't speak on that," Ravena tells me. "However, you and Rel get them when you're awake, and you normally just stand frozen until you snap out of it."

"Exactly," Aurelia says. "My mind drifts to the clouds, but my body remains on Earth, perfectly well."

"My mind finds the darkness, then finds my body the same

way it was when it left it," I explain indifferently. I observe Asher's face, imploring him to wake. "He's taking a while to come back. Maybe we should call for a healer."

"Do you want me to go fetch help?" Aurelia proposes, already taking a step closer to the door.

In the time it takes Aurelia to reach for the handle, Asher gasps loudly, his arms coming to life as they pinwheel around me. I steady him, clasping his waist. He blinks several times, then looks to the side to find what is indeed an unimpressed look, courtesy of *moi*.

"Am I in Oasòs?" he questions, his mouth quirking.

I huff, relinquish my hold, and let him fall. He catches himself on the bed's poster before anything can happen.

Ash tsks. "Naughty little angel…"

His mischievous grin compels me to punch him square in the shoulder. "You scared me, you giant oaf!"

Asher chuckles. "So, she does care for me."

"Why did you collapse?" I interrogate him, crossing my arms over my chest.

"It is unfortunate but typical when Ahemì greets me."

"You received a guidance from the Celestial of Death?" Ravena asks, quietly coming closer to us.

"Yes," he responds brusquely.

My heart thunders back to life, a force that nearly knocks me over. Ahemì's divinatory guidances are few and far between. When he has something to say, it usually pertains to fast-approaching death.

"Was it bad?" Ravena asks, voice small and fragile.

Asher rubs his chin in thought before replying, "It depends on how we use the information."

"Lovely," I mutter, pacing before the large gothic window. The cool wind soothes my searing temper.

"*I don't believe Ravena's heart is well enough to hear the guidance,*" Asher tells me through our mind-link.

"*Understood.*"

"We should all have breakfast and prepare ourselves for this day," Asher announces, gesturing to the pastries and fruit he'd brought to Aurelia and Ravena's room. "It is ten past seven, and we convene with the Fae Council at eight."

"I don't think my stomach can handle eating right now," Ravena whines, her pallor blanching.

Aurelia dutifully withdraws out a chair for our sister, pouring Ravena a glass of orange juice without question.

I smirk tauntingly at my mate, who I'd watched squeeze at least twenty oranges himself to obtain said juice.

"*It was hardly twenty,*" he argues, cocking his perfect brow at me.

"At least eat something small," Aurelia suggests to Ravena, who tentatively chooses a croissant and begins ripping small pieces from its corner, placing them in her mouth.

"Oh, these are delicious," she mumbles, eating a little more ravenously.

"That's the magic of the fae," Asher sings, grabbing one for himself.

"Please tell me we're not stuck in some strange bargain now that I've accepted faerie food." Ravena gulps.

"That is an outlandish myth." Asher chuckles, then passes me the croissant he'd taken. "*Oh, as if this is out of character. Eat, Mate.*"

I purse my lips before taking it from his claws. "*Gladly.*"

"*I'm going to recite the divinatory guidance I received, but I would ask that you refrain from reacting so as not to signal to your sisters that we are having a private conversation.*"

"*You've got it,*" I answer, eating my croissant and humming a tune as I search the closet for something to wear. Asher had thoroughly nagged me about wearing leggings, saying the Council members would be dressed formally and I should try to match his attire.

"To embrace your beloved is akin to embracing your death, for she shall unify with the boundless realm of Oblivion. In your pursuit to keep a star, be prepared to relinquish all that you hold dear. Yet, rest assured, for in your resolute choice, loyal eterìan rulers stand by your side, unwavering and steadfast. The moon fast approaches. Which path will it light?"

As Asher's voice dims, my hands skim across a sleek black dress adorned with silver detailing. I quietly remove it from its hanger and close the closet door behind me to change away from prying eyes.

"Astraea?" Asher searches.

"I'm fine," I tell him. *"I'm just... thinking."*

"There is nothing to think about," he replies curtly.

I slip each of my feet into the dress and slide it up, reaching behind to zip the back. I am flexible and manage to get the bottom half up. I groan, frustrated as I lose my grasp on the slider.

A small crack of light filters into the closet, and I turn to find Ash looking down at me with concern. *"Let me help you."*

I scuttle backward, my face tingling with shame. *"I... I don't want my sisters to see my back."* I never want them to see the scars I've received and the pain I've suffered in protecting our people.

"They're both in the restroom applying rouge," he informs me, his brows lowering. *"Let me in, Astraea."*

I exhale a shaky breath, then turn so he can help me with the dress.

"You should leave, Asher," I insist, feeling the thoughtfulness he puts into zipping the dress up. He trails his fingers up my spine, then moves my hair to the side, resting it over my shoul-

der. I feel him draw closer, my skin prickling as he presses a featherlight kiss to the top of my spine.

"My soul made a decision about you long before I even knew it." He breathes, then gently turns me around to face him. *"Do you really think I could let you go, knowing what it is to love you?"*

I shudder beneath his touch. *"Ahemì said you're going to die at my side."*

Asher frowns. *"No. I don't think he did."*

I scoff. *"Sounds to me like I'm destructive, and if you stay, I'll take you down with me."*

Asher tugs on my hair before returning it to hang down my back. *"I think,"* he begins, leaning down until our lips are but a breath away, *"when you piece our messages together, you'll find that they all beckon you to claim your position with Oblivion."*

I gulp, searching his gaze as his lips teasingly brush against mine.

"You want to know what I think?" he asks, his voice low.

"What?"

"I think Nemesis was wrong about Phaðs, and they eagerly await your arrival."

I step back, hitting the rack of clothes. *"Wait, what?"*

Asher purses his lips, thinking. *"I believe Phaðs is alive and well, and they are the answer to all our problems."*

"But they're supposed to be dead."

"No," he corrects. *"They didn't go into Oblivion—they've become it."*

CHAPTER 79
ASTRAEA

The sparkling Council Chamber lies in the heart of the Fae Court's Capitol. Atop a giant hill stands a tall, gothic cathedral, lofty vines trying to swallow it whole. There is only one room inside the cathedral, so the Chamber is large and echoey as we accept our seats.

The Council has already taken their places in a rounded row on a platform. The table is slim, connecting them together as they sit in highbacked silver chairs. It seems the rumors are true —the fae love their shiny silver.

Asher helps me and my sisters take a seat, moving extra chairs for us and adding them to his right. Naturally, Ash takes his place in the center. Aspen tries giving me their seat, but I politely decline. There's no reason for me to take their place, as there's a seat on Ash's right for me. My sisters are fine next to me. None of us need to sit next to Asher when it is Aspen's rightful place. Aspen has earned it. We legacies are just happy to be included.

"Esteemed Council, I express my gratitude for gathering with me and my companions. Before we proceed, would you be so kind as to present yourselves along with your distinguished titles, allowing us to become better acquainted?"

The person furthest to the left stands, a petite blond with shorn hair. "Greetings, and may I be the first to say, welcome to the Fae Court."

I incline my head, giving them my best smile.

"I am Sun, I use ze/zir pronouns, and I am the Minister of Immigration and Citizenship," ze says, beaming at us with a gap-toothed grin. Ze appears incredibly friendly; I hadn't expected that from the Fae Council. I assumed they'd be severe, but they appear contented, visibly absorbed in this meeting and unbothered by our presence.

"Hello," says the kind-eyed council member next to Sun. "I'm Tariq, he/him, and I'm the Minister of Health." Tariq's happy expression grows, his brows slanting into his headscarf, his hazel eyes conveying how honored he is to be here.

Next stands a tall, lean, and heavily tattooed member. "I'm River, and I go by he/him. I'm the Coastal Minister. I oversee the fishing industry, manage waterways, and supervise the Coast Guard and Freshwater Fish Marketing Corporation."

"Basically, he always smells like seaweed," someone snorts. The rest of the Council snickers, making River roll his dark, monolid eyes.

"Enough about fish," says a pale, blue-eyed, round-faced member. "I'm Zoya, she/her, and I am Minister of Public Services." Zoya rests her hands on her hips, as if incredibly impressed by her role here. I internally chuckle—her mannerisms remind me of Aurelia.

"They're either going to love or hate each other," Asher comments.

"Great."

"Hi! It's nice to meet you all," chirps a sweet-voiced member, their blue eyes astoundingly bright in contrast to their light brown skin. They have a very soft appearance that suits their voice. "My name is Parineeti, and I am the Minister of Science and Innovation. I go by she/her." She smiles shyly, her eyes lowering. She doesn't seem to like attention. Strange for someone of such importance.

"She's new at this," Ash informs me. *"She's only twenty-three."*

"That's how old Aurelia is. Wow... Well, good for her." That is impressive. The fae can potentially live to one hundred and fifty, even two hundred years old. It's shocking for a twentysomething fae to be so advanced in their career.

"You're advanced and in your twenties," Asher remarks.

"Well, that's different."

"Whatever you say, Starlight."

"The name's Freya," a tall, muscular redhead rises, giving us a two-fingered salute. Their hair is long, save for the right side, which is shaved to their shining white scalp. "I'm content with she/they for pronouns, and my specialty is in Workforce Development."

Aurelia shrinks a little further into her seat, and I watch her reaction from the corner of my eye. *Looks like someone's got a crush.*

The person beside Ravena waves from their seat, almost matching her height. It's rare to see fae any shorter than five foot five.

"Good to meet you all," they say, their pouty lips forming a genuine smile. "I'm Zoren, he/him, and I'm the Minister of Fae Court Revenue and Finance."

Ahh. So, he's the money guy.

"Don't go getting any ideas, Mate. The money's technically mine. He only handles it."

"Oaf." I gingerly reach over and pinch Asher's thigh.

He flinches, chuckling darkly in my mind. *"Violent little thing."*

"*Shut up and let me pay attention. Someone else is talking, and I didn't get their name.*"

"*That's Aziz. He's the Minister of Public Safety.*"

I nod, pretending I heard the dark, bearded man's introduction. He seems a little more reserved.

"*His mind is likely on the several dragons that lay in my castle courtyard,*" Asher supposes. "*He handles public safety.*"

"*Right. That would be worrisome.*"

"Hello," speaks a calm, smooth voice. My eyes immediately draw to the lips that had uttered the greeting.

They might be a siren with a voice like that.

"I am Imani, she/her, and Minister of National Defense," she drawls, leaning forward to rest her dark, muscled forearms on the table. Her long black twists sway, joining her arms in front of her.

"*She is a siren fae,*" Asher says. "*I'm surprised you can tell.*"

I scoff. "*Seriously? She might as well be singing her words. They're so melodic.*"

"*I hadn't noticed,*" he replies, and I sense he's being honest.

I eye him. "*You didn't notice the beautiful enchantress' beckoning call?*"

"*Nothing is beckoning to me, my Star. Nothing but your light.*"

"*Ash,*" I whisper, squirming in my seat. Can my organs melt from too much sweetness?

"*Let's not find out,*" he answers, laughing.

"She/her," says a golden-skinned goddess, returning our attention to the room.

Shit. "Who's she?" I ask.

"*Indigo.*"

Indigo points her aquiline nose up high, her long brown hair tumbling in loose waves around her shoulders. "I am Minister of Agriculture, and my business is prioritizing the welfare of farming families, the prosperity of the Fae Court, and the preser-vation of our environment."

"Hi, I'm Jade—she/her," announces an enthusiastic council member. Her hands are animated in greeting, her gorgeous afro bouncing atop her head. She has a bright red piece dyed in the front, framing her pretty, angular face. "And I am the Minister of International Development and Trade!" she exclaims, clasping her hands together. Her smile is infectious, and if I weren't so sullen of a person, I might have returned an excited beam. Instead, I control myself, nodding with a polite smile.

"And last, but hopefully not least," the member furthest to the right begins, causing the group to chuckle. "My name is Devi. I go by she/her, and I'm the Minister of Emergency Preparedness. Essentially, you need me, but you don't *want* to need me," she remarks, smirking. Her black curtain bangs shake when she laughs, falling into her coffee-colored eyes, which are slightly darker than her smiling cheeks.

"You all know Aspen and I, so I'll graciously give the floor to Astraea," Asher decides, sweeping his large hand toward me. "My mate and your queen."

Murmurs sound raucously, echoing up into the cathedral, making my ears ring. Everyone immediately stands from their chairs, the metal scraping against the marble floors. They all take a knee, lowering their heads.

"Umm..." I swallow, feeling a little too warm in my seat.

Asher smirks. *"They'll stay down till you tell them to rise, Queen Aidos."*

"Uh, please get up." I cough. *So much for being queenly.*

My mate lifts my hand and kisses my knuckles. *"No matter what you do or say, you are still queen of the Fae Court."* He pats my hand, and I'm glad to see everyone retake their seats, though it is piercingly quiet.

"Well, this is an uncomfortable introduction, to say the least," I mutter. I then widen my eyes, my heart hammering. "I mean, not that I don't appreciate this... this—" I stammer, gesturing to the Council, who listens attentively to my ramblings. I take a steadying breath. "Sorry," I huff, shaking my head. "I am new to this."

"You're doing fine," Tariq assures me, his gentle gaze encouraging.

"You're the general of the Legacy Legion," Imani drawls. "This should be a walk in the garden compared."

I snort. "You might be right."

Everyone snickers lightly, helping put me at ease.

"Okay, let's try this again," I insist. "Hello, esteemed Council," I begin, trying to imitate Asher's regal tone. It stirs a few more giggles from the council members, and I feel the strain in my body alleviate. "I am Astraea, she/her, and it sounds as though you already know who I am, so I'll save you the gory details. Just know that I'm the general of the Legacy Legion—or so I *was*, before they cast me out."

"What?" Freya gasps. Many of the members seem just as shocked as she looks.

"We've got a lot to catch you up on," I speak frankly. "Before we do, I'd like to introduce you to my sisters," I hold, pointing to Aurelia and Ravena, who hang off the edge of their seats, engrossed in the happenings of the Fae Council.

Aurelia waves awkwardly, trying to avoid Freya's gaze. "My name's Aurelia," she starts, then looks down into her lap before adding, "But I like being called Lia."

What? Since when?

Aurelia, or *Lia*, flicks her long blonde hair over her shoulder and continues, "My pronouns are she/her, and I used to be a healer for the Legacy Compound."

Used to be... There is so much I've fucked up in the last few days, but the worst of it is realizing I've single-handedly ruined my sisters' lives.

"You didn't ruin their lives."

I ignore Asher, knowing well the consequences of my actions.

"Hi, everyone," Ravena says, fixing her glasses on her round, tawny face. "I'm Ravena, she/her, and I'm the head botanist of the Legacy Compound's Healer Division." Ravena flinches, throwing a hand over her mouth in shock. "Oh." She exhales. "Well, I guess I *used* to be, too."

CHAPTER 80
ASHER

Now that the Council is up to speed with everything that happened in the past week, we can focus on action.

"So, our goal is to get the Compound to reconsider their actions," Astraea explains, her arms crossed and pursing her perfect lips. "If the legacies fall in line, we have a better chance of overpowering Urðra. We know she won't end this willingly, and we'll likely need to involve the other celestials, but that's an issue for another time." The lights above illuminate her prominent cupid's bow, and I yearn to kiss it.

"Like Nemesis said, the more people we have on our side, the better the outcome," I tell the Council. "To be frank, it's highly probable we won't succeed with the legacies, so we need to devise a strategy to get as many people as possible from each species to fight with us if and when the time comes. We need to spread the truth about the Asherian War and the dragons, so that everyone understands what's needed in order to stop Urðra and save our world."

"And that is giving the dragons the same freedom we all have

—the freedom they deserve," Astraea proclaims. My chest fills with pride as I watch her assume a leader role at my side. She is a natural-born torchbearer, and I am all the more enamoured by her for it.

"We need to join forces with as many fae, nymphs, orcs, lycanthropes, and vampires as possible, in hopes that many will fight at our sides when the day comes to battle the celestials, not only their underlings. The best way to do that is to go to each territory ruler and ask them to lead their people in the right direction. We also want to be sure that the vulnerable are informed, and can hide if they cannot fight."

"So, we divide and conquer," Imani states coolly.

I nod. "Just so. I have good-standing relations with the Highlands Enclave and the Vampire Empire. Nasir and Leander won't be difficult to sway."

"The vampires do have a knack for violence," Astraea huffs, smirking.

I chuckle knowingly. "Their emperors especially."

"The lycanthropes never put their snouts in danger, though," Astraea remarks. "What makes you think they'll join us so easily?"

I smirk, reclining in my chair before putting an arm around my mate. She tries to shrug me off, but I won't budge.

"Because Atlas Loupart is my closest acquaintance," I state casually.

Astraea grimaces. "Are you telling me the leader of the highlands is your friend? He's a hermit."

I shrug nonchalantly. "Most would think."

"He's not going to come out of hiding for something like this. If we want a chance at getting a pack on our side, we should be going straight to Spain and request Fenrir Vale's support," Astraea maintains. "Especially if we want numbers and fighters."

"Trust me. *That*, you definitely don't want to do."

Astraea looks at me questioningly but evidently decides not to pursue it further—for now, of course.

"You know me so well," she quips through our thoughts.

"You wouldn't believe how well."

"All right," Sun replies. "Since you know the whole fae population will undoubtedly support you, we don't need to worry about that."

"Since the Compound is so close to our territory," I say, "I suggest we evacuate our people."

"We'll be sure to inform the Court and catch everyone up to speed," Aziz promises.

"Absolutely," Jade agrees, nodding.

"If you and the queen will cover the vampire and lycanthrope territories, that leaves the nymphs and the orcs," Zoya lists on her fingers.

"We'll want to have someone go to the capitol to request an audience with the queens in both respective territories," I state.

"My sisters can handle going into the Capitol of the Nymph Wilds, since they are both members." Astraea looks at them expectantly. "You two go there occasionally and can certainly manage, correct?"

"Yes, absolutely," Ravena answers, surprising me. I can sense her soul is filled with sadness, but perhaps making herself useful will help give her purpose. "But is it really safe for us to split up?" she continues.

"I'll be sending guards with you both," I assure them. "And, of course, you'll fly with your bonded dragons."

"Thanks," Astraea whispers.

"Um, actually…" Aurelia stammers, raising her hand as if she's in a classroom setting.

"Yes, Aurelia?" I ask, seeing that she won't speak until someone allows it.

"If it's all right, I think I'll take care of working with the Orcs."

I watch as the entire Council whips their heads in Aurelia's direction. My sister-in-law shrinks under their baffled regard.

"And why might you do that, Aurelia Nox?" Astraea asks, her voice hard.

Aurelia waves her hand casually, though her face shines with anxiety. "Oh, you know... I've got *connections*."

Ravena gasps. "Oh, my gods, Relie! Is that who you were talking about the other night?"

Aurelia swallows hard, making a sad attempt to cover her embarrassment with a smile. Her cheeks turn a bright red and I instantly come to understand the inuendo.

"An orc?!" Ravena screeches.

"Do you have relations with an orc?" Astraea asks, confounded.

"Orcs, plural," she corrects.

Ravena pinches Aurelia's arm, laughing at her sister's expense. "Girl, you are brave."

Aurelia flicks her hair and crosses her arms. "They aren't all bad."

"They eat nymphs like you," Ravena counters exasperatedly.

"That they do," Aurelia mumbles under her breath.

"Relie!" Ravena huffs, trying to hide a blushing smirk. "Not appropriate."

"Well," I speak, clearing my throat. "I guess that settles that. Who do you know in the Orc Lands? Can they take you to their fortress to speak with a noble?"

"Well, here's the thing," Aurelia begins, darting her eyes uncomfortably. "One of them *is* of noble blood."

"No way," Ravena murmurs excitedly. "Who?"

"Well, you know Keziah Shadesteele?" Aurelia asks coyly.

"The orc princess?!" Astraea and Ravena exclaim in unison.

Their sister rolls her eyes, visibly becoming annoyed. "Well, her and a few of her friends."

"I think that settles it." Freya whistles, cocking a knowing brow at Aurelia.

"Yeah," Astraea huffs, a slight smirk tugging at her lips as she assesses her youngest sister. "I guess so." From what I can gather of her thoughts, Astraea is equally impressed and concerned that her youngest sister has the bravery to involve herself with orc nobility. Every territory is protective of their royals, the orcs especially.

"Well, now that that's settled, I'd like to introduce you to the dragons," I tell the Council, earning their exchanged murmurs of curiosity. "Unfortunately, you won't be able to hear what they're saying because, as I've explained, they can only communicate with bonded riders. But I would like to include them in our conversation, since they have much to do with our current situation and future."

"It's only right," says Sun, overtly eager to see the legendary beasts.

"Will they try to attack us?" asks Aziz.

"No, no," I assure them all. "They are on our side. They are looking forward to meeting their allies."

With a bright smile, Devi says, "I don't know about you lot, but I'm certainly looking forward to this introduction."

"Follow me."

CHAPTER 81

AURELIA

As I follow Asher and Astraea through the castle grounds, the Council and Ravena at my side, judgment seems to tangibly emanate off my sisters. This is precisely why I didn't ever tell them about my extracurricular activities. So what if I enjoy a little danger? Besides, they know Keziah from her years of studying at the Compound. She's safe enough. It's her friends who are a little unrestrained, but, to be fair, they don't spend much time outside of the Orc Lands, and aren't used to fraternizing with people outside of their species.

Keziah Shadesteele is the princess of the orcs. Vizhen, Queen of the Orcs, wed a naiadian legacy, therefore making their daughter Keziah a legacy, too. She'd only spent her early years at the Compound, deciding to move to the Orc Lands immediately after graduating.

We'd bonded a few years back on a camping trip. Some jerks were chasing birds for fun, and Keziah and I quickly put a stop to it. The bird had stayed to play with us for a while, drifting serenely in my air eterì. It was peaceful.

Keziah is peaceful, but she is definitely not gentle—especially in the bedroom. My cheeks heat as I reminisce about our involvements—alone and with her friends. I like her friends. They are always in good spirits, though the drink could have something to do with that. Therein lies the issue. When we're sober, it's like our intimacy doesn't exist, which is why I didn't tell my sisters about Keziah, nor Oshin and Storm.

I'm beginning to realize I desire more from them. I want a real relationship with feelings and affection, not just sexual intimacy. I want it all with them, but when morning comes, they all pretend like nothing happened. I'm stuck in a dream.

"Lia," Idris greets me as I enter the back courtyard, where the dragons wait.

"Hey, Idris," I say on an exhale, making my way to him before leaning against his massive leg.

"Why so glum?" he wonders.

"It's nothing." I shrug, looking down at my feet.

"Ahh..." he hums. **"They will only understand what you desire from them if you tell them so, Lia. If you haven't spoken of it, you cannot assume they do not want a romantic relationship."**

"Ever the wise, Idris." I snort. He has a point. But I'm too scared to bring it up. I have a dark suspicion that, if I do, I'll lose the illusion in my head and my friends, too.

"We are going to the Orc Lands," says Idris.

I peer up at him through my blonde bangs. *"How did you know?"*

"Not only are your thoughts loud, but King Asher and Nemesis have been conversing with us all." Idris huffs a plume of smoke which surrounds me and his feet. *"Have you not been listening?"*

"Should I be?" I kick a few loose rocks with the toe of my shoe.

"Clear your mind, Lia. We have a mission ahead of us."

I sigh heavily, looking up at the group. *"I know."*

"We leave at first light tomorrow," Asher announces, drawing me out of my stupor. "Aspen will lead the Fae Court in my absence. I trust you will all care for our home while I am gone."

"Yes, King," the Council agrees in unison.

"Very good," Asher responds, then turns to me.

My eyes widen, and I tuck my long hair behind my ear.

"I'll assign your guards tonight and get you acquainted as soon as possible," he says, looking to me and Ravena for approval.

"Thank you, King Asher," Ravena says.

I nod, smiling uneasily. "Sounds good."

A few Council members laugh, and I blink away my humiliation. Regal life is not meant for me. I am made for the forest, where no one judges, and all are welcome. It's too bad I'm not going to the Nymph Wilds with Ravena. It would have been nice to step into that familiar wood.

"You are being helpful by going to the orcs," Idris encourages me. **"It is unlikely any of the others have such good relations with a noble of their kind. You are doing something good, Lia."**

"I know, I know. It's why I offered."

"I'll be at your side, my bonded. Do not trouble your mind with your restless thoughts."

I pat Idris' leg. *"Will you be fine tonight?"*

"Indeed. I am with my horde. Do not worry for us, little legacy. We are strong and mighty. It is others who should worry for themselves in our presence."

"Says the softest dragon I know," I say, raising my brow at him.

Idris shifts his head, his chest puffing out as he sniffs. **"We shall see who is soft."**

I giggle, smirking.

Suddenly, Idris lifts his paw and flicks me with the back of his claw, sending me tumbling several feet away. I land on my ass, dust stirring as I sit and stare at Idris.

"Not nice, dragon."

Idris raises his head, making audible chortling sounds.

He's laughing at me.

"It's not funny!" Thankfully, the Council have departed, but unfortunately, my sisters and the fae king are left to torment me.

"What the hell did you do to deserve that?" Astraea asks, a ridiculous smirk on her face.

"Nothing at all!"

"Nemesis says you called Idris soft," Asher comments, picking imaginary dirt from his shoulder. "Which is likely less than a compliment to a dragon."

Ravena snorts, holding a hand in front of her mouth. "Oh, Relie..." She sighs, then offers her hand to help me to my feet. "He's literally the opposite of soft," she apprises me, eyeing the dragon horde.

"Stop it! He *is* soft," I counter, staring up at the green beast with onyx eyes as I dust myself off. "You *are*."

"Not as soft as you," he answers, his own dragon-smirk playing on his scaly face.

CHAPTER 82

RAVENA

When alone, I drown in sorrow. The shower's steam is kind to my lungs, but each breath is never quite satisfactory.

Calix is dead.

I can still hear the sickening squelch of the arrow piercing him. Malek had meant for it to hit *me*. It makes me sick to think about it.

I spend longer than necessary combing conditioner through my locks, letting the warm water cascade down my back. Calix's last words replay in my mind, echoing through the large shower stall.

"Keep wishing on stars. I'll always answer your call."

I exhale, the water turning from warm to room temperature, a sign I've used all the hot water. I grudgingly rinse my hair and step out, preparing for the day.

Once we moved into his castle, Asher provided everything we'd ever need and more. The clothes I wear are a perfect fit. My dress is lavender, the lightness contrasting my complexion. I love bright colors. I don't especially feel like wearing my favorite color today, feeling guilty for finding any pleasure, but after much consideration, I acknowledge that Calix wouldn't want me to be so sorrowful.

He'd always been so kind and thoughtful. He wouldn't want me to linger on his death. Perhaps I could give him a proper funeral tonight before we leave for our next mission. The idea settles a bit of peace in my heart, and I decide it's a worthy idea.

I lean closer to the bathroom mirror, applying mascara and warm brown lip gloss. After scrunching my hair in a towel, I plop my curls with a bit of curl cream. They'll dry naturally, and fairly quickly, so I don't have to worry about styling my hair. Grabbing my glasses, I set them atop the bridge of my nose and give myself a once-over in the mirror. I still look tired, but more refreshed than the night before.

Turning to face the door and grabbing the knob, I steel my spine, closing my eyes. I can do this. I'll tell Astraea I'd like to hold a small funeral for Calix, and we will celebrate his life. I twist the door handle and step into Aurelia's and my room. My sisters perch on the edge of the bed, facing me, looking stunned as I approach. It doesn't evade me that those two have kept secrets regarding the man I was falling in love with. He's gone now, and though I know I shouldn't think it, I wonder if the outcome would've been different if my sisters had come to me with the concerns instead of keeping it to themselves. I would've told them Calix surely wasn't the conniving backstabber they assumed he was.

When Aurelia explained the situation to me earlier, telling me about the journal, I wanted to tear my heart out. The words written in the journal were so evidently similar to what Malek had been muttering all along. How hadn't they seen that? Why would they just assume that Calix was planning to kill one of us?

The better question would be, why didn't we realize Aurelia had succeeded in healing Malek when she'd given over her eterì? He fooled all of us, pretending he was still ill from the broken bond between him and his deceased dragon, Erebus. All this time, we had had an enemy in our midst, wholly unaware and trying our best to aid him. I coddled him, hand-feeding him when he pretended that he couldn't do it for himself. Just the thought of it makes me nauseous.

We're still unable to figure out how Malek planned his trickery. Who is working with him here on Earth? We know from Astraea's divinatory guidance—from Urðra—that our mother had known this day would come, and had planned whatever this was long ago. How Malek knew, how Malek worked to get the Compound against us while he was away in Freìre with us, I can't fathom.

"You look nice, Vena," Aurelia says to me.

I look down at myself, then back up to them with determination. "I would like to hold a funeral for Calix tonight."

Astraea's brows furrow, her mouth pressed tight. "I understand, but I hope you know we cannot hold a true funeral here, Ravena."

"I don't want a crowd of people giving insincere sympathies to people they don't know."

"Rightfully so," Astraea says. "So, what do you want?"

"Just us," I tell her. "And Asher."

"That can certainly be arranged," Astraea states. "His body's being kept in their morgue. It hasn't been cremated. Ash thought you should be the one to decide what's done."

I swallow hoarsely, the air in the room growing cold. "Calix was a naiad and a water wielder. He should be sent into the water if he cannot be buried at the Compound."

"That's a good idea, V," Aurelia encourages me softly.

"We could spread his ashes off the coast."

"Then it's settled," Astraea vows, standing and straightening her posture. "I'll make the arrangements and come find you when all is prepared."

A single tear trails down my cheek. I wipe it away, feeling the quiver in my voice before I speak. "Thanks, Raea."

"Of course."

CHAPTER 83
AURELIA

When a knock sounds at our door, I swiftly rise and hurry to answer it. I'm shocked to find three strangers, accompanied by the king.

"Aurelia, may we come in?" asks Asher.

"Of course," I respond, opening the door a little wider and backing away.

Astraea glides to my side, her usual daunting pose at the ready. "Who are they?"

"These are Eagan, Zade, and Rana," Asher explains, pointing to the strangers. "They're the guards I have appointed to you both."

Ravena creeps closer, quiet on her toes. "Hello," she says in greeting.

"Good evening," answers the fae closest to her.

"Hello," greets a tall blond with beaming eyes. "I'm Eagan, the fellow assigned to whichever one of you is called Ravena."

Ravena waves shyly. "That would be me," she reveals, nervously fixing her glasses.

Eagan bows with a tattooed hand on his stomach. "Lovely to make your acquaintance."

"And you must be the special Aurelia," says a tall, slim, dark-haired fae, their eyes seeming to size me up. The way they'd called me *special* was prickly. What in the world had I done to piss this one off?

"Um, in the flesh," I say, my throat dry.

"I'm Rana," they state irritably, their body language full of agitation.

Astraea cocks an unimpressed brow at Rana, who wears a bored expression. "Congratulations."

The other guard stifles a laugh. "I'm Zade," they say, reaching out a strong-armed hand. I take it, shaking their firm grasp. Their medium-length brown hair falls forward into their hazel eyes.

"Why do I have two guards, but Ravena only gets one?" I ask, pointing out the apparent difference.

"Precisely my question." Rana huffs.

"It's because you're heading to the Orc Lands which are not your home territory, Aurelia. I felt it better to be safe than sorry," says Asher.

Rana scoffs, unimpressed. "I told you I could take care of it myself. What trouble could one measly girl get herself into?"

Wow. What a lovely first impression.

"Ignore her," Zade insists. "I usually do."

"Because he's an idiot," Rana retorts with a hiss.

"Enough." Asher sighs, irritated, throwing a tired hand against his forehead. "Am I going to have to separate you two, or will you behave and take your duties seriously?"

"I always take my duties seriously," Rana answers, straightening her back. "You can count on me to get the job done."

I catch Zade closing his eyes and pinching the bridge of his nose before he gives me a knowing look. I'm thankful he's accompanying me, too. I don't know how well my trip would have gone with just Rana at my side.

"Good," says Asher. "Does anyone have any questions?" He looks from me to Ravena, giving us this chance. I don't know about V, but I have a million questions, none of which are important. I understand what I'm meant to accomplish, and that's all I need to know.

"Do we have a plan for where and when we'll all reconvene?" asks Ravena.

Right. Oasòs above. I should have thought of that.

"I planned to ask you all if you'll agree to meet back here by Sunday," Asher returns.

"The seventeenth?" Astraea clarifies.

"Indeed. By flying with the dragons, the five days should give us enough time to sort things out. Even so, we shouldn't linger in the other territories for too long. The full moon is fast approaching. We'll have but a week to gather our strength and approach the compound and, concurrently, the celestials. Whether you manage to get your designated territories on our side or not, we'll need to make plans for further action soon."

"Agreed," says Astraea. There's no room for argument. These are the facts.

"Yes, that's fine," Ravena confirms.

I nod. "Sounds good to me."

Rana regards me, peeved, and I feel like shrinking into myself. I square my shoulders, trying my best not to show my cowardice.

"Then it's decided," Asher proclaims, clapping his hands together. "I trust that you'll all rest as much as possible before we begin our next adventures. Should you need anything, just ask."

"Thank you, King Asher," Ravena says.

"Yes, thank you," I add. "We appreciate all your help. Really."

I know the thanks isn't enough for what he's done for me and my sisters, but I don't have anything else to offer him. He doesn't seem to mind as he shrugs, smiling brightly.

"It is my pleasure," he says. "And the least I can do for family."

King Asher is too kind. Astraea is lucky. I peer at my eldest sister, amorously regarding her mate. They are good for each other.

"Very well," says Asher. "If that is all, I shall leave you to your affairs while I prepare for this evening. I will come find you when it's time."

CHAPTER 84

ASHER

"Everything is ready for us," I tell Astraea, who paces back and forth in our room.

"He's been cremated?" she asks, biting her lip.

"Yes."

"What about the urn? Do we have one for him?" she asks. "We can't just pack him up in a box. Ravena will want something nice."

"I hand-selected the urn myself."

"Good, good," she mutters, still burning a track in my floor. "Did you get the permit?" she questions, stopping to point an interrogative finger at me.

"River made sure we're following code. He's told us where to go and where we are allowed to scatter Calix's ashes."

Astraea groans, her shoulders so tight I can feel it myself just by looking at her. "Okay. All right."

I stand, staring at my fearsome mate—the woman made of spirit, the brightest star in all the galaxies. "Come here," I insist, beckoning her toward me as I reach out my hand. She hesitates, but finally places her delicate fingers into my palm. I note how her knuckles have reddened, the skin around her joints turning white when she flexes. "Have you been taking your medication, love?"

Astraea's hand stiffens in mine, but she doesn't withdraw. "Yes." Her answer is short but adequate.

"You look like you're in pain."

That causes her to wince, and she backs away from me. "I am not weak, Aidos. Do not act like you haven't seen me fight through far worse."

"There has never been a day in my life that I've ever thought of you as anything less than strong."

"Then why point out this flaw?" she snaps, folding her arms over her chest.

"You are not flawed because you live with illness. You didn't give yourself lupus nor arthritis."

"You just told me that I look like I am in pain. I don't appreciate being called weak."

"Gods, Astraea. Experiencing pain doesn't make you weak. That I've seen you injured countless times and watched you continue to fight should tell you I know how resilient you are. Fighting, living, and breathing through pain is a sign of strength in itself. You are intimidatingly tough. Do not put words in my mouth."

Astraea flicks her eyes away, refusing to meet my gaze.

"You are the strongest person I know."

My mate scoffs, a tiny but encouraged smirk trying its best to tug her lip up. "You'd best believe it."

I chuckle. "Stop shutting me out, and let me worship you how you deserve."

"Worship, you say?" Astraea hums, turning on her heel to face me better.

"Yes, my queen."

"You just love throwing that title around, don't you?" Astraea thinks through our mind-link.

"It is my second favourite," I admit.

"And the first?"

"Mate. *My* mate." I stride toward her, loving how she remains tall, looking down at me even though I am much taller. I smirk, watching her eyes light. I grab her by the waist and pull her to me, our bodies flush against one another. "*My* Astraea."

Astraea laughs an utterly divine laugh.

I lift up her defiant chin. "Do that again."

Astraea's tongue sneaks out, wets her lips. Her eyes search mine, and I let her look her fill.

"Your laugh is bliss, and your smile is Earth-shattering."

"Of course, I got stuck with a romantic fool," she jeers weakly, her true thoughts shining through the surface.

"Fool?" I feign a blow. "You take that back."

Astraea snickers, that smile illuminating her face again. "Never."

CHAPTER 85
RAVENA

The ocean waves undulate, creating a symphony as if to pay tribute to the reason behind our presence. We find ourselves under the cover of night, the peace and quiet of the Fae Court solace to my pounding head. I walk with my sisters, one on either side of me, as I tenderly enfold Calix in my hands. His urn is beautiful, a silver vessel with ornate detailing depicting the sea, the edges rounded with vines. It's very fitting for Calix, and though I can't imagine he'd like that he is in there now, he would have appreciated its beauty.

We arrive at the edge of a rock cliff, only a few feet above the shore. The wind blows caressingly, my hair floating about my face. I have cried a thousand tears, and still they come, causing my curls to stick to my cheeks.

"Would you like to say anything, V?" Asks Astraea. "Or would you like some privacy?"

I shoot my head up, eyes wide. "N—no," I stammer. "Don't leave."

Astraea squeezes my shoulder.

"We're with you," Aurelia assures me, her voice gentle.

"We all are," Nyx says from behind me.

"Thank you," I whisper, closing my eyes and taking in the crisp night air. The sea breeze is cool, a refreshing salty wind.

I step closer to the threshold, peering down at the dancing sea. The waves are dark yet full of life. I hug Calix to my chest, letting myself feel everything. It's the only way I will grieve healthily, and it will allow me to let go in time.

I hear an achingly broken whimper, and know Orion has joined us. By the sound of his cries, Calix's bonded dragon suffers immensely. I hadn't even thought of him while I was wrapped in my grief. I turn to look at him; his once-deep indigo scales now a pale blue. His head rests on the ground, smoke puffing from his mouth and nose with each distressed sniff. My heart breaks for him.

"I'm sorry, Orion." I start to weep.

He whines, turning his head into himself.

I face the ocean again, trying my best to muster courage. My chest clenches as I close my eyes, letting the saltwater breeze cool my tears.

"Calix Lightcrest was, as his namesake implies—a light over this starving, gloomy world," I speak, my voice growing stronger. I smile into the distance. "He was kind, the gentlest of souls, and clever. Gods, was he ever clever? That man was the smartest, most thoughtful person I've ever known. He dedicated his life to learning and had a real passion for helping others, even when no one was watching."

I swallow hard, my tears flowing freer as I choke on a sob. "He was trying to protect us, and we didn't get to appreciate him for it. And he died because of it. I will forever be grateful for his efforts, even if they were his demise. Calix gave us a chance to save the world. And—" I sniff, removing the lid from his urn. "And he sacrificed himself to save me. I promised him that, no matter the outcome, I would always fight for what was right.

He allowed me to continue fighting, and I will not let him down."

I raise Calix's urn to the skies, staring at the stars. *I hope you're okay up there, Calix. Thank you for saving me.*

The weight beneath my hands lessens as my eyes catch the beautiful green vines wrapping around Calix's urn. I gasp, and turn to find Nyx kneeling in respect, vinery growing from the crown of her head and helping me carry this heavy burden. It's the first time I witness her eterì manifesting, and it's touching that she's called it to aid me in this moment of strife.

"Are you ready, my bonded?" Nyx asks gently.

I sob and bow my head, my fingers tightening against the silver metal. The wind gusts from behind, and my hair tumbles forward to follow Calix's ashes into the sea. I stare as they dance in the sky, the stars brightening as the ashes scatter.

Aurelia nears from behind, wrapping her arms around my shoulders and turning me into her. I cry in her embrace, my emotions high as I bid farewell to my sweet, brown-eyed, dimple-cheeked friend.

"I'm so sorry, V," Aurelia whispers as she hugs me close.

"I know," I reply, my voice wobbly, but the tears have finally begun fading.

"I am sorry for your loss, Ravena," Asher tells me. "For what it's worth, I'm glad he protected you. He was good."

I wipe my face, looking up at my sisters and Asher, who stand at my side. I am hurt that they kept their secret from me, but I can see their regrets and sorrow in the depths of their souls. I understand they were looking out for me, just as they are now.

Astraea gazes wistfully up at the sky, her face aglow in the moonlight. She inhales deeply. "May Oasòs greet you among the stars," she whispers. "Thank you for saving my sister. May you find peace in the afterlife."

My heart weeps as I stare up at the stars with Astraea. "Do

you think he's looking down at us from up there?" I wonder, hiccupping on my words.

"Absolutely," Aurelia answers, definite.

"I wish I could see him, just to know he's all right," I whisper longingly.

"Look," Asher exclaims, pointing up toward a vivid light.

My hand flies to my chest. A large, brilliant star shines wildly, flying across the sky.

Orion bellows, his head lifted to the stars, the light illuminating his precious face. His call is a sound of liberation and relief—it's how I feel, too. I watch as he closes his eyes, tilting his nose up as far as it can go.

I move closer to him, resting my palm against his leg.

Orion's muscles relax, but he keeps his head to the skies.

"Hi, Calix." I wave at the star, my lip quivering into a watery smile. "You're so bright." I laugh, feeling it warm my soul. "I'm glad you are safe. Thank you for everything."

CHAPTER 86

AURELIA

The moon shines through the open bedroom window, a cool breeze ruffling the long silver curtains. My sisters and I spent the evening packing for the days to come. Astraea's clothes were moved into her and Asher's room the night before, so she opted to help V and me in here first. The fae king graciously granted us an entire wardrobe of custom-made clothing. I would never know how *he* knew exactly what we needed and what would fit. He seems to have a knack for the finer things in life. Perhaps clothes and shopping are his passions. I snort, thinking about Raea, my training-attire-only sister, soul-bound to a prissy king.

"What's so funny over there?" Astraea asks, as if she can hear my thoughts.

"Nothing," I answer demurely.

"Do you have enough socks and underwear, Relie?" Ravena probes, rummaging through my rucksack.

"Worrywart."

"It is a valid question," Astraea helps me fold my pants into compact piles so they'll fit better in the bag.

"*Do you* have enough socks and underwear?" I ask, turning the question around on Ravena.

"Of course." She pushes her glasses up the bridge of her nose, her brows raised matter-of-factly.

Hypocrite.

Astraea dusts off her hands before placing my bag at the foot of the bed. "I think that's everything. We'll pack the food in the morning before we head out."

I nod. "Sounds good."

"Knock, knock," calls Asher, rather than rapping at the door.

"Come in," Astraea responds, meeting his stride halfway.

"Do you have all you need?" he asks us.

"And more." Ravena whistles, looking about the room.

Since we'd moved in, Ravena and I had made ourselves comfortable, leaving our new things strewn about. The room is tidy now that we've gone through our things, packing what we need and returning the things we don't.

Asher hums thoughtfully. "Good, good."

"I already told them we'd take care of the food come morning," Astraea explains.

Asher chuckles. "Always one step ahead of me."

Astraea smirks, a response on its own.

"Well, if you don't need anything more, I think I'll leave for respite now," Asher says, his hand moving to rest on Raea's waist. "Will you come now, or should I leave our door unlocked?"

Astraea looks at me and Vena questioningly.

"We're going to get ready for bed, too," I assure her.

"Go get your beauty sleep," Ravena teases, throwing a wink at Raea.

She scoffs in turn, throwing a thumb over her shoulder at Asher. "He's the one who likes that crap."

Asher pretends to be offended, lightly tugging on Astraea's

hair. "Come along, Sleeping Beauty, before I curse you to sleep for a hundred years."

Astraea rolls her eyes, walking away with the swish of her hips with Asher trailing behind. Looking over her shoulder, she says, "If I'm to sleep for a hundred years, who would win this war?"

Asher shakes his head. "Good point."

Their voices fade as I hear the click of their door across the hall.

Ravena hops into bed, pulling the covers up under her chin and sighing heavily. After locking our bedroom door, I move to the giant window, shutting and securing it.

"They're really in love, aren't they?" Ravena murmurs reflectively.

I turn a smile at her. "I think so."

"You think you and I will find that someday?" she asks.

I exhale, kicking off my fluffy green slippers. "I hope."

"Me too," she replies dreamily, pulling back the silk covers so I can slip in beside her.

I reach for the lamp and turn the light off, throwing us into darkness. The room is lit only by the moon, which slips past the heavy curtains.

"Tomorrow..." she begins.

"Yeah," I murmur.

"Are you sure you want to go to the Orc Lands instead of coming to the Nymph Wilds with me?"

I roll onto my side, facing her. She does the same, her hair a curly masterpiece atop her head as she rests her cheek on her folded hands.

"I've been there a couple of times," I justify, trying to put her at ease. "It won't be any different than going to the Nymph Wilds."

"It's not your territory, Rel. Not only that, but Malek and

whoever else he's working with could attack you and we'd be none the wiser."

"Yeah. Same goes for you."

Ravena sinks further into the bed. "I know, and I'm scared."

"You have every right to be," I assure her, though it can't be comforting, for it has the opposite effect on me. "Thankfully, you'll have Nyx for transportation and Eagan guarding your side. Odds are you'll be fine."

Ravena blows a dry laugh. "Odds...the likelihood of something going wrong is far too probable for my liking these days."

"You can't think like that, V. You're only setting yourself up for failure." I sigh, laying back to stare at the ceiling. "We're going to make it. We have to."

"I hope you're right."

CHAPTER 87

ASHER

"Do you need anything, love?" I offer.

Astraea strides out of the restroom, her long ash-colored hair freshly blown out and her skin refreshed and glowing. "I am fine, Ash."

"Fine isn't good," I counter, pursing my lips. "Do you need anything? Better yet, do you *want* anything?"

She pads over to the bed, a slight limp to her step before she jumps up and flops onto her back, her arms splaying out like a star. "I *need* to sleep. I *want* to lie awake and review strategy and prospects."

I look at her fondly as I caress her long, golden legs. I lift them, before sitting at her side and placing her feet on my thighs. I hold her swollen ankles carefully, spreading my warmth into the joints.

"Mmm," Astraea hums, closing her eyes. I admire her long lashes, which fan her prominent cheekbones. "That feels nice." Her lithe form melts into the bed, the muscles in her legs finally relaxing.

"Have you taken your medication?" I ask.

She nods, her eyes still closed. "Before my shower."

I rub her feet, taking extra care to show her joints the love they need. My poor mate aches, and there isn't much I can do to help. "You're shaking more than usual."

"It's the steam from the shower. I'm fine."

"How is it that you're able to train and fight morning 'til night with aches such as yours?" I ask. I cannot help myself.

"Because my eterì is strong and heals me as I go. You know that's how it works."

"Yet it only heals that which is inflicted by an outside cause. How do you manage the fight while your trembling, or while your joints ache?"

Astraea grumbles, punching the comforter. "I just do. Stop pitying me, Aidos."

"Astraea, I worry about you," I admit, running my hand up her leg. "I care for you, and it hurts me to see you in pain. Whether it be as small as a paper cut or that giant gash you were hiding from everyone before you let me help you."

"I am used to pain. It's manageable. I am clearly stronger than you think."

I chuff. "Then you're the strongest being in all the realms, because I already think quite highly of you."

Astraea slowly sits up, reclining on her forearms, her lean torso stretched before me. "Then stop worrying about me."

I offer her a tender, sad smile, one I hope she understands. "That, I'm afraid, will never happen. But I'll try to do it in a better fashion."

She rolls her eyes, tugging on her feet. *"Sap."*

I chuckle, watching her crawl up toward the pillows, relishing the way her back curves, her perfect ass held high for my viewing.

"*Trouble.*" She tucks herself into bed, seemingly content. Her leg snaps out and kicks me in the rear, startling me.

I toss the blankets up, jumping into bed with her. "*Wicked little witch.*"

CHAPTER 88
ASTRAEA

s we lay together, sharing in the warmth of our embrace, Asher lightly runs his fingers through my hair, playing with the ends between his fingers.

"You know, I've been thinking," he begins. "Since I can hear your mind whirring, why don't we go over all the divinatory guidances you've received as of late? Now that we have more information, we may find something that wasn't there before when we were still entirely in the dark."

I worry my lip, watching Ash's hands flex as he gently glides them from my hair to my face, cupping my jaw. His thumb lightly brushes my lips, sending a warm, tingling sensation to the tips of my toes.

"Will you share them with me, Starlight?" Asher requests. It's a gentle nudge, and though I know he could simply filch them from my mind, he respects me enough to ask permission.

I kiss the pad of his thumb, earning myself a sweet smile from my mate. *My mate.* That is still going to take some getting used to.

Asher watches me tentatively. "You're awfully quiet."

I sigh, shutting my eyes and appreciating his closeness. "I'm savoring this moment."

Asher chuckles, and I sense him drawing closer, the bed moving beneath us. He presses a gentle kiss to my eyelid. My lashes flutter, surprised by the touch. Asher moves to do the same to the other, softening my heart.

"What was that for?" I ask breathily, opening my eyes to find his aligned with mine. The icy blue never seizes to take my breath away.

"Savoring the moment," Ash answers, repeating my sentiment.

"I—" I begin, my words choking my throat. *I love you, Ash.*"

Asher beams at me with pride, pulling me closer with one big hand wrapped around the back of my head. "I'll never tire of hearing that."

I laugh. "I didn't even say it aloud," I remark, trailing my finger over his tattooed heart, committing the patterns to memory with every stroke.

"But you *meant* it," he tells me, reaching for my hand and pressing it firmly against his chest. His heart beats beneath my palm, a steady rhythm, strong, just like him. "That means the world to me, Astraea." Ash strokes his thumb over the back of my hand, the motion extremely soothing. "And I love you, *all* of you, just the way you are."

Impishly, I slap at his chest. "Okay, Mushy-Mush. Enough of this, or else I'll barf." I smile coyly at Asher, who pretends to be appalled. *"Or maybe I'll never find a reason to leave this bed."*

Asher grins wolfishly. The predatory smirk reminds me that my fae mate would gladly accept that invitation—if it weren't for our mission come morning.

I sigh, rolling onto my back and out of his reach, flopping my arms out on either side of me. "The divinatory guidances began coming to me more frequently the night of the battle in Dieppe," I say, turning my mind to more important things.

"Not more important, just more pressing," Asher corrects, following my thoughts.

"Anyway, the one I received on the cliffs was from the Celestial of Wisdom," I state. "Though she seldom counsels my carnage, I can't imagine that guidance being from anyone but her." I'd thought it over many times since I'd first heard it, and though it was odd for C'tarð to involve herself in my violence, I really couldn't imagine it coming from anyone else.

"What was it?" he questions, lying on his side with a hand beneath his head and looking down at me.

"*Embrace not death. Seek instead solace in knowledge. Let wisdom be your guiding light as you navigate the challenges ahead. Have faith in your instincts, for they will lead you to greatness.*"

"I agree. That's Wisdom," says Ash. He likely has a good understanding of this since he, too, is ruled by the spirit eterìan sector. "What else? Count them all."

"Well, this one you already know," I tell him. "*Never trust fire, for your fate is to be consumed by its destructive flames. The vast expanse of Oblivion eagerly awaits your arrival, beckoning you to claim your rightful position amidst the celestial tapestry among the stars. You, Astraea the Star, Spirit of my Spirit, shall forge your own path and shape your destiny, transcending the limitations imposed by mere Earthly existence. Be prepared.*"

"Yes. That one, I clearly remember. It's struck a chord with me." Ash frowns. "I've been trying to uncover all its hidden messages since you spoke it."

"You really think Phaðs is alive?" I ask. He nods, and it lights my curiosity. "If it is them, why haven't I ever received a divinatory guidance from them before now?"

"I imagine they've been waiting for the right time," Ash supposes.

"Do you think Nemesis knows?"

"Doubtfully. But I do think we should tell him."

I cock a brow at him. "You fully, unreservedly trust him?"

"We can see into his mind, Astraea. What more could you ask for you to give him your trust?"

I ponder that momentarily, and though Nemesis hasn't shown any signs of malice toward us, I don't necessarily trust that that couldn't change at any point.

"He's our bonded. That should count for something."

"It does," I assure him, exhaling a long, exhausted breath. Even though we didn't know bonded existed until a handful of days ago. "But," I say, "if Phaðs is alive, who's to say Nemesis will keep us instead of them?"

"That is a problem for another time, love. Besides, I think Phaðs is on our side. I think they've been planning all of this, right down to this very moment between us, for a very long time."

I roll my eyes. "They're not the Celestial of Fate."

"They're the Celestial of Creation," Asher counters. "That is far more than fate could ever be."

"And you think the Celestial of Creation, or, now Oblivion, gave me a divinatory guidance," I reply thoughtfully.

"I do, indeed."

I bite my lip, considering all it could mean. I work through the guidances word for word, shifting each, searching for their meaning and landing on one particular phrase.

"Did you notice most of the people who were against us at the Compound had fire eterì?" I note, running my mind through that day, play-by-play. I sit up quickly, my hair fluttering around my shoulders and face as all dawns on me. "That guidance warned against fire, Ash. Perhaps the celestials of the fire sector are working with Urðra."

"This…" he considers, mulling it over. "Fuck." He sits up with me. "You might be onto something, Astraea."

"If that's the case, we are running out of luck."

"For Malek to have been conspiring against us with Urðra, his ruling celestial would have had to play some part in sharing their initiative."

"Well, shit."

"Do you know who they are? Which astrological sign does his birthdate fall under?" Asher asks.

"Take a guess." I cross my arms over my chest, pushing my breasts up, entirely disheveled. I am so damn irritated that I didn't see this until now.

"Sagittarius?" he asks cautiously.

"Ruled by Zephrðn, the God of War himself."

"Well, shit," Asher mimics me.

"Yup." I tilt my head to stare at the canopy, following the patterns of black wisps sewn into the Aegean Sea-blue fabric.

"What was the next guidance you received?" Asher asks, doing his best to keep my mind on track.

"The one from my mother," I hiss, feeling the tension and rage simmering in me. "*I have long foreseen the day when you would betray me, accompanied by dragons at your traitorous side. Should you persist in your defiance and refuse to yield, Fate shall be the harbinger of your demise. Vanquish the beasts. Respite is yours 'til the arrival of the next lunar cycle. Consider this guidance as your lone warning.*"

"Urðra is the traitor. Not you," Ash declares defiantly, defending my honor without hesitation. I stare up at his proud nose, admiring his face's perfect, sharp angles. I appreciate that Asher Aidos is so resolute in his opinion.

"Thank you," I murmur, trying my best to diffuse my anger

and anxiety. I reach out my hand, my heart melting when he hurriedly accepts it, cradling it like it was sacred.

Asher tugs me toward him, and I willingly oblige, enjoying the comfort. He envelops me with his tall, powerful frame, protecting me even in sleep. "For what do you thank me for, my star?"

"For being my anchor," I say, curling into him, my head against his chest, the beat of his heart lulling me to sleep.

CHAPTER 89
RAVENA

Walking into the dining hall is like entering a magical kingdom of its own. Standing inside this spacious room solidifies just how rich and royal my brother-in-law is. The walls around us are perfectly carved brick, extravagant torches and ornaments lining each tall, green stain-glass window that brightens the room. The table in the center of the room is long—without counting, I know there are at least forty chairs, if not more.

Of course, everything is made of silver.

The scent of freshly baked bread guides our noses toward breakfast. We are already packed and ready for our journey ahead. Aspen, Asher's sibling, came to find Ravena and me, showing us the way. Astraea was busy taking care of things with the king.

What I didn't expect was to find a giant, fresh feast, waiting for us to dig in.

Astraea smirks with her arms folded under her bust, shaking her head at her mate.

He ignores her, instead turning to us. In a grand gesture, he opens his arms, a great smile plastered on his face. "Who's hungry?"

"You didn't have to go to all this trouble," I insist, though my mouth waters at the sight of all the delicious foods. There are berries, cream, jams, cheeses, thinly carved slices of meats, and my favorite thing since coming here, croissants. There are water and orange juice pitchers, which I know from experience is the most fresh and delicious juice I've ever tasted. This breakfast looks divine.

"It was no trouble at all," he replies, offering Astraea a seat by pulling out her chair.

"No," she drawls, rolling her eyes. "No trouble at all."

"Ignore her," Asher says, taking the seat Astraea refused and hauling her onto his lap. She yelps and throws her weight into his lap. "She's just angry I made her wake up early to bake these croissants with me."

She laughs dryly. "If only that were all."

Asher chuckles. "She doesn't like cleaning."

"Astraea?" I ask, confused.

Aurelia and I burst into laughter, and Astraea grumbles as she snatches a piece of cheese off a wooden board and shoves it into her mouth.

"That doesn't sound like our sister," Aurelia comments. "That girl's a clean freak."

"Still am," Raea snaps. "That's why I didn't enjoy the mess."

Asher tsks. "Please. It was only one bag of flour."

"That you dumped on my head! I had to clean your mess and take another shower." Her hands fly out with frustration.

"Ahh, yes. Such wonderful memories." Asher kisses her cheek, which reddens.

"Ew." Aspen groans, shoving their plate away.

Astraea seems prepared to respond, but the door to the hall swings open, turning our attention to the guards walking in.

"Good morning," says Asher. "Please. Come join us."

"Don't mind if I do," Eagan answers, pulling up a chair and digging in.

Rana and Zade take places opposite each other, glaring across the table.

"Eat," Eagan orders them, nudging Zade in the arm. "Thank you, King Asher."

"You're most welcome," says the fae king.

"Yes, thank you," Rana joins.

"The biggest thanks," Zade adds, grabbing a buttery pastry for himself. "You always make the best croissants."

Asher snickers, the tips of his pointed ears flushing slightly. "Don't tell the kitchens that. They'll kick me out."

Eagan whistles, but it turns into a laugh. "They could try."

Asher nods, picking up a deep-red strawberry and handing it to Astraea, who gives him a false vexed look. She takes the berry and chomps down in an exasperated manner.

All jokes aside, Astraea's changed, and it's for the better. I would never have imagined seeing her sitting willingly in some-one's embrace. In my lifetime, I could count the times she allowed me to hug her on my hands. Asher is good for her. I'm glad she's learning to accept love—even if she's still grumpy about it.

"How is everyone feeling about today?" Asher asks, ensuring Astraea eats as he hands her pieces of fruit.

"Very well, my king," Rana replies. "Confident as ever that we'll get the job done efficiently."

"That's what I like to hear," Asher answers. "Are there any concerns or questions before we head out? We've only this time to speak on them, so please, if there's anything at all, voice it."

"Yeah, just wondering if we're still meeting back here by the seventeenth," Aurelia mentions.

Asher nods. "Yes. That would be best. And tell those who

agree to fight at our side that they have a place to stay here on the castle grounds."

"Perfect," Eagan agrees. "Will do."

I exhale weightily, looking around the table. Things are light and breezy here, and forgetting what we've seen and done can be easy. It isn't hard to imagine I'm going on an ordinary visit to the Nymph Wilds, but I know deep down that this can go wrong for any one of us. I honestly feel like my sisters and the fae aren't being cautious enough. If it were up to me, I'd choose not to separate into groups, but I do understand that it will be beneficial to accomplish as much as possible with haste. Who knows when Malek and the others, whoever they are, plan to strike next?

"What about you, Ravena?" asks Asher.

"No, I don't have any questions. I know the goal, and I'll do my best to bring back good news."

"Thank you," Asher replies. "I've packed up some food supplies for everyone." He points toward the door where three brown burlap sacks sit full. "I've already spoken with the dragons, and though they were not pleased, they allowed me to set them up with chains linked around their necks, which our bags can hang from."

That's brilliant. I'm not insensible—I know I'm not built to carry heavy weight for too long. Perhaps I could learn to manage with training, but I am out of shape from spending all my time in labs. A four-foot-eleven legacy, with a reverence for sitting and snacking, doesn't bode well for the journey ahead. I'm glad I have Nyx to help me out with transportation.

"I can't imagine Idris was pleased," says Aurelia.

Astraea snorts. "I'm sorry, but your dragon's as vicious as a poodle at best. Have you seen Nemesis?"

My eyes widen, imagining those sharp teeth snapping at

Asher at every turn as he insisted the giant black dragon wear chain.

Asher waves his hand dismissively. "He's all bark and no bite."

Astraea flicks the king's ear, irritated. "Do you forget I fought that motherfucker, and he slaughtered all the soldiers I was with?"

"That's in the past, love." Asher brushes a kiss atop her head. "Things are going to be better now."

Astraea huffs, her brows raised. "Not before they get way, way worse."

"That's some positive thinking, right there," Aurelia admonishes.

Astraea reclines, stretching her legs out and propping her feet on the chair beside her and Asher. "Where's the lie?"

"Raea," I hiss, eyeing her shoes. "That's not polite."

Asher throws his head back with laughter, his chest rumbling so hard it shakes Astraea. He wipes his eyes, leaning over to look at me in bewilderment. "Have you met your sister?"

Everyone at the table joins in the amusement, giving Astraea the drive to push her luck further as she throws her legs up on the table, disturbing the cheese before her.

"Take a good look," she says, plucking a blueberry from a small bowl. She pops it into her mouth and smirks. "This is what you're stuck with for a queen."

CHAPTER 90
AURELIA

"You'll be careful," Astraea insists, pointing at my face. She's agitated, worried to the brim, and taking it out on Asher, who, for his part, is taking it in stride. He's accustomed to Raea's conduct, having worked with her for years when she was Lieutenant-General. The king knows just as well as Vena and I that Astraea is doing her best to keep herself together, trying not to fall apart in front of us.

I give my eldest sister a crooked smirk. "Love you too, Raea."

Her brows knit, her lips forming a hard line. "Don't you dare get hurt," she warns, her voice breaking. I watch dazedly as a tear falls through her lashes, staining her freckled cheek. She wipes it away hurriedly, straightening her spine. "Else, I'll come to find you, and you'll wish you'd listened to me."

I snicker, swatting her pointy hand away, dragging her in for a hug. She goes ramrod straight, her arms stiff at her sides, but I don't care. "You be safe too, Sis."

She retreats, placing a rough hand on my shoulder and squeezing. "Always."

"Okay, enough!" Ravena whines, running toward us on her

short legs, bumping into me and Raea with a thud. Her arms encase us in the tightest hug known to man, making us laugh. She's tiny, but she is mighty.

"You're squishing me," Astraea barks, causing Ravena to cling even tighter.

"Shut up and accept it! I'm going to miss you guys."

I squeeze her right back. "I'll miss you too."

She reluctantly releases us, holding Raea and me by the hand. "Promise me you'll do everything it takes to get back to this castle safely," she demands, her eyes watery beneath her glasses. "Promise, no matter what happens, we'll see each other again."

"Of course, we will, V," I assure her.

Astraea smiles, though it doesn't meet her eyes, causing my heart to sink into my chest. I realize this could potentially be dangerous. There could be people looking for us, ready to strike while we're on our own. I'm thankful we have guards with us— even more pleased by the dragons at our sides. But nothing is really promised, whether my sisters and I say so or not.

"It is time," Nemesis proclaims, his heavy footsteps shaking the ground beneath our feet.

Astraea glances up at him. "Tell your horde to protect our family."

"They will protect them with their lives," he promises for all of us to hear.

Astraea turns to face us again, looking us both in the eyes with a determined look within hers. "I believe in you both." With that, she squeezes our hands and lets go.

She turns to face her dragon, King Asher already astride its back. My sister hops on, accepting Asher's help without a thought. She's come such a long way in just this short week. I hope to see even more of her guard down when next I see her.

Asher waves down at us. "See you Sunday."

Ravena returns the gesture before climbing up Nyx's shoulder, settling atop her purple back.

"Ready, Lia?" asks Idris.

I exhale a breath, steeling my spine as best I can. "I have to be."

CHAPTER 91
ASTRAEA

I can't tell if my lupus is acting up, or if I'm so worried sick about my sisters that it's making me unwell. As I sit atop Nemesis, watching Idris and Nyx fly away with my family on their backs, my lungs constrict, as if there is no air in this world. Sweat trickles down my back as I loosen my collar, trying to let the breeze flow through my leathers. I am overheating, dizzy as hell, and Nemesis readies to propel us into the air.

"Lean on me, love," Asher soothes, gently tugging my shoulders back. "I've got you."

My tongue slows in my mouth, and I barely mumble the agreement that comes out.

"Close your eyes, Starlight."

I accept his command, my back rigid against his chest, the warmth between us almost too much to bear. Just when I think I can no longer take it, Nemesis springs into the clouds, the cool air a balm to the scorching heat.

I swallow hoarsely, the strain in my muscles lessening as Nemesis levels out, the clouds dissipating around us. "I'm going soft," I croak, trying to laugh, though dread is ever present.

"You?" Asher scoffs. "Never."

I blow out my nerves, turning my head to look at him. The banter between us always helps.

He grins. "I am so proud of you, Astraea."

My brows lift, the threat of tears stinging my eyes. "Why?" I whisper.

Asher devotedly wraps me in his arms, and with a heavy exhale, I realize my body is regulating, though the tremor in my hands is ever-present. I need to keep my anxiety in check if I'm going to make it through this. My sisters will survive—I'll make sure of it.

"I am proud of you for everything you've done, how you handle yourself, and how you care for and protect your family. I know it's hard watching them go off into other territories, and I understand that they are not trained to protect themselves like we are. But they do have guards and, most impressively, dragons. Even if something were to go wrong, I can't imagine an enemy getting through Idris or Nyx."

I feel panic stirring, though I pretend otherwise. "Careful not to speak too soon, Trouble. We both know the unimaginable has become more and more realistic by the day. Odds are, something's going to go wrong."

Asher hums, tucking me under his chin. "Then we'll just have to beat the odds."

CHAPTER 92
RAVENA

When I see how close we are to the new patch of land, I know Nyx, Eagan, and I are almost at our destination. The Isle of Man floats dreamily in the Irish Sea, a deserted little island that marks a usual three-hours-left time stamp on my trips to the Nymph Wilds.

Since we're flying by dragon, though, it will take no time at all.

"How long have we been flying?" I ask Eagan over my shoulder for the millionth time. He sports a special solar-powered army watch, which I use to my benefit. For his part, my constant repetitiveness doesn't seem to bother him.

"It's been three hours, ma'am."

"Three?" I gawk. That's incredible.

"I am exceptionally fast, my bonded," Nyx boasts proudly.

"No kidding. You're faster than the speed of light. You must be flying two hundred miles per hour, at minimum."

"Is that good?"

I giggle, petting her purple scales. *"Very, Nyx."*

She whinnies, shaking her head with satisfaction. **"We are almost there."**

"I'd like to stop on that island before we part ways," I say, pointing below. "That's Isle of Man!" I holler over to Aurelia, who rides atop her shiny green dragon with her long blonde hair flowing behind her. Aurelia appears in her element. Rana and Zade sit a few feet behind her, barely avoiding the brush of her strands when Idris twists. "Want to touch down on the island and take a break together before you leave for the Orc Lands?"

We won't have to worry about distressing people, as the place is deserted. It will be a safe place to land with two dragons, without having to dive into explanations.

"Sounds good!" Aurelia calls, a jolt of relief freeing the tension in my shoulders.

Since Relie has to fly over the Nymph Wilds to get to the Orc Lands, Idris and Nyx have stayed together. I can hardly believe we've reached this point so quickly. If Relie were to travel without the help of Idris, she'd have to endure several days' worth of travel. We have to take trains and ferries to get to the Nymph Wilds and Orc Lands. When I visit with my uncle and cousins, the over thousand-mile distance feels like a tedious lifetime. These dragons are supernaturally fast, and I'm grateful.

Now that we've reached the Isle of Man, Aurelia and Idris will leave for Iceland, a much farther distance. I enjoyed these last hours with my sister, and I'm not quite ready to let her go. I'm exceptionally averse to being alone with a stranger and my untrained dragon, and even more worried about sending my little sister off into the Orc Lands.

I pat Nyx's neck, and she aims downward, following Idris's tail.

"Everything all right?" Eagan asks behind me.

"Yes," I tell him, turning to face his direction. "Aurelia wanted to take a break with us before continuing their flight."

He smiles empathetically. "And you needed to see your sister."

I give him a lopsided grin. "She's my baby sister. I worry."

"I understand." He nods thoughtfully. "She'll be okay, though. Don't worry too much. The king sent his best to guard her. I guarantee she'll be well protected."

"Thank you, Eagan. That's reassuring."

Nyx lands softly, and Eagan helps me down. My legs are sore from flying for so long, but they'll feel better after a stretch.

"I am so glad we stopped, because I seriously need the bathroom," Relie says, running toward me and tugging on my hand.

Elms, spruce and the like surround us—nothing else for miles. I trail my sister through the brush, jumping over fallen trees and trying my best to keep up.

"Gods, your bladder is weak," I chide her. She finally slows when the bushes become thicker and the trees grow taller here. This is surely good enough for hiding and squatting.

"It's not my bladder," she groans, holding her stomach.

I chortle, wheezing as I laugh at her expense. "You shouldn't have eaten the cheese at breakfast."

"But it was so delicious." Aurelia sighs with relief when she spots a small hill behind the bushes. This isn't her first time improvising, and anyone who's ever done this in the woods knows you want the stream to flow down and away from your feet.

"Did you think about bringing toilet paper?" I ask.

"Shit."

I chuckle, removing the backpack I'd thought to bring with me and stealthily pass it to her.

She sighs. "Oh, thank Oasòs."

I hurriedly depart, giggling. I'm assuredly not in the mood to listen to her buffoon baboon tune. "How are Zade and Rana treating you?" I ask from an acceptable distance.

"I think they hate each other, and I know Rana hates me," she hollers. "So, obviously, I'm set to have a joyous time."

I laugh at her obvious sarcasm.

When she returns from the brush, she rolls her eyes. "I'm not exaggerating. She's strange."

I nudge Relie's arm. "You can handle her. You're Little Miss Sassy Pants."

Aurelia grumbles, throwing her hands on her hips as we exit the forest.

"Seriously, Rel," I stop her at the treeline before we get too close to our group. "Don't take crap from anyone. What you're doing, going to the Orc Lands, that's difficult enough. You don't need to deal with someone nagging on the back of your dragon. Don't be afraid to stand your ground. Idris has your back."

"Trust me. If Rana keeps her shit up, Idris will be the one to put her in her place. My dragon's sassier than me. Don't forget." She winks, turning on her heel to find him. I trail behind, watching her long blonde hair sway with each step. My little sister is valiant. I wish I were as half as brave as she.

"Idris says they must go now," Nyx informs me. **"The clouds are darkening, and it will be too cold for your companions to fly in the rain."**

As if on cue, thunder strikes off in the distance. I lament, though I understand.

"I guess this is the part where we say goodbye," Aurelia says, a sad smile on her pretty face.

I take her into my arms, hugging the very life out of her.

"I need to breathe, V!" she squeals.

I let go, reluctant, grabbing her hands and squeezing them with all my love. "This is not goodbye. You hear me?" I give her a stern look.

Aurelia sticks her tongue out at me and blows a raspberry.

I withdraw, relinquishing my hold. "Be serious, child. I am worried about you."

Relie rolls her eyes. "I'm not a child anymore, V. I've been trying to tell you all along. I'll be fine." I grumble when she pats my head, taunting me. "You be safe. You hear me?"

"Whatever you say, Relie Bean."

Aurelia smacks my shoulder, then bolts toward her dragon, pretending to fear my wrath. Whether I want to or not, I can't pretend to be angry and muster the courage to chase her, as if today were any regular day.

I watch as Zade offers my sister help, the pair settling atop Idris like they're born for it. Rana folds her arms across her chest, clearly grumpy. I let out a dry laugh as I regard the fae. Rana is in for a treat, if I know my sister. And with that dragon at her side, who knows what kind of trouble they'll get into?

"Later, V!" Aurelia calls, waving goodbye as Idris takes to the skies.

I raise my palm to the sky, my heart aching at the loss of her presence. "Later, Rel," I whisper.

"Are you ready, my bonded?" asks Nyx.

"Yes," I reply, trudging back to my dragon. When Eagan offers me a hand, I realize I forgot to collect my backpack. I think back to my sister climbing Idris and realize she hadn't had it on her. She must have left it in the woods.

"I forgot my bag." I exhale. "I'll be right back," I tell Nyx and Eagan, then spin on my heels and jog toward the trees.

"Hurry, Ravena. The clouds are angry."

"I'm hurrying," I call back to Nyx, picking up my pace as I enter the brush. I do my best to keep my feet forward, usually quite comfortable in Earthy places. My sense of direction is good, and I am glad for it.

I pass tree after tree, the leaves crunching beneath my feet as I finally find the place we'd been. I peer around the foliage where

Relie had gone, finding my bag at the bottom of the hill. *Great*, I gripe, complaining to myself as I steady my footing, trekking downward. Thankfully, the bag is spotless, except for a few twigs caught in the net pockets. I pick them out, strap the bag on my shoulder, then turn to climb back up. I stare up, admiring the height of the trees. They are breathtaking, gnarled and ancient, and I'd love to stay a while, but the clouds above steadily darken, and I hasten my pace.

A flash of red sparks my attention, and I slow my walk as I near the plant. It's a rowan shrub, full of tiny red berries—but I hadn't seen it there before. A sudden tchup sounds piercingly loud, making my heart pound violently. I snap my eyes to find a large black bird beating its wings and dashing away.

A black bird's alarm.

A reverberating growl silences the woods, the trees going eerily still. Branches crack and snap, my back locking up as a spine-chilling nightmare approaches me from behind. I have to run.

Run.

In this fading moment, my foot hovers above the earth, suspended in a spell. An excruciating jolt clips my time, the merciless fangs of a predator ensnaring me, tearing me from existence.

EPILOGUE

To win the war, one must lose the battle.
A star fast approaches its zenith; burning brightly, she journeys
higher, beyond Oasòs.
Have you prepared, Grandchild?

ACKNOWLEDGMENTS

Wow, do I ever have lots to be grateful for?

I am incredibly grateful for the individuals who assisted me with this book. To have alpha readers was a new experience for me, and having their help and encouragement made the process of writing this book far more enjoyable!

I am lucky to have two soul sisters who greatly impacted my experience with writing this book. The three of us got together for video chats and even read through the first draft together, which warmed my heart and helped me get this book out to readers.

To Jaclyn Bourque, my cousin, my best friend, my Aurelia, who stayed up late video-chatting with me to help me work through plot holes. She is the ultimate hype girl for when I want to reign chaos, and I love her for it. Jaclyn assisted with those first days of plotting and alpha-reading the book, providing invaluable help that made the entire process much smoother. Thanks, Cuz.

Next, to Megan Bourque, my cousin, my best friend, my Ravena, who kept the magic (and desperately tried to keep the characters) alive throughout the process. (Sorry, girl.) Megan joined in on the video chats and enthusiastically supported my sometimes wild ideas. She also alpha-read the book, making the whole experience more enjoyable and seamless. Thanks, Cuz.

I'd like to thank my grandmother (Mémère), Theresa Gallant, my #1 hype-woman. Thank you for alpha-reading my book and ensuring it was ready for the world. You've probably read my books more times than anyone else, and I'm forever grateful for your unwavering love and encouragement in all my artistic endeavors. As you already know, I get my artistic flair from you. So, thank you.

I want to extend a huge thank you to the sensitivity readers (Alexia, Jaclyn, & Megan), who reviewed Nemesis and helped me create an inclusive novel. It's essential for me to write stories that reflect the diversity of our shared world. Thank you for helping ensure I did it the best way possible.

Alexia went above and beyond to help with my novel. She is exceptionally professional and kind, and her attention to detail is lovely and refreshing. Thank you for all your help and notes; I couldn't have asked for a better sensitivity reader!

Thanks to my brother, Justin, for chatting all things dragons with me.

Thanks to my husband, Carlo, for supporting me. You help me make my dreams a reality. There is no one like you. Je t'aime.

I want to express my deepest gratitude to all the readers who took a chance on my book. Your support means the world to me.

It brings me immense joy to share my stories with fellow story-lovers like yourself, and I sincerely hope you had a wonderful time on this journey.

Known to many as "Shania Fillmore" of YTV's THE NEXT STAR SEASON 4 and THE NEXT STAR: SUPERGROUP, this small-town girl from New Brunswick, Canada, has taken a turn from singing on television to pursuing her writing dreams.

Music, visual arts, reading, and writing are what she lives and breathes. The art world is her truest passion.

Settled back in her hometown, Shania Scichilone has spent her time as Musical Director during show season, and the rest of her time has been filled with writing and learning digital arts.

ALSO BY SHANIA SCICHILONE

Want to read more of my books?

Check out the FATES DIVINE series!

- A Fate of Smoke and Ash/Un Destin de Fumée et de Cendres
- A Fate of Gods and Fire

Want to join me on social media? You can find me here:

FACEBOOK: Shania Scichilone

INSTAGRAM: @ShaniaScichilone

TIKTOK: @ShaniaScichilone

THREADS: @ShaniaScichilone

YOUTUBE: Shania Scichilone

WEBSITE: www.shaniascichilone.com